The Literary Ghost

The Literary Ghost

GREAT CONTEMPORARY GHOST STORIES

Edited and with an Introduction by
Larry Dark

THE ATLANTIC MONTHLY PRESS
NEW YORK

Published simultaneously in Canada
Printed in the United States of America
FIRST EDITION

Library of Congress Cataloging-in-Publication Data

The Literary ghost: great contemporary ghost stories/edited and with an introduction by Larry Dark.—1st ed.
ISBN 0-87113-474-8
1. Ghost stories, English.   2. Ghost stories, American.   I. Dark, Larry.
PR1309.G5L57   1991   823'.0873308—dc20   91-15052

Design by Laura Hough

The Atlantic Monthly Press
19 Union Square West
New York, NY 10003

FIRST PRINTING

Contents

CONTENTS

CONTENTS

CONTENTS

The Literary Ghost

LARRY DARK

Introduction

I initially saw little potential for confluence between contemporary short stories and stories with ghosts in them. Contemporary short fiction called to mind a world of trailer parks, tract houses, and strip shopping centers. I heard rock-and-roll music, the din of television, and the muted rhythms of inarticulate speech. In contrast, the thought of ghost stories evoked musty castles and rattling chains, wronged nobility stubbornly but eloquently maintaining tiresome grudges from beyond the grave. This isn't to say that I perceived a lack of ghosts in contemporary popular culture —they just didn't seem the stuff of which literature was made. Comedian Stephen Wright asks, "Who was Caspar the Friendly Ghost before he died?" and the joke is that there is no answer.

I exaggerate my initial misgivings to make a point about contemporary writing and about the long tradition of the literary ghost, namely that both are richer in possibilities than the reductive truisms associated with them. After all, many great writers have trotted out a revenant spirit at least once. Charles Dickens, Henry James, and Edith Wharton immediately come to mind, but there are also ghosts in *Look Homeward, Angel* by Thomas Wolfe and in James Joyce's *Ulysses*. One of the great prototypes of the modern short story, Mr. Joyce's "The Dead," is essentially a ghost story without the ghost. And what about novels by the likes of Alice Walker, Toni Morrison, and William Kennedy?

To introduce a ghost into a contemporary short story, with credibility, is to posit a world beyond the scope of a purely empirical sensibility. The

1

writers whose work is included in this collection are writers closely connected to a tradition of imaginative storytelling. It takes a certain amount of daring for a literary writer to employ a device as powerful and obvious as a ghost, and a great deal of talent and self-assurance to pull it off. The fact that these stories are so different from one another and that no two ghosts in them are alike is a testament to the power of the individual imagination to appropriate established myths without assuming the associated clichés.

In the traditional ghost story a protagonist experiences strange phenomena which he or she can't explain; a ghost is encountered; the ghost reveals its purpose; that purpose is, more often than not, addressed; the ghost is released. Of the stories in this collection, only two, R. K. Narayan's "Old Man of the Temple" and Robertson Davies's "The Ghost Who Vanished by Degrees," follow this form. Davies, however, uses these elements to create a humorous pastiche of the traditional ghost story.

Other stories present further departures from the traditional form. In some, the ghost itself narrates, as in stories by Muriel Spark, Anne Sexton, Padgett Powell, and Nadine Gordimer. In Paul Bowles's "The Circular Valley," the ghost is the point-of-view character. We see everything through its eyes and experience the vivid sensations it feels as it inhabits the bodies of a succession of humans and other living creatures. At the other end of the spectrum from these ghost-centered stories are those in which ghosts make only a brief appearance, such as "Eisenheim the Illusionist" by Steven Millhauser, and Tim O'Brien's "The Ghost Soldiers," in which ghosts inform the story metaphorically, never literally materializing.

The settings of the stories in this collection are as diverse as the range of approaches: from London to East Africa to Toronto to seventeenth-century Seville to the Louisiana Bayou to Vietnam to Austria during the reign of the Hapsburgs to India to Poland at the turn of this century. As might be expected, the British tradition of the ghost story is well represented by seven stories in *The Literary Ghost,* but the collection also includes work by two writers of South African origin (Nadine Gordimer and Barry Yourgrau), two Canadians (Robertson Davies and Mavis Gallant), and an Indian (R. K. Narayan), as well as diverse American writers. Still, it is the British tradition, more than any other, that casts its shadow over this anthology.

In describing the great-niece she has chosen to haunt, the ghostly narrator of Anne Sexton's story makes an astute observation about the difference between the traditional English ghost and the contemporary American ghost:

> . . . she is unwilling to move into a house that is not newly made, she is unwilling to live within the walls that might whisper and tell stories of other lives. It is her ghost theory. But like many she has made the perfect mistake; the mistake being that a ghost belongs to a house, a former room. . . . I think the English believe it because their castles were passed on from generation to generation. Indeed, perhaps an American ghost does something quite different, because the people of the present are very mobile, the executives are constantly thrown from city to city, dragging their families with them.

Even in contemporary settings, British writers continue to link ghosts to houses and specific rooms, as in the stories here by V. S. Pritchett, Fay Weldon, and Penelope Lively. The mobile American ghost, on the other hand, is in evidence in "Ghostly Populations" by Jack Matthews, in which ghosts roll by in passing cars, and Joyce Carol Oates's "The Others," in which they unexpectedly appear in public places, including a passageway connecting various commuter lines. M. F. K. Fisher's "The Lost, Strayed, Stolen," with its American protagonist and English setting, provides a bridge between the sedentary British ghosts and their migratory American cousins, delivering both varieties.

Because diversity is a strength of this collection, I arranged the stories in an order designed to underscore it and to provide a varied reading experience for that rare individual who reads the stories in an anthology in order, from first to last. There are a few subtle connections between sequential stories, but generally the order was dictated by concerns of balance in length and tone, subjectively determined. Other than this my only aim was to begin and end with particularly good sequences of stories.

If anything else surprised me as I compiled this collection, it was that even in this hyperrational age of bits and bytes and subsubatomic particles, ghost stories still have the power to enthrall even the most skeptical among us. Freud identified the unfulfilled wish as the engine of our dreams. Fiction in general, and ghost stories in particular, are similarly inspired by the need for psychic satisfaction. In dreams and literary fiction, the unfulfilled wish is usually transformed by symbols and metaphors. Ghosts, powerful symbols themselves, allow the writer to state the unfulfilled wish or unmet need overtly. Through their agency, wrongs are righted, broken trajectories completed, and justice, of a sort, achieved. The literary ghost story can be frightening, engrossing, clever, ironic, mysterious, funny—any or all of these—but at its best, it can also be immensely satisfying to our mortal souls and their yearnings for completion.

M. F. K. FISHER

The Lost, Strayed, Stolen

The few people who did not like Mr. and Mrs. Beddoes laughed, perhaps jealously, at their ambience of golden wedding, their greeting-card happiness. Even friends teased a little, half irked by the feeling that, in spite of the Beddoeses' hospitality and warmth, all they really needed was themselves. "What is your secret?" friends would ask. "Tell us how you managed to stand it all these years!" But the Beddoeses would smile the secret smile of any long marriage and close the door gently, just as they had been doing ever since he made the trip to England, soon after the depression.

At first, on board ship, Mr. Beddoes felt upset to be without his wife for the first time in his married life. Then he remembered Perry MacLaren, a tall Scot whom he had met ten years before on this very same ship. They had exchanged speakeasy addresses and had suddenly felt like brothers—as happens occasionally, both on and off ships. Since then, there had been a few disappointing notes, formal and forced. But impulsively Beddoes sent MacLaren a cable, and now there was a wire waiting at his hotel in London: "DELIGHTED CAN PROMISE YOU INTERESTING WEEKEND MEET YOU CARLISLE FRIDAY AFTERNOON."

As Beddoes unpacked his bags, he was stirred by an almost skittish thrill. Before he knew it, he had broken two appointments with representatives of his firm and one date with a lovely Swedish woman from the boat and was stepping in a rumpled, excited state onto the gray platform at Carlisle. "Mac, old boy!" he shouted heartily.

5

"Beddoes, you . . . you son of a gun!"

The two men stood in a sweat of embarrassment, each listening to his own attempt to make the other feel easy—and then everything was all right and MacLaren picked up the suitcase, smiling, and Beddoes said, "My God! Excuse me, Mac, but I forgot you were a minister—a priest, I mean. Or do I mean a padre?"

"No, not padre. It's quite all right. Come along, Beddoes. I've got a neat little buggy since I last wrote—a real beauty."

Beddoes tucked himself into the tight tiny car that stood near the station, and wondered if his legs would go to sleep. They headed into disjointed traffic and then were in the country, and he felt fine, as if time had not come between the two of them.

MacLaren looked sideways at him, sharply. "You mustn't bother about the clericals, will you? These collars are really quite comfortable, you know. Sometimes they help in crowds. And there are other things that are good, too."

"Sure," said Beddoes. "Sure. Fine."

They headed north. The sun slanted over increasing hills, with great rocks and sweeps of high meadowland—moors, Beddoes reminded himself pleasurably. Mac drove hard, with a gleeful look on his bony red face. They stopped at a tavern and drank some bitter ale and ate an awful snack of cold canned American beans from the bar, and then tooled ahead as if they were pursued. It grew dark. Their talk was spotty and meaningless through the speed until the minister said, "Beddoes, I don't plan to take you home to Askhaven tonight. Of course we could make it, and Sally hopes we will. But I've a job to do. I thought perhaps you'd not mind helping me."

Beddoes clucked and murmured. "Sure thing," he said. He felt comfortable, spiritually if not physically, and his cramped legs and buzzing bones only heightened an inner coziness. He liked Mac, and the thought of being useful to him. He liked the almost sensual way Mac drove the silly little roadster.

"You see," Mac said, "I told some people—a very nice simple woman, as a matter of fact—that I'd come to help her. And since she's on our way home from Carlisle and I was meeting you . . ."

The country grew mountainous. Beddoes swayed sleepily with the skill-fully violent cornering of his driver, and was half aware of bare steppes and sudden shouting streams and long heady straight stretches where Mac let out the little car like a demon. Then they pulled up before a dimly lighted inn. "The Queen's Head," it said in a small box with a light in it, the black paint cracking off and blurring the letters.

"Here we are, then." Mac's voice sounded falsely hearty, like an echo in a cave. "That's the village, over there."

Beddoes looked into blackness, and then hopefully back at the dour tavern sign. He untwined his prickling legs. He felt tired and vaguely peevish, and yet there stirred in his mind a strange excitement: he, son of the wide Midwestern prairies, stood at last in the heart of an English village, on a green. "God, it's wonderful to be an American—to have this heritage, to come back to it," he told himself solemnly.

Mac walked toward the black closed door, and slapped at it. The peremptory sound echoed across the darkness and settled thinly down. Somewhere a toad croaked. Mac pounded again. "Mrs. Protheroe," he said. His voice was sharp but low, almost secretive. "Mrs. Protheroe, are you there?" His voice was still low but now deeply urgent.

Then the door clanked open and warm light poured out, and Beddoes, who had begun to feel uncomfortable, blinked and staggered into it, with bags in either hand.

"Here, sir. Let me help you." A short woman with dark eyes took the bags. He followed her up a flight of narrow stone steps harshly lighted, to a small bedroom. The woman poured water into a basin, and left him.

He sat for a minute on the side of his bed. He was dog tired. His hands dropped between his legs, and his lips felt as if they were made of feathers. Mac is quite a driver, he thought wryly. There was a banging on his door. He jumped up, and then laughed at his nervousness as he recognized MacLaren's quiet, full voice calling him to open. Soon, washed and slicked, Beddoes felt better—strong and in an odd way excited.

The two men went down the stairs, which seemed friendly now, and into a small parlor. There was a fire burning in the tiny grate. It caught with gold the corners of the fussy antimacassared chairs and the ugly piano and the round table laid with silver and plates. A lamp on a chain hung over the table.

"My God, Mac, it's like a fairy tale! You can't possibly know what this means to me." He saw MacLaren looking at him remotely, and he stopped, choked by a thousand conditioned reactions, from Christmas cards and history in school to his own mother's saccharine reminiscences of her "trip through the Lake Country." He wanted to tell Mac what England meant to a middle-class, sentimental, moderately sensitive American salesman. Instead, he gulped awkwardly, feeling young and naïve before the minister's tired friendliness, and said, "Well, Mac, I'm certainly glad to be here!"

"So am I, Beddoes, glad you're here. It's been too long. I asked Mrs. Protheroe— Ah! Here she is!"

Before he knew it, Beddoes had slipped back in his chair under the delightful impact of a double Scotch and was watching Mrs. Protheroe's black shadow come and go in the lamplight, and then was tucking into two chops and some crisp pickles and pretty plum tart with cheese. He felt like a million dollars. Almost at once, it seemed, he was in bed, and comfortably, to his mild surprise. He had meant to talk with Mac—what about Chamberlain, and this business of Hitler or whatever his name was, and L'Entente Cordiale, and . . .

Then Mac was sitting on the edge of his bed, with a candle. It seemed quite natural.

"What's up?" Beddoes asked.

Outside in the dark of the village green, the toad honked and gargled. Mac sat for a minute. His eyes were shadowed, but Beddoes felt the trouble in them. His head was clear as a bell. Nothing like good liquor, he thought.

"Beddoes, I need your help." Mac's voice did not sound solemn, but at the same time it was not light. He looked down at the candle in his hand, which flared and sputtered in the window's draft and lighted the bony solidity of his good Scottish face. "I meant to tell you before—Mrs. Protheroe wrote me to come. She's had to close the Queen's Head, and she needs my help."

As Mac talked quietly, his friend thought of the silent dark-eyed woman who had unlocked the inn door for them and led them to their rooms and served them.

". . . and I knew that as a man of God it was my duty. And you, Beddoes . . ." Perry MacLaren hesitated, and looked full into the other's eyes. He sighed sharply. "Your coming was an answer to my prayer. I need you—your good, honest, unspoiled soul—for company. Come along." The candle flickered as he stood up.

Beddoes, confused but keenly awake, pushed his legs into his trousers, feeling almost virtuously sane and sensible.

They walked in their stocking feet down a cold, silent corridor. It seemed longer than Beddoes remembered—or were they going into another part of the inn? He was bewildered. He put his hand on MacLaren's strong thin shoulder and felt comforted and indirectly hilarious, as if he were a character in a French comedy in a dream. The candle lit numbers on dark, heavy-looking doors. The corridor turned, and grew even colder.

"Here we are," Mac muttered. "It's this one."

As they stood for a moment while the candle wax formed slowly into a burred tongue over his fingers, MacLaren turned irrevocably into a priest. Beddoes, facing him before the closed door in the guttering light, knew probably for the first time in his life that he was in the company of a vessel of the Lord. He felt overwhelmed, not with shyness as at the railroad station but with an inchoate terrible respect, as before a great stone or a sudden inexplicable light.

"Yes, this is the door," the priest muttered again. He stared calmly at Beddoes. "Are you ready? You can help me, perhaps. We can try." He turned the handle of the door.

The bed in the room was like something in a movie—tall, with a flat tent top, and curtains half pulled around its high mattress. Queer, but even in the candlelight, steady now though feeble in the cold, still air, the curtains were pure blue, with silver threads woven here and there through their stiff folds. MacLaren set the candle on a table and stood at the foot of the bed. His face was long and dreadful. He raised his hand.

Beddoes' heart seemed to flop like a trout against his ribs, and his breath moved cautiously over his dry lips.

"Thomas and Martha Gilfillan!" The priest spoke earnestly, entreating someone named or something unnamed to listen to him.

Beddoes' eyes saw more and more clearly: the fluted lines of the paneling and of the chimney, and the soft impenetrable blueness of the bed curtains; his old friend, straight and thin, standing with head bent into his hands; the bedspread, dimly white; and at last he saw the things beneath the bedspread. There in the blue-hung bed lay two people. Or were they dead bodies? Or were they shadows? They made sharp mounds, surely, under the coverlet. The lengths of their thighs, the sharp peaks of their feet and pelvic bones pushed up the cloth and shifted in the candlelight. But over their two still skulls it did not move.

Beddoes put out his hand again, like a child, for his friend's shoulder, but MacLaren stood away from him, tall and stern. His hands hung now at his sides. His head dropped like a ripe fig from the stem of his spine. *"Remember not, Lord, our iniquities,"* he prayed, *"nor the iniquities of our forefathers . . . neither take thou vengeance . . ."*

Beddoes looked wildly at the ridges and mounds and hollows under the counterpane and then at the emerging shell of the room. There was an electric clock on the wall. He could see it, round and plain as a piepan, and it said twelve-twenty and then whirred tinnily, so that he wondered why he had not heard it before. It made him feel almost real again.

". . . and be not angry with us forever," MacLaren went on, and then answered himself, *"Spare us, good Lord. Let us pray!"*

Beddoes kneeled, peering up into the well of light around the candle on the table. He watched MacLaren now with trust and a kind of hypnotized belief, and thought, This isn't the Burial Service. For prisoners, is it? Or dead murderers? *"Christ, have mercy upon us,"* he heard himself responding.

The two men prayed there by the bed, as unselfconscious as savages, and after they had said the Lord's Prayer, MacLaren went on in his flat, somber voice through all the Visitation of Prisoners and the mighty words for those under sentence of death, and Beddoes sweated beside him, knowing that he was wrestling with the Devil. The electric clock whirred occasionally, and outside on the black village green the old toad croaked. *"O Saviour of the World, save us and help us."*

Beddoes held his hands before his face now, and his eyes were shut, but still he saw like fire on fire the outlines of the two ghosts beneath the coverlet. They lay there, finite and evil, resisting him and MacLaren and all the words of God. "No!" he cried out. He could stand no more.

The priest stopped his supplication. He seemed not to be breathing. *"Save us and help us!"* he cried toward the dreadful bed. *"Save us and help us!"*

The electric clock whirred. The toad belched again in the weeds outside. Sweat started from the men's armpits and foreheads and spines. And from the bed rose such a wave of hatred, such foul resistance, that they backed away, Beddoes still kneeling, until they touched the stone of the hearth.

Hurriedly, MacLaren raised Beddoes to his feet. "I have failed," he said softly. With his left hand he pulled the American after him. His right he raised high, and his voice shouted out, stern, flat, awesome, *"In the name of the Father . . . and of the Son . . ."* From the bed rose a horrible feeling—like a stench, like a shriek. But the bony shapes still lay under the coverlet. The curtains were unruffled. The clock whirred. *". . . and of the Holy Ghost."*

Beddoes never knew how he found his way back to his room. The priest followed him blindly, his hand on Beddoes' shoulder, and then lay on Beddoes' narrow bed. His face looked like a death mask. Beddoes covered him with an ugly, lump-filled quilt, and went to the washstand and stood for a long time in the dark, listening to the priest's exhausted breathing, forgetting England and his friend and even himself in the abysmal realization that some souls are lost souls.

The next morning, Beddoes felt bright as a dime, although he had spent the remnant of the night sitting in various agonized positions on a prickly black horsehair chair. Mac had lain like a snoring corpse on the narrow bed, and only once did Beddoes feel any of the earlier horror, when his friend's raucous breathing suddenly beat in his sleepless ears with the same whirring as the clock. He straightened in the discomfort of the armchair and pulled his topcoat sensibly over his knees.

Now, as the little car roared out through the dim, dawn-bound village, the struggle of the night seemed misty. He made himself forget it. He listened to the engine with fresh ears, and smelled the brightening air delightedly. "That was a good breakfast!" he shouted, grinning.

Mac laughed and drove faster. "You're right there, old boy. Mrs. Protheroe—poor woman, I failed her. She knew my father, you know. She'd never let us creep out, as I wished, without waking her."

The silent woman with tear-reddened eyes had lighted the lamp in the sitting room and blown on the warm coals and set before them such a breakfast as Beddoes had never had. Tea, and a round fat loaf of country bread with a great knife stuck in it, and butter in a pat! And bacon as thick and lean as ham. They ate, and as the fire mounted and Mac's face took on its usual ruddiness and his eyes looked less pained, Beddoes felt exhilaration creep like smoke or some strong wine into all his intimate corners. "That little lady admires you, all right," he said now, his belt snug and his mind serene. "You say she knew your father? Was he a—that is, have you followed in his foot-steps?"

Perry MacLaren let out a good yell of laughter, tightened one arm on the steering wheel to bang Beddoes roughly on the back with his other, and said, "Old boy, you're wonderful! Sally will love you. Yes, by damn, she will!" He laughed again, and the little car swerved upward merrily into the mist. As the sun touched the hills with a thin light, bluish and pure, snippets of fog caught on the occasional oaks in the glens, and on the bushes, and then, like music or perfume, disappeared. Once, a lark sang, startlingly near and clear above the impertinent racketing of the car. And then suddenly they went through a kind of gorge and Mac stopped the car. "Askhaven," he said.

Below them, in a narrow valley, lay a village so much like all the things that meant "village" in Beddoes' somewhat muddled Anglophilic mind that he almost shouted. The wee houses, rosy brick and tile, straggled along a grassy street, and smoke rose from their doll-like chimneys, and there was a tiny church with a steeple, and there was a green in front of it, with a fountain and a cross—and then, miraculous and perfect, in the still air rose the jeweled, dream-familiar notes of a hunting horn. Beddoes drew in his breath sharply. "God, Mac," he said softly. "It's—it's England!"

"Yes, yes, it's a decent little spot. Bad drains, of course."

Mac started the car, resolutely British, and Beddoes felt silly. Then, as they coasted down into the valley and the houses became sturdy reality, he peered keenly about him. He saw children and old people at the windows, and once a woman flapped her apron in the doorway to scare away three pecking hens. There were early-summer flowers everywhere. The church door was open. They were off the street now, and wheeling into a lane behind the small buttressed chancel of the church. Then Mac stopped violently, sprang out of the car, and ran up the path toward a small ugly house, his face young and dazzling with love. "Sally!" he called.

Beddoes watched without any modesty while his friend folded himself around and against the woman in the doorway. Their embrace was in itself so without shame that it never occurred to him to turn away his eyes. Instead, he smiled dazedly, and then crawled with stiff joints from the car and carried the two suitcases up the path.

"Beddoes—Sally." Mac kept his arms for a minute around his wife, and then the three of them laughed and scrambled into the narrow darkness of the hallway, which smelled, like narrow dark hallways of English literature, of wet woolens and cabbage.

Soon Beddoes was alone in his room, which smelled faintly like the hall and had one window looking across and through some yews into the stoniness of the church wall. It was a cheery cubbyhole, with a high narrow bed and a small fireplace twinkling with polished brass fittings, and an armchair drawn up, cramped but comfortable, between the fire and the dresser. There was chintz all over everything, just as it should be in the vicar's guest room of a village in—yes, Beddoes assured himself happily—in the heart of England. He opened his bag, yawned, and stood looking down into its familiar tidiness, its sterile order of a salesman's allotted shirts and ties and razor blades, with the cabinet photograph of his wife on top.

Beddoes' mind filled, suddenly and completely, with his first real sight of Sarah MacLaren. Now *there,* he thought helplessly. Now *there!* Ripe and beautiful, her voice like warm honey . . . He shook his head. Then, as he listened to new sounds in the tight little house, his thoughts swerved toward normal nothingness again.

There was a subdued tussling and giggling outside his door, and a kind of whispering, as if two or three children were in the midst of some secret. A voice said, "The water's hot for your bath, sir."

"All right. Thanks!" Beddoes felt like adding jovially, "O.K., you kids. No more fooling around out there, either!" He pulled open the door to speak to them, but they had gone. He felt foolish, and stood rather crossly for a minute, certain the next door hid his watchers. The hall was too dim to see whether there was a crack open. He laughed self-consciously, and went back into his room. A bath at eleven-thirty in the morning was nonsense anyway. He soon flapped obediently down the hall to the bathroom, though. It was a bleak barn, probably once meant for beds and now draftily occupied by an ancient oak flush toilet on a raised platform, a shabby armchair with a huge towel draped over it, and the tub. It was of green tin, and enormous. The geyser heater above it hissed and let occasional blobs of soot drop into the water. For some reason, the whole place was delightful.

With the good hot water running slowly into the tub, Beddoes lay back and felt like Leviathan awash. It was damn nice of Mrs. Mac to think of this for him. Funny he hadn't seen the children. But *hey!* Whose children? That wasn't a thing people kept quiet about. Certainly there had been giggling and tussling outside the door before one of them said, "The water's hot for your bath, sir." Beddoes sat up in the tub. He suddenly felt chilly. *Had* he heard a voice say that? Or had he just thought so?

He dried himself hurriedly and, not waiting with his usual tidiness to wipe the tub, flapped back to his room. He closed his door firmly, forcing himself not to look back at the other closed doors in the dark hall, and went straight to the bottom of his suitcase for his flask of good bourbon. He lifted the bottle with practiced courtesy to his wavy image in the mirror, took a firm pull, and shuddered pleasurably. Never take baths so early in the day, he decided; steam gets in the brain.

He dressed quickly, strapped on his watch and found that it marked past noon, started downstairs, and then remembered the tub. But in the bathroom it was as neat—and almost as cold—as if he had not sloshed about in it a few minutes before. Damned efficient maid, he thought wryly, even if she runs off tittering. Rather to his surprise—for he was a moderate man—he took another ceremonious swig from his flask, and then descended almost gaily into the increasing cabbaginess of the vicarage.

And true enough, there was cabbage for lunch, or dinner, or whatever the badly cooked meal was called. Beddoes hated the stuff, but this noon, for some reason, it tasted very good. Perhaps it was the way it lay all higgledy-piggledy with onions and carrots in the big bowl of stew, or perhaps it was the bottle of ale that he drank with it—or the bourbon he had drunk before. Probably, though, it was because he was eating it with the MacLarens.

He had never been with two people like them. Everything they said sounded musical to his enchanted ears. When they looked at each other, which was often, their eyes darkened and widened with an almost audible protestation of love. They seemed wrapped around with bliss, so that the whole stuffy little dining room was transfigured. He felt a part of their passion, just as he had when he first saw them melt into each other in the doorway, and the fact that he now found himself in love for the only time in his life, and with Sarah MacLaren, was a part of the whole. He did not feel disturbed, only a little dizzy. He ate solidly of the watery, ill-cooked stew, and clicked glasses now and then with Mac, and spooned his way in a kind of happy vertigo through a tough apple tart with some clotted cream that had waited on the sideboard.

"Agatha made it," Sarah said, laughing softly and looking sideways at her husband from her long brown eyes.

"Then no wonder it's so . . . That is, my dear Sally, you must admit it's pretty dreadful." MacLaren stared at the glutinous pile on his plate.

"Yes," she said placidly. "That's why I got the cream. I thought it might help. But you know Agatha's so anxious. . . ."

"Of course, darling. It's just that I do love decent tarts."

"Yes, I know. Mr. Beddoes, Perry's really rather a humbug. He idealizes himself as the simple parish priest, but often he has to pretend dreadfully hard that he's having supper at the Café de Paris in order to stand it. And, of course, I'm a rotten cook."

"Rotten, my dear. But Agatha's worse." Mac pushed back his chair. "Let's get out of here before I begin to idealize myself as a peppery old colonel and call for my digestive powders."

Beddoes looked with some faint worry at Sarah, expecting that she might seem unhappy, but she smiled at him and pushed her hair from her forehead gently with her plump hands. "I thought Mr. Beddoes might like to watch me show off with my Turkish coffeepot," she said vaguely. "I told Agatha, so everything's ready for it in the parlor. Now, Perry," she exclaimed, laughing so that her cheeks shook up and down, "you know very well that she can boil water!"

Beddoes followed them across the hall and into a surprisingly comfortable room, somewhat cluttered with small tables but with all Mac's books at one end in a kind of study, and a big couch in front of the fire, so that it seemed intimate and pleasant. It looks lived in, he decided with serene banality.

"Milk, too," Sarah added, after she had stuffed a pillow with absent-minded hospitality behind Beddoes on the couch and seated herself in front of her low coffee table. "Agatha boils milk well, too."

"Yes, that she does, darling. Where in hell's my pipe? Any mail while I was gone?" Mac rummaged about on the top of his desk, humming gently; then he wandered back to the hearth and folded himself into a big chair.

The fire burned with clear flame in its grate, so different from the fireplaces at home, and Beddoes stuck his feet as far toward it as he dared without appearing oafish, and managed to wiggle Sarah's well-meant pillow into a less uncomfortable spot. He watched her tenderly as she sat, completely absorbed with the various boilings and fussings and spoonings of her coffee routine. She was beautiful and, he decided, very much like a little fat hen at the moment. He started to ask, "Who's this Agatha?" but, instead, said mildly, "I heard the children in the hall this morning."

There was complete silence.

Beddoes did not realize it for a few seconds, and then he sat up straighter and looked miserably at the MacLarens. They did not notice him, but seemed as if they were talking silently to each other. Finally, Mac sighed and shook his head a little, and Sarah poured three cups of coffee almost nervously, and Beddoes said, "What did I—"

"Yes, quite," Mac interrupted him firmly. "And Beddoes old boy, I was hoping for a couple of rounds with you this afternoon—there's a decent little course near here—but I see a note saying that old Mrs. Timpkins has 'come over worse, suddenlike,' as she says."

"Again? That old silly! Mrs. Timpkins is always coming over worse when we have visitors." Sarah frowned, and then went on brightly, "How's the coffee? *I* think it's delicious!"

"I do, too," Beddoes said. It was strange and awful, but he echoed quite sincerely that it *was* delicious.

"Delicious, darling. You get better all the time. When you're an old lady, you can wear a veil—or several might be better, good thick ones—and you can make coffee in a seraglio or a big French restaurant. Don't you think so, Beddoes?"

Beddoes giggled shrilly, and then before he could help it he yawned an enormous, engulfing, noisy yawn. He was sickly embarrassed and put down his cup, trembling, blinking his wet eyes. "I'm *sorry*," he said. "*Please* excuse me. It—"

"It come over you worse, suddenlike," Sarah said. "I know. It's just as well Perry can't drag you around the golf course. Perry, you go comfort old Mrs. Timpkins—she's in love with *you*, not the Church—and Mr. Beddoes and I will curl up on the couch. That is, he'll curl up for a nap, and I'll sit here and mend every damned sock in the whole house!" She took one last sip of coffee, licked her full lower lip delicately, murmured "Delicious!" again, and withdrew into a kind of trance, like a cat.

Beddoes saw Mac kiss her forehead and then the back of her neck, and tiptoe out of the room. But almost before he put his feet up onto the soft couch he was asleep, with Sarah MacLaren's image, like a brown butterfly, behind his peaceful eyelids.

When he wakened, it was to the sound of coal embers falling whisperingly from the grate under the weight of fresh fuel. Someone was poking the fire.

But when he opened his eyes, almost at once, Sarah sat quietly across the hearth from him, and the coals burned all by themselves in the odd little iron basket. He lay looking at her, and in spite of a strong sense of bewilderment he was very content. His eyes felt as fresh as a child's and, indeed, his whole body tingled and cooled as if a gentle wind blew privately over it from some other world. He had never felt so alive. He lay easily within his skin, and if anyone had told him that he looked the same as ever—an average man—he would not have understood.

He gazed calmly at Sarah and thought without pain of his love for her. It was strange, of course, but in some way quite natural that he should have waited so long to fall so utterly in love with any woman, let alone with this chubby little hen of a creature. What would his wife think of her? Sarah's hair was long and unstylish and seemed to slip out of its pins pretty easily, and her knitted dress had a definite and matronly bag behind. He smiled and stirred, and veiled his eyes as she looked up quickly at him from her darning. He wanted not to talk for a few minutes longer. It seemed to him that he had talked all his life and never said anything until today—and at that he could not remember what it was that he had said. Perhaps nothing. But he felt potentially able to say, to utter at last, some of the thoughts that all his years had been lying like eggs in a nest, ready for this hatching. What they would be he did not know and certainly did not care. It was enough to realize that they were there.

He must have dozed again, because he woke to hear Sarah scolding, in a muted, exasperated voice. "No, Tom! You've been very good today, and I'm proud of you, and indeed you've managed beautifully with the others. But *no!*"

Beddoes watched her poking her needle against the sock she darned, frowning and clucking as she did it.

My love is a madwoman, he thought, and asked quietly, "Who are you talking to, Mrs. MacLaren?"

"Tom's pestering me to play the gramophone," she said, and then dropped her mending and put both hands against her lips. Her eyes stared at him. They no longer looked placid or merry or mysteriously deep, but round as plums with consternation. Finally, she put down her hands and folded the mending carefully into the basket and then came over and sat on the floor beside Beddoes.

He lay absolutely still, not fearful at all but listening as if every pore in his skin were a little ear.

"Go away now, Tom," Sarah said clearly. "That's a good soul." She waited a minute, and then started to talk, in a rather strained way at first and then almost eagerly. "I *told* Perry we'd have to explain to you. You're a friend, or I suppose we'd never have let you come at all. These last few months, we've been so absorbed in this job that we've rather forgotten how strange it may look to people who don't know about it. Of course, here in Askhaven every-one understands. Everyone knows Perry for the dear godly man he is. He *is* a man of God, you know, Mr. Beddoes. He could be a bishop if he wished—a *good* bishop. But I've no ambition for him—and I'd be such a ninny as a bishop's wife! And Askhaven is his whole life. Mine, too."

Beddoes held out a cigarette to her, and she lit it for herself and then said, "They really seem to like me, too. Vicars' wives are often disliked. Of course, I do most of the things I'm supposed to—Girls' Friendly, and Guild, and those ghastly boxes for the missions. And I visit. That helps Perry. I'm really a *very* good vicar's wife, now I think of it." She leaned sensuously against the couch, and let the smoke curl up her cheekbones from her slackened fine lips.

"What about Tom?" Beddoes asked it softly, as if afraid to scare her away—or into plain friendliness again.

"Oh, Tom." She looked vaguely at him, and then shook herself. "Yes, Tom. Well—it's rather hard to start. I do hope he is not listening. He's so terribly sensitive lately. You see, it's getting time for him to leave us, and he doesn't want to. But of course Perry says he must. Oh dear! Mr. Beddoes—Mr. Beddoes, Tom is . . ." Sarah looked earnestly at him, as if she was praying that it was all right to hurt him in some way or frighten him, and without even knowing that he did it he took one of her hands. She smiled at him. "Tom is a lost soul. There are a lot of them, everywhere. When they're really lost, completely, hopelessly, they're usually what people call ghosts. They're terribly unhappy, Mr. Beddoes, and they do mischievous things, or bad things. It's a kind of rage they're in. They haunt people. It's wretched. The two at Mrs.

Protheroe's—Perry feels so depressed about them that he's almost ill, Mr. Beddoes. Poor darling. You see, Mrs. Protheroe called him because she knows how he is helping, and of course she has to support herself and run the inn alone, and the two . . . They were a man and woman in about 1620 who owned the Queen's Head and sent all the decent women who stopped there to London, doped, for the sailors. These two horrible souls have come back, and they are driving away all the trade. They just lie in that bed, which isn't really there, of course, and . . ." Sarah shuddered, and threw her cigarette into the grate.

Beddoes closed his eyes for a moment. He felt nauseated and cold, remembering the waves of hatred that had risen from the blue-canopied high couch last night, and hearing his own voice heavy with prayer against the impossible whirring of the electric clock upon the wall. "Yes, those were damned souls," he said at last, and looked at Sarah.

"Well, Perry will try again. And he has helped many, you know. Agatha is one of the best. She *came* to us! Usually Perry discovers where there is trouble and goes and rescues the poor tormented thing and brings it here. But Agatha came by herself, and asked to stay. Of course, she's more like a guest, you know. It's a queer mess. We hardly feel that we can ask her about herself. But she's never been sly, like some of the others, and she's getting clearer all the time. She insists she was a cook! She'll soon leave us, too. You see, they grow clearer as they find themselves. Some of them, even if you can't see them, you know they're tiny and hideous, more like ideas than things—ideas of pain, perhaps. And then as they find themselves they grow straighter and clearer until they're almost like children, but with old minds, of course. I can see Agatha lately. Today, when she wanted so much to make the tart, she was *there*, Mr. Beddoes—so little and sincere that I knew she'd be honest about it. It was a *terrible* tart, but it was a *tart*. Some of them, even when they promise to be good, do naughty things, and might use salt instead of sugar. Or rat poison. Or drain cleanser . . ."

"My God!" Beddoes looked angrily at her. "You're in danger, then!"

"Of course. It's risky business, really. But we must do it. You could tell, couldn't you, the dreadful suffering of those two at Mrs. Protheroe's, caught

20

as they were in their own evil? And Perry can save them. He has had worse. He'll bring them here, and gradually—I think it's probably my quiet nature, and of course I'm patient when eggs get broken because I *often* break eggs myself—gradually they begin to be less cruel and twisted, and I give them little jobs to do. In fact, they can become very helpful. I don't hire anyone at all now." She smiled at him.

He could see her only dimly against the soft glow of the fire, but her eyes looked sure and steady into his. He gave her another cigarette and then said fretfully, "But I don't like your being in danger. I don't like it."

"There isn't much, really. And of course Tom is here."

"Yes. What about Tom?"

Sarah watched smoke rise from her cigarette toward the chimney, and then she laughed. "It's really simple, you know. He's been with us several months now—almost since Perry began this. But every time Perry tells him it is nearly time to go, Tom breaks something, or pretends to be naughty, and then we have to start all over again. At least, he means us to. And of course I have to be stern with myself, because really I wish he could stay forever. I depend on him—too much, I know. He should have a real home, one he could run correctly. Number One Boy. But he's wonderful with the others. I told him this afternoon about the silliness outside your door. I think it must have been Lady Donfellows and the Negro girl, Odessa. They've only been here a few weeks. They're not bad at all, just idiotic—completely zany. Nitwits. They got lost before they died, and then fluttered around wondering what was wrong with everybody else—for *centuries*, probably. I told Tom. He felt rather badly. But he'll keep them in order. I'm sure of him."

Once more the soft sound of falling coal ash whispered in Beddoes' ears, and he felt a little prickly, as he had once after an injection of adrenaline. "Where is Tom now?" he whispered.

Sarah looked around. "I can't always see him, you know," she answered rather impatiently. "And I can only feel him here if he wants me to. Tom, are you here?" They waited for a minute, Sarah on the floor, with her soft plump hand warmly in Beddoes', which suddenly felt rather damp. "No, he isn't here. Or else he is but is shy with you." She grinned. "You don't have to *hear* them, you know. I know it's annoying. It annoys me sometimes. Even Tom will tease me a little. I'll think I'm alone and suddenly he'll steal the last bite of a bonbon I've been saving for after supper." She jerked her hand away. "Oh, Mr. Beddoes! Tea! I haven't even told them about tea for you!"

Beddoes laughed. "I'm not used to afternoon tea," he said. "We don't have it much back home, except for company from England!"

"But Perry will be furious with me! Don't tell him, eh?"

He felt delightfully secretive, and grabbed her hand hard. "In cahoots!" he cried. "The tea was delicious, ma'am! As I live and breathe, it was indeed!"

Sarah laughed excitedly, and then bit at her lip, her eyes bemused. "Yes," she murmured. "Today's Saturday. I have some beautiful fresh eggs. We'll have up an egg to our tea, as Mrs. Timpkins says. And that'll be instead of supper. And you and Perry can go down to the Golden Duck and play darts. He likes to go Saturday nights. The men are easier then. They can tell him about—"

The door into the hall opened quietly, and Mac stood dark against the light that streamed in past him. Beddoes started to sit up, feeling vaguely guilty, but Sarah held his hand tighter. "Perry!" she called. "Perry, I've been telling him about our ghoulies. He knows about them."

"Good," Mac said. "That's all right, then. Beddoes, old boy, how about a wee nip before supper? I could stand one myself."

"And I'll go see about things," Sarah said. "I'll tell Agatha about the eggs."

The rest of Beddoes' weekend passed in a pleasant blur. He helped clear the table after meals, at which he ate heartily of the bad food, and he never went into the kitchen, feeling shyly that Agatha and the others might not like it, but instead stacked dishes and cups with his customary neatness on the sideboard. They always disappeared soon after.

Saturday night, he played interminable darts in a crowded smoky saloon—pub, he should say. He drank an astonishing number of double Scotches, but none of them seemed to hit him, and afterward, in a solemnly clearheaded mood, he walked home through the sleeping village with Mac. He thought a long time and finally started to say that it was queer how well he understood the garbled accent of the village men, but Mac cut into his half-formed words. "Wait here, Beddoes, eh? I'll be but a minute." And, in his tweeds and round white collar, MacLaren hurried into the church through the unlocked door.

Beddoes waited, leaning against the cross by the sweetly dripping fountain. He knew Mac was right to leave him; he was drunk, even if he did not feel so in the least. "Tipsy souls must go to pray all by themselves, inside themselves, if they can find the door," Beddoes said.

Mac came out in a few minutes, his face serene, and they went home to bed.

After morning services the next day (Beddoes did not go, feeling strangely shy about seeing his friend in vestments at the altar), they played golf a few miles from the village with a pair of fat tweedy old boys who scowled for eighteen holes and made Beddoes feel stiffly foreign and oafish, and then relaxed completely in the stuffy little clubhouse and told innumerable jokes so fast and mumblingly that he could only guess when to laugh.

He went to Evensong, rather to his surprise. The church was dim and musty, and two musty dim old women prayed alone on one side of the aisle, while he and Sarah sat, discreetly parted by an untidy pile of hymnals, in a pew across from them. At the back of the church, an ancient man—the sexton, perhaps—snuffled and creaked. Beddoes found himself following automatically the ritual that meant his childhood and then an occasional service with his wife back home. It was wonderful how some things never faded. And it was queer how little he felt at the sight of Mac up there, hunched like a great white quiet bird over the lectern. He had counted on being awed, and instead he felt only a desire to yawn. It was disappointing.

"*The grace of our Lord Jesus Christ,*" Mac was saying deeply, his voice echoing from the damp walls, "*and the love of God, and the fellowship of the Holy Ghost, be with us all, evermore.*"

"Amen," said Beddoes and Sarah and the two old dim shadows in the pew across the aisle. The invisible sexton at the back of the church cleared his throat sanctimoniously and threw open the doors as for a fine wedding. Beddoes hurried away from Sarah. He felt wildly, urgently depressed. He almost ran around the buttresses of the little church and into the twilit garden, which lay somberly between the high stone structure and the vicarage.

A few minutes later, when Sarah came slowly to join him, she found him sitting on a bench under a tall privet tree. He stared strangely at her, and she saw even in the twilight that his face was almost luminous with emotion. "What is it, my dear Mr. Beddoes? What is it?" she cried, sitting quickly down beside him.

"Mrs. MacLaren—I have just seen Tom!"

For a minute, neither spoke, and then Sarah laughed. "But how good! That is wonderful. Tom must like you very much. As we do, Mr. Beddoes, you know. That's really dear of Tom, I think!"

"I didn't think it dear at all, at first," Beddoes answered rather severely. "I was damned upset, I can tell you. I was sitting here, wondering why Perry didn't have some of his . . . his . . ."

"His ghoulies?"

"Yes, why he didn't have them go to church. And then Tom said—and I heard him as clearly as I'm sitting here—Tom said, 'Because we ain't ready yet, you damn fool!' And damn it, Mrs. MacLaren, he's as American as I am! He's no Limey. What's he doing over here?"

Sarah only shook her head, smiling softly, her eyes dark in the gentle round fullness of her face.

"And then I sat down here feeling sort of queer, and I looked up and there he stood. It's pretty dark, but I *saw* him, all right. He's short and twisted, like a little old jockey, only smaller. There was a sort of blue outline. Oh, hell!"

Sarah sighed, as if she felt tired. "Yes, he's like that. But they all are, for a while, Mr. Beddoes. They all are. But it's good that you saw him. He trusts you. He's still very lost, poor ghoulie, but he's beginning to trust Perry, and me most of the time, and now you. He's beginning to find himself." She sighed again, and stood up. "Let's go in. Perry's not coming for a time; he's helping the doctor with a poor woman in labor. I wish I'd had children. I'd have been a fine mother, I think."

She walked up the path, talking as if to herself, and Beddoes, following

24

her, felt a deep wrench at his heart. Poor Sarah! She was right. All that rich fullness of her body should have fed something other than lost souls.

"Turn on the switch there, dear Mr. Beddoes," she went on. "Right by your hand. We'll find a plate of cold toast. I like cold toast, especially when it grows a bit chewy, don't you?"

He had never thought about it, but now it was plain to him that he did, indeed, like cold toast. I wouldn't mind a good drink to wash it down, though, he thought.

"Tom says you'd like a drink." She stood in the doorway of the kitchen, with the toast on a blue plate in her hand. "Get a glass, then, and we'll pour a wee bit more from the vicar's bottle. We'll blame it on Tom." There was a faint sound of giggling in the hall, and she laughed, too. "He's a canny one," she added, and disappeared.

Beddoes found a tumbler and half filled it with water and then followed Sarah down the narrow musty hall to the parlor. He felt tired, but when he saw her sitting as if broken in the low chair by the hearth he wanted to cry out and fold her to him tenderly and mightily, like a cloud or a giant. Her little round arms lay down along her sides, and she looked up at him with a faint frown, as if she were trying to remember who he was and what he expected her to say. "Where is Mac's bottle?" he asked her.

"In the cupboard on the left—or is it on the right? On *your* right of his desk. Isn't it nice there's a fire? I think we'll have a storm soon. Poor Perry. But he loves to drive in storms. He took the doctor in his car with him."

Beddoes poured himself a good wallop from the bottle, and swirled the glass around. Then he walked down the long room to Sarah and said, "Here, you take a little of this."

She smiled, and sipped generously. "I like it," she said. "Thank you, Mr. Beddoes. It's fine now and again, I think, and I could easily do more of it. There's my position to think of, though." She sat up, quickly refreshed. "And now, what do you think of a little music until Perry's here again? Would you like Haydn, or are you noisy and disordered after your sight of poor Tom and ready for Tchaikovsky, perhaps?"

Beddoes felt dull. "I don't know much about music. My wife—she always goes to the Philharmonic, of course. But I haven't had much time for music myself."

"I've heard that of you American men. It's a pity, isn't it? I can tell, Mr. Beddoes, by the bumps on your brow, that you would have a fine feeling for it if you had the chance. We'll start with Tchaikovsky, then; he'll stir you and not bother your brain much. That's always best at first—not too much thought."

She went quietly to the study end of the room, and he could hear her sliding records out of their envelopes and fussing in a measured way, and then, as she walked back through the half-lighted room nearer to the fire, the first tempestuous strains of a piano playing with an orchestra crashed against his ears. He felt his hair prickling all over his head, and even under his arms. He lay back and let himself wash like seaweed in the tide of the music. Now and then, he sipped at his Scotch, but he did not think. He didn't even feel anything identifiable, but only a great weakness and fulfillment. Then, gradually, he began not to hear. His untrained ears were exhausted; the music became noise, and he looked about him once more. "Is it a Panotrone changer?" he whispered. "I knew a producer in Hollywood with one. It flashed red and green lights, I remember, when it was running out of records. Scared hell out of me."

"No," Sarah murmured. "It's Tom. He loves to change them. But listen—this is 'Eine Kleine Nachtmusik.'" She bent her head back again, so that it rolled slowly sideways.

Instead of listening, Beddoes looked at the smooth flow of her cheek. There must be a tiny down upon it, to catch the firelight with such gold. He wished he could see it more clearly, or perhaps touch it.

The music went on, with hardly a pause between records, and then there was a small crash, which sounded sharply in the peaceful room. Sarah stiffened, and Beddoes sat up nervously, the empty glass jerking in his hand.

"It's a record, I'm afraid," she murmured. "Tom, I'm coming. Never mind. Never mind, my dear!" she called out as she hurried to the other end of the room. "It will be all right," Beddoes heard her whisper urgently. "I'll tell Mr. MacLaren. Think no more of it, my darling, but play us the Mozart again. Then we'll stop. Come along now, don't mope!" She walked back to the fire again, and Beddoes, who had thoughtfully kept his eyes away from the phonograph, saw that she was shaking her head a little. "He feels dreadfully. This time it wasn't on purpose," she told him. "We'll listen to just one more, to buck him up a bit, don't you think?"

"Sure, poor fellow." It did not seem at all queer to Beddoes to be commiserating over the hurt pride of a ghoulie.

They listened dutifully, and then sat without talking. The man watched the woman and she watched the fire. "I'm sorry you must go tomorrow," she said finally. "Perry will have to call you at five, I'm afraid. The train leaves Carlisle early. We'll miss you, all of us."

They talked for a minute or two of trains and travel, but Beddoes had no feeling that he was actually leaving, and so soon. It was like reading a book—the words were all there, but he himself was not.

The train trip down to London was longer than he had remembered. Fog hid the landscape, except for quick hideous flashes of factories and an occasional hedgerow leading thornily into more fog. He twisted and steamed alone in his compartment until about noon, when an old man in a silk hat climbed angrily in beside him and, after one bitter stare, hid himself behind a paper.

A steward brought Beddoes a piece of cold ham with little pickles, and a bottle of stout. It tasted fine, and there was not enough of it. In spite of that, he was on the point of offering a part of it to the silent old man across from him when he saw a crumb or two fall between the discreetly striped thighs and realized that all the time the man had been eating, like a secretive rabbit, at bread and cheese, without another sign than the few crumbs from behind his stiffly held paper. Beddoes laughed to himself. Tea was the same—hot and bitter and welcome to the American, and a matter of hidden nibblings to the silent old man. British reserve, Beddoes decided; if he can stick it, I can.

Once, between luncheon and tea, something that had been mounting in him for more hours than he could count rose like a frightful wave, and for the first time since he had met Sarah MacLaren two days before, desire conquered him. He lay back palely against the cushions, his eyes closed. Every bone in his body ached as if he were catching influenza, and his brain swam. He was helpless, drowning, and he knew that although he had slept well with his slender wife, and would again, he had never felt passion for a woman until now. Gradually, he grew calm, resigned.

It was after dark, with steam on the windows and the old gentleman still inflexible behind his paper, when Beddoes first knew that Tom was in the compartment. He could not remember later whether Tom spoke to him or not, but there he was. Beddoes, who was wondering whether it was worth a glare from his fellow traveler to get up and open his suitcase and pull out the flask and take a good swig, clearly felt Tom say, "I'll get it down for you, sir."

"You will not," he snapped.

"What's that?" The paper finally lowered itself, and the old gentleman looked rather shyly over the top of it. "Did you speak, sir?"

Beddoes cleared his throat, rather like a butler being discreet in a bed-room farce, and smirked apologetically. It worked. The old man disappeared again.

From then on, the conversation was silent, but no less violent. "What in hell are you doing here, Tom?" Beddoes asked furiously.

"Well now, sir. Well, listen. I summed you up, see, Mr. Beddoes? And I figured—"

"Oh, you figured, did you? And what do you suppose Mrs. MacLaren is going to do without you? Who's going to keep them in line—Odessa and the old Duchess or whatever she is, and Agatha and all of them? So you walk out! A *fine* way to treat a woman who's—"

"We'd say 'lady' here in England, sir," Tom interrupted slyly, showing himself with a faint blue grin just above the seat level.

"Oh, you would, would you? 'We,' you say? You're no more English than I am, damn it! What in— Tom, what am I going to do with you? That's the hell of it." Beddoes saw the old gentleman lower his paper perhaps an inch and peer at him with a timid bloodshot eye.

"That's just it," Tom said softly. "You don't know yet, sir. But you may sometime. The hell of it, I mean."

Beddoes felt him grow sad and dim, and he was humiliated to remember Sarah's kind, tender ways. "O.K.," he said gruffly. "O.K., Tom. But you'll have to go back to Askhaven, you know. I mean it." And that was the end of the incident, as far as Beddoes could remember later.

In London, he felt the muted exhilaration he always knew there, as if he were a happy ghost himself. He sent his bags on to the hotel, and took a cab to the New Clarges on Half Moon Street for a small bottle of rather warm champagne at one of the little green tables in the street bar. Then he went back to his room, with only a sleepy nod from the night clerk and not a thought in his head of Tom. Inside his room, though, he saw that the stolen ghoulie—lost, strayed, *and* stolen, he thought solemnly—had been hard at work. Pajamas lay neatly ready, and on the marble dresser top were his toothbrush, his tubes of toothpaste and shaving cream, and the cabinet photograph of Mrs. Beddoes.

He felt coldly furious. The nerve of the fellow, to follow him to London and then try to weasel his way into things so that he could stay, when all the time Sarah needed him in Askhaven, and God knows what his wife would think, to have him land home with a ghoulie! He stood for a minute before he closed the door, cursing. There was no sight of Tom.

At last Beddoes saw the letter, which was leaning up against the photograph. It was smudged and cheap-looking, and he turned it over curiously a few times before he saw that the postmark was Askhaven. Askhaven, Thursday. Then it had been written before he went up there—mailed a day before he even started. "Dear Mr. Beddoes and Honor'd Sir," it said, in a sloping, pompous hand:

I regret to inform you that as postmaster and former keeper of the public house none nown known as ye Golden Duck now closed that your telegram being duly received re your visit I regret to inform you that the reverend Mr. Perry MacLaren our dear pastor and his good wife were immediately killed some eleven months five days ago in a dreadful motor accident in the high-lands near us. Please believe me honor'd sir your ob't servant and hoping to serve you if I but had the pub still but trade has gone to nothing lately so I remain,

Yours the postmaster,
JOHN GATES

P.S. The accident was in new car and all knew Mr. MacLaren was not a slow driver.

Yrs.
J. G.

Beddoes sat quietly for a long time. Outside the windows, partly open, an occasional taxi tooted, and, inside, the little glowing tube of the electric fireplace glowed like a scar against the wall. He felt, without thinking about it, as if he had in the last few days or minutes lived more than a thousand years. The letter lay like a grimy leaf upon his knee, and he looked dispassionately at it and at his hand beside it—his hand still firm and strong. He thought wearily of Mac and Sarah, and of the cold toast on the blue plate, and the whiskey and the music.

"O.K.," he said at last. "All right, Tom. Come on. My wife and I . . ."

MURIEL SPARK

The Portobello Road

One day in my young youth at high summer, lolling with my lovely companions upon a haystack, I found a needle. Already and privately for some years I had been guessing that I was set apart from the common run, but this of the needle attested the fact to my whole public: George, Kathleen and Skinny. I sucked my thumb, for when I had thrust my idle hand deep into the hay, the thumb was where the needle had stuck.

When everyone had recovered George said, "She put in her thumb and pulled out a plum." Then away we were into our merciless hacking-hecking laughter again.

The needle had gone fairly deep into the thumby cushion and a small red river flowed and spread from this tiny puncture. So that nothing of our joy should lag, George put in quickly.

"Mind your bloody thumb on my shirt."

Then hac-hec-hoo, we shrieked into the hot Borderland afternoon. Really I should not care to be so young of heart again. That is my thought every time I turn over my old papers and come across the photograph. Skinny, Kathleen and myself are in the photo atop the haystack. Skinny had just finished analyzing the inwards of my find.

"It couldn't have been done by brains. You haven't much brains but you're a lucky wee thing."

Everyone agreed that the needle betokened extraordinary luck. As it was becoming a serious conversation, George said,

31

"I'll take a photo."

I wrapped my hanky round my thumb and got myself organized. George pointed up from his camera and shouted,

"Look, there's a mouse!"

Kathleen screamed and I screamed although I think we knew there was no mouse. But this gave us an extra session of squalling hee-hoo's. Finally we three composed ourselves for George's picture. We look lovely and it was a great day at the time, but I would not care for it all over again. From that day I was known as Needle.

One Saturday in recent years I was mooching down the Portobello Road, threading among the crowds of marketers on the narrow pavement, when I saw a woman. She had a haggard, careworn, wealthy look, thin but for the breasts forced up high like a pigeon's. I had not seen her for nearly five years. How changed she was! But I recognized Kathleen, my friend; her features had already begun to sink and protrude in the way that mouths and noses do in people destined always to be old for their years. When I had last seen her, nearly five years ago, Kathleen, barely thirty, had said,

"I've lost all my looks, it's in the family. All the women are handsome as girls, but we go off early, we go brown and nosey."

I stood silently among the people, watching. As you will see, I wasn't in a position to speak to Kathleen. I saw her shoving in her avid manner from stall to stall. She was always fond of antique jewelry and of bargains. I wondered that I had not seen her before in the Portobello Road on my Saturday-morning ambles. Her long stiff-crooked fingers pounced to select a jade ring from among the jumble of brooches and pendants, onyx, moonstone and gold, set out on the stall.

"What do you think of this?" she said.

I saw then who was with her. I had been half conscious of the huge man following several paces behind her, and now I noticed him.

"It looks all right," he said. "How much is it?"

"How much is it?" Kathleen asked the vendor.

I took a good look at this man accompanying Kathleen. It was her husband. The beard was unfamiliar, but I recognized beneath it his enormous mouth, the bright sensuous lips, the large brown eyes forever brimming with pathos.

It was not for me to speak to Kathleen, but I had a sudden inspiration which caused me to say quietly.

"Hallo, George."

The giant of a man turned round to face the direction of my face. There were so many people—but at length he saw me.

"Hallo, George," I said again.

Kathleen had started to haggle with the stall-owner, in her old way, over the price of the jade ring. George continued to stare at me, his big mouth slightly parted so that I could see a wide slit of red lips and white teeth between the fair grassy growths of beard and mustache.

"My God!" he said.

"What's the matter?" said Kathleen.

"Hallo, George!" I said again, quite loud this time, and cheerfully.

"Look!" said George. "Look who's there, over beside the fruit stall."

Kathleen looked but didn't see.

"Who is it?" she said impatiently.

"It's Needle," he said. "She said 'Hallo, George.'"

"*Needle,*" said Kathleen. "Who do you mean? You don't mean our old friend *Needle* who—"

"Yes. There she is. My God!"

He looked very ill, although when I had said "Hallo, George" I had spoken friendly enough.

"I don't see anyone faintly resembling poor Needle," said Kathleen, looking at him. She was worried.

George pointed straight at me. "Look *there.* I tell you that is Needle."

"You're ill, George. Heavens, you must be seeing things. Come on home. Needle isn't there. You know as well as I do, Needle is dead."

I must explain that I departed this life nearly five years ago. But I did not altogether depart this world. There were those odd things still to be done which one's executors can never do properly. Papers to be looked over, even after the executors have torn them up. Lots of business except, of course, on Sundays and Holidays of Obligation, plenty to take an interest in for the time being. I take my recreation on Saturday mornings. If it is a wet Saturday I wander up and down the substantial lanes of Woolworth's as I did when I was young and visible. There is a pleasurable spread of objects on the counters which I now perceive and exploit with a certain detachment, since it suits with my condition of life. Creams, toothpastes, combs and hankies, cotton gloves, flimsy flowering scarves, writing paper and crayons, ice-cream cones and orangeade, screwdrivers, boxes of tacks, tins of paint, of glue, of marmalade; I always liked them but far more now that I have no need of any. When Saturdays are fine I go instead to the Portobello Road where formerly I would jaunt with Kathleen in our grown-up days. The barrow-loads do not change much, of apples and rayon vests in common blues and low-taste mauve, of silver plate, trays and teapots long since changed hands from the bygone citizens to dealers, from shops to the new flats and breakable homes, and then over to the barrow-stalls and the dealers again: Georgian spoons, rings, ear-rings of turquoise and opal set in the butterfly pattern of true-lovers' knot, patch boxes with miniature paintings of ladies on ivory, snuffboxes of silver with Scotch pebbles inset.

Sometimes as occasion arises on a Saturday morning, my friend Kathleen, who is a Catholic, has a Mass said for my soul, and then I am in attendance, as it were, at the church. But most Saturdays I take my delight among the solemn crowds with their aimless purposes, their eternal life not far away, who push past the counters and stalls, who handle, buy, steal, touch, desire and ogle the merchandise. I hear the tinkling tills, I hear the jangle of loose change and tongues and children wanting to hold and have.

That is how I came to be in the Portobello Road that Saturday morning when I saw George and Kathleen. I would not have spoken had I not been inspired to it. Indeed it's one of the things I can't do now—to speak out, unless inspired. And most extraordinary, on that morning as I spoke, a degree of visibility set in. I suppose from poor George's point of view it was like seeing a ghost when he saw me standing by the fruit barrow repeating in so friendly a manner, "Hallo, George!"

* * *

We were bound for the south. When our education, what we could get of it from the north, was thought to be finished, one by one we were sent or sent for to London. John Skinner, whom we called Skinny, went to study more archaeology, George to join his uncle's tobacco farm, Kathleen to stay with her rich connections and to potter intermittently in the Mayfair hat shop which one of them owned. A little later I also went to London to see life, for it was my ambition to write about life, which first I had to see.

"We four must stick together," George said very often in that yearning way of his. He was always desperately afraid of neglect. We four looked likely to shift off in different directions and George did not trust the other three of us not to forget all about him. More and more as the time came for him to depart for his uncle's tobacco farm in Africa he said,

"We four must keep in touch."

And before he left he told each of us anxiously,

"I'll write regularly, once a month. We must keep together for the sake of the old times." He had three prints taken from the negative of that photo on the haystack, wrote on the back of them "George took this the day that Needle found the needle" and gave us a copy each. I think we all wished he could become a bit more callous.

During my lifetime I was a drifter, nothing organized. It was difficult for my friends to follow the logic of my life. By the normal reckonings I should have come to starvation and ruin, which I never did. Of course, I did not live to write about life as I wanted to do. Possibly that is why I am inspired to do so now in these peculiar circumstances.

I taught in a private school in Kensington for almost three months, very small children. I didn't know what to do with them but I was kept fairly busy escorting incontinent little boys to the lavatory and telling the little girls to use their handkerchiefs. After that I lived a winter holiday in London on my small capital, and when that had run out I found a diamond bracelet in the cinema for which I received a reward of fifty pounds. When it was used up I got a job with a publicity man, writing speeches for absorbed industrialists, in which the dictionary of quotations came in very useful. So it went on. I got engaged to Skinny, but shortly after that I was left a small legacy, enough to keep me for six months. This somehow decided me that I didn't love Skinny so I gave him back the ring.

But it was through Skinny that I went to Africa. He was engaged with a party of researchers to investigate King Solomon's mines, that series of ancient workings ranging from the ancient port of Ophir, now called Beira, across Portuguese East Africa and Southern Rhodesia to the mighty jungle-city of Zimbabwe whose temple walls still stand by the approach to an ancient and sacred mountain, where the rubble of that civilization scatters itself over the surrounding Rhodesian waste. I accompanied the party as a sort of secretary. Skinny vouched for me, he paid my fare, he sympathized by his action with my inconsequential life although when he spoke of it he disapproved. A life like mine annoys most people; they go to their jobs every day, attend to things, give orders, pummel typewriters, and get two or three weeks off every year, and it vexes them to see someone else not bothering to do these things and yet getting away with it, not starving, being lucky as they call it. Skinny, when I had broken off our engagement, lectured me about this, but still he took me to Africa knowing I should probably leave his unit within a few months.

We were there a few weeks before we began enquiring for George, who was farming about four hundred miles away to the north. We had not told him of our plans.

"If we tell George to expect us in his part of the world he'll come rushing to pester us the first week. After all, we're going on business." Skinny had said.

Before we left Kathleen told us, "Give George my love and tell him not to send frantic cables every time I don't answer his letters right away. Tell him I'm busy in the hat shop and being presented. You would think he hadn't another friend in the world the way he carries on."

We had settled first at Fort Victoria, our nearest place of access to the Zimbabwe ruins. There we made enquiries about George. It was clear he hadn't many friends. The older settlers were the most tolerant about the half-caste woman he was living with, as we found, but they were furious about his methods of raising tobacco which we learned were most unprofessional and in some mysterious way disloyal to the whites. We could never discover how it was that George's style of tobacco farming gave the blacks opinions about themselves, but that's what the older settlers claimed. The newer immigrants thought he was unsociable and, of course, his living with that nig made visiting impossible.

I must say I was myself a bit off-put by this news about the brown woman. I was brought up in a university town to which came Indian, African and Asiatic students in a variety of tints and hues. I was brought up to avoid them for reasons connected with local reputation and God's ordinances. You cannot easily go against what you were brought up to do unless you are a rebel by nature.

Anyhow, we visited George eventually, taking advantage of the offer of transport from some people bound north in search of game. He had heard of our arrival in Rhodesia and though he was glad, almost relieved, to see us he pursued a policy of sullenness for the first hour.

"We wanted to give you a surprise, George."

"How were we to know that you'd get to hear of our arrival, George? News here must travel faster than light, George."

"We did hope to give you a surprise, George."

At last he said, "Well, I must say it's good to see you. All we need now is Kathleen. We four simply must stick together. You find, when you're in a place like this, there's nothing like old friends."

He showed us his drying sheds. He showed us a paddock where he was experimenting with a horse and a zebra mare, attempting to mate them. They were frolicking happily, but not together. They passed each other in their private play time and again, but without acknowledgment and without resentment.

"It's been done before," George said. "It makes a fine strong beast, more intelligent than a mule and sturdier than a horse. But I'm not having any success with this pair, they won't look at each other."

After a while, he said, "Come in for a drink and meet Matilda."

She was dark brown, with a subservient hollow chest and round shoulders, a gawky woman, very snappy with the houseboys. We said pleasant things as we drank on the stoep before dinner, but we found George difficult. For some reason he began to rail at me for breaking off my engagement to Skinny, saying what a dirty trick it was after all those good times in the old days. I diverted attention to Matilda. I supposed, I said, she knew this part of the country well?

"No," said she, "I been a-shellitered my life. I not put out to working. Me nothing to go from place to place is allowed like dirty girls does." In her speech she gave every syllable equal stress.

George explained, "Her father was a white magistrate in Natal. She had a sheltered upbringing, different from the other coloreds, you realize."

"Man, me no black-eyed Susan," said Matilda, "no, no."

On the whole, George treated her as a servant. She was about four months advanced in pregnancy, but he made her get up and fetch for him, many times. Soap: that was one of the things Matilda had to fetch. George made his own bath soap, showed it proudly, gave us the recipe, which I did not trouble to remember; I was fond of nice soaps during my lifetime and George's smelt of brilliantine and looked likely to soil one's skin.

"D'yo brahn?" Matilda asked me.

George said, "She is asking if you go brown in the sun."

"No, I go freckled."

"I got sister-in-law go freckles."

She never spoke another word to Skinny nor to me, and we never saw her again.

Some months later I said to Skinny,

"I'm fed up with being a camp follower."

He was not surprised that I was leaving his unit, but he hated my way of expressing it. He gave me a Presbyterian look.

"Don't talk like that. Are you going back to England or staying?"

"Staying, for a while."

"Well, don't wander too far off."

I was able to live on the fee I got for writing a gossip column in a local weekly, which wasn't my idea of writing about life, of course. I made friends, more than I could cope with, after I left Skinny's exclusive little band of archaeologists. I had the attractions of being newly out from England and of wanting to see life. Of the countless young men and go-ahead families who purred me along the Rhodesian roads, hundred after hundred miles, I only kept up with one family when I returned to my native land. I think that was because they were the most representative, they stood for all the rest: people in those parts are very typical of each other, as one group of standing stones in that wilderness is like the next.

I met George once more in a hotel in Bulawayo. We drank highballs and spoke of war. Skinny's party were just then deciding whether to remain in the country or return home. They had reached an exciting part of their research, and whenever I got a chance to visit Zimbabwe he would take me for a moonlight walk in the ruined temple and try to make me see phantom Phoenicians flitting ahead of us, or along the walls. I had half a mind to marry Skinny; perhaps, I thought, when his studies were finished. The impending war was in our bones: so I remarked to George as we sat drinking highballs on the hotel stoep in the hard bright sunny July winter of that year.

George was inquisitive about my relations with Skinny. He tried to pump me for about half an hour and when at last I said, "You are becoming aggressive, George," he stopped. He became quite pathetic. He said, "War or no war I'm clearing out of this."

"It's the heat does it," I said.

"I'm clearing out in any case. I've lost a fortune in tobacco. My uncle is making a fuss. It's the other bloody planters: once you get the wrong side of them you're finished in this wide land."

"What about Matilda?" I asked.

He said, "She'll be all right. She's got hundreds of relatives."

I had already heard about the baby girl. Coal black, by repute, with George's features. And another on the way, they said.

"What about the child?"

He didn't say anything to that. He ordered more highballs and when they arrived he swizzled his for a long time with a stick. "Why didn't you ask me to your twenty-first?" he said then.

"I didn't have anything special, no party, George. We had a quiet drink among ourselves, George, just Skinny and the old professors and two of the wives and me, George."

"You didn't ask me to your twenty-first," he said. "Kathleen writes to me regularly."

This wasn't true. Kathleen sent me letters fairly often in which she said, "Don't tell George I wrote to you as he will be expecting word from me and I can't be bothered actually."

"But you," said George, "don't seem to have any sense of old friendships, you and Skinny."

"Oh, George!" I said.

"Remember the times we had," George said. "We used to have times." His large brown eyes began to water.

"I'll have to be getting along," I said.

"Please don't go. Don't leave me just yet. I've something to tell you."

"Something nice?" I laid on an eager smile. All responses to George had to be overdone.

"You don't know how lucky you are," George said.

"How?" I said. Sometimes I got tired of being called lucky by everybody. There were times when, privately practicing my writings about life, I knew the bitter side of my fortune. When I failed again and again to reproduce life in some satisfactory and perfect form, I was the more imprisoned, for all my carefree living, within my craving for this satisfaction. Sometimes, in my impotence and need I secreted a venom which infected all my life for days on end and which spurted out indiscriminately on Skinny or on anyone who crossed my path.

"You aren't bound by anyone," George said. "You come and go as you please. Something always turns up for you. You're free, and you don't know your luck."

"You're a damn sight more free than I am," I said sharply. "You've got your rich uncle."

"He's losing interest in me," George said. "He's had enough."

"Oh well, you're young yet. What was it you wanted to tell me?"

"A secret," George said. "Remember we used to have those secrets."

"Oh, yes we did."

"Did you ever tell any of mine?"

"Oh no, George." In reality, I couldn't remember any particular secret out of the dozens we must have exchanged from our schooldays onwards.

"Well, this is a secret, mind. Promise not to tell."

"Promise."

"I'm married."

"Married, George! Oh, who to?"

"Matilda."

"How dreadful!" I spoke before I could think, but he agreed with me.

"Yes, it's awful, but what could I do?"

"You might have asked my advice," I said pompously.

"I'm two years older than you are. I don't ask advice from you, Needle, little beast."

"Don't ask for sympathy, then."

"A nice friend you are," he said, "I must say after all these years."

"Poor George!" I said.

"There are three white men to one white woman in this country," said George. "An isolated planter doesn't see a white woman and if he sees one she doesn't see him. What could I do? I needed the woman."

I was nearly sick. One, because of my Scottish upbringing. Two because of my horror of corny phrases like "I needed the woman," which George repeated twice again.

"And Matilda got tough," said George, "after you and Skinny came to visit us. She had some friends at the Mission, and she packed up and went to them."

"You should have let her go," I said.

"I went after her," George said. "She insisted on being married, so I married her."

"That's not a proper secret, then," I said. "The news of a mixed marriage soon gets about."

"I took care of that," George said. "Crazy as I was, I took her to the Congo and married her there. She promised to keep quiet about it."

"Well, you can't clear off and leave her now, surely," I said.

"I'm going to get out of this place. I can't stand the woman and I can't stand the country. I didn't realize what it would be like. Two years of the country and three months of my wife has been enough."

"Will you get a divorce?"

"No, Matilda's Catholic. She won't divorce."

George was fairly getting through the highballs, and I wasn't far behind him. His brown eyes floated shiny and liquid as he told me how he had written to tell his uncle of his plight, "Except, of course, I didn't say we were married, that would have been too much for him. He's a prejudiced hardened old colonial. I only said I'd had a child by a colored woman and was expecting another, and he perfectly understood. He came at once by plane a few weeks ago. He's made a settlement on her, providing she keeps her mouth shut about her association with me."

"Will she do that?"

"Oh, yes, or she won't get the money."

"But as your wife she has a claim on you, in any case."

"If she claimed as my wife she'd get far less. Matilda knows what she's doing, greedy bitch she is. She'll keep her mouth shut."

"Only, you won't be able to marry again, will you, George?"

"Not unless she dies," he said. "And she's as strong as a trek ox."

"Well, I'm sorry, George," I said.

"Good of you to say so," he said. "But I can see by your chin that you disapprove of me. Even my old uncle understood."

"Oh, George, I quite understand. You were lonely, I suppose."

"You didn't even ask me to your twenty-first. If you and Skinny had been nicer to me, I would never have lost my head and married the woman, never."

"You didn't ask me to your wedding," I said.

"You're a catty bissom, Needle, not like what you were in the old times when you used to tell us your wee stories."

"I'll have to be getting along," I said.

"Mind you keep the secret," George said.

"Can't I tell Skinny? He would be very sorry for you, George."

"You mustn't tell anyone. Keep it a secret. Promise."

"Promise," I said. I understood that he wished to enforce some sort of bond between us with this secret, and I thought, "Oh well, I suppose he's lonely. Keeping his secret won't do any harm."

I returned to England with Skinny's party just before the war.

I did not see George again till just before my death, five years ago.

After the war Skinny returned to his studies. He had two more exams, over a period of eighteen months, and I thought I might marry him when the exams were over.

"You might do worse than Skinny," Kathleen used to say to me on our Saturday-morning excursions to the antique shops and the junk stalls.

She too was getting on in years. The remainder of our families in Scotland were hinting that it was time we settled down with husbands. Kathleen was a little younger than me, but looked much older. She knew her chances were diminishing but at that time I did not think she cared very much. As for myself, the main attraction of marrying Skinny was his prospective expeditions to Mesopotamia. My desire to marry him had to be stimulated by the continual reading of books about Babylon and Assyria; perhaps Skinny felt this, because he supplied the books and even started instructing me in the art of deciphering cuneiform tablets.

Kathleen was more interested in marriage than I thought. Like me, she had racketed around a good deal during the war; she had actually been engaged to an officer in the U.S. navy, who was killed. Now she kept an antique shop near Lambeth, was doing very nicely, lived in a Chelsea square, but for all that she must have wanted to be married and have children. She would stop and look into all the prams which the mothers had left outside shops or area gates.

"The poet Swinburne used to do that," I told her once.

"Really? Did he want children of his own?"

"I shouldn't think so. He simply liked babies."

Before Skinny's final exam he fell ill and was sent to a sanatorium in Switzerland.

"You're fortunate after all not to be married to him," Kathleen said. "You might have caught T.B."

I was fortunate, I was lucky . . . so everyone kept telling me on different occasions. Although it annoyed me to hear, I knew they were right, but in a way that was different from what they meant. It took me very small effort to make a living; book reviews, odd jobs for Kathleen, a few months with the publicity man again, still getting up speeches about literature, art and life for industrial tycoons. I was waiting to write about life and it seemed to me that the good fortune lay in this, whenever it should be. And until then I was assured of my charmed life, the necessities of existence always coming my way and I with far more leisure than anyone else. I thought of my type of luck after I became a Catholic and was being confirmed. The Bishop touches the candidate on the cheek, a symbolic reminder of the sufferings a Christian is supposed to undertake. I thought, how lucky, what a feathery symbol to stand for the hellish violence of its true meaning.

I visited Skinny twice in the two years that he was in the sanatorium. He was almost cured, and expected to be home within a few months. I told Kathleen after my last visit.

"Maybe I'll marry Skinny when he's well again."

"Make it definite, Needle, and not so much of the maybe. You don't know when you're well off," she said.

This was five years ago, in the last year of my life. Kathleen and I had become very close friends. We met several times each week, and after our Saturday-morning excursions in the Portobello Road very often I would accompany Kathleen to her aunt's house in Kent for a long weekend.

One day in the June of that year I met Kathleen specially for lunch because she had phoned me to say she had news.

"Guess who came into the shop this afternoon," she said.

"Who?"

"George."

We had half imagined George was dead. We had received no letters in the past ten years. Early in the war we had heard rumors of his keeping a night club in Durban, but nothing after that. We could have made inquiries if we had felt moved to do so.

At one time, when we discussed him, Kathleen had said,

"I ought to get in touch with poor George. But then I think he would write back. He would demand a regular correspondence again."

"We four must stick together," I mimicked.

"I can visualize his reproachful limpid orbs," Kathleen said.

Skinny said, "He's probably gone native. With his coffee concubine and a dozen mahogany kids."

"Perhaps he's dead," Kathleen said.

I did not speak of George's marriage, nor of any of his confidences in the hotel at Bulawayo. As the years passed we ceased to mention him except in passing, as someone more or less dead so far as we were concerned.

Kathleen was excited about George's turning up. She had forgotten her impatience with him in former days; she said,

"It was so wonderful to see old George. He seems to need a friend, feels neglected, out of touch with things."

"He needs mothering, I suppose."

Kathleen didn't notice the malice. She declared, "That's exactly the case with George. It always has been, I can see it now."

She seemed ready to come to any rapid new and happy conclusion about George. In the course of the morning he had told her of his wartime night club in Durban, his game-shooting expeditions since. It was clear he had not mentioned Matilda. He had put on weight, Kathleen told me, but he could carry it.

I was curious to see this version of George, but I was leaving for Scotland next day and did not see him till September of that year, just before my death.

While I was in Scotland I gathered from Kathleen's letters that she was seeing George very frequently, finding enjoyable company in him, looking after him. "You'll be surprised to see how he has developed." Apparently he would hang round Kathleen in her shop most days: "It makes him feel useful," as she maternally expressed it. He had an old relative in Kent whom he visited at weekends; this old lady lived a few miles from Kathleen's aunt, which made it easy for them to travel down together on Saturdays, and go for long country walks.

45

"You'll see such a difference in George," Kathleen said on my return to London in September. I was to meet him that night, a Saturday. Kathleen's aunt was abroad, the maid on holiday, and I was to keep Kathleen company in the empty house.

George had left London for Kent a few days earlier. "He's actually helping with the harvest down there!" Kathleen told me lovingly.

Kathleen and I planned to travel down together, but on that Saturday she was unexpectedly delayed in London on some business. It was arranged that I should go ahead of her in the early afternoon to see to the provisions for our party; Kathleen had invited George to dinner at her aunt's house that night.

"I should be with you by seven," she said. "Sure you won't mind the empty house? I hate arriving at empty houses, myself."

I said no, I liked an empty house.

So I did, when I got there. I had never found the house more likable. A large Georgian vicarage in about eight acres, most of the rooms shut and sheeted, there being only one servant. I discovered that I wouldn't need to go shopping, Kathleen's aunt had left many and delicate supplies with notes attached to them: "Eat this up please do, see also fridge" and "A treat for three hungry people see also 2 bttles beaune for yr party on back kn table." It was like a treasure hunt as I followed clue after clue through the cool silent domestic quarters. A house in which there are no people—but with all the signs of tenancy—can be a most tranquil good place. People take up space in a house out of proportion to their size. On my previous visits I had seen the rooms overflowing as it seemed, with Kathleen, her aunt, and the little fat maidservant; they were always on the move. As I wandered through that part of the house which was in use, opening windows to let in the pale yellow air of September, I was not conscious that I, Needle, was taking up any space at all; I might have been a ghost.

The only thing to be fetched was the milk. I waited till after four, when the milking should be done, then set off for the farm which lay across two fields at the back of the orchard. There, when the byreman was handing me the bottle, I saw George.

"Hallo, George," I said.

"Needle! What are you doing here?" he said.

"Fetching milk," I said.

"So am I. Well, it's good to see you, I must say."

As we paid the farm hand, George said, "I'll walk back with you part of the way. But I mustn't stop, my old cousin's without any milk for her tea. How's Kathleen?"

"She was kept in London. She's coming on later, about seven, she expects."

We had reached the end of the first field. George's way led to the left and on to the main road.

"We'll see you tonight, then?" I said.

"Yes, and talk about old times."

"Grand," I said.

But George got over the stile with me.

"Look here," he said. "I'd like to talk to you, Needle."

"We'll talk tonight, George. Better not keep your cousin waiting for the milk." I found myself speaking to him almost as if he were a child.

"No, I want to talk to you alone. This is a good opportunity."

We began to cross the second field. I had been hoping to have the house to myself for a couple more hours and I was rather petulant.

"See," he said suddenly, "that haystack."

"Yes," I said absently.

"Let's sit there and talk. I'd like to see you up on a haystack again. I still keep that photo. Remember that time when—"

"I found the needle," I said very quickly, to get it over.

But I was glad to rest. The stack had been broken up, but we managed to find a nest in it. I buried my bottle of milk in the hay for coolness. George placed his carefully at the foot of the stack.

'My old cousin is terribly vague, poor soul. A bit hazy in her head. She hasn't the least sense of time. If I tell her I've only been gone ten minutes she'll believe it.'

I giggled, and looked at him. His face had grown much larger, his lips full, wide and with a ripe color that is strange in a man. His brown eyes were abounding as before with some inarticulate plea.

"So you're going to marry Skinny after all these years?"

"I really don't know, George."

"You played him up properly."

"It isn't for you to judge. I have my own reasons for what I do."

"Don't get sharp," he said, "I was only funning." To prove it, he lifted a tuft of hay and brushed my face with it.

"D'you know," he said next, "I didn't think you and Skinny treated me very decently in Rhodesia."

"Well, we were busy, George. And we were younger then, we had a lot to do and see. After all, we could see you any other time, George."

"A touch of selfishness," he said.

"I'll have to be getting along, George." I made to get down from the stack.

He pulled me back. "Wait, I've got something to tell you."

"O.K., George, tell me."

"First promise not to tell Kathleen. She wants it kept a secret so that she can tell you herself."

"All right. Promise."

"I'm going to marry Kathleen."

"But you're already married."

Sometimes I heard news of Matilda from the one Rhodesian family with whom I still kept up. They referred to her as "George's Dark Lady" and of course they did not know he was married to her. She had apparently made a good thing out of George, they said, for she minced around all tarted up, never did a stroke of work and was always unsettling the respectable colored girls in their neighborhood. According to accounts, she was a living example of the folly of behaving as George did.

"I married Matilda in the Congo," George was saying.

"It would still be bigamy," I said.

He was furious when I used that word bigamy. He lifted a handful of hay as if he would throw it in my face, but controlling himself meanwhile he fanned it at me playfully.

"I'm not sure that the Congo marriage was valid," he continued. "Anyway, as far as I'm concerned, it isn't."

"You can't do a thing like that," I said.

"I need Kathleen. She's been decent to me. I think we were always meant for each other, me and Kathleen."

"I'll have to be going," I said.

But he put his knee over my ankles, so that I couldn't move. I sat still and gazed into space.

He tickled my face with a wisp of hay.

"Smile up, Needle," he said; "let's talk like old times."

"Well?"

"No one knows about my marriage to Matilda except you and me."

"And Matilda," I said.

"She'll hold her tongue so long as she gets her payments. My uncle left an annuity for the purpose, his lawyers see to it."

"Let me go, George."

"You promised to keep it a secret," he said, "you promised."

"Yes, I promised."

"And now that you're going to marry Skinny, we'll be properly coupled off as we should have been years ago. We should have been—but youth!—our youth got in the way, didn't it?"

"Life got in the way," I said.

"But everything's going to be all right now. You'll keep my secret, won't you? You promised." He had released my feet. I edged a little further from him.

I said, "If Kathleen intends to marry you, I shall tell her that you're already married."

"You wouldn't do a dirty trick like that, Needle? You're going to be happy with Skinny, you wouldn't stand in the way of my—"

"I must, Kathleen's my best friend," I said swiftly.

He looked as if he would murder me and he did. He stuffed hay into my mouth until it could hold no more, kneeling on my body to keep it still, holding both my wrists tight in his huge left hand. I saw the red full lines of his mouth and the white slit of his teeth last thing on earth. Not another soul passed by as he pressed my body into the stack, as he made a deep nest for me, tearing up the hay to make a groove the length of my corpse, and finally pulling the warm dry stuff in a mound over this concealment, so natural-looking in a broken haystack. Then George climbed down, took up his bottle of milk and went his way. I suppose that was why he looked so unwell when I stood, nearly five years later, by the barrow in the Portobello Road and said in easy tones, "Hallo, George!"

The Haystack Murder was one of the notorious crimes of that year.

My friends said, "A girl who had everything to live for."

After a search that lasted twenty hours, when my body was found, the evening papers said, " 'Needle' is found: in haystack!"

Kathleen, speaking from that Catholic point of view which takes some getting used to, said, "She was at Confession only the day before she died—wasn't she lucky?"

The poor byre hand who sold us the milk was grilled for hour after hour by the local police, and later by Scotland Yard. So was George. He admitted walking as far as the haystack with me, but he denied lingering there.

"You hadn't seen your friend for ten years?" the Inspector asked him.

"That's right," said George.

"And you didn't stop to have a chat?"

"No. We'd arranged to meet later at dinner. My cousin was waiting for the milk, I couldn't stop."

The old soul, his cousin, swore that he hadn't been gone more than ten minutes in all, and she believed it to the day of her death a few months later. There was the microscopic evidence of hay on George's jacket, of course, but the same evidence was on every man's jacket in the district that fine harvest year. Unfortunately, the byreman's hands were even brawnier and mightier than George's. The marks on my wrists had been done by such hands, so the laboratory charts indicated when my post-mortem was all completed. But the wrist-marks weren't enough to pin down the crime to either man. If I hadn't been wearing my long-sleeved cardigan, it was said, the bruises might have matched up properly with someone's fingers.

Kathleen, to prove that George had absolutely no motive, told the police that she was engaged to him. George thought this a little foolish. They checked up on his life in Africa, right back to his living with Matilda. But the marriage didn't come out—who would think of looking up registers in the Congo? Not that this would have proved any motive for murder. All the same, George was relieved when the enquiries were over without the marriage to Matilda being disclosed. He was able to have his nervous breakdown at the same time as Kathleen had hers, and they recovered together and got married, long after the police had shifted their enquiries to an Air Force camp five miles from Kathleen's aunt's home. Only a lot of excitement and drinks came of those investigations. The Haystack Murder was one of the unsolved crimes that year.

Shortly afterward the byre hand emigrated to Canada to start afresh, with the help of Skinny, who felt sorry for him.

After seeing George taken away home by Kathleen that Saturday in the Portobello Road, I thought that perhaps I might be seeing more of him in similar circumstances. The next Saturday I looked out for him, and at last there he was, without Kathleen, half worried, half hopeful.

I dashed his hopes. I said, "Hallo, George!"

He looked in my direction, rooted in the midst of the flowing market-mongers in that convivial street. I thought to myself, "He looks as if he had a mouthful of hay." It was the new bristly maize-colored beard and mustache surrounding his great mouth which suggested the thought, gay and lyrical as life.

"Hallo, George!" I said again.

I might have been inspired to say more on that agreeable morning, but he didn't wait. He was away down a side street and along another street and down one more, zigzag, as far and as devious as he could take himself from the Portobello Road.

Nevertheless he was back again next week. Poor Kathleen had brought him in her car. She left it at the top of the street, and got out with him, holding him tight by the arm. It grieved me to see Kathleen ignoring the spread of scintillations on the stalls. I had myself seen a charming Battersea box quite to her taste, also a pair of enameled silver earrings. But she took no notice of these wares, clinging close to George, and, poor Kathleen—I hate to say how she looked.

And George was haggard. His eyes seemed to have got smaller as if he had been recently in pain. He advanced up the road with Kathleen on his arm, letting himself lurch from side to side with his wife bobbing beside him, as the crowds asserted their rights of way.

"Oh, George!" I said. "You don't look at all well, George."

"Look!" said George. "Over there by the hardware barrow. That's Needle."

Kathleen was crying. "Come back home, dear," she said.

"Oh, you don't look well, George!" I said.

They took him to a nursing home. He was fairly quiet, except on Saturday mornings when they had a hard time of it to keep him indoors and away from the Portobello Road.

But a couple of months later he did escape. It was a Monday.

They searched for him in the Portobello Road, but actually he had gone off to Kent to the village near the scene of the Haystack Murder. There he went to the police and gave himself up, but they could tell from the way he was talking that there was something wrong with the man.

"I saw Needle in the Portobello Road three Saturdays running," he explained, "and they put me in a private ward but I got away while the nurses were seeing to the new patient. You remember the murder of Needle—well, I did it. Now you know the truth, and that will keep bloody Needle's mouth shut."

Dozens of poor mad fellows confess to every murder. The police obtained an ambulance to take him back to the nursing home. He wasn't there long. Kathleen gave up her shop and devoted herself to looking after him at home. But she found that the Saturday mornings were a strain. He insisted on going to see me in the Portobello Road and would come back to insist that he'd murdered Needle. Once he tried to tell her something about Matilda, but Kathleen was so kind and solicitous, I don't think he had the courage to remember what he had to say.

Skinny had always been rather reserved with George since the murder. But he was kind to Kathleen. It was he who persuaded them to emigrate to Canada so that George should be well out of reach of the Portobello Road.

George has recovered somewhat in Canada but of course he will never be the old George again, as Kathleen writes to Skinny. "That Haystack tragedy did for George," she writes, "I feel sorrier for George sometimes than I am for poor Needle. But I do often have Masses said for Needle's soul."

I doubt if George will ever see me again in the Portobello Road. He broods much over the crumpled snapshot he took of us on the haystack. Kathleen does not like the photograph, I don't wonder. For my part, I consider it quite a jolly snap, but I don't think we were any of us so lovely as we look in it, gazing blatantly over the ripe cornfields, Skinny with his humorous expression, I secure in my difference from the rest, Kathleen with her head prettily perched on her hand, each reflecting fearlessly in the face of George's camera the glory of the world, as if it would never pass.

ROBERTSON DAVIES

The Ghost Who Vanished by Degrees

Some of you may have wondered what became of our College Ghost. Because we had a ghost, and there are people in this room who saw him. He appeared briefly last year at the College Dance on the stairs up to this Hall, and at the Gaudy he was seen to come and go through that door, while I was reading an account of another strange experience of mine. I did not see him then, but several people did so. What became of him?

I know. I am responsible for his disappearance. I think I may say without unwarrantable spiritual pride that I laid him. And, as is always the case in these psychic experiences, it was not without great cost to myself.

When first the Ghost was reported to me, I assumed that we had a practical joker within the College. Yet—the nature of the joke was against any such conclusion. We had had plenty of jokes—socks in the pool, fish in the pool, funny notices beside the pool, pumpkins on the roofs, ringing the bell at strange hours—all the wild exuberance, the bubbling, ungovernable high spirits and gossamer fantasy one associates with the Graduate School of the University of Toronto. The wit of a graduate student is like champagne—Canadian champagne—but this joke had a different flavor, a dash of wormwood, in its nature.

You see, the Ghost was so unlike a joker. He did not appear in a white sheet and shout "Boo!" He spoke to no one, though a Junior Fellow—the one who met him on the stairs—told me that the Ghost passed him, softly laying a finger on its lips to caution him to silence. On its lips, did I say? Now this

54

is of first importance: it laid its finger where its lips doubtless were, but its lips could not be seen, nor any of its features. Everybody who saw it said that the Ghost had a head, and a place where its face ought to be—but no face that anybody could see or recognize or remember. Of course there are scores of people like that around the university, but they are not silent; they are clamoring to establish some sort of identity; the Ghost cherished his anonymity, his facelessness. So, perversely I determined to find out who he was.

The first time I spotted him was in the Common Room. I went in from my study after midnight to turn out the lights, and he was just to be seen going along the short passage to the Upper Library. I gave chase, but when I reached the Upper Library he had gone, and when I ran into the entry, he was not to be seen. But at last I was on his trail, and I kept my eyes open from that time.

All of this took place, you should know, last Christmas, between the Gaudy and New Year. Our Gaudy last year was on December the seventeenth; I first saw the Ghost, and lost him, on the twenty-first. He came again on the twenty-third. I woke in the night with an odd sensation that someone was watching me, and as this was in my own bedroom I was very angry; if indeed it were a joker he lacked all discretion. I heard a stirring and—I know this sounds like the shabbiest kind of nineteenth-century romance, but I swear it is true—I heard a sigh, and then, on the landing outside my door, a soft explosion, and a thud, as though something had fallen. I ran out of my room, but there was nothing to be seen. Over Christmas Day and Boxing Day I had no news of the Ghost, but on the twenty-eighth of December matters came to a head.

December the twenty-eighth, as some of you may know, is the Feast of the Holy Innocents, traditionally the day on which King Herod slaughtered the children of Bethlehem. In the Italian shops in this city you can buy very pretty little babies, made of sugar, and eat them, in grisly commemoration of Herod's whimsical act.

I was sitting in my study at about eleven o'clock that night, reflectively nibbling at the head of a sugarbaby and thinking about money, when I noticed that the lights were on in the Round Room. It troubles me to see electric current wasted, so I set out for the Round Room in a bad humor. As I walked across the quad, it seemed that the glow from the skylight in the Round Room was more blue and cold than it should be, and seemed to waver. I thought it must be a trick of the snow, which was falling softly, and the moonlight which played so prettily upon it.

I unlocked the doors, walked into the Round Room, and there he was, standing under the middle of the skylight.

He bowed courteously. "So you have come at last," said he.

"I have come to turn out the lights," said I, and realized at once that the lights were not on. The room glowed with a fitful bluish light, not disagreeable but inexpressibly sad. And the stranger spoke in a voice which was sad, yet beautiful.

It was his voice which first told me who he was. It had a compelling, cellolike note which was unlike anything I was accustomed to hear inside the College, though our range is from the dispirited quack of Ontario to the reverberant splendors of Nigeria. The magnificent voice came from the part of his head where a face should be—but there was no face there, only a shadow, which seemed to change a little in density as I looked at it. It was unquestionably the Ghost!

This was no joker, no disguised Junior Fellow. He was our Ghost, and like every proper ghost he was transporting and other-worldly, rather than merely alarming. I felt no fear as I looked at him, but I was deeply uneasy.

"You have come at last," said the Ghost. "I have waited for you long— but of course you are busy. Every professor in this university is busy. He is talking, or he is pursuing, or he is in a journey, or peradventure he sleepeth. But none has time for an act of mercy."

It pleased me to hear the Ghost quote Scripture; if we must have apparitions, by all means let them be literate.

"You have come here for mercy?" said I.

"I have come for the ordeal, which is also the ultimate mercy," he replied.

"But we don't go in for ordeals," said I. "Perhaps you can tell me a little more plainly what it is you want?"

"Is this not the Graduate School?" said he.

"No indeed," said I; "this is a graduate college, but the offices of the Graduate School are elsewhere."

"Don't trifle with me," said the Ghost sternly. "Many things are growing very dim to me, but I have not wholly lost my sense of place; this is the Graduate School; this is the Examination Room. And yet"—the voice faltered—"it seemed to me that it used to be much higher in the air, much less handsome than this. I remember stairs—very many stairs. . . ."

"You had been climbing stairs when you came to me in my bedroom," said I.

"Yes," he said eagerly. "I climbed the stairs—right to the top—and went into the Examination Room—and there you lay in bed, and I knew I had missed it again. And so there was nothing for it but to kill myself again."

That settled it. Now I knew who he was, and I had a pretty shrewd idea where, so far as he was concerned, we both were.

Every university has its secrets—things which are nobody's fault, but which are open to serious misunderstanding. Thirty or more years ago a graduate student was ploughed on his Ph.D. oral; he must have expected something of the kind because when he had been called before his examiners and given the bad news he stepped out on the landing and shot himself through the head. It is said, whether truly or not I cannot tell, that since that time nobody is allowed to proceed to the presentation and defense of his thesis unless there is a probability amounting to a certainty that he will get his degree.

Here, obviously, was that unfortunate young man, standing with me in the Round Room. Why here? Because, before Massey College was built, the Graduate School was housed in an old dwelling on this land, and the Examination Room was at the top of the house, as nearly as possible where my bedroom is now. Before that time the place had been the home of one of the Greek-letter fraternities—the Mu Kau Mu, I believe it was called.

"The Examination Room you knew has gone," said I. "If you are looking for it, I fear you must go to Teperman's wrecking yard, for whatever remains of it is there."

"But is this not an Examination Room?" said the Ghost. I nodded. "Then I beg you, by all that is merciful, to examine me," he cried, and to my embarrassed astonishment, threw himself at my feet.

"Examine you for what?" I said.

"For my Ph.D.," wailed the Ghost, and the eerie, agonized tone in which it uttered those commonplace letters made me, for the first time, afraid. "I must have it. I knew no rest when I was in the world of men, because I was seeking it; I know no rest now, as I linger on the threshold of another life, because I lack it. I shall never be at peace without it."

I have often heard it said that the Ph.D. is a vastly overvalued degree, but I had not previously thought that it might stand between a man and his eternal rest. I was becoming as agitated as the Ghost.

"My good creature," said I, rather emotionally, "if I can be of any assistance—"

"You can," cried the Ghost, clawing at the knees of my trousers with its transparent hands; "examine me, I beg of you. Examine me now and set me free. I'm quite ready."

"But, just a moment," said I; "the papers—the copies of your thesis—"

"All ready," said the Ghost, in triumph. And, though I swear that they were not there before, I now saw that all the circle of tables in the Round Room was piled high with those dismal, unappetizing volumes—great wads of type-written octavo paper—which are Ph.D. theses.

"Be reasonable," said I. "I don't suppose for a minute I can examine you. What is your field?"

"What's yours?" said the Ghost, and if a Ghost can speak cunningly, that is exactly what this one did now.

"English Literature," I said; "more precisely, the drama of the nineteenth-century, with special emphasis on the popular drama of the transpontine London theaters between 1800 and 1850."

Most people find that discouraging, and change the subject. But the Ghost positively frisked to one of the heaps, drew out an especially thick thesis, and handed it to me.

"Shall I sit here?" he asked, pointing to the red chair, which, as you know, has a place of special prominence in that room.

"By no means," said I, shocked by such an idea.

"Oh, I had so hoped I might," said the Ghost.

"My dear fellow, you have been listening to University gossip," said I. "There are people who pretend that we put the examinee in that chair and sit around the room in a ring, baiting him till he bursts into tears. It is the sort of legend in which scientists and other mythomaniacs take delight. No, no; if you will go away for a few hours—say until tomorrow at ten o'clock—I shall have the room set up for an examination. You shall have a soft chair, cheek by jowl with your examiners, with lots of cigarettes, unlimited water to drink, a fan, and a trained nurse in attendance to take you to the Examinees' W.C. and bring you back again, should the need occur. We are very well aware here that Ph.D. candidates are delicate creatures, subject to unaccountable metaphysical ills—"

The Ghost broke in, impatiently. "Rubbish," he said; "I'm quite ready. Let's get to work. You sit in the red chair. I'm perfectly happy to stand. I think I'm pretty well prepared"—and as he said this I swear that something like a leer passed over the shadow that should have been a face—"and I'm ready as soon as you are."

There was nothing for it. The Ghost had taken command. I sat down in the red chair—my chair—and opened the thesis. *Prologomena to the Study of the Christ Symbol in the Plays of Thomas Egerton Wilks*, I read, and my heart, which had been sinking for the last few moments, now plunged so suddenly that I almost lost consciousness. I have heard of Wilks—it is my job to have heard of him—but of his fifty-odd melodramas, farces, and burlesque extravaganzas I have not read a line. However, I have my modest store of professor-craft. I opened the thesis, riffled through the pages, hummed and hawed a little, made a small mark in the margin of one page, and said—"Well, suppose, for a beginning, you give me a general outline of your argument."

He did.

Forty-five minutes later, when I could get a word in, I asked him just where he thought the Christ symbol made its first appearance in *My Wife's Dentist, or The Balcony Beau*, which is one of Wilks' dreary farces.

He told me.

Before he had finished he had also given me more knowledge than I really wanted about the Christ symbol in *Woman's Love or Kate Wynsley the Cottage Girl, Raffaelle the Reprobate, or the Secret Mission and the Signet Ring, The Ruby Ring, or The Murder at Sadlers Wells,* and another farce named, more simply, *Bamboozling.*

By this time I felt that I had been sufficiently bamboozled myself, so I asked him to retire, while the examination board—me, me, and only me, as the old song puts it—considered his case. When I was alone I sought to calm myself with a drink of water, and after a decent interval I called him back.

"There are a few minor errors in this thesis which you will undoubtedly notice during a calm rereading, and a certain opaqueness of style which might profitably be amended. I am surprised that you have made so little use of the great Variorum Edition of Wilks published by Professors Fawcett and Pale, of the University of Bitter End, Idaho. Nevertheless I find it to be a piece of research of real, if limited, value, which, if published, might be—yes, I shall go so far as to say, will be—seminal in the field of nineteenth-century drama studies," said I. "I congratulate you, and it will be a pleasure to recommend that you receive your degree."

I don't know what I expected then. Perhaps I hoped that he would disappear, with a seraphic smile. True enough, there was an atmosphere as of a smile, but it was the smile of a giant refreshed. "Good," he said; "now we can get on to my other subjects."

"Do you mean to say that nineteenth-century drama isn't your real subject?" I cried, and when I say "I cried," I really mean it; my voice came out in a loud, horrified croak.

"Sir," said he; "it is so long ago since my unfortunate experience at my first examination that I have utterly forgotten what my subject was. But I have had time since then to prepare myself for any eventuality. I have written theses on everything. Shall we go on now to History?"

I was too astonished, and horrified, and by this time afraid, to say anything. We went on to History.

My knowledge of History is that of a layman. Academically, there is nothing worse, of course, that can be said. But professor-craft did not wholly desert me. The first principle, when you don't know anything about the subject of a thesis, is to let the candidate talk, nodding now and then with an ambiguous smile. He thinks you know, and are counting his mistakes, and it unnerves him. The Ghost was an excellent examinee; that is to say, he fell for it, and I think I shook his confidence once with a little laugh, when he was talking about Canada's encouragement of the arts under the premiership of W. L. Mackenzie King. But finally the two hours was up, and I graciously gave him his Ph.D. in History.

Next came Classics. His thesis was on *The Concept of Pure Existence in Plotinus.* You don't want to hear about it, but I must pause long enough to say that I scored rather heavily by my application of the second principle of conducting an oral, which is to pretend ignorance, and ask for explanations of very simple points. Of course your ignorance is real, but the examinee thinks you are being subtle, and that he is making an ass of himself, and this rattles him.

And so, laboriously, we toiled through the Liberal Arts, and some of the Arts which are not so liberal. I examined him in Computer Science, and Astronomy, and Mediaeval Studies, and I rather enjoyed examining him in Fine Art. One of my best examinations was in Mathematics, though personally my knowledge stops short at the twelve-times table.

Every examination took two hours, but my watch did not record them. The night seemed endless. As it wore on I remembered that at cockcrow all ghosts must disappear, and I cudgeled my brain trying to remember whether the kosher butchers on Spadina keep live cocks, and if so what chance we had of hearing one in the Round Room. I was wilting under my ordeal, but the Ghost was as fresh as a daisy.

"Science, now!" he positively shouted, as a whole new mountain of theses appeared from—I suppose from Hell. Now I know nothing whatever of Science, in any of its forms. If Sir Charles Snow wants a prime example of the ignorant Arts man, who has not even heard of that wretched law of thermodynamics, which is supposed to be as fine as Shakespeare, he is at liberty to make free with my name. I don't know and I don't care. When the Ghost moved into Science I thought my reason would desert me.

I needn't have worried. The Ghost was as full of himself as a Ghost can possibly be, and he hectored and bullied and badgered me about things I had never heard of, while my head swam. But little by little—it was when the Ghost was chattering animatedly about his work on the rate of decay of cosmic rays when they are brought in contact with mesons—I realized the truth. The Ghost did not care whether I knew what he was talking about or not. The Ghost was a typical examinee, and he wanted two things and two things only—an ear into which he could pour what he believed to be unique and valuable knowledge, and a license to go elsewhere and pour it into the ears of students. Once I grasped this principle, my spirits rose. I began to nod, to smile, to murmur appreciatively. When the Ghost said something especially spirited about the meiosis function in the formation of germ cells, I even allowed myself to say "Bravo"—as if he had come upon something splendid that I had always suspected myself but had never had time to prove in my laboratory. It was a great success; I knew that dawn could not be far away, for as each examination was passed, the Ghost seemed to become a little less substantial. I could see through him now, and I was happily confident that he could not, and never would, see through me. As he completed his last defense of a doctoral dissertation, I was moved to be generous.

"A distinguished showing," I said. "With a candidate of such unusual versatility I am tempted to go a little beyond the usual congratulations. Is there anything else you fancy—a Diploma in Public Health, for instance, or perhaps something advanced in Household Science?"

But the Ghost shook his head. "I want a Ph.D. and that only," said he. "I want a Ph.D. in everything."

"Consider it yours," said I.

"You mean that I may present myself at the next Convocation?"

"Yes; when the Registrar kneels to take upon him the degrees granted to those who are forced by circumstances to be absent, I suggest that you momentarily invest him with your ectoplasm—or whatever it is that people in your situation do," said I.

"I shall; oh, I shall," he cried, ecstatically, and as he faded before my eyes I heard his voice from above the skylight in the Round Room, saying, "I go to a better place than this, confident that as a Ph.D. I shall have it in my power to make it better still."

So at last, as dawn stole over the College, I was alone in the Round Room. The night of the Holy Innocents had passed. Musing, my hand stole to my pocket and, pulling out the sugarbaby, I crunched off its head. Was it those blessed children, I wondered, who had hovered over me, protecting me from being found out? Or had it perhaps been the spirit of King Herod, notoriously the patron of examiners?

All things considered, I think it was both great spiritual forces, watching over me during the long night. Happy in the thought that I was so variously protected, I stepped out into the first light, the last crumbs of the sugarbaby still sweet upon my lips.

JOYCE CAROL OATES

The Others

Early one evening in a crowd of people, most of them commuters, he happened to see, quite by accident—he'd taken a slightly different route that day, having left the building in which he worked by an entrance he rarely used—and this, as he'd recall afterward, with the fussy precision which had characterized him since childhood, and helped to account for his success in his profession, because there was renovation being done in the main lobby—a man he had not seen in years, or was it decades: a face teasingly familiar, yet made strange by time, like an old photograph about to disintegrate into its elements.

Spence followed the man into the street, into a blowsy damp dusk, but did not catch up to him and introduce himself: that wasn't his way. He was certain he knew the man, and that the man knew him, but how, or why, or from what period in his life the man dated, he could not have said. Spence was forty-two years old and the other seemed to be about that age, yet, oddly, older: his skin liverish, his profile vague as if seen through an element transparent yet dense, like water; his clothing—handsome tweed overcoat, sharply creased gray trousers—hanging slack on him, as if several sizes too large.

Outside, Spence soon lost sight of the man in a swarm of pedestrians crossing the street; and made no effort to locate him again. But for most of the ride home on the train he thought of nothing else: who was that man, why was he certain the man would have known him, what were they to each other, resembling each other only very slightly, yet close as twins? He felt stabs of excitement that left him weak and breathless but it wasn't until that night, when he and his wife were undressing for bed, that he said, or heard himself

64

say, in a voice of bemused wonder, and dread: "I saw someone today who looked just like my cousin Sandy—"

"Did I know Sandy?" his wife asked.

"—my cousin Sandy who died, who drowned, when we were both in college."

"But did I know him?" his wife asked. She cast him an impatient sidelong glance and smiled her sweet-derisive smile. "It's difficult to envision him if I've never seen him, and if he's been dead for so long, why should it matter so much to you?"

Spence had begun to perspire. His heart beat hard and steady as if in the presence of danger. "I don't understand what you're saying," he said.

"The actual words, or their meaning?"

"The words."

She laughed as if he had said something witty, and did not answer him. As he fell asleep he tried not to think of his cousin Sandy whom he had not seen in twenty years and whom he'd last seen in an open casket in a funeral home in Damascus, Minnesota.

The second episode occurred a few weeks later when Spence was in line at a post office, not the post office he usually frequented but another, larger, busier, in a suburban township adjacent to his own, and the elderly woman in front of him drew his attention: wasn't she, too, someone he knew? or had known, many years ago? He stared, fascinated, at her stitched looking skin, soft and puckered as a glove of some exquisite material, and unnaturally white; her eyes that were small, sunken, yet shining; her astonishing hands—delicate, even skeletal, discolored by liver spots like coins, yet with rings on several fingers, and in a way rather beautiful. The woman appeared to be in her mid-nineties, if not older: fussy, anxious, very possibly addled: complaining ceaselessly to herself, or to others by way of herself. Yet her manner was mirthful; nervous bustling energy crackled about her like invisible bees.

He believed he knew who she was: Miss Reuter, a teacher of his in elementary school. Whom he had not seen in more years than he wanted to calculate.

Miss Reuter, though enormously aged, was able, it seemed, to get around by herself. She carried a large rather glitzy shopping bag made of a silvery material, and in this bag, and in another at her feet, she was rummaging for her change purse, as she called it, which she could not seem to find. The post-office clerk waited with a show of strained patience; the line now consisted of a half-dozen people.

Spence asked Miss Reuter—for surely it was she: while virtually unrecognizable she was at the same time unmistakable—if she needed some assistance. He did not call her by name and as she turned to him, in exasperation, and gratitude—as if she knew that he, or someone, would come shortly to her aid—she did not seem to recognize him. Spence paid for her postage and a roll of stamps and Miss Reuter, still rummaging in her bag, vexed, cheerful, befuddled, thanked him without looking up at him. She insisted it must be a loan, and not a gift, for she was, she said, "not yet an object of public charity."

Afterward Spence put the incident out of his mind, knowing the woman was dead. It was purposeless to think of it, and would only upset him.

After that he began to see them more frequently. The Others—as he thought of them. On the street, in restaurants, at church; in the building in which he worked; on the very floor, in the very department, in which his office was located. (He was a tax lawyer for one of the largest of American "conglomerates"—yes and very well paid.) One morning his wife saw him standing at a bedroom window looking out toward the street. She poked him playfully in the ribs. "What's wrong?" she said. "None of this behavior suits you."

"There's someone out there, at the curb."

"No one's there."

"I have the idea he's waiting for me."

"Oh yes, I do see someone," his wife said carelessly. "He's often there. But I doubt that he's waiting for you."

She laughed, as at a private joke. She was a pretty freckled snub-nosed woman given to moments of mysterious amusement. Spence had married her long ago in a trance of love from which he had yet to awaken.

Spence said, his voice shaking, "I think—I'm afraid I think I might be having a nervous breakdown. I'm so very, very afraid."

"No," said his wife, "—you're the sanest person I know. All surface and no cracks, fissures, potholes."

Spence turned to her. His eyes were filling with tears.

"Don't joke. Have pity."

She made no reply; seemed about to drift away; then slipped an arm around his waist and nudged her head against his shoulder in a gesture of camaraderie. Whether mocking, or altogether genuine, Spence could not have said.

"It's just that I'm so afraid."

"Yes, you've said."

"—of losing my mind. Going mad."

She stood for a moment, peering out toward the street. The elderly gentleman standing at the curb glanced back but could not have seen them, or anyone, behind the lacy bedroom curtains. He was well dressed, and carried an umbrella. An umbrella? Perhaps it was a cane.

Spence said, "I seem to be seeing, more and more, these people—people I don't think are truly there."

"*He's* there."

"I think they're dead. Dead people."

His wife drew back and cast him a sidelong glance, smiling mysteriously. "It does seem to have upset you," she said.

"Since I know they're not there—"

"*He's* there."

"—so I must be losing my mind. A kind of schizophrenia, waking dreams, hallucinations—"

Spence was speaking excitedly, and did not know exactly what he was saying. His wife drew away from him in alarm, or distaste.

"You take everything so personally," she said.

One morning shortly after the New Year, when the air was sharp as a knife, and the sky so blue it brought tears of pain to one's eyes, Spence set off on the underground route from his train station to his building. Beneath the city's paved surface was a honeycomb of tunnels, some of them damp and befouled but most of them in good condition, with, occasionally, a corridor of gleaming white tiles that looked as if it had been lovingly polished by hand. Spence preferred aboveground, or believed he should prefer aboveground, for reasons vague and puritanical, but in fierce weather he made his way underground, and worried only that he might get lost, as he sometimes did. (Yet, even lost, he had only to find an escalator or steps leading to the street—and he was no longer lost.)

This morning, however, the tunnels were far more crowded than usual. Spence saw a preponderance of elderly men and women, with here and there a young face, startling, and seemingly unnatural. Here and there, yet more startling, a child's face. Very few of the faces had that air, so disconcerting to him in the past, of the eerily familiar laid upon the utterly unfamiliar; and these he resolutely ignored.

He soon fell into step with the crowd, keeping to their pace—which was erratic, surging, faster along straight stretches of tunnel and slower at curves; he found it agreeable to be borne along by the flow, as of a tide. A tunnel of familiar tear-stained mosaics yielded to one of the smart gleaming tunnels and that in turn to a tunnel badly in need of repair—and, indeed, being noisily repaired, by one of those crews of workmen that labor at all hours of the day and night beneath the surface of the city—and as Spence hurried past the deafening vibrations of the air hammer he found himself descending stairs into a tunnel unknown to him: a place of warm, humming, droning sound, like conversation, though none of his fellow pedestrians seemed to be talking. Where were they going, so many people? And in the same direction?—with only, here and there, a lone, clearly lost individual bucking the tide, white-faced, eyes snatching at his as if in desperate recognition.

Might as well accompany them, Spence thought, and see.

V. S. PRITCHETT

A Story of Don Juan

One night of his life Don Juan slept alone. Returning to Seville in the spring, he was held up, some hours' ride from the city, by the floods of the Quadalquivir, a river as dirty as an old lion after the rains, and was obliged to stay at the finca of the Quintero family. The doorway, the walls, the windows of the house were hung with the black and violet draperies of mourning when he arrived there. Quintero's wife was dead. She had been dead a year. The young Quintero took him in and even smiled to see Don Juan spattered and drooping in the rain like a sodden cockerel. There was malice in his smile: Quintero was mad with loneliness and grief. The man who had possessed and discarded all women was received by a man demented because he had lost only one.

"My house is yours," said Quintero, speaking the formula. There was bewilderment in his eyes; those who grieve do not find the world and its people either real or believable. Irony inflects the voices of mourners, and there was malice, too, in Quintero's further greetings; he could receive Don Juan now without that fear, that terror which he brought to the husbands of Seville. It was perfect, Quintero thought, that for once in his life Don Juan should have arrived at an empty house.

There was not even (as Don Juan quickly found out) a maid, for Quintero was served only by a manservant, being unable any longer to bear the sight of women. This servant dried the guest's clothes and in an hour or two brought in a bad dinner, food which stamped up and down in the stomach, like people waiting for a coach in the cold. Quintero was torturing his body

69

as well as his mind, and as the familiar pains arrived they agonized him and set him off about his wife. Grief had also made Quintero an actor. His eyes had the hollow, taper-haunted dusk of the theater as he spoke of the beautiful girl. He dwelled upon their courtship, on details of her beauty and temperament, and how he had rushed her from the church to the marriage bed like a man racing a tray of diamonds through the streets into the safety of a bank vault. The presence of Don Juan turned every man into an artist when he was telling his own love story—one had to tantalize and surpass the great seducer—and Quintero, rolling it all off in the grand manner, could not resist telling that his bride had died on her marriage night.

"Man!" cried Don Juan. He started straight off on stories of his own. But Quintero hardly listened; he had returned to the state of exhaustion and emptiness which is natural to grief. As Don Juan talked, the madman followed his own thoughts like an actor preparing and mumbling his next entrance; and the thought he had had, when Don Juan first appeared at the door, returned to him: a man must be a monster to make a man feel triumphant that his own wife was dead. Half listening, and indigestion aiding, Quintero felt within himself the total hatred of all the husbands of Seville for this diabolical man. And as Quintero brooded upon this it occurred to him that it was probably not by chance that he had a vengeance in his power.

The decision was made. The wine being finished, Quintero called for his manservant and gave orders to change Don Juan's room.

"For," said Quintero dryly, "His Excellency's visit is an honor and I cannot allow one who has slept in the most delicately scented rooms in Spain to pass the night in a chamber which stinks to heaven of goat."

"The closed room?" said the manservant, astonished that the room which still held the great dynastic marriage bed and which had not been used more than half a dozen times by his master since the lady's death was to be given to a stranger.

Yet to this room Quintero led his guest and there parted from him with eyes so sparking with ill-intention that Don Juan, who was sensitive to this kind of point, understood perfectly that the cat was being let into the cage only because the bird had long ago flown out. The humiliation was unpleasant. Don Juan saw the night stretching before him like a desert.

What a bed to lie in: so wide, so unutterably vacant, so malignantly inopportune! He took off his clothes, snuffed the lamp wick. He lay down knowing that on either side of him lay wastes of sheet, drafty and uninhabited except by bugs. A desert. To move an arm one inch to the side, to push out a leg, however cautiously, was to enter desolation. For miles and miles the foot might probe, the fingers or the knee explore a friendless Antarctica. Yet to lie rigid and still was to have a foretaste of the grave. And here, too, he was frustrated; for though the wine kept him yawning, that awful food romped in his stomach, jolting him back from the edge of sleep the moment he got there.

There is an art in sleeping alone in a double bed, but this art was unknown to Don Juan. The difficulty is easily solved. If one cannot sleep on one side of the bed, one moves over and tries the other. Two hours or more must have passed before this occurred to him. Sullen-headed, he advanced into the desert, and the night air lying chill between the sheets flapped and made him shiver. He stretched out his arm and crawled towards the opposite pillow. The coldness, the more than virgin frigidity of linen! He put down his head and, drawing up his knees, he shivered. Soon, he supposed, he would be warm again, but, in the meantime, ice could not have been colder. It was unbelievable.

Ice was the word for that pillow and those sheets. Ice. Was he ill? Had the rain chilled him that his teeth must chatter like this and his legs tremble? Far from getting warmer, he found the cold growing. Now it was on his forehead and his cheeks, like arms of ice on his body, like legs of ice upon his legs. Suddenly in superstition he got up on his hands and stared down at the pillow in the darkness, threw back the bedclothes and looked down upon the sheet; his breath was hot, yet blowing against his cheeks was a breath colder than the grave, his shoulders and body were hot, yet limbs of snow were drawing him down; and just as he would have shouted his appalled suspicion, lips like wet ice unfolded upon his own and he sank down to a kiss, unmistakably a kiss, which froze him like a winter.

In his own room Quintero lay listening. His mad eyes were exalted and his ears were waiting. He was waiting for the scream of horror. He knew the apparition. There would be a scream, a tumble, hands fighting for the light, fists knocking at the door. And Quintero had locked the door. But when no scream came, Quintero lay talking to himself, remembering the night the apparition had first come to him and had made him speechless and left him choked and stiff. It would be even better if there were no scream! Quintero lay awake through the night, building castle after castle of triumphant revenge and receiving, as he did so, the ovations of the husbands of Seville. "The stallion is gelded!" At an early hour Quintero unlocked the door and waited downstairs impatiently. He was a wreck after a night like that.

Don Juan came down at last. He was (Quintero observed) pale. Or was he pale?

"Did you sleep well?" Quintero asked furtively.

"Very well," Don Juan replied.

"I do not sleep well in strange beds myself," Quintero insinuated. Don Juan smiled and replied that he was more used to strange beds than his own. Quintero scowled.

"I reproach myself; the bed was large," he said.

But the large, Don Juan said, were necessarily as familiar to him as the strange. Quintero bit his nails. Some noise had been heard in the night—something like a scream, a disturbance. The manservant had noticed it also. Don Juan answered him that disturbances in the night had indeed bothered him at the beginning of his career, but now he took them in his stride. Quintero dug his nails into the palms of his hands. He brought out the trump.

"I am afraid," Quintero said, "it was a cold bed. You must have *frozen*."

"I am never cold for long," Don Juan said, and, unconsciously anticipating the manner of a poem that was to be written in his memory two centuries later, declaimed: "The blood of Don Juan is hot, for the sun is the blood of Don Juan."

Quintero watched. His eyes jumped like flies to every movement of his guest. He watched him drink his coffee. He watched him tighten the stirrups of his horse. He watched Don Juan vault into the saddle. Don Juan was humming, and when he went off was singing, was singing in that intolerable tenor of his which was like a cockcrow in the olive groves.

Quintero went into the house and rubbed his unshaven chin. Then he went out again to the road where the figure of Don Juan was now only a small smoke of dust between the eucalyptus trees. Quintero went up to the room where Don Juan had slept and stared at it with accusations and suspicions. He called the manservant.

"I shall sleep here tonight," Quintero said.

The manservant answered carefully. Quintero was mad again and the moon was still only in its first quarter. The man watched his master during the day looking toward Seville. It was too warm after the rains, the country steamed like a laundry.

And then, when the night came, Quintero laughed at his doubts. He went up to the room and as he undressed he thought of the assurance of those ice-cold lips, those icicle fingers and those icy arms. She had not come last night; oh, what fidelity! To think, he would say in his remorse to the ghost, that malice had so disordered him that he had been base and credulous enough to use the dead for a trick.

Tears were in his eyes as he lay down and for some time he dared not turn on his side and stretch out his hand to touch what, in his disorder, he had been willing to betray. He loathed his heart. He craved—yet how could he hope for it now?—that miracle of recognition and forgiveness. It was this craving which moved him at last. His hands went out. And they were met.

The hands, the arms, the lips moved out of their invisibility and soundlessness toward him. They touched him, they clasped him, they drew him down, but—what was this? He gave a shout, he fought to get away, kicked out and swore; and so the manservant found him wrestling with the sheets, striking out with fists and knees, roaring that he was in hell. Those hands, those lips, those limbs, he screamed, were *burning* him. They were of ice no more. They were of fire.

MAVIS GALLANT

Up North

When they woke up in the train, their bed was black with soot and there was soot in his Mum's blondie hair. They were miles north of Montreal, which had, already, sunk beneath his remembrance. "D'you know what I sor in the night?" said Dennis. He had to keep his back turned while she dressed. They were both in the same berth, to save money. He was small, and didn't take up much room, but when he woke up in that sooty autumn dawn, he found he was squashed flat against the side of the train. His Mum was afraid of falling out and into the aisle; they had a lower berth, but she didn't trust the strength of the curtain. Now she was dressing, and sobbing; really sobbing. For this was worse than anything she had ever been through, she told him. She had been right through the worst of the air raids, yet this was the worst, this waking in the cold, this dark, dirty dawn, everything dirty she touched, her clothes—oh, her clothes!—and now having to dress as she lay flat on her back. She daren't sit up. She might knock her head.

"You know what I sor?" said the child patiently. "Well, the train must of stopped, see, and some little men with bundles on their backs got on. Other men was holding lanterns. They were all little. They were all talking French."

"Shut up," said Mum. "Do you hear me?"

"Sor them," said the boy.

"You and your bloody elves."

"They was people."

"Little men with bundles," said Mum, trying to dress again. "You start your fairy tales with your Dad and I don't know what *he'll* give you."

74

It was this mythical, towering, half-remembered figure they were now traveling to join up north.

Roy McLaughlin, traveling on the same train, saw the pair, presently, out of his small red-lidded eyes. Den and his Mum were dressed and as clean as they could make themselves, and sitting at the end of the car. McLaughlin was the last person to get up, and he climbed down from his solitary green-curtained cubicle conspicuous and alone. He had to pad the length of the car in a trench coat and city shoes—he had never owned slippers, bathrobe, or pajamas—past the passengers, who were drawn with fatigue, pale under the lights. They were men, mostly; some soldiers. The Second World War had been finished, in Europe, a year and five months. It was a dirty, rickety train going up to Abitibi. McLaughlin was returning to a construction camp after three weeks in Montreal. He saw the girl, riding with her back to the engine, doing her nails, and his faculties absently registered "Limey bride" as he went by. The kid, looking out the window, turned and stared. McLaughlin thought "Pest," but only because children and other men's wives made him nervous and sour when they were brought around camp on a job.

After McLaughlin had dressed and had swallowed a drink in the wash-room—for he was sick and trembling after his holiday—he came and sat down opposite the blond girl. He did not bother to explain that he had to sit somewhere while his berth was being dismantled. His arms were covered with coarse red hair; he had rolled up the sleeves of his khaki shirt. He spread his pale, heavy hands on his knees. The child stood between them, fingertips on the sooty windowsill, looking out at the breaking day. Once, the train stopped for a long time; the engine was being changed, McLaughlin said. They had been rolling north but were now turning west. At six o'clock, in about an hour, Dennis and his mother would have to get down, and onto another train, and go north once more. Dennis could not see any station where they were now. There was a swamp with bristling black rushes, red as ink. It was the autumn sunrise; cold, red. It was so strange to him, so singular, that he could not have said an hour later which feature of the scene was in the foreground or to the left or right. Two women wearing army battle jackets over their dresses, with their hair piled up in front, like his mother's, called and giggled to someone they had put on the train. They were fat and dark—grinny. His mother looked at them with detestation, recognizing what they were; for she hated whores. She had always acted on the desire of the moment, without thought of gain, and she had taken the consequences (Dennis) without complaint. Dennis saw that she was hating the women, and so he looked elsewhere. On a wooden fence sat four or five men in open shirts and patched trousers. They had dull, dark hair, and let their mouths sag as though they were too tired or too sleepy to keep them closed. Something about them was displeasing to the child, and he thought that this was an ugly place with ugly people. It was also a dirty place; every time Dennis put his hands on the windowsill they came off black.

"Come down any time to see a train go by," said McLaughlin, meaning those men. "Get up in the *night* to see a train."

The train moved. It was still dark enough outside for Dennis to see his face in the window and for the light from the windows to fall in pale squares on the upturned vanishing faces and on the little trees. Dennis heard his mother's new friend say, "Well, there's different possibilities." They passed into an unchanging landscape of swamp and bracken and stunted trees. Then the lights inside the train were put out and he saw that the sky was blue and bright. His mother and McLaughlin, seen in the window, had been remote and bodiless; through their transparent profiles he had seen the yellowed trees going by. Now he could not see their faces at all.

"He's been back in Canada since the end of the war. He was wounded. Den hardly knows him," he heard his mother say. "I couldn't come. I had to wait my turn. We were over a thousand war brides on that ship. He was with Aluminium when he first came back." She pronounced the five vowels in the word.

"You'll be all right there," said McLaughlin. "It's a big place. Schools. All company."

"Pardon me?"

"I mean it all belongs to Aluminium. Only if that's where you're going you happen to be on the wrong train."

"He isn't there now. He hates towns. He seems to move about a great deal. He drives a bulldozer, you see."

"Owns it?" said McLaughlin.

"Why, I shouldn't *think* so. Drives for another man, I think he said."

The boy's father fell into the vast pool of casual labor, drifters; there was a social hierarchy in the north, just as in Heaven. McLaughlin was an engineer. He took another look at the boy: black hair, blue eyes. The hair was coarse, straight, rather dull; Indian hair. The mother was a blonde; touched up a bit, but still blond.

"What name?" said McLaughlin on the upward note of someone who has asked the same question twice.

"Cameron. Donald Cameron."

That meant nothing, still; McLaughlin had worked in a place on James Bay where the Indians were named MacDonald and Ogilvie and had an unconquered genetic strain of blue eyes.

"D'you know about any ghosts?" said the boy, turning to McLaughlin. McLaughlin's eyes were paler than his own, which were a deep slate blue, like the eyes of a newly born child. McLaughlin saw the way he held his footing on the rocking train, putting out a few fingers to the windowsill only for the form of the thing. He looked all at once ridiculous and dishonored in his cheap English clothes—the little jacket, the Tweedledum cap on his head. He outdistanced his clothes; he was better than they were. But he was rushing on this train into an existence where his clothes would be too good for him.

"D'you know about any ghosts?" said the boy again.

"Oh, sure," said McLaughlin, and shivered, for he still felt sick, even though he was sharing a bottle with the Limey bride. He said, "Indians see them," which was as close as he could come to being crafty. But there was no reaction out of the mother; she was not English for nothing.

"You seen any?"

"*I'm* not an Indian," McLaughlin started to say; instead he said, "Well, yes. I saw the ghost, or something like the ghost, of a dog I had."

They looked at each other, and the boy's mother said, "Stop that, you two. Stop that this minute."

"I'll tell you a strange thing about Dennis," said his mother. "It's this. There's times he gives me the creeps."

Dennis was lying on the seat beside her with his head on her lap.

She said, "If I don't like it I can clear out. I was a waitress. There's always work."

"Or find another man," McLaughlin said. "Only it won't be me, girlie. I'll be far away."

"Den says that when the train stopped he saw a lot of elves," she said, complaining.

"Not elves—men," said Dennis. "Some of them had mattresses rolled up on their backs. They were little and bent over. They were talking French. They were going up north."

McLaughlin coughed and said, "He means settlers. They were sent up on this same train during the depression. But that's nine, ten years ago. It was supposed to clear the unemployed out of the towns, get them off relief. But there wasn't anything up here then. The winters were terrible. A lot of them died."

"He couldn't know that," said Mum edgily. "For that matter, how can he tell what is French? He's never heard any."

"No, he couldn't know. It was around ten years ago, when times were bad."

"Are they good now?"

"Jeez, after a *war?*" He shoved his hand in the pocket of his shirt, where he kept a roll, and he let her see the edge of it.

She made no comment, but put her hand on Den's head and said to him, "You didn't see anyone. Now shut up."

"Sor 'em," the boy said in a voice as low as he could descend without falling into a whisper.

"You'll see what your Dad'll give you when you tell lies." But she was halfhearted about the threat and did not quite believe in it. She had been attracted to the scenery, whose persistent sameness she could no longer ignore. "It's not proper country," she said. "It's bare."

"Not enough for me," said McLaughlin. "Too many people. I keep on moving north."

"I want to see some Indians," said Dennis, sitting up.

"There aren't any," his mother said. "Only in films."

"I don't like Canada." He held her arm. "Let's go home now."

"It's the train whistle. It's so sad. It gets him down."

The train slowed, jerked, flung them against each other, and came to a stop. It was quite day now; their faces were plain and clear, as if drawn without shading on white paper. McLaughlin felt responsible for them, even compassionate; the change in him made the boy afraid.

"We're getting down, Den," said his Mum, with great, wide eyes. "We take another train. See? It'll be grand. Do you hear what Mum's telling you?"

He was determined not to leave the train, and clung to the windowsill, which was too smooth and narrow to provide a grip; McLaughlin had no difficulty getting him away. "I'll give you a present," he said hurriedly. But he slapped all his pockets and found nothing to give. He did not think of the money, and his watch had been stolen in Montreal. The woman and the boy struggled out with their baggage, and McLaughlin, who had descended first so as to help them down, reached up and swung the boy in his arms.

"The Indians!" the boy cried, clinging to the train, to air; to anything. His face was momentarily muffled by McLaughlin's shirt. His cap fell to the ground. He screamed, "Where's Mum? I never saw *anything*!"

"You saw Indians," said McLaughlin. "On the rail fence, at that long stop. Look, don't worry your mother. Don't keep telling her what you haven't seen. You'll be seeing plenty of everything now."

JOHN GARDNER

The Warden

1

The Warden has given up every attempt to operate the prison by the ancient regulations. Conditions grow monstrous, yet no one can bring them to the Warden's attention. He paces in his room, never speaking, never eating or drinking, giving no instructions of any kind. He dictates no letters, balances no accounts, never descends to the dungeons or inspects the guards. At times he abruptly stops pacing and stands stock still, listening, his features frozen in a look of vengeful concentration. But apparently nothing comes of it. He looks down from whatever his eyes have chanced to fix upon, his stern and ravaged face relaxes to its usual expression of sullen ennui. (I speak not of what I see but of what I used to see, in the days when he occasionally called me in, in the days when sometimes he would even smile grimly and say, "Vortrab, you and I are the only hope!") After a moment's thought he remembers his pacing and at once, doggedly, returns to it. His pacing has become a kind of heartbeat of the place. Even when I'm far from here, lying in my cottage in the dead of night, I seem to hear that beat come out of the stones, then ominously stop, then at last start up again, the old man walking and walking in his room, like a gnome sealed up in a mountain. I, his mere amanuensis, am left to do what little I can to keep the institution functioning. I pay the guards and give them encouragement; I visit the cells and arrange for the changing of straw and the necessary burials. When we lose personnel, which happens often—sweepers and gravediggers loading up their satchels with government equipment and slinking away like wolves in the night—I go to the village and find, if possible, replacements. It's a touchy arrangement. They all know I have no authority. They doubt that they themselves have any. It seems to me at times that we have nothing to go on but our embarrassment. That and the money that still comes, from time to time, from the Bureau of Correctional Institutions. I have a subterfuge that I've fallen into using, though I doubt that anyone's convinced by it. I tell the guards and supervisors that the Warden has commanded so-and-so. I say, for instance, "The Warden is concerned about the smell down here. He's asked me to organize a clean-up detail." At times, when morale is unusually low, I pretend that the Warden is angry, and I give them stern orders, supposedly from him. They look down, as if afraid, and accept what I say, though they do not believe it and certainly stand in no awe of me—a small, balding fat man forever short of breath. It gives them a reason to continue.

How long this can last I do not know. Let me set down here, for whoever may follow, a full report of how things stand with us, though none of this touches on the cause of our troubles—a thing so complex that I scarcely know how to comprehend it.

Some weeks ago, finding one of our older and more loyal guards asleep at his post, and being, perhaps, a trifle edgy and self-righteous from worry, lack of sleep, and irritation at being required to do more than I'm trained to do. I stepped briskly to the sleeping man's side and shouted directly in his ear, "Heller! What's the meaning of this?"

Heller jumped a foot, then looked angry, then sheepish. "I'm sorry, sir," he said. He's a small man, narrow-chested, with a thin, nervous face like a comic mask—large-eyed, large-eared, beneath the long nose a beard and mustache, and to the sides of it, rectangular spectacles. He was obviously distressed at his lapse of vigilance—at least as distressed as I was, in fact. If I'd been fully myself, I'd have let the matter drop. But I couldn't resist pressing harder, the way I myself am pressed.

I jabbed my face at him. "What will the Warden think of this?"

He lowered his eyes. "The Warden," he said.

I said, "What would happen if some prisoner got into the corridor?" I came close to shaking my fist at the man. He looked past me, morose. They always know more than you do, these Jews. You see them shuffling along the roadside, hats sagging, beards drooping, eyes cast down as if expecting the worst. They tempt you to swing your team straight at them, let them know for once how matters stand. No doubt that's what Mallin would have done—the man we had here some time ago. A nihilist, destroyer of churches, murderer of medical doctors.

At the thought of Josef Mallin I pretended to soften, but it was really from cruelty not unlike his, a sudden wish that the accident had happened. "You wouldn't be the first guard killed by his own reckless laziness, Heller. You know what they're like. Wild animals! Whatever touch of humanness they may ever have possessed . . ."

Heller nodded, still avoiding my eyes. He refused to say a word.

"Well?" I said. I struck the stone floor with my stick and stamped my foot. The idea of Mallin, even now that he'd been dead for months, made my indignation seem reasonable. Guards *had* been murdered, from time to time. And there *were* certain men so bestial, so black of heart . . .

Heller's eyes swung up to mine, then down, infinitely weary. Immediately, I was ashamed of myself, slapped back to sense and sick to death of the whole situation. I turned from him in stiff, military fashion, though I have nothing to do with the military, and started away. I knew well enough that he had no answer. No one has an answer for a question, a manner of behavior, so grotesque. But as I started up the dark, wet stairs, self-consciously dignified, full of rage which no longer had anything to do with Heller, he called after me: "Herr Vortrab!"

I stopped, despite myself. I waited, squeezing the handle of my stick, and when he said nothing more, I turned to look at him, or turned partway. The tic which troubles me at times like these was jerking in my cheek.

"I'm sorry to have troubled you," he said.

His foolish, weak face made me angrier yet, but for all his meekness he managed to make me more helpless and ludicrous than ever. Nor was it much comfort that in the flimmer of the lamp he too looked childlike, clownlike, absurdly out of place. The flat, heavily initialed stones glistened behind him, wet as the bedwork of the moat. He had his hands out and his shoulders hunched, like a scolded tailor. It was impossible to meet his eyes, but also impossible not to, in that ghastly place. The corridor winding through the shadow of chains and spiderwebs toward increasing darkness was like a passage in a dream leading endlessly downward toward rumbling coal-dark waterfalls, sightless fish.

"You haven't talked to them, sir," he said.

I stared at him, eyebrows lifted, waiting.

He raised his hands, the center of his forehead, his narrow shoulders in a tortuous shrug, as if pulling upward against centuries. "I *do* talk to them," he said. "If they're animals—"

"It's forbidden to talk with the prisoners," I said. I squeezed harder on the handle of my stick.

He nodded, indifferent. "Doesn't it strike you that we—we too are prisoners? I go home at night to my wife and children, but I never leave the prison. That makes no sense, I suppose." His shoulders slumped more.

"It certainly doesn't," I said, though I understood. I too go home every evening to the same imprisonment. My senile father, who's ninety, paints pictures in the garden, thoroughly oblivious to my worries; amused by them. My two small children cackle over jokes they do not explain to me, watching as if through high windows, great square bars. My wife . . .

"Heller, you need a vacation," I said.

His smile, for all its gentleness, was chilling. Centuries of despair, determination to continue for no clear reason, some ludicrous promise that all would be well though nothing had ever been well or ever would be. A brief panic flared up in me.

I took a step down, moving toward him, then another, and another. The panic was fierce now, icy, irrational, a sense of being led toward ruin and eagerly accepting it. "What prisoners do you talk to?" I asked.

Again, this time more thoughtfully, he looked at me, his fingers on his beard. With a slight shrug he turned and moved down the corridor, then timidly glanced back, looking over his spectacles, inquiring whether I'd follow. At the first turn, he lifted a lamp from its chain and hook, glancing back again. I nodded impatiently. He held the lamp far forward, at eye-level. Rats looked up at us. We came to the worn stone steps leading downward to the deepest of the dungeons. The walls were so close we had to walk single file, the ceiling so low that even a man of my slight stature was forced to walk cocked forward like a hunter.

At the foot of the steps, the cells appeared, door after door, dark iron-barred crypts. Most of the barred doors supported great silvery spiderwebs like spectral tents, their sagging walls gaudied by moisture drops that shone in the glow of the lantern like sapphires and rubies. The stink was unspeakable. Old straw, human feces, old age, and the barest trace, like some nagging guilt, of the scent of death. At the fourth door on the righthand side, he held up the lantern, and, obeying his gesture, I cautiously peeked in.

What I saw, when my eyes had adjusted to the gloom, was a naked old man seated in his chains—seated or propped, I couldn't make out which—in the corner of the cell. Beside him lay a pan of uneaten food and his lumpy, musty sleeping-pallet. He was a skeleton awkwardly draped in veined, stiff parchment. His hair and beard, which reached to the floor, were as white as snow, or would have been except for the bits of straw and dirt. One could see at a glance that his luminous eyes were useless to him. His hands, closed to fists, were like the feet of a bird; his wrists and ankles were like crooked pairs of sticks. I could not tell for certain whether or not the man was still alive, but my distinct impression—the smell perhaps—was that he wasn't. I thought I felt something behind us and turned to look. There was no one. A flurry of rats.

Heller called out, "Professor, you have a visitor." The words were distorted by echoes running down the long stone corridor and bouncing from the lichen-covered walls of the cells. The prisoner made no response. Heller called out the same words again, more slowly this time, as if speaking to a child hard-of-hearing. And now it seemed to me that a kind of spasm came over the face—not an expression, not even a movement of features suggestive of human intelligence, but some kind of movement, all the same. I watched in horror, pierced to the marrow by the sight of that dead face awakening. Then—still more terrible—the skull of a head turned slowly to the right, straining, perhaps, to decipher some meaning in the echoes. Heller called out a third time, leaning forward, hand on beard, calling this time still more slowly, and as the echoes died, there came from the creature in the cell or from the walls around him a windy, moaning syllable almost like a word.

"He's saying 'Friend,'" Heller whispered, at my shoulder. Then, to the prisoner: "Professor, tell the visitor your crime."

Again the prisoner seemed unable to grasp what the guard was saying. He swiveled his head like an old praying mantis, translucent white. But when Heller had asked the same question three times, the prisoner brought out a series of noises, hoarse, reedy grunts—his stiff, dark tongue seemed locked to his palate—and Heller interpreted: "'No crime,' he says. 'Was never accused.'" Heller studied me, looking over his spectacles, trying to see what I made of it. But I had no time to consider that now. I was beginning to understand, myself, the prisoner's noises. I needed to hear more, test my perceptions against Heller's. I struggled against distraction. I had, more strongly than before, the impression that someone was behind us. Except when I looked closely, I was aware of a bulky, crouching shadow. No doubt it was merely a trick of my nerves; at any rate Heller was unaware of it. I nailed my attention to the prisoner.

"Why do you call him 'Professor'?" I whispered.

The guard looked away from me, annoyed by the question, then changed his mind. He asked the prisoner, "Professor, tell us of Matter and Mind."

The prisoner sat perfectly still, as before, but it did not seem to me now that he was struggling to make sense of Heller's words. He seemed to consider with his weakened wits whether to respond or relax his attention, drift deeper into death. Then, little by little, I saw him laboring back toward thought. He began to speak, if you could call it speaking, and Heller interpreted word for word until, by my touching his arm, he perceived that I no longer needed his assistance.

I can suggest only faintly and obscurely what I felt, listening in darkness to the tortuous syllables of that spiritless old man. The lamp threw the shadows of bars across his body, and I had a sense—a conviction related to his words—that insubstantial shadows alone were sufficient to pin him in his place.

"There is no immateriality," he said. "Mere word. Mere sound." He ran his thick, dry tongue around his lips. His eyebrows lifted, part of an attempt to get his jaw muscles working. For all his difficulty in expressing himself, it was plain that he had his words by heart. He'd delivered the lecture a hundred—more like a thousand—times. Not merely to students; to himself more often; to the rats, the spiders, the bats, the darkness and emptiness around him, perhaps to neighboring felons, while they lasted. The lecture was doubtless the anchor of his sanity, or had been once. Such tricks are common among prisoners. As long as he could still put the words in order, still grasp some part of their significance, he was himself, a man, not yet reduced to the level of beasts, whose suffering, if not unconscious, is soon forgotten. I could see by his pauses and the accompanying expression of bafflement and panic that the power of the magic was draining away. A ghostly pallor lay over his features, his voice trembled, and his blind eyes stared fixedly, as if he were listening intently to every word.

I no longer recall the exact phrasing, but I remember very well the general argument—that and the terrible struggle in his voice, like the labor of the prematurely buried. As Heller and I have reconstructed it, the lecture went as follows:

"There are gradations of matter of which man knows nothing, the grosser impelling the finer, the finer pervading the grosser. The atmosphere, for example, impels the electric principle, while the electric principle permeates the atmosphere. These gradations increase in rarity until we arrive at matter unparticled; and here the law of impulsion and permeation is modified. The ultimate, unparticled matter not only permeates all things but impels all things, and thus *is* all things within itself. This matter is God. What men attempt to embody in the word *thought* is this matter in motion.

"There are two bodies, the rudimental and the complete, corresponding with the two conditions of the worm and the butterfly. What we call 'death' is the painful metamorphosis. Our present incarnation is progressive, preparatory, temporary. Our future is perfected, ultimate, immortal. The ultimate life is the full design.

"But of the worm's metamorphosis, you may object, we are palpably cognizant. I answer: *We*, certainly—but not the worm. Our rudimental organs

86

are adapted to the matter of which is formed the rudimental body, but not to that of which the ultimate is composed. We thus perceive only the shell which falls from the inner form, not the inner form itself. Yet consider. In certain states—in states of entrancement, as for instance when we have been mesmerized—we perceive independent of rudimental organs: we employ the medium we shall fully employ in the ultimate, unorganized life.

"Only in the rudimental life is there any experience of pain, for pain is the product of impediments afforded by number, complexity, and substantiality. That is not to say that the rudimental life is bad, however painful in a given case. All things, after all, are good or bad only by comparison. To be happy at any one point we must have suffered at the same. Never to suffer would be never to have been blessed. But in the inorganic life, pain cannot be; thus the necessity for the organic."

I have no idea how long it took him to get all this out, nor what I thought of his opinions at the time—though I've had fearful occasion to think back to them since. I stood motionless, clinging to the square iron bars as if the slightest movement might shatter his delicate hold on sense. Heller, too, stood motionless, staring at the floor, his hand closed on one end of his mustache, his bearded chin pressed firmly to his chest. When the lecture broke off, the guard shot a glance at me, then moved the lamp closer to the bars and peered in at the prisoner. The sudden alteration of the shadows was alarming, as if something alive had slipped closer to us. Then, without a word, the guard stepped back from the door of the cell, gave me a nod, and started toward the stairway we'd come down.

When we reached the relatively less dismal passage above—a corridor six feet wide and eight feet high, lighted, every twenty feet or so, by flickering, smoke-dulled hanging lamps and etched, like all our prison walls, with the initials of a thousand miserable souls long since departed—Heller dropped back to walk beside me, his head bowed and his long hands folded in front of him.

"So now you've seen," he said.

I nodded, not certain what it was that he meant I'd seen. My mind turned over the Professor's ideas—those and the irony of his present condition, his whole life of pain grown remote, unreal, a cold refutation of his optimistic theory.

"The man's innocent," Heller said. "A keen, metaphysical mind; and yet through all these years—"

"On the contrary," I said, "we've no notion whatever of his innocence or guilt. He was no doubt legally sentenced to this dungeon."

The guard stopped and looked at me, holding the lamp up to see me more clearly—exactly, I noticed with a shudder, as he'd held up the lamp to inspect the old man. "Why would he deny his guilt at this stage? Surely he's aware—"

"Habit, perhaps." I said it too sharply, as if for the benefit of the darkness behind us. I could hardly blame the guard for his quick little shrug of exasperation. I looked away, toward the steps that would lead me to higher, wider corridors and at last to my chamber, remote from this graveyard of the living. The guard waited, not even bothering to scoff at my suggestion. Again I could hardly blame him.

"I must speak to the Warden about this," I said, clipped and official, and looked over his head. The guard leaned toward me with a jerk and a bewildering smile, and caught my arm. "Do!" he whispered. His fingers dug into me. (I have seen it before, the guilt the men feel about the horrors they help to perpetuate.) Though I know the importance of keeping the forms in a place like this, I did not shake Heller's hand from my arm. "I'll see to the matter at once," I said. My voice was accidentally stern.

And so I left him, my step as metallic as an officer's, my walking stick a weapon. As I passed the guards in the passageways above I gave to each of them a crisp salute. Some responded, looking up from their half-sleep, their dice games, their lunch baskets; some did not. I let it pass, secretly listening already for the sound of pacing that would prove that the Warden had been all the while in his chamber and knew nothing of our breach of regulations.

And so I came to the Warden's door and stood listening. My knock brought no change to the rhythm of his step. I knocked again, and then again. It was unthinkable that the Warden couldn't hear the banging of that great brass knocker—the figure of a lion with eyes worn blank by a century of hands. But the Warden continued pacing.

2

The sky ahead of me, as I walked home that evening, was a thing of sublime and fearsome beauty. The sun was still high—it was the middle of summer—and the weather had for weeks been alternating between hot, dense, muggy days and twilight cloudbursts. Mountainous thunderheads towered all around me, some miraculously white, where the sunlight struck them, some—the lower clouds—glowering, oppressive. The sky in the glodes between masses of cloud was irenic blue, and down through some of them came shafts of light that transmuted the ripening wheatfields, the pastures, the plane trees, hedges, and haycocks to images from a dream. Here and there on the horizon, sheet lightning flickered.

I hurried. The rain was not far off. I might easily have gotten transportation if I'd wished—with one of the guards relieved of duty; with the lumbering, creaking supply wagon that went back each night from the prison to the village; with some kindly stranger in his touring carriage; or even with one of the farmers bringing in hay. But I preferred to risk a soaking; I valued, almost superstitiously, the long walk home, transition from the world of officials to the world of men. Tonight especially I hadn't yet shaken the image of the wasted, enfeebled "Professor" or that ominous burden on my soul, the Warden's self-confinement.

The land was becalmed. Shadows lengthened almost visibly, and the light grew fiery green. Moment by moment the landscape around me darkened more. The river vanished, then the hedges, soon all but the hills. I would hear now and then the low warble of a bird, a sound that seemed to come from all directions, like sounds heard under water. Gradually even the hills sank away. All the more impressive, even awesome, then, that directly above me stood a window of somber sky, its frame edged by moonlight, and in the infinite depths of that sky, three stars. Despite the warning of thunder in the distance, I stopped in my tracks—as stirred to wonder as my father would have been, a foolish old man, but one with all his sensibilities refined by landscape painting. Something of what the old prisoner had said came back to me. Not

89

words, exactly. A sense; an impression. I had a feeling of standing outside myself, as if time and space had stopped and in one more second would be extinguished. As quickly as the queer impression came it passed, faded back into shadow like a fish. And for some reason impossible to name, I was left with a feeling of indescribable, senseless horror, a terrible emptiness, as if I'd penetrated something, broken past the walls of my consciousness and discovered . . . what? But perhaps the cause was above me, not within. The walls of the open, moonlit glade were collapsing violently toward one another, blotting the stars out, tumbling downward like a falling roof. I seemed to hear a step, and I turned to look back. In all that darkness there was nothing to be seen—neither on the hills nor on the road behind me—nothing but the smoldering torches on the prison walls.

3

I do not ordinarily mind the burden of my father's senility. It provides distraction from those other problems I have no power or authority to solve. In any case, I'm the dutiful, respectful sort. If I'd meant to question or judge the old man, I'd have done so long since. He has his opinions, and I have mine. I let it go at that. On this particular evening, however, his whimsy took an extraordinary turn.

We had finished supper and were seated in the parlor, except for my wife, who was washing dishes. I've told her time and time again that the children are old enough for that, if only she'd give them some discipline. But she prefers to do all the work herself. She enjoys work, no doubt. It frees her from the rest of us. So tonight, as usual, they lay scribbling, gouging great holes in the paper, on the floor beside my father's shoes. Every now and then they would glance through the window, keeping watch on the storm like creatures in secret league with it. My father was sorting through old canvases—paintings of craggy precipices; huge-boled hickories, walnuts, oaks; sunlight bursting through chasms, orange and purple. Whatever the quality of the paintings— I'm no judge—the old man certainly had the look of an artist, irrumpent white hair ferociously shaggy, eyes deep set as two caves in an overhung cliff. When he clamps his mouth shut, the tip of his nose and chin come together. You'd think, from the looks of him—the heavy-veined temples, the glittering eyes—

that the old man misses nothing; but not so. One can have no notion, from moment to moment, where his mind will surface next.

He jerked his head up, cracked lips pursed, staring at me as if angrily in his attempt to remember what it was that, a moment earlier, had occurred to him. I lowered my treatise—the *Discourse* of Descartes, I think it was—and at last, with another little jerk, abandoning the paintings stacked beside his chair, he said, "Ah! So you're executing Josef Mallin!"

I was so startled I nearly dropped my book. There are times when his senility seems purposeful, malicious. Worse than that, there are times when, for all his confusion, he seems to see with perfect clarity what troublesome thoughts are astir at the edge of your consciousness. "Mallin's been dead for months," I said sharply. The tic came over me, flickering like lightning. I covered it with my hand.

"Impossible!" he snorted, but the next instant he looked unsure of himself, then cunning. "An interesting man," he said quickly and firmly, like a good liar shifting his ground. He leaned toward me, bent-backed, slightly drooling, and in the lamplight it seemed his head grew larger. His eyes were like a tiger's. "A man could learn a good deal from that Josef Mallin," he said. "Tried to burn down my studio once."

It happened to be true, though how it fit with the subject at hand was impossible to determine unless, like my father, you were addled. He suddenly jerked still nearer to me, as if he'd hit on something. "He's an atheist!" he said.

I sighed, still covering the tic, then sadly nodded to prevent his continuing. I did not appreciate (to say the least) his insistence on bringing Josef Mallin back to life. The period of Mallin's imprisonment, first while he awaited trial, then while he awaited execution, was a terrible strain on all of us. He was a brilliant devil, black-haired and handsome and deadly as a snake, so cunning at bribing or persuading his guards that at last the Warden himself took charge of holding him. It was shortly after his death that the Warden began that interminable pacing in his chamber. Mallin's execution, I might add, was unpleasant. His crimes were the worst of the three main kinds of which the laws speak, so that, after the decapitation, his head was thrown to the sawdust in the village square, to be eaten by dogs, as the law requires.

But my nod did nothing to check my father's babblings. "He claims the

Bible is a pack of lies,'' he said, squinting, tightening his fists to get the thought exact. "The man's not merely indifferent to religion, he *hates* it, heart and soul!'' He struck his knee with his fist, as if some great point were scored.

I could not help but glance at my children, sprawled on the floor with their coloring papers and candies. One of these days I must force them back to their Bible lessons. My wife, unfortunately, can see no reason for reading the Bible if one does not like it. She enjoys it herself, and she merely laughs—as she laughs at everything I stand for—when I insist that religion is no natural impulse but a thing to be acquired. (I know only too well. It's a thing I myself never properly acquired, despite my father's love of Scripture and his labor, when I was a boy, to make me study it. I could profit by religion's consolations, I think, if only I'd reached them at the proper age, the age when trust is as reasonable as reason. If I'd known what troubles this world affords . . .)

"I admit," my father said abruptly, "that I've never seen a ghost myself, that I know of." I blinked, grasping in vain for the connection, and I felt my heartbeat speeding up. Needless to say, I'd said nothing to my father of my foolish idea, in the dungeon this morning, that something was watching us. My father continued soberly, "But I know a little something of states of entrancement. Sometimes when you're painting, a kind of spell comes over you, and you know—you positively *know*—that there's no chance of erring with the picture at hand. You're nailed directly to the universe, and the same force that moves in the elm tree is moving your brush." He nodded.

Again I nodded back; I hardly knew what else to do. I'm always uncomfortable when he speaks of himself as a master craftsman. His paintings in recent years have been clumsy and confused as a child's. Not even kind old ladies buy them. I listened with the back of my mind to my wife in the kitchen, rhythmically washing and rinsing plates. She works, always, in a pleasant daze, humming to herself, her mind as empty as a moonbeam.

My father said, "He hates Swedenborg, too, and the politics of Spinoza. 'The essence of life is suffering,' says he."

Once again I gave a start, thinking of Heller's pathetic "Professor"; but my father didn't notice, engrossed in the pleasure of pontificating. "Says Mallin, 'I can say at least this for myself. I have steadily resisted illusion.' " My father smiled wickedly, as if he'd just made some vicious joke at my expense. I pursed my lips, watching him closely, but of course the whole thing was lunatic. I took off my spectacles and sighed.

Now both of us listened to the kitchen sounds, and the sound of the children's chewing. After a time he began nodding his head. "It will be a great blow to the Warden, no doubt. The minute the axe comes down on Joe Mallin, the Warden's life will go *fssst!*" He grinned.

I was positive, for an instant, that the old man knew perfectly well that Josef Mallin, "Laureate of Hell," as he called himself, was dead. I suspected that he brought the matter up just to torture me, remind me of my worrisome troubles at the prison. But then, as before, I was unsure. I saw—so vividly that I winced away—the image of Mallin's head rolling from the block into sawdust, spraying blood. The mustached lips were curled back, furious, raging their pain and indignation even now, and the black eyes—small flecks of sawdust hung on them—stared, now, full of hatred as ever, at the clouded sky.

My father looked down, disconcerted for some reason. "The prophets leap backward and forward in time," he said loudly, and slammed the arm of the chair with his fist. "There is no past or future in the grammar of God."

The children looked up at him and laughed. There was candy between their teeth. I felt giddy, pulled crazily in diverse directions. I was suddenly reminded, looking at my children, of those bestial creatures at the prison—your usual criminal, I mean; not "the Professor," as Heller calls him, and not some outraged philosopher-poet like Mallin. They live, the more usual criminal lot, for nothing but pleasure, like animals. They wallow in their food; when you let them together, they attack one another sexually; when you let them out into the exercise yard they snap at the sunlight, roll in the mud, and provoke horrible fights, even killings. I must have been fond of my children once, but if so, I had now forgotten it. They were completely out of hand. I had tried to correct them—I'd tried many times—but my wife and father undid all my labors, she because she saw no point in correcting them—"Let them be, let them be!" she'd say lightly, with that foolish, carved-wood smile. As for my father, he disapproved of my *mode* of correcting them. He preferred tiresome argument to switchings. What time have I for argument, a man overworked, in an impossible situation? Between my wife and my father, I was hopelessly walled in.

He was about to speak again—he was raising his hand to shake his finger at me. To sidetrack his ravings I learned forward quickly and began telling about Heller's "Professor." He closed his mouth tight and listened carefully, his heavy white eyebrows so low they completely hid his eyes. While I spoke, he turned his head, apparently looking out the window, not at me. I too looked out.

It was a violent, sternly beautiful night. A whirlwind had apparently collected its force in our vicinity, for there were frequent and severe alterations of wind, and even the brief illumination the lightning gave was sufficient to show the velocity with which the great black tons of cloud careened and collided. When I'd told the whole story, including as much as I remembered of the lecture on Matter and Mind, my father nodded, his eyes screwed up tight, and said, perplexingly—"Some poets get to the heart of the matter. Most just fool around with language." I could not help but wonder, that instant, who was more lonely, more desperately helpless—the prisoner whispering in his pitch-dark dungeon, or myself.

Fortunately, however, our conversation ended there. My wife came in, wiping her hands together, smiling vaguely, passing her eyes like a casual benediction over all of us. "Father," she said, "it's bedtime. The same for you, children."

My father looked hard at her, thinking about whether or not to consent, then got up, stiffly, and shuffled toward the far end of our cottage, where he sleeps. Halfway there he paused, noticing his violin, and, as if he were curious, discovering some object never seen before, he bent to pick it up off the table. The children, meanwhile, had for some reason decided that they too would obey, and had started in the direction of their bedroom. They too, however, found some pretext for changing their minds. Though she still went on smiling, two lines of consternation appeared between my wife's eyebrows. "Children, *do* go to bed," she said. They did nothing, of course, and she merely put the tips of her fingers together. "They're just like Grampa," she said to me, and smiled, exactly like a picture of a hang-dog saint. I studied her thoughtfully, saying not a word.

My father told her, raising a trembling arm and pointing. "They're not like me at all. They're like *you.*"

It was not strictly fair, of course: my wife is the soul of diligence, and she's sensitive besides. She prays nightly; she cooks, cleans, darns our stockings for us; she has a remarkable natural feeling for music. Nevertheless, I was perversely delighted at hearing him speak so crossly to her. I closed the volume over my finger, rose from my chair, and bent down to pick up the children's horrible scribblings.

"Good heavens!" my wife cried, staring out the window. Her face had gone white. I straightened up quickly. I had an impression, for an instant, that there was a man out there—a man in a great black coat and black boots, someone I would know, if I could make myself think calmly. But we were both mistaken, for the next instant there was nothing; it was merely an illusion manufactured by the storm. Yet when the children squealed, an instant later, my first thought was that now they too had seen it. It turned out to be nothing of the kind. The little girl was trying to pull down her brother's trousers. Without a word to their mother (I had never spent a more miserable evening) I went after the little criminals, spanked them soundly with my shoe, and put them to bed. I now felt much better. My father's look of outrage had no effect on me. My wife's alarm was a pleasure. I stood at the window, smiling out at the storm with satisfaction. But there was a flaw in my comfort. I could not seem to rid myself of the feeling that he was still watching us, standing behind some tree, perhaps, or peering in from the darkness of the shuddering grape arbor. I watched for some time but saw nothing in the least suspicious, neither on my grounds, nor on the rainslick road, nor on the serpentine lane beyond the stone gateposts, rising past lindens and maples toward the old church.

4

The situation at the prison grew desperate. Though I tried repeatedly, I could get no response whatever to my knocks at the Warden's door. It was a case altogether without precedent, and so, though I knew the risks in appearing insubordinate, I wrote to the Bureau of Justice. After two weeks, I had still received no answer. At even greater risk to myself, I wrote a second letter. I might as well have dropped my complaints into a cistern. I closely questioned the courier—a man I have always found, in the past, to be dutiful and efficient. He spoke of an iron-studded door in an unlighted hallway, a huge brass plate bearing the single word JUSTICE, and beside the door a bill of instructions, among them instructions for the delivery of petitions. These last had a deadly simplicity: *Deposit petition in slot. No exceptions.* I studied him, looking severe, no doubt. "Could you hear anything through the door?" I asked. "Nothing, sir," he said and touched his cap as if in sign that he must leave. "Not a *sound?*" I said. His blue, button eyes stared straight ahead. His turned-up nose was like a halt signal reared in my roadway. "Do not press me, sir," the nose seemed to say. "It's none of my affair." I couldn't help but compare the man to my troublesome friend Heller. Heller, too, knew what was his business and what was not, but he never put that knowledge in the way of his lugubrious humanity. However, I sent the courier on his way, and I did not trouble myself about sending more letters. As a matter of fact, I'd heard before of the inefficiency and corruption of the Justice Department. It was one of the Warden's chief complaints. He, luckily, had strings he could pull.

Meanwhile, we had one near-calamity after another at the prison. The cook was found murdered. All evidence suggested that the murder was the fruit of a long-standing feud between the cook and his assistant. Being unable to rouse the Warden, I took action myself, placing the assistant in confinement to await his trial. I did this, of course, upon no legal authority; but I could see no reasonable alternative.

Hardly was that ugly matter resolved, and a new cook installed, before a second crisis struck. A sizable group of the guards revolted. I asked, in the absence of any other authority, for a conference with their spokesman. The meeting was arranged, a ridiculous melodramatic affair, since the leader of the rebellious faction was convinced—surly, double-dealing peasant that he was— that my intent was to get him alone and unceremoniously shoot him. I scarcely bothered to protest the opinion, but met him, as required, at the prison front gate, at the hour of noon, with all the guards loyal to him on one side, with their guns aimed at me, and all those loyal to me on the other side, training their guns on him. Even if we'd met as friends, it would have been a dreary spectacle. The guards' uniforms were faded and threadbare, here an epaulette missing, there an off-color elbow patch. Coats lacked buttons, trousers and boots were no longer standard; if treachery came along, it was doubtful that more than a few of the rifles on either side would fire.

Clownish and base as all this was, I sweated profusely throughout that meeting. What assurance could I have that men so disloyal would not hazard a further disloyalty, and shoot me for their sport? The rebellious guards' demand was simple. I must double their pay. "Impossible!" I said—as it most certainly was. If I hadn't been so frightened, I might have laughed. My opponent declared the meeting ended; he would speak no further except with the Warden himself. I found a delaying tactic: I would relay to the Warden the rebels' demand and would meet them in twenty-four hours with the Warden's response. With some mutterings, they accepted. The guards on each side lowered their rifles, and I went briskly back to my chambers next to the Warden's. I did not bother, this time, to knock on his door.

As I was unlocking my own, a hand touched my elbow. I jumped. It was Heller. "Good heavens!" I said. He nodded, his bearded mask-face smiling sadly down at me, and he took off his cap.

I'd been avoiding Heller, I need hardly explain. I had given my assurance that I would speak to the Warden about his so-called Professor, and for reasons outside my control (though I could hardly admit that to Heller), I had not done it. I was certain, now, that he was here to ask what the Warden had decided with regard to his friend.

"Come in, Heller," I said, and cleared my throat. "I've been meaning to speak with you."

He must have known well enough that that was untrue. I'd been ducking and fleeing at sight of him for a week. But he nodded, still smiling sadly, and stepped ahead of me into the room.

"Very elegant," he said, pretending to look around for a moment, then staring at his cap. Though it was plain that he wasn't much interested, in fact, in the elegance of my chambers, I seized on his remark to stall the embarrassing question I expected. "So it is," I said. "In former times, the prison used to have important visitors. In those days cases were in constant review. In certain situations, the chief justices themselves would come down. But of course it's no longer practical. With the seat of government so much farther away . . ."

Heller nodded. I saw that he relished our meeting as little as I did. I too now fell silent, knowing there was no escape. We stood like two miserable children gazing apprehensively around us. I remembered my own first impression of the place. Though smaller than the Warden's, the central chamber is enormous. Exactly as in the Warden's chamber, the windows are long, narrow, and pointed—situated so high above the black-oak floor as to be altogether inaccessible from within. Feeble gleams of encrimsoned light fall from the trellised panes to warm small patches below. Ancient, dark draperies hang on the walls. The furniture is sparse, comfortless, antique. The general effect, I felt at the beginning and I now felt more strongly, was one of oppressive, irredeemable gloom. One has an occasional, rather eerie sense of something moving in the corners of the chamber—an effect, perhaps, of cloud banks passing between the windows and the sun.

Heller drifted toward the far end of the room, hands behind his back, head tipped forward and to one side. When he came to the bust of Plotinus on its high black-marble base, he paused and looked at it. I waited, perspiring, wringing my hands.

He turned and said, "Do you know why the guards want higher pay?"
"Do you?" I asked. Again I waited, rigid and official to hide my uneasiness.

"They lose everything they make through gambling. Stop the fellow who empties their pockets, and all the rest will resolve itself."

"You're quite certain of this?"

"I can show you," he said.

I agreed at once, and Heller led me down the great dark stairway to the first of the lower passages, and thence to a large, communal cell which had not been in use for many years. At the back of the cell a large stone had been removed, as I saw at once by the reddish light breaking through from somewhere lower. At Heller's direction, I stepped to this patch of light and looked through it. Below lay a windowless room without furniture of any kind: an abandoned cell whose door was directly beneath us, out of sight.

Four guards in shirtsleeves hunkered on the floor, shooting dice. It was clearly not one of those ordinary games, the kind I break up in the corridors.

All four were sweating, their shirts pasted to their chests and backs. Beside each man stood a small pile of pebbles. One man's pile was slightly larger than the others, but not significantly so.

"Keep your eye on the fat man," Heller said.

I nodded.

The fat man—a guard named Stuart, a man with hair longer than regulations allow, and a neatly trimmed beard, small fingers like a woman's—threw the dice several times and lost. He seemed unconcerned. On the other hand, those who took his money, represented by the stones, did not seem as cheered by their success as one might normally have expected. The others threw, sometimes winning, sometimes not. I began to feel Heller was wasting my time. He apparently sensed it. "Keep watching," he said. I did so, mentally telling myself that after five more rolls of the dice I would insist upon leaving.

Then something happened. The guard named Stuart began to glow. Call it hallucination if you will, a trick played by the oil lamps around them, but I *saw* the glow, and so did Heller, whose hand immediately tightened on my arm. The fat man was glowing like a lamp-chimney. "Stuart can't tell you himself how it happens," Heller whispered. "All he knows is that for four or five minutes he knows exactly what the dice will do."

He stared at the dice now, white as new bone against the lamp-reddened floor. He patted them, smacked them, fussed with them as a mother fusses with a baby. Suddenly he snapped them up and flung them the length of the room. "Five and two!" he yelled while the dice were in the air. Five and two came up. The other three gasped. Once more Stuart fidgeted with the dice, then flung them. "Hard six!" he yelled. Two threes showed. The others were trembling.

"Get out of the game, fools!" Heller whispered.

But it was impossible.

Next Stuart called out eleven and made it. Then four. Then nine. I felt a weird urge to go down to them, join in.

"Come away," Heller whispered.

I resisted.

"Come at once."

That evening I called the fat guard to my chamber. Simply, brutally, rapping the table with my walking stick, I gave him my imperative—which I attributed, of course, to the Warden. He would return all his winnings to those he had robbed and would depart the prison forever, or I would jail him. He expressed indignation, outrage. I was firm. He wheedled, spoke of "divine gift." I said nothing. Heller sat across from us, toying with his pistol. Stuart whimpered, begged, called me irreligious. I read him the regulations on gambling in the prison. I did not mention that I had no authority to confine him to the dungeon. The simple truth was in any case that, authority or no authority, I would do it. At last, he was persuaded. And so the second of our near-calamities was averted.

5

Less than an hour after my meeting with the spokesman for the rebels (the second meeting by the prison gate, the meeting which resolved our differences), Heller came to my chamber, where I lay resting a moment, and, when I answered his knock, expressed a desire to speak with me. I met him more guiltily than before, since now I felt that not only had I failed to fulfill my promise with regard to "the Professor," but had failed him though owing him a favor. When I'd ushered Heller to an old tattered sofa and had seated myself across from him, he brought himself immediately to the point—that is to say, to the first of his points. Looking sadly at his knees, he said, "Have you spoken to the Warden, Herr Vortrab?"

I could see no alternative but to confess the truth. "I'm afraid I have not. The plain fact is, I can't get to him."

His eyebrows went up in an inverted v, but despite that, he did not seem surprised. "He refuses to listen?"

I held back for a fraction of a second, and then came out with it. "He refuses to answer his door," I said. I felt so curiously relieved at having unburdened myself of that dreadful secret that on an impulse I told him more: "In fact, Heller, I haven't laid eyes on the Warden in months!"

The guard was stunned. But the next instant, to my astonishment, he laughed. "Why then," he cried, "what makes you think he's there?" Almost merrily, he threw out his hands. I could hardly account for his look of joy. It was as if my revelation . . .

But I said firmly, "I hear him pacing."

"Impossible," he scoffed. "What does he eat? Does he sneak away for supplies in the dead of night?"

I had gone, of course, too far; I must now go all the way. "Believe what I say or not," I told him, bending toward him, my hands raised, fingers interlaced, to hide that infuriating tic, "but the Warden never leaves his room—at least not by the one door I know of."

He stared at me as if convinced I'd gone mad. At last he said, "How can you be sure?"

After a pitiful flicker of hesitation, I rose, keeping my face turned away, saying, "Come, I'll show you," and led him to the great studded door, showed him how firmly the door pressed down on the smooth oak sill, and directed his attention to the undisturbed dust. He studied it all with the fascination of a scientist. At last, with another queer shake of the head and that same odd smile, he said, "Apparently it's all up to us, then."

I was at the point of agreeing when I sensed something left unstated in his words. He glanced at me and saw my hesitation. He smiled, more lugubrious than usual, and shrugged. "The prisoner you met—the Professor—has passed away," he said.

I made no attempt to hide my embarrassment. "Poor devil," I said, and snatched off my spectacles and bit my lip. "I'm not surprised," I added, merely to be saying something. "It's a miracle he lasted so long."

Heller nodded.

As I turned back toward my chamber, he said gently, "We must give him a proper burial, sir. We must, so to speak, put his soul at rest. He belongs in the churchyard, where he would have gone, as a Christian citizen, if it weren't for this terrible judicial mistake."

I saw that he was serious. I might have laughed at the outlandish idea if I did not already owe so much to Heller—and if, moreover, I had not just now placed myself in his power by my ill-considered admissions. I said, at last: "Only the Warden can order such a thing."

He looked down, rubbed his mustache. "But it seems the Warden has abandoned us."

It brought me to my senses. "Not so!" I said. "Listen!" Catching his arm a trifle roughly, I led him back to the door and bent my head to it, indicating by a gesture that Heller do the same. For an instant, I heard nothing. Then, listening still more intently, I caught the faint, familiar sound of the Warden's footsteps pacing the carpet, louder as the Warden came near, then softening as he retreated to the further wall. "You hear?" I said.

He listened, neither convinced nor unconvinced. His ears, unfortunately, were considerably less acute than mine. After a time he said, thoughtfully studying me, "I don't hear a thing." A flurry of panic swept through me, and I pressed my ear tighter to the door. But there was no mistaking it: he was there, still pacing. At times, as he'd done in the old days, he would pause—I remembered again the way he would stare, fierce with concentration—and then he would begin to pace again. "Take my word for it, Heller, he's in there," I said.

For a long moment he looked at me, absentmindedly smoothing his beard. At last he accepted it, or seemed to. "Then we must rouse him," he said. Before I knew he would do it, he snatched up the lion's-head knocker and banged it on the iron plate with such force that it rang like a blacksmith's maul. I did nothing to check him, though I was sick with fear. Obviously he had no memory of the Warden's wrath.

When he stopped, I bent, trembling all over, to listen at the door. The Warden had stopped pacing, but he did not come to us. The longer we waited, the greater my apprehension grew. Heller said: "You see? It's up to us." He smiled again, but his thoughts were far away, his long, thin hand still mechanically moving on his beard.

I agreed in haste and, catching his arm, virtually hurled him away from the door and back to my chambers. Almost unaware that I was doing it, I allowed myself once more to be guided by Heller. As soon as we were secure, I pushed the door shut behind us and locked it, then immediately crossed to the brandy closet, where I poured a glass for myself and one for Heller. When I'd taken a sip, which did not calm me, I turned to my conspirator. "What are we to do?" I whispered. It no longer mattered to me, in fact, that if we did as Heller wished we were throwing the ancient regulations to the winds. I had no more authority to grant a pardon than to flap my arms and fly. Indeed, formal pardon was out of the question. But we could perhaps entomb Heller's friend, if we were circumspect.

Heller sipped his brandy and ignored my agitation. "My people," he said, "have a long history of dealing with absurd situations. Leave everything to me."

"Gladly!" I said, and gave a laugh as hollow and despairing as Heller's own.

He sat stroking his bearded chin, looking up over his glasses at the shadows in the room's dim corners, as if reading there, in indefinite shapes, the outline of his plan. At length he said, "This evening a large parcel will be delivered to your cottage. From there it's only a stone's throw to the church-yard."

"Whatever you say," I said helplessly. I drank off the brandy and returned to the closet for more. My whole chamber rang, it seemed to me, with the sound of the Warden's footsteps.

"A burial detail," my friend said then, with the same queer smile, "will meet at your gate after sunset."

The footsteps paused. I was sure he could hear every word we said.

"Good," I whispered. "I agree." We shook hands in haste, guiltily, and parted.

6

What anxiety I suffered, waiting in my cottage that evening! My family seemed determined to drive me mad—the children quarreling endlessly, my father more fantastic than I could remember ever having seen him. Shortly before sunset I caught sight of the great black supply-wagon coming from the prison to the village. I tried to show no particular interest as it lumbered down toward my gate, drawn by four gray horses ruled more by mindless habit than by the sleepy old peasant who held the reins. The wagon listed on its broken springs like a foundering ship, and with every pothole the wooden wheels struck (the road has been in shameful disrepair for years), I was sure the whole hulk would topple, and our secret come clattering out. I fixed my eyes on whatever tract I was pretending to read—my father had his fierce eyes fixed upon me—and I did not look up until the clumsy structure paused in front of my gate. The nearer horses nibbled at my tulip tree. The driver slept on. And then, as if of its own volition, the wagon started up again. I cleared my throat, closed my book as if casually, and ambled toward the door.

"Smells are strange things," my father said.

My heart leapt; but I was sure an old man could not smell, from this distance, the corpse that now lay, I knew, beside my gatepost. I strolled out onto the porch and down to the road. When I glanced past my shoulder I saw my father, my wife, and the children peering through the window. Perspiration poured down my inner arms. Heller would feel no such guilt, I was sure. I was determined that before this was over I would learn his secret.

When I reached the road (the sky was now red, and evening birds had begun to sing), I found an old, innocent-looking trunk, its clasps unnaturally gleaming in the decaying light. The stone wall beside the road and the long-dead climbing roses hid it from my family's view. I drew it into the shadow of the wall, holding my breath against the stench. I hastily covered it with branches and leaves, then hurried back up to the cottage. My father was sitting in the kitchen, tamping his pipe with a nail.

"It's a beautiful evening," I remarked as naturally as possible.

"It's a *good* evening," the old man said, pursing his lips and squinting at me, wicked eyes glittering.

My panic increased by the minute. I'd be a very unsuccessful criminal! I remembered Josef Mallin's ungodly calm, the smile of scorn, the self-righteous conviction that was visible even on his decapitated head. Halfheartedly, I made conversation with my palely smiling, abstracted wife as she prepared our supper. She was later than usual, which alarmed me. If Heller's burial detail should arrive while we were still at table, I had no idea how I'd escape my family's watchfulness. Between dreary, absentminded remarks to my wife and father, I asked myself a thousand questions. Was I right to trust Heller to arrange the detail? Obviously I'd been out of my wits! It was a hundred to nothing that sooner or later one of the guards he'd persuaded to help would disclose what we'd done. But it was no use thinking about such things now. In my agitated state, I felt downright relief when my father turned, for no discernible reason, to the subject ordinarily more distressing to me than all others.

"I'll tell you what it is with Josef Mallin," he said. He drew in pipe smoke, savored it, and let it out again. I actually leaned forward, eager to hear him, "He's convinced all ideals are a flight from reality. The unpleasant facts of life, he claims, charge the human soul with longing. They drive a man to make up a world that's better than ours. But that better world is mere illusion, says Mallin; and illusion, being false, a mere cowardly lie, is as foul as actuality. So he goes at the universe with dynamite sticks. It's a natural mistake." He leered, showing his crooked, gray teeth. His eyes came into me like nails.

"Well, he's paid for his mistake," I said too loudly.

My father nodded, presumably to keep peace. He lit another match, and held it over the cracked, black pipe bowl. He said, "The Warden, now, he *believes* in the mystical experience. But, unfortunately, he's never had one. He wastes his life anticipating. It's a terrible crime. A mortal sin, I judge."

"That's true," I said eagerly, senselessly. But it did not persuade the old man to babble on. He fell silent, as if everything were settled.

At just that moment, my wife announced supper. I went to the parlor to call in the children. They came at once, not from obedience, of course; from hunger. As I was about to follow, I glanced out, hardly thinking, toward the lane. They were there—Heller's burial detail! I could see nothing but their shapes, dark blocks against the gray of the road, standing motionless as tombstones, waiting. A curious feeling of calm came over me, a mingled indifference and determination that reminded me of Heller. Without a word to those expecting me for dinner, I stepped to the door, opened it, and went out.

7

My mind was curiously blank, climbing, with my walking stick, up the old stone lane toward the churchyard; and blank as I took my turn at the shovel. We would have been, to a passerby, a curious sight. Of the dozen or more of us, only I myself was beardless, the rest of them shaggy with orthodoxy. Two of them at least must have been rabbis; they were not only bearded but wore tattered robes. No one spoke. They were a company born for undertakings, sad-eyed, stoop-shouldered, all their faces the mirror images of a single expression: shrugging surprise and mild pleasure that they too were not dead. They worked in rhythm with one another, or stood harmoniously silent. It was as if they were performing a religious duty—though the churchyard was Christian and the man we were burying certainly no Jew. The night above us was immense, majestic. Except for the graveyard itself, all the grounds of the church were shrouded in darkness, shadowed by the interlocking limbs of chestnut trees and oaks. Above the open space of the graveyard, the full moon shone serene, mysterious. The grave was chest-deep when, panting heavily, sticky with sweat and slightly dizzy from my unusual exertion, I handed the spade to the old man seated in the grass above me and prepared to climb out for my period of rest. A hand reached down out of the group to help me; I accepted it. When I was free of the grave I recognized Heller. "Thank you," I said. He said nothing. He led me to a crooked, low tombstone wide enough that both of us could sit on it. The old man who had taken my place shoveled steadily, his upper teeth closed on his bearded lower lip, three younger men standing above him, waiting their turns.

"He was a strange man," Heller said. I merely looked at him, too winded to comment. "He never ate," he said. He took a deep breath and looked up into the night. "It's amazing he lasted as long as he did."

I nodded, a trifle reluctantly, glanced over toward the gravediggers.

Heller frowned, silent for a moment, then at last continued: "I think of something he used to say: 'In the inorganic life, pain cannot be; thus the necessity for the organic.' There's the secret of the man. He relished his pain because of, you know, his mysticism." He looked away from me, down at the grass, then sighed deeply and looked up at the moon again. "He hated life, you know, yet delighted in it, because of what its horrors would do for him later."

Something my father had said crossed my mind, flitting softly, like a bat at dusk, almost too swift for me to catch it.

"Perhaps he was guilty after all," I said.

Heller turned his face toward me.

I rose from the tombstone, less giddy now, though still short of breath, just perceptibly lightheaded. He too rose. I walked, hands in pockets, down the aisle between graves. Neither of us spoke. At length we came to the slope declining to the moonlit pool. The shadow of willow trees lay on the water, motionless, snatched out of time. We could hear the faint crunch of the spade behind us. On the opposite side of the pool the old stone church stood brooding, as patiently still as its reflection. Beyond the church, where the dark trees began, there was motionless fog. We stood for a long time saying nothing. At length, following some train of thought of his own, Heller said, "It was a terrible injustice."

I said nothing, watching the reflection of the church.

"He clung to his pain, but in the end he lost all sense of it. If there are angry ghosts, envious prowlers in the shadow of the living—" He stared across the pool, smiling thoughtfully, perhaps unaware that he was smiling. It was not, I saw, a matter of great importance to him. Merely another of life's ironies. I felt a queer irritation and found myself squeezing the handle of my cane. I calmed myself, listening to the rhythmical crunch of the spade.

"There's no such thing as a ghost," I said suddenly.

"I don't believe in them either," he said, "but I'm afraid of them."

I moved closer to the water, head bowed, musing. He followed. We looked at the dead-still reflection of the church. No one had used it regularly for years. Doors hung loose, some of the windows were broken. People who came to the graveyard would repair it, from time to time, for the sake of the dead or for those who were yet to be buried here, but the repairs were pitiful at best. A wired-up sash, a softwood patch where the door had been broken, a supporting stake to prop a sagging iron fence. Heller said: "Or is it the Mallins of the world who come back—the enemies of 'illusion'? Maybe the unexpected fact of their survival—maybe it makes them more furious than before at the particled world of sticks and stones, the obstruction blocking—"

"*No* one comes back," I said, and struck the ground with my stick.

He smiled, looking at the grass. "No doubt you're right. Not the Mallins, at any rate." He sat mechanically nodding. "How could a man like Josef Mallin live more intensely than he did?—boiling like a cauldron from the cradle to the grave!"

Nothing, it seemed, would drive him from the subject. Why it was important that we speak of other things, I could not say; but it was. I felt as I'd felt on the road, walking home from the prison that night—that any moment I might slip outside myself, become no one, everyone, the drifting universe.

"Enough of this," I said, and gave a false little laugh. "Heller, this is hardly the time or place—" I let it trail off. I was thinking suddenly: *Which is more appalling, the crude stone church on land or the one upside down in the pool?*

Heller touched my arm and tipped his head down to study me. "You're in earnest," he said.

"We're grown men," I said, and laughed again. "Talk of ghosts is for children."

He too laughed, watching me. His teeth, in the darkness, were misty white. "Come now, Herr Vortrab. Look at the fog in the trees, the glitter of stars in the windows of the church. Surely such stubborn realism does them an injustice!" But he paused, seeing my agitation. "Well—" he said. He turned his hands palms up, a harmless tailor once more.

Behind us, the crunch of the spade, old men's voices, the black hole awaiting the world's latest victim, persuading him to rest.

"What man can say what he really believes about these things?" Heller said lightly.

I felt unwell. I'm too old, too fat to be shoveling graves. My heartbeat was a little wrong somehow; my tongue was dry.

Heller said, downright merry now, "No one comes back, of course. You've convinced me, Herr Vortrab! Neither the unfeeling nor the hypersensitive, neither idiots—"

I touched his arm.

Everything was silent. The pool was so still the night itself seemed dead. The gravedigging was finished and Heller's burial detail stood across from us. I counted them. Eleven.

I gazed at the upside-down image of the church. Tangled vines crawled down toward the steeple and pushed against the windows. The still air was wintry, not as if cold had come but as if all warmth in the area had lost its vitality, decayed. I was aware of someone standing to my right, and I glanced over, casually. It was the Warden, standing with one hand in his pocket, the other cradling a revolver. He stood with one highly polished boot thrown forward. I saw, without alarm, that a part of his forehead was blasted away, as if by some violent explosion. He noticed my glance and nodded, severe, withdrawn—laboring, despite some inner turmoil, to be sociable. Dried blood from his wound lay over his left eye and cheek. "Good heavens," I said, with a quick, no doubt somewhat obsequious smile, and leaped back a step. I threw a look at Heller. When I turned to look back at the Warden, he was walking away, moving hurriedly around the rim of the pond in the direction of the church. Heller was touching his beard, looking over his spectacles at me.

"Impossible!" I whispered—probing, perhaps, to learn for certain whether Heller too had seen it.

But Heller had no answer, as silent as the eleven across from us, watching—all twelve of them watching: grim, moonlit jury.

"We're finished here," I said abruptly, my voice rather shrill in that midnight stillness. I pointed with the tip of my stick toward the grave mound.

Heller nodded, still not commenting. What was I to do?

Stiff-legged, ridiculous, my back still tingling, I led them past headstones to the iron gates and down the pitch-dark lane to my cottage, where I left them with a crisp good night and a click of my heels. No doubt they smiled at that later.

What was I to do? I too had my laugh. From the darkness of my parlor I peeked out at them, trudging down the road, the rabbis' skirts dragging, the younger men clinging to the elbows of the old.

That is how things stand with us. I no longer bother to deny that I am frightened, hopelessly baffled, but neither do I pretend to believe that sooner or later he will answer my knock. I need rest, a change of air, time to sort out my thoughts . . . but each day provides new calamities. . . .

We no longer go home nights; it wouldn't be safe to leave the prison in the hands of the guards we have now, except, of course, Heller.

A fool came to visit me, to sell me a book. It began, as I remember,

Modern thought has made considerable progress by reducing the existent to the series of appearances which manifest it. Its aim was to overcome certain dualisms which have embarrassed philosophy, and to replace them by the singleness of the phenomenon. . . .

I drove the man out with my walking stick. Heller looked on with his cap in his hands, mournful of eye but not altogether disapproving. He thinks I'm mad, of course. Each new regulation I bring "from the Warden," each new pardon or death sentence, increases his despair. I understand his feelings. I do what I can for him. "If Order has value, you and I are the only hope!" I whisper. He nods, mechanically stroking his beard.

I worry about him. Late at night, when he should be asleep, I hear Heller pacing, occasionally pausing, deep in thought.

DONALD BARTHELME

The Death of Edward Lear

The death of Edward Lear took place on a Sunday morning in May 1888. Invitations were sent out well in advance. The invitations read:

> Mr. Edward LEAR
> *Nonsense Writer and Landscape Painter*
> *Requests the Honor of Your Presence*
> *On the Occasion of His DEMISE.*
>
> San Remo   2:20 a.m.
> The 29th of May   Please reply

One can imagine the feelings of the recipients. Our dear friend! is preparing to depart! and such-like. Mr. Lear! who has given us so much pleasure! and such-like. On the other hand, his years were considered. Mr. Lear! who must be, now let me see . . . And there was a good deal of, I remember the first time I (dipped into) (was seized by) . . . But on the whole, Mr. Lear's acquaintances approached the occasion with a mixture of solemnity and practicalness, perhaps remembering the words of Lear's great friend, Tennyson:

> *Old men must die,*
> *or the world would grow mouldy*

and:

For men may come and men may go,
But I go on forever.

People prepared to attend the death of Edward Lear as they might have for a day in the country. Picnic baskets were packed (for it would be wrong to expect too much of Mr. Lear's hospitality, under the circumstances); bottles of wine were wrapped in white napkins. Toys were chosen for the children. There were debates as to whether the dog ought to be taken or left behind. (Some of the dogs actually present at the death of Edward Lear could not restrain themselves; they frolicked about the dying man's chamber, tugged at the bedclothes, and made such nuisances of themselves that they had to be removed from the room.)

Most of Mr. Lear's friends decided that the appropriate time to arrive at the Villa would be midnight, or in that neighborhood, in order to allow the old gentleman time to make whatever remarks he might have in mind or do whatever he wanted to do, before the event. Everyone understood what the time specified in the invitation meant. And so, the visitors found themselves being handed down from their carriages (by Lear's servant Giuseppe Orsini) in almost total darkness. Pausing to greet people they knew, or to corral straying children, they were at length ushered into a large room on the first floor, where the artist had been accustomed to exhibit his watercolors, and thence by a comfortably wide staircase to a similar room on the second floor, where Mr. Lear himself waited, in bed, wearing an old velvet smoking jacket and his familiar silver spectacles with tiny oval lenses. Several dozen straight-backed chairs had been arranged in a rough semicircle around the bed; these were soon filled, and later arrivals stood along the walls.

Mr. Lear's first words were: "I've no money!" As each new group of guests entered the room, he repeated, "I've no money! No money!" He looked extremely tired, yet calm. His ample beard, gray yet retaining patches of black, had evidently not been trimmed in some days. He seemed nervous and immediately began to discourse, as if to prevent anyone else from doing so.

He began by thanking all those present for attending and expressing the hope that he had not put them to too great an inconvenience, acknowledging that the hour was "an unusual one for visits!" He said that he could not find words sufficient to disclose his pleasure in seeing so many of his friends gathered together at his side. He then delivered a pretty little lecture, of some twelve minutes' duration, on the production of his various writings, of which no one has been able to recall the substance, although everyone agreed that it was charming, graceful, and wise.

He then startled his guests with a question, uttered in a kind of shriek: "Should I get married? Get married? Should I marry?"

Mr. Lear next offered a short homily on the subject Friendship. Friendship, he said, is the most golden of the affections. It is also, he said, often the *strongest* of human ties, surviving strains and tempests fatal to less sublime relations. He noted that his own many friendships constituted the richest memory of a long life.

A disquisition on Cats followed.

When Mr. Lear reached the topic Children, a certain restlessness was observed among his guests. (He had not ceased to shout at intervals, "Should I get married?" and "I've no money!") He then displayed copies of his books, but as everybody had already read them, not more than a polite interest was generated. Next he held up, one by one, a selection of his watercolors, views of various antiquities and picturesque spots. These, too, were familiar; they were the same watercolors the old gentleman had been offering for sale, at £5 and £10, for the past forty years.

Mr. Lear now sang a text of Tennyson's in a setting of his own, accompanying himself on a mandolin. Although his voice was thin and cracked frequently, the song excited vigorous applause.

Finally he caused to be hauled into the room by servants an enormous oil, at least seven feet by ten, depicting Mount Athos. There was a murmur of appreciation, but it did not seem to satisfy the painter, for he assumed a very black look.

At 2:15 Mr. Lear performed a series of actions the meaning of which was obscure to the spectators.

At 2:20 he reached over to the bedside table, picked up an old-fashioned pen which lay there, and died. A death mask was immediately taken. The guests, weeping unaffectedly, moved in a long line back to the carriages.

People who had attended the death of Edward Lear agreed that, all in all, it had been a somewhat tedious performance. Why had he seen fit to read the same old verses, sing again the familiar songs, show the well-known pictures, run through his repertoire once more? Why invitations? Then something was understood: that Mr. Lear had been doing what he had always done and therefore, not doing anything extraordinary. Mr. Lear had transformed the extraordinary into its opposite. He had, in point of fact, created a gentle genial misunderstanding.

Thus the guests began, as time passed, to regard the affair in an historical light. They told their friends about it, reenacted parts of it for their children and grandchildren. They would reproduce the way the old man had piped "I've no money!" in a comical voice, and quote his odd remarks about marrying. The death of Edward Lear became so popular, as time passed, that revivals were staged in every part of the country, with considerable success. The death of Edward Lear can still be seen, in the smaller cities, in versions enriched by learned interpretation, textual emendation, and changing fashion. One modification is curious; no one knows how it came about. The supporting company plays in the traditional way, but Lear himself appears shouting, shaking, vibrant with rage.

PAUL BOWLES

The Circular Valley

The abandoned monastery stood on a slight eminence of land in the middle of a vast clearing. On all sides the ground sloped gently downward toward the tangled, hairy jungle that filled the circular valley, ringed about by sheer, black cliffs. There were a few trees in some of the courtyards, and the birds used them as meeting-places when they flew out of the rooms and corridors where they had their nests. Long ago bandits had taken whatever was removable out of the building. Soldiers had used it once as headquarters, had, like the bandits, built fires in the great windy rooms so that afterward they looked like ancient kitchens. And now that everything was gone from within, it seemed that never again would anyone come near the monastery. The vegetation had thrown up a protecting wall; the first story was soon quite hidden from view by small tress which dripped vines to lasso the cornices of the windows. The meadows roundabout grew dank and lush; there was no path through them.

At the higher end of the circular valley a river fell off the cliffs into a great cauldron of vapor and thunder below; after this it slid along the base of the cliffs until it found a gap at the other end of the valley, where it hurried discreetly through with no rapids, no cascades—a great thick black rope of water moving swiftly downhill between the polished flanks of the canyon. Beyond the gap the land opened out and became smiling; a village nestled on the side hill just outside. In the days of the monastery it was there that the friars had got their provisions, since the Indians would not enter the circular valley. Centuries ago, when the building had been constructed, the Church

115

had imported the workmen from another part of the country. These were traditional enemies of the tribes thereabouts, and had another language; there was no danger that the inhabitants would communicate with them as they worked at setting up the mighty walls. Indeed, the construction had taken so long that before the east wing was completed the workmen had all died, one by one. Thus it was the friars themselves who had closed off the end of the wing with blank walls, leaving it that way, unfinished and blind-looking, facing the black cliffs.

Generation after generation, the friars came, fresh-cheeked boys who grew thin and gray, and finally died, to be buried in the garden beyond the courtyard with the fountain. One day not long ago they had all left the monastery; no one knew where they had gone, and no one thought to ask. It was shortly after this that the bandits and then the soldiers had come. And now, since the Indians do not change, still no one from the village went up through the gap to visit the monastery. The Atlájala lived there; the friars had not been able to kill it, had given up at last and gone away. No one was surprised, but the Atlájala gained in prestige by their departure. During the centuries the friars had been there in the monastery, the Indians had wondered why it allowed them to stay. Now, at last, it had driven them out. It always had lived there, they said, and would go on living there because the valley was its home, and it could never leave.

In the early morning the restless Atlájala would move through the halls of the monastery. The dark rooms sped past, one after the other. In a small patio, where eager young trees had pushed up the paving stones to reach the sun, it paused. The air was full of small sounds: the movements of butterflies, the falling to the ground of bits of leaves and flowers, the air following its myriad courses around the edges of things, the ants pursuing their endless labors in the hot dust. In the sun it waited, conscious of each gradation in sound and light and smell, living in the awareness of the slow, constant disintegration that attacked the morning and transformed it into afternoon. When evening came, it often slipped above the monastery roof and surveyed the darkening sky: the waterfall would roar distantly. Night after night, along the procession of years, it had hovered here above the valley, darting down to become a bat, a leopard, a moth for a few minutes or hours, returning to rest immobile in the center of the space enclosed by the cliffs. When the monastery had been built, it had taken to frequenting the rooms, where it had observed for the first time the meaningless gestures of human life.

And then one evening it had aimlessly become one of the young friars. This was a new sensation, strangely rich and complex, and at the same time unbearably stifling, as though every other possibility besides that of being enclosed in a tiny, isolated world of cause and effect had been removed forever. As the friar, it had gone and stood in the window, looking out at the sky, seeing for the first time, not the stars, but the space between and beyond them. Even at that moment it had felt the urge to leave, to step outside the little shell of anguish where it lodged for the moment, but a faint curiosity had impelled it to remain a little longer and partake a little further of the unaccustomed sensation. It held on; the friar raised his arms to the sky in an imploring gesture. For the first time the Atlájala sensed opposition, the thrill of a struggle. It was delicious to feel the young man striving to free himself of its presence, and it was immeasurably sweet to remain there. Then with a cry the friar had rushed to the other side of the room and seized a heavy leather whip hanging on the wall. Tearing off his clothing he had begun to carry out a ferocious self-beating. At the first blow of the lash the Atlájala had been on the point of letting go, but then it realized that the immediacy of that intriguing inner pain was only made more manifest by the impact of the blows from without, and so it stayed and felt the young man grow weak under his own lashing. When he had finished and said a prayer, he crawled to his pallet and fell asleep weeping, while the Atlájala slipped out obliquely and entered into a bird which passed the night sitting in a great tree on the edge of the jungle, listening intently to the night sounds, and uttering a scream from time to time.

Thereafter the Atlájala found it impossible to resist sliding inside the bodies of the friars; it visited one after the other, finding an astonishing variety of sensation in the process. Each was a separate world, a separate experience, because each had different reactions when he became conscious of the other being within him. One would sit and read or pray, one would go for a long troubled walk in the meadows, around and around the building, one would find a comrade and engage in an absurd but bitter quarrel, a few wept, some flagellated themselves or sought a friend to wield the lash for them. Always there was a rich profusion of perceptions for the Atlájala to enjoy, so that it no longer occurred to it to frequent the bodies of insects, birds and furred animals, nor even to leave the monastery and move in the air above. Once it almost got into difficulties when an old friar it was occupying suddenly fell back dead. That was a hazard it ran in the frequenting of men: they seemed not to know when they were doomed, or if they did know, they pretended with such strength not to know, that it amounted to the same thing. The other beings knew beforehand, save when it was a question of being seized unawares and devoured. And that the Atlájala was able to prevent: a bird in which it was staying was always avoided by the hawks and eagles.

When the friars left the monastery, and, following the government's orders, doffed their robes, dispersed and became workmen, the Atlájala was at a loss to know how to pass its days and nights. Now everything was as it had been before their arrival: there was no one but the creatures that always had lived in the circular valley. It tried a giant serpent, a deer, a bee: nothing had the savor it had grown to love. Everything was the same as before, but not for the Atlájala; it had known the existence of man, and now there were no men in the valley—only the abandoned building with its empty rooms to make man's absence more poignant.

Then one year bandits came, several hundred of them in one stormy afternoon. In delight it tried many of them as they sprawled about cleaning their guns and cursing, and it discovered still other facets of sensation: the hatred they felt for the world, the fear they had of the soldiers who were pursuing them, the strange gusts of desire that swept through them as they sprawled together drunk by the fire that smoldered in the center of the floor, and the insufferable pain of jealousy which the nightly orgies seem to awaken in some of them. But the bandits did not stay long. When they had left, the soldiers came in their wake. It felt very much the same way to be a soldier as to be a bandit. Missing were the strong fear and the hatred, but the rest was almost identical. Neither the bandits nor the soldiers appeared to be at all conscious of its presence in them; it could slip from one man to another without causing any change in their behavior. This surprised it, since its effect on the friars had been so definite, and it felt a certain disappointment at the impossibility of making its existence known to them.

Nevertheless, the Atlájala enjoyed both bandits and soldiers immensely, and was even more desolate when it was left alone once again. It would become one of the swallows that made their nests in the rocks beside the top of the waterfall. In the burning sunlight it would plunge again and again into the curtain of mist that rose from far below, sometimes uttering exultant cries. It would spend a day as a plant louse, crawling slowly along the underside of the leaves, living quietly in the huge green world down there which is forever hidden from the sky. Or at night, in the velvet body of a panther, it would know the pleasure of the kill. Once for a year it lived in an eel at the bottom of the pool below the waterfall, feeling the mud give slowly before it as it pushed ahead with its flat nose; that was a restful period, but afterward the desire to know again the mysterious life of a man had returned—an obsession of which it was useless to try to rid itself. And now it moved restlessly through the ruined rooms, a mute presence, alone, and thirsting to be incarnate once again, but in man's flesh only. And with the building of highways through the country it was inevitable that people should come once again to the circular valley.

A man and a woman drove their automobile as far as a village down in a lower valley; hearing about the ruined monastery and the waterfall that dropped over the cliffs into the great amphitheater, they determined to see these things. They came on burros as far as the village outside the gap, but there the Indians they had hired to accompany them refused to go any farther, and so they continued alone, upward through the canyon and into the precinct of the Atlájala.

It was noon when they rode into the valley; the black ribs of the cliffs glistened like glass in the sun's blistering downward rays. They stopped the burros by a cluster of boulders at the edge of the sloping meadows. The man got down first, and reached up to help the woman off. She leaned forward, putting her hands on his face, and for a long moment they kissed. Then he lifted her to the ground and they climbed hand in hand up over the rocks. The Atlájala hovered near them, watching the woman closely: she was the first ever to have come into the valley. The two sat beneath a small tree on the grass, looking at one another, smiling. Out of habit, the Atlájala entered into the man. Immediately, instead of existing in the midst of the sunlit air, the bird calls and the plant odors, it was conscious only of the woman's beauty and her terrible imminence. The waterfall, the earth, and the sky itself receded, rushed into nothingness, and there were only the woman's smile and her arms and her odor. It was a world more suffocating and painful than the Atlájala had thought possible. Still, while the man spoke and the woman answered, it remained within.

"Leave him. He doesn't love you."

"He would kill me."

"But I love you. I need you with me."

"I can't. I'm afraid of him."

The man reached out to pull her to him; she drew back slightly, but her eyes grew large.

"We have today," she murmured, turning her face toward the yellow walls of the monastery.

The man embraced her fiercely, crushing her against him as though the act would save his life. "No, no, no. It can't go on like this," he said. "No."

The pain of his suffering was too intense; gently the Atlájala left the man and slipped into the woman. And now it would have believed itself to be housed in nothing, to be in its own spaceless self, so completely was it aware of the wandering wind, the small flutterings of the leaves, and the bright air that surrounded it. Yet there was a difference: each element was magnified in intensity, the whole sphere of being was immense, limitless. Now it understood what the man sought in the woman, and it knew that he suffered because he never would attain that sense of completion he sought. But the Atlájala, being one with the woman, had attained it, and, being aware of possessing it, trembled with delight. The woman shuddered as her lips met those of the man. There on the grass in the shade of the tree their joy reached new heights; the Atlájala, knowing them both, formed a single channel between the secret springs of their desires. Throughout, it remained within the woman, and began vaguely to devise ways of keeping her, if not inside the valley, at least nearby, so that she might return.

In the afternoon, with dreamlike motions, they walked to the burros and mounted them, driving them through the deep meadow grass to the monastery. Inside the great courtyard they halted, looking hesitantly at the ancient arches in the sunlight, and at the darkness inside the doorways.

"Shall we go in?" said the woman.

"We must get back."

"I want to go in," she said. (The Atlájala exulted.) A thin gray snake slid along the ground into the bushes. They did not see it.

The man looked at her perplexedly. "It's late," he said.

But she jumped down from her burro by herself and walked beneath the arches into the long corridor within. (Never had the rooms seemed so real as now when the Atlájala was seeing them through her eyes.)

They explored all the rooms. Then the woman wanted to climb up into the tower, but the man took a determined stand.

"We must go back now," he said firmly, putting his hand on her shoulder.

"This is our only day together, and you think of nothing but getting back."

"But the time . . ."

"There is a moon. We won't lose the way."

He would not change his mind. "No."

"As you like," she said. "I'm going up. You can go back alone if you like."

The man laughed uneasily. "You're mad." He tried to kiss her.

She turned away and did not answer for a moment. Then she said: "You want me to leave my husband for you. You ask everything from me, but what do you do for me in return? You refuse even to climb up into a little tower with me to see the view. Go back alone. Go!"

She sobbed and rushed toward the dark stairwell. Calling after her, he followed, but stumbled somewhere behind her. She was as sure of foot as if she had climbed the many stone steps a thousand times before, hurrying up through the darkness, around and around.

In the end she came out at the top and peered through the small apertures in the cracking walls. The beams which had supported the bell had rotted and fallen; the heavy bell lay on its side in the rubble, like a dead animal. The waterfall's sound was louder up here; the valley was nearly full of shadow. Below, the man called her name repeatedly. She did not answer. As she stood watching the shadow of the cliffs slowly overtake the farthest recesses of the valley and begin to climb the naked rocks to the east, an idea formed in her mind. It was not the kind of idea which she would have expected of herself, but it was there, growing and inescapable. When she felt it complete there inside her, she turned and went lightly back down. The man was sitting in the dark near the bottom of the stairs, groaning a little.

"What is it?" she said.

"I hurt my leg. Now are you ready to go or not?"

"Yes," she said simply. "I'm sorry you fell."

Without saying anything he rose and limped after her out into the court-yard where the burros stood. The cold mountain air was beginning to flow down from the tops of the cliffs. As they rode through the meadow she began to think of how she would broach the subject to him. (It must be done before they reached the gap. The Atlájala trembled.)

"Do you forgive me?" she asked him.

"Of course," he laughed.

"Do you love me?"

"More than anything in the world."

"Is that true?"

He glanced at her in the failing light, sitting erect on the jogging animal.

"You know it is," he said softly.

She hesitated.

"There is only one way, then," she said finally.

"But what?"

"I'm afraid of him. I won't go back to him. You go back. I'll stay in the village here." (Being that near, she would come each day to the monastery.) "When it is done, you will come and get me. Then we can go somewhere else. No one will find us."

The man's voice sounded strange. "I don't understand."

"You do understand. And that is the only way. Do it or not, as you like. It is the only way."

They trotted along for a while in silence. The canyon loomed ahead, black against the evening sky.

Then the man said, very clearly: "Never."

A moment later the trail led out into an open space high above the swift water below. The hollow sound of the river reached them faintly. The light in the sky was almost gone; in the dusk the landscape had taken on false contours. Everything was gray—the rocks, the bushes, the trail—and nothing had distance or scale. They slowed their pace.

His words still echoed in her ears.

"I won't go back to him!" she cried with sudden vehemence. "You can go back and play cards with him as usual. Be his good friend the same as always. I won't go. I can't go on with both of you in the town." (The plan was not working; the Atlájala saw it had lost her, yet it still could help her.)

"You're very tired," he said softly.

He was right. Almost as he said the words, that unaccustomed exhilaration and lightness she had felt ever since noon seemed to leave her; she hung her head wearily, and said: "Yes, I am."

At the same moment the man uttered a sharp, terrible cry; she looked up in time to see his burro plunge from the edge of the trail into the grayness below. There was a silence, and then the faraway sound of many stones sliding downward. She could not move or stop the burro; she sat dumbly, letting it carry her along, an inert weight on its back.

For one final instant, as she reached the pass which was the edge of its realm, the Atlájala alighted tremulously within her. She raised her head and a tiny exultant shiver passed through her; then she let it fall forward once again.

Hanging in the dim air above the trail, the Atlájala watched her indistinct figure grow invisible in the gathering night. (If it had not been able to hold her there, still it had been able to help her.)

A moment later it was in the tower, listening to the spiders mend their webs that she had damaged. It would be a long, long time before it would bestir itself to enter into another being's awareness. A long, long time—perhaps forever.

WILLIAM FERGUSON

The Third Voice

There are two hills on my farm, both heavily wooded. One is near the house; the other is at the far end of the property, down by the river. When I climb the near hill in the early morning, there seems to be a man shouting from the far one. I shout back, but he never answers. So I hike down toward the river and up the other slope, but no one is ever there, and I hear the shouting again from the first hill. This has been going on, winter and summer, since my son moved his family to Boston, seven years ago this March.

I know the man I hear is the ghost of a suicide: my grandfather, John Rudd, who owned this farm before I was born. He was a good man, but given to alcohol. One day his wife and children left him for better things; a week later, John hanged himself in the barn—the one I still use today.

In the evenings, I get to thinking about John Rudd; I go into the barn after supper and stare up at the rafters, wondering what it would be like to die.

Before my son left, I remember, we all used to walk up on the hill at dusk and hoot at the great horned owl that lived in the hemlocks. We had no idea what we were saying, of course, but whatever it was, the bird was saying it back.

The exchange with my grandfather is more disturbing. One word from me is enough to quiet him; his silence makes me giddy, like the dizziness that comes over me when I'm plowing the middle field and the woodlot begins to go yellow and brittle at the edges, like a page in an old book.

It bothers me to think that my grandfather and I may be striding through each other's bodies as we cross in the morning, as insubstantial, at least to each other's eyes, as dust off the summer fields.

"Hold your horses," he seems to be saying. "Hold your horses!"

Is he telling me to wait? Why should I wait?

There is a third voice, sometimes, that comes from the field across the river. It is certainly not an echo of John Rudd's; it sounds more like a child calling its father.

The land is beautiful over there, rich and level, with no stones. When my son comes back, he should buy it any way he can and repair the bridge, because it would make all the difference, and maybe then he'd have something worthwhile to give his children.

I've told him so.

But he doesn't answer letters.

I lean on a fencepost, gazing across the river.

"Coming!" says the voice from over there. "I'm coming!"

I hear it, as I hear John Rudd; but I say nothing. What good would it do? These voices, by now, are as familiar and useless as wind in the swaying trees.

PATRICK McGRATH

Marmilion

1

Have you ever eaten monkey? The Cajuns have long considered Louisiana spider monkey a great delicacy. I should know: my husband was a Cajun. They serve it in the traditional manner, heavily spiced with Tabasco. It's probably for this reason that the creatures move so soundlessly; all you hear is an occasional soft "swoosh" as they swing through the trees, and then the telltale patter of falling water droplets. I was once lucky enough to observe a group of them gathered for the night. What a charming spectacle of domestic tranquility they presented! Clustered along a stout bough, they were engaged in mutual grooming when I came drifting down the bayou. I saw them all huddled together, with their tails twined and dangling beneath the branch in a great thick furry knot. It's been suggested that tail twining enhances balance, but the primary function, in my opinion, is social. Then they went to sleep, and I shot them—with my camera.

Slavers brought them up from Brazil in the eighteenth century, is my conjecture. When the ships docked at New Orleans, a few of the creatures slipped off into the wilderness and adapted to conditions there. Nature was bountiful and predators few; in fact, their only real predator is Man, which accounts, as I say, for their shyness today and the infrequency of sightings. But they're there, all right, way back in the dankest region of the Charenton Swamp, and all you need is a boat, and a great deal of patience, and you'll find them. I did; I went out to photograph them for a book called *Our Endangered Species.* It was in the course of this assignment that I first laid eyes on Marmilion.

Marmilion! How sweet the sound—and yet . . . !

I came upon it one warm evening in early September after crossing a blind lake. I had located through my binoculars a wharf on the far shore, and I hoped to find somewhere nearby a fisherman's shack in which to spend the night. The water was as flat and still as a sheet of glass; behind me the ripples from the boat spread out in long furrows, and only the buzz of the outboard broke the deep silence of the evening. On every side the water was fringed with trees, black against the crimson-streaked sunset.

I reached the far shore. After securing the boat I clambered up the levee and found myself, to my astonishment, at the foot of a great avenue of spreading oaks, from the branches of which hung sheets of fleecy, drifting moss. At the far end, white and shining, stood a pair of pillars flanking the deep-set doorway of what appeared to be a large plantation house. The avenue was thick with shadows and formed a sort of arboreal tunnel. The glimpse of those shining pillars was strangely dramatic, in that lonely place. I shouldered my pack and set off into the obscurity.

It was indeed a plantation house, a massive structure in the Greek Revival style, though in a state of advanced decay. It stood in the center of a patch of cleared ground, and the last light caught it in such a way that the pillars literally *glowed* against the darkened galleries, with such a lovely soft luminosity that they seemed almost to be immanent with a life of their own. Everything was disintegrating but for a pair of stout brick chimneys, thrusting up through the rafters on either side.

A feeling of great desolation clung to the house, but I decided nonetheless to shelter for the night beneath its roof, such as it was; and, coming again to the front, I ascended a short flight of crumbling steps, crossed the lower gallery, and so over the threshold.

I am not a superstitious woman. But as soon as I crossed that threshold I felt something in the house react to my presence, and I stood dead still. But nothing stirred, nothing at all, and after a few moments I went cautiously forward into the gloom.

It was foul with the smell of nesting rodents and rotting plaster. Directly ahead of me, at the far end of the hallway, reared what had once been a grand staircase. I turned off into the front room, which was full of dust and shadows, and in which I found an open fireplace with tall brick pillars on either side. I dared not use it, for fear of setting ablaze the rubbish with which the chimney was undoubtedly clogged. I built a fire on the hearth instead, and cooked a simple supper. Then I leaned my back against the bricks and drank my bourbon in the firelight.

By this time it was completely dark outside. The birdsong of the evening had died away, and the only sounds were those of the insects, a sort of low, steady hiss produced by the rubbing together of thousands of gossamer wings. Nothing else.

The fire burned down, and I must have drifted off. Then suddenly I was wide awake, frozen with fear and with every sense straining into the darkness. The insects had ceased their hissing, and a profound silence lay upon the house. And then I heard it: a scratching sound, close to my head. It lasted for a few seconds, and then fell silent. It was like a nail being scraped by a very feeble hand against a brick. Slowly my terror subsided. The sound persisted, intermittently, for about an hour. By that time I was not so much frightened as perplexed. Was there some sort of creature in the chimney? Was it—absurd question—the creature that had stirred when I crossed the threshold at dusk?

Before I left the house the next morning I crawled into the fireplace and lit a match. The flame threw a brief flickering glow upon blackened bricks crusted with the droppings of birds and bats. A couple of feet above my head the flue sloped away sharply, leaving me only an oblique glimpse of the mouth of the chimney. I crawled out again, still puzzled, and made my way back down the oak alley, where sunlight sifted through the murmuring leaves and splashed in golden puddles on the grass. I was soon upon the water once more, and heading back toward the Charenton Swamp, and its elusive simian residents. I was ill at ease the rest of the day, and had scant success with the monkeys. You see, I had the bizarre impression that something had been trying to *communicate* with me in the night.

2

When I got back to New Orleans I spent a morning finding out what I could about the ruined house. Its name, I discovered, was Marmilion, and it was built by a planter called Randolph Belvedere. Randolph had settled the land in 1820 and founded a great fortune on sugar; then in middle age he became a prominent figure in Louisiana politics. A stout man, he was apparently endowed with huge reserves of energy and imagination, and Marmilion proudly reflected his appetite for ostentatious splendor. By the time the house was finished, he had spent six years and $100,000 on it. All the building materials were manufactured on the spot, the bricks baked from local river clay and the great framing timbers cut by slaves from stands of giant cypress in the Charenton Swamp. The furniture was imported from Europe, and was said to have cost as much as the house itself.

Randolph did not have a large family, which struck me as unusual, given the man's temperament and class. Perhaps the delicacy of his wife, Camille, was the reason. She had been a legendary Creole belle, and apparently retained into old age a petite and fragile beauty. I was intrigued to learn that her correspondence with a sister, Mathilde, in Virginia, had survived, and was stored in the Louisiana State Archives, in Baton Rouge; and I resolved that when I next visited the state capital I would look them up, those letters of the long-dead mistress of Marmilion.

But in the meantime, the publishers of *Our Endangered Species* were so impressed with the work I had done that they decided it merited a book of its own, to be called *The Spider Monkeys of Louisiana.* I was delighted, if for no other reason than that it justified another visit to Marmilion. For my casual interest in the old ruin was becoming, I could feel it, somewhat obsessive; you see, I had come upon a very curious fact about Randolph Belvedere's death— the fact that nobody knew anything about it.

What happened was this: late one afternoon in the summer of 1860 a stranger galloped up to the front door of Marmilion and, without dismounting, announced to a houseboy that he must speak to the master. Randolph was doing plantation accounts in his study; he came to the door in his shirtsleeves, and there the two men whispered together for some minutes. Then Randolph called for his horse, and without a word to anyone, without even taking his coat and hat, he rode away with the stranger. He was never seen again.

3

It did not take me long to find a pretext for going to Baton Rouge; and once there, it did not take me long to realize that Camille Belvedere was, like the wives of so many planters in the Old South, a deeply unhappy woman. (Perhaps this accounts for my intuitive attraction to her.) *"These lines,"* she wrote in one of the last letters to Mathilde, *"are the effusions of a pen directed by the Hand of a Woman whose life has been occupied solely with drudgery."* Much of the correspondence concerns the unending round of domestic chores that were the lot of the plantation mistress, and with those I need not weary you. What also emerges is that Randolph was away for long periods, and to combat Camille's "disposition to despondency" the family physician, a man called Oscar de Trot, prescribed laudanum—tincture of opium—the effects of which were little understood at the time. In a letter written several months before her husband's disappearance, Camille tells Mathilde: *"I resort nightly to a liberal dose of the black drops. It so relieves my mind, I fear it is impossible for me to exist in tolerable comfort without it."*

My sympathy for the woman was immeasurably strengthened when I read those lines.

Neither of her children, it appears, provided any "tolerable comfort" to Camille. Her daughter, Lydia, was thirty-four and unmarried when Randolph rode away; Camille refers to her always as "poor Lydia." In 1846, at the age of twenty, she had loved a man called Simon Grampus Lamar, whom Randolph, however, forbade her to marry. One night Simon and Lydia eloped. In the course of their flight to Natchez they encountered a flooded stream, and Simon—a gallant fellow, but lacking, unfortunately, both money and land—carried Lydia across in his arms. Six weeks later he was dead of pneumonia, and Lydia never recovered from the shock.

She returned to Marmilion and assumed spinsterhood. It was clear to all that never again would passion touch her, and no suitor ever came calling on Miss Lydia again. She drifted about the plantation like a ghost, entirely immured in her melancholy; and the disappearance of her father had no apparent effect on her at all.

4

Lydia's profound lethargy was quite clearly the result of a broken heart; but what are we to think of her brother, William? In the summer of 1860 William was thirty-two years old, a fat, idle, ill-tempered, and dissolute man who seldom left the plantation; and in the face of Camille's anguish at Randolph's sudden disappearance he affected a careless nonchalance that "grievously vex'd and plagued" his mother. He rarely appears in the letters, and this in itself is odd. I would hazard that he had been a difficult boy; the task of rearing him would have fallen largely on Camille's shoulders, and no doubt the relationship of mother and son began to deteriorate at an early stage. (I should know; I've had a son of my own.) Southern society has always been rigidly patriarchal, and it must have been clear to young William that his mother's authority was by no means absolute. He realized that she was merely carrying out Randolph's orders, and this aroused in him a contemptuous defiance. In fact, it soon becomes clear that William's personality was a warped and stunted thing, and as he grew older, and became conscious of his moral defects, we can be fairly sure that he lashed out at anyone or anything weaker than himself. The slaves hated him; horses reared and dogs slunk off at his approach. Randolph Belvedere was deeply disappointed in the son upon whom he had hoped to found a dynasty, and no doubt tormented himself with the thought that it was his fault William had turned out as he had. But be that as it may, the upshot was that when her husband disappeared, Camille had no one to turn to but Dr. de Trot and his ready supply of "black drops."

And then, in January 1861, Louisiana seceded from the Union. Three months later Fort Sumter was shelled, and the War Between the States began.

5

I'm what they call in the business a monkey woman. I can photograph anything, but it's monkeys I'm best at and monkeys I've built my reputation on. I owe a lot to monkeys; and helping to publicize the plight of an endangered species like the Louisiana spiders is my attempt to repay some part of that debt. I am, incidentally, utterly opposed to the eating of monkeys.

I am also a Southerner, and like all Southerners I'm obsessed with history. But unlike most, I'm not interested in glory and romance. I'm not interested in resurrecting the Old South in a hazy splendor that far outshines the historical reality. Nor do I cling to the Lost Cause. The Old South is to me an example of a society dedicated to the greatest good for the smallest number. Endorsing such a society I consider the moral equivalent of eating monkeys.

Have you ever noticed, for example, how the slaveowners of the Old South emulated Classical Antiquity? They copied the architecture of ancient Greece and named their slaves after Roman statesmen. Like the Romans they also made sure the women stayed at home and had no control over their own affairs. The Southern gentleman who "sheltered" and "protected" his women—those fragile blossoms, spotless as doves—in fact shackled them; in a very real sense they were slaves, and that young William Belvedere should have detected this, and sought to exploit it, doesn't surprise me in the least; he was merely imitating his father.

The war changed all that. The war turned everything upside down. Randolph was gone, and William, lacking any inclination to take up arms for the cause, took to his bed with a "nervous fatigue" instead. Lydia Belvedere remained mired in apathetic melancholy, and all the slaves deserted save one, a taciturn fellow called Caesar. Upon his shoulders, and Camille's, now rested Marmilion's fate. Many of the great houses had been burned to the ground by the advancing Union army; how could these two, the woman and the slave, hope to turn back such an implacable foe?

It is with this tantalizing question that Camille's correspondence with

Mathilde abruptly ceases. No explanation was available; simply, there were no more letters. Imagine my frustration. After three days spent deciphering Camille's spidery hand in a dusty, subterranean reading room—after immersing myself in the intimate details of her day-to-day existence, and constructing a plausible picture of her unhappy family—just as she faces the major crisis of her life, the letters stop. The source dries up. It was not to be borne. I walked the shady streets of Baton Rouge like a woman demented. One question alone burned in my brain: what happened next?

Late that night, as I sat, by myself, in a little bar on Pinel Street, an idea made its tentative way into the parlor of consciousness. I entertained it; grew warm over it; and went to bed nursing a small flame of hope. The next morning, early, I again presented myself at the Archives and asked, with beating heart, to see the letters of Dr. Oscar de Trot. The archivist came back shaking his head. My heart sank. There were no such letters. There were, however, the doctor's journals; but they were kept in New Orleans.

I left within the hour.

6

How did Caesar and Camille turn back the Union army? With charm and hospitality—the old Southern virtues. When the inevitable troop of soldiers appeared, Camille was ready for them. The officers were treated as honored guests; they slept in the beds that Randolph had imported from Paris, drank the finest wines in his cellar, dined on wild duck, she-crab, and roast quail. Quite predictably they looted the furniture and plundered the storehouse; but when they rode away Marmilion was still standing, intact but for a few smashed window shutters and a broken pillar by the fireplace. William was in a state of collapse, for he had feared for his life every hour the Northerners were under his roof; and Lydia had been rather roughly handled by a drunken captain from New Jersey one evening. But otherwise there was no damage done. Camille handled the situation superbly, wrote the doctor. *"She rose to the occasion fully mindful of the responsibility she bore both toward her children and toward her house. She is indeed a plucky little woman, a woman of unsuspected fortitude."* Patronizing ass.

Marmilion survived the war; but when it ended, the "plucky little woman's" troubles were far from over. The South lay prostrate, exhausted, a wasteland across which roamed bands of desperate men—landless farmers, liberated slaves, and various shabby remnants of the Confederate army. On several occasions Marmilion was visited by such scavengers. Each time, Camille appeared at the front door and shouted at them to get away, if they valued their lives. Her words at first had no effect; but when she told them that the house had been used by Union forces as a yellow-fever hospital, they soon drifted off. Camille went back inside—where Caesar was waiting with a loaded shotgun, as a defense of last resort.

7

As you see, I wasted no time in getting at de Trot's journals. I often tell people that the secret to locating monkeys in the wild is to think like a monkey. It was the same with those journals; it was all a question of *sympathetic imagination.* For to construct a cohesive and plausible chain of events from partial sources like letters and journals requires that numerous small links must be forged—sometimes from the most slender of clues—and each one demands an act of intuition. It's a project fraught with risk, but it's the only means we have for constructing a credible representation of historical reality.

Take William. It was for him, now, that Oscar de Trot supplied laudanum, Camille having abandoned the habit soon after Randolph's disappearance. William, we may be sure, was by this stage little better than a parasite, providing nothing of moral or material value to Marmilion. He was tolerated, I would guess, only because he was Camille's child, and a Belvedere; precisely the same could be said of Lydia, though she did manage some needlework, and now, it appeared, might even be instrumental in propagating that curious little society inhabiting Marmilion. The one blessing, you see, that Lydia's apathy had bestowed was that it enabled her to suffer the war less traumatically than others of her class. In fact, apart from the incident with the officer from New Jersey, the war did not touch her at all. Nothing did. It was for this reason that she responded with compliance to the sexual attentions of Caesar.

This development I quickly gleaned from de Trot's journals. You may imagine the doctor's emotions as he records the disgraceful information. Imagine, then, his utter horror when Camille subsequently informed him that her daughter was *pregnant* by Caesar!

As for William, when he heard the news he became hysterical. It was probably the last straw; for I'm sure he was aware, at least to some extent, of just how wide was the gulf between himself and the sort of man his father had been. Perhaps, with the laudanum, he still maintained illusions about himself, rationalized his failure in some manner. But the news that his sister had been impregnated by Caesar—whom William still considered a *slave*—would have punctured those illusions and revealed to him just how low he had sunk: that he could permit his own sister, under his own roof . . . but I hypothesize. The fact is, William became hysterical and went after Caesar with a bullwhip. It was probably the first time since Randolph's day that he had attempted to exercise authority in Marmilion; and it was a fiasco. Dr. de Trot tells us that William—who was very overweight—came upon Caesar behind the house, and attempted to thrash him there. Without difficulty Caesar took the whip from him, and then lashed him with it three or four times before the fat man went howling like a child back into the house, to his mother, who was the only one who could have persuaded Caesar to desist from inflicting a punishment that had long been deserved. It seems that from then on, William's pathetic lassitude began to take an increasingly malicious turn, and the object of the new flame of hatred that smoldered in him was, of course, Caesar.

8

The time came for me to return to the Charenton Swamp and shoot more monkeys. I've told you my technique for locating the timorous creatures, and on this occasion I expended more than my usual amount of sympathetic imagination; but for some reason they eluded me completely. Perhaps I expended *too much* sympathetic imagination, if such a thing is possible. Anyway, I crossed the blind lake and then for hours I drifted through the swamp, but not once did that sudden stirring in the treetops, that soft "swoosh," alert me to their presence. I passed through one of the weird dead forests of Louisiana—the trees turned to gaunt skeletal frames, and the moss hanging from the branches in strips and sheets, all mirrored in the glassy still waters of the aimlessly wandering bayou. By late afternoon the failure to find any monkeys had somewhat dispirited me, and I consoled myself with a few artful shots of dead, moss-draped swamp maples rising from the quiet water. In the Louisiana climate, outdoor exposures have to be relatively heavy, as the high percentage of water vapor in the air acts to absorb and scatter light. It is the same light-absorbing quality that enables the moss effectively to kill off entire forests.

I returned to Marmilion at sunset. In the light of what I had learned about the Belvederes, I was intrigued, as you might imagine, to reenter the theater in which those strange and tragic lives had been enacted. Emerging from the oak alley, however, I was momentarily startled by the sharply defined profiles of the chimneys. How sinister they looked against the darkening sky, rising up quite blackly on either side of the house—which in some subtle way seemed unwelcoming this time, malevolent even—though doubtless my own ill-temper, the weather—which was cloudy and windy—and, in retrospect, the events of the night all conspired to influence my memory of those moments before I entered Marmilion again.

It was the worst night of my life. God alone knows what was up that chimney, but when darkness had fallen, and the wind came up, there was a wailing fit to wake the dead. Not until the first pale gleam of day came creeping through the shutters, which had wheeled and slammed on their hinges all night, did I manage to drift off for an hour or so; the rest of that night I sat up in my sleeping bag, with my back against the pillar, in a state of gradually intensifying unease, as what at first had seemed simply the eerie sounds that the wind always produces in an extensive chimney system slowly turned into a sustained shriek, as of some being in terrible, unending agony; and when it was at its fiercest, and the shutters were banging and from everywhere around me came howls and whimpers and groans—then it was that I seemed to hear, above and beyond it all, the scratching of that infernal nail. That was the worst moment of all. By then the rain had started—I could hear it drumming on the corrugated tin, and dripping through the ceiling—and from somewhere so close that I even began to think it came from inside my own skull, that hideous sound kept grinding and scraping away, on and on through the wildest hours of the night.

When the dawn came the wind died a little and, as I say, I dozed off for an hour or so. I awoke desperately tired, and felt as though I'd barely survived a storm at sea; and I gathered my things and left in haste. I turned to gaze at Marmilion before entering the oak alley; and against the sky of that gray morning, against the driven clouds, the old house heaved and rattled like a thing in pain, like a broken engine, like a ruined heart.

9

Lydia gave birth to a baby girl in the summer of 1871, on August 24 to be precise; three days later she died. The delivery was long and painful. Dr. de Trot had no chloroform with which to ease the mother's ordeal; nor, one suspects, was he as scrupulous as he could have been about the complete and antiseptic removal of the afterbirth. He was an old man now, and his medical training had been undertaken in the 1820s. In any event, Lydia became infected, and de Trot stood by helplessly as puerperal fever ran its implacable course. Toward the end she apparently began to scream for her dead lover, Simon Grampus Lamar, until the convulsions exhausted her; on several occasions she even saw him at the end of her bed, and rose from her pillow, and beckoned him to come close . . . until, as the doctor records, *"soul and body could remain together no longer, and she was transplanted to flourish in a more congenial soil."*

In the Old South the aftermath of a death was governed by ritual; both conduct at the death scene and reporting of the death itself reflected strict rules of decorum. Relatives gathered, last words were carefully recorded, and coffin and funeral were chosen to demonstrate the wealth and status of the deceased's family. That was in the Old South; this was Reconstruction. Lydia died at the center of the bizarre microcosm Marmilion had become, a small world of anguished and embittered individuals, and her funeral was humble indeed. Caesar built the coffin, and an Episcopalian minister rode out to conduct the ceremony. The procession consisted of William and Camille,

Caesar, and Oscar de Trot; the doctor's old nag drew the wagon; and poor Lydia went to her rest beneath a simple wooden cross behind the disused sugar mill in the field beyond the kitchen garden. Her death did nothing to allay the animosity that crackled almost palpably now between the two men in the house—rather, the reverse, for William held Caesar directly responsible for the loss of his sister.

And now the story of Marmilion begins to move toward its grim, inexorable climax. Lydia's child was christened Emily, and Camille cared for her while Caesar labored in the garden. Almost single-handedly that silent man had brought forth fruit and vegetables from the wilderness Marmilion had been at the end of the war. There were pigs now, and chickens, and a cow; and he planned soon to replant the good field beyond the sugar mill with cane. Perhaps in the closeness of his heart Caesar entertained a vision of Marmilion returned to its former glory—with himself as master. Perhaps he even shared that vision with Camille. The old doctor gives us a picture of the household in this, its last period before the tragedy, with Caesar the devoted father returning each evening from the fields to gaze with mute adoration on the coffee-colored baby Camille tended as if she were her own; while upstairs, soaking in the venom secreted by his own vile heart, William Belvedere bitterly schemed the black man's destruction. We sometimes forget that the Creole aristocracy was descended from thieves, prostitutes, and lunatics—Parisian scum forcibly recruited to populate the colony in the reign of Louis XIV. We are about to witness the spectacle of one such aristocrat reverting to type.

10

(May 17, 1872)

The night was no worse than usual. I rose at eight o'clock and read two chapters in Hebrew and some Greek in Thucydides. I said my prayers and ate cake and boiled milk for breakfast. The weather was warm and sunny. I read a sermon and then took a little nap. I ate cowpeas and grits for dinner. In the afternoon I sat upon the necessary chair with scant result. I sat then upon my verandah and read a little Latin. Shortly before five o'clock I saw Caesar the Negroe coming across the fields. He walked like a sleeping man. He carried in his arms a bloody sheet that draped a corpse, and upon his back the swaddled form of his infant daughter. He entered my house without a word, and laid his burden on my table. I was forced to drive off the flies that clustered about it. It was with an exclamation of the deepest sorrow that I lifted the sheet and recognized thereunder the lifeless clay of the mistress of Marmilion. She had been dead some days. The Negroe gazed silently at his mistress for many minutes and though I ardently questioned him as to the circumstances of the tragedy he made no answer. Soon after he left my house, and I was unable to prevent his going. He made off toward the river. God help us all.

Despite the extensive searches that were mounted in the days that followed, Caesar and Emily were never found. Perhaps they got clear away, and started a new life in the North. Perhaps they were swallowed by the Mississippi.

11

I have no more documentary evidence to offer. What follows is the construction of a sympathetic imagination.

It began, three days earlier, in the big room at the front of the house. Caesar was working there. He was sweeping out the ashes of last night's fire; or more probably—almost certainly—and this is a leap of the purest intuition—he was working with mortar and trowel, rebuilding the great pillar by the fireplace. William entered from the gallery with the shotgun. He stood in the doorway, and as Caesar went about his work he began to taunt him. I need not go into the precise character of his taunts; white men have been insulting black men in a manner essentially unchanged, I would guess, since—when?— Prince Henry's African expeditions? The wars between Rome and Carthage? The neolithic revolution of 1250 B.C.? William Belvedere stood taunting Caesar with a shotgun in the crook of his arm.

Caesar ignored him. William grew excited. Caesar at last rose to his feet, and turned toward his persecutor. It was at this moment that Camille, who had heard William's cries from upstairs, entered from the hallway. She saw her son pointing the shotgun at Caesar; and she saw Caesar standing by the broken pillar, a big man, physically strong, and unintimidated.

"Caesar!" she cried.

This is decisive. This is of crucial importance. For you see, Camille had not cried out to William to desist, to put aside the weapon; she had, instead, seen Caesar as the dangerous man, the dominant man; she had cried out to Caesar to back down, not William—and to that weak, contemptible creature this was the deepest cut of all: that even as he apparently held all the power in the situation, standing under his own roof with a shotgun pointing at a *slave*, his mother called upon the other to back down.

They both, Camille and Caesar, must have realized her mistake. Caesar stepped forward to take the gun from William; Camille darted between the two men; William, with his eyes closed, fired at his black nemesis—and his mother fell dead at his feet.

Oh, there is irony here, tragic irony; but what happened next? This is a mystery, for William, like his father, like Caesar and Emily, disappeared. They found bloodstains by the fireplace, and a discharged shotgun leaned against the wall. But they never found William.

Randolph Belvedere, in the opinion of Oscar de Trot, was killed in a duel. But what happened to William? I will tell you my conjecture. Consider: Caesar was a black nemesis, an agent of retributive justice; and he saw before him a vicious, despicable wretch, a wretch who stood for all the misery and oppression suffered by his race. That vile creature had just killed his, Caesar's, only friend and ally; and with her had died his dream of restoring Marmilion to its former glory—with himself as master! Oh, Caesar punished William, of this I have not the slightest doubt, for I've had a son of my own. And he made him suffer terribly, I have no doubt of that, either. And he made certain that no one would find him, that the bloodhounds and Klansmen that took up the chase would find no trace of William Belvedere. And William's spirit would know no rest, this was Caesar's intention; never would he lie in the soil with his sister, never would his spirit find peace. No, William's spirit would be trapped, it would be bricked up, to howl in endless torture in some prison of Caesar's construction—and there, close at hand, lay the tools to do it with!

This was my conjecture—that Caesar bricked him up in that pillar by the fireplace, buried him alive, upright and conscious!

Maybe he chained him up in the pillar first, so that William could watch every single brick being fitted into its allotted place. God knows, there were enough chains, and shackles, and manacles, all the grim hardware of slavery, in Marmilion to enchain an army. Or possibly he drugged him first, so that when William emerged from an opiated daze he found himself sealed up tight in his tomb. I am certain he did not kill him first. William died slowly. He deserved to.

And it took three days for the plaster to dry. I am not a superstitious woman, but this was my conjecture. I'd heard him in there, you see.

12

The last time I saw Marmilion I came in broad daylight; and as I emerged from the dappled shade of the oak alley, what a quiet glory the old house offered to my eye! The walls were of faded lemon-yellow, and where the plaster had crumbled the exposed brickwork was a beautiful soft red into which, in places, had seeped the grayness of moss. The window shutters and the railings of the galleries were a pale, weathered green; but loveliest of all was the woodwork of the entablature atop the pillars, which had been painted first sky-blue, then pink, then given a final wash of lavender such that it flushed in the sunshine with a delicate, roseate glow. No stone or metal, I now noticed, had been used in the construction of the house; entirely built of brick and timber, and lately touched by the encroaching vegetation, it rose from the soil, so it seemed, organically; and I was awed that despite the heat and damp of the semitropical climate, despite the ravages of neglect, and looting, and war, it yet retained in its decadence such dignity and strength.

I entered. The years had been less kind to Marmilion's interior. No line was straight; everything sagged and crumbled, and the walls were scabrous with mold, for the rainfall had loosened both plaster and woodwork. I realized, as I picked my way through the ruined rooms, that only the brickwork had resisted the damp. The two great chimneys rose through the structure like a pair of stanchions, or spines.

There were twenty-eight pillars girdling Marmilion, Corinthian pillars with fluted columns of plastered brick and elaborate, leafy capitals. The interior pillars echoed the design, even to the acanthus-leaf motif on the capitals. They were beautiful objects; it was a shame to destroy even one of them.

It was a day's work with crowbar and hammer to hack and claw that pillar by the fireplace to pieces. But finally I did it, and I found my skeleton. It was beautifully preserved, with not a bone out of place; it was delicate, fragile, white as china; but it was not the skeleton of William Belvedere. Perhaps, once again, I'd exercised too much sympathetic imagination. You see, what I'd found was the tiny, perfect skeleton—of a spider monkey.

MELISSA PRITCHARD

Spirit Seizures

Based on *The Watseka Wonder,* an authenticated narrative of spirit manifes-
tation by Dr. E. W. Stevens, 1908

July 1882: The Binning farm three miles outside Watseka, Illinois

Purplish soil receded in motionless, combed waves from around the frame house. The ripening corn surged, had an oily river sheen over it. . . .

Holding her newest baby, Lurancy walked again to the road's edge, shielding her eyes, her sunbonnet tied but swinging against her damp back. Deep clay ruts crisscrossed the road, old wheel ruts, but no dust was building in the distance, no buggy approached from town. Mr. Asa B. Roff, a wealthy lawyer, and his wife, Anne, former residents of Watseka, had come from Emporia, Kansas, to visit their eldest daughter. News that they would also be visiting the Binnings had bred a quarrel with Lurancy's husband. Thomas had gone down to the river to fish and lay traps, and to evade further argument. That morning Lurancy had attended both to the baby and their daughter, Lucia, with overscrupulous attention, had stiffly set down Thomas's plate of breakfast, avoided watching him eat.

Thomas Binning. In overalls and cracked shoes, that black shingle of hair laid flat across his broad plank of forehead, that infrequent laughter forever reminding her of a saw drawn backward. Now he was coldly separate; her hands served, his took. There could be little else with the Roffs about to visit them again.

Two summers before, the Roffs had returned to Watseka from their new home in Emporia. Lurancy Vennum Binning, as a new bride, had been proud to show her new home, that first child lifting up her belly. Thomas had nearly

144

undone that pride, sitting in their barren front parlor, his knees sprung like an iron scissors, his hands flopped like wrung hens. He sat, stonily ignorant, in that darkened room with Mr. and Mrs. Roff and their daughter Minerva, leaving with a hard curse when Minerva Roff tremblingly proposed that the soul of her sister Mary be brought forward through the able instrument of their dear Lurancy.

Lurancy had already confessed to Thomas about the summer she was thirteen, the night in July 1877 when the voices had started. Hissing voices, breaths clawing over her face . . . *Lurancy, Rancy* . . . a dissonant choir of the dead stopped only by her mother's presence. Then followed seizures, trances, ecstasies, her body rigid while her voice roamed among the contents of heaven. Dead but unreconciled souls borrowed her voice, pressed grievance through her, sour from desuetude.

With everyone, family, physicians, ministers, neighbors, banded under the sad resolve to commit Lurancy Vennum to the Springfield asylum, the Roffs, whose own daughter Mary had been subject to similar seizures before she died in 1865, brought a spiritualist down from Janesville. In the presence of Dr. E. W. Stevens, Mr. and Mrs. Vennum, and Asa Roff, the soul of Mary Roff, dead twelve years, asserted its benign, wonderful residence within Lurancy's flesh. From February to May 1878, Mary's spirit read like wildest news out of the living envelope of Lurancy Vennum. While living at the Vennum house, Mary asked repeatedly to be taken home. With the Vennums' consent, Mary was returned "home," to the Roffs. In late May this personality, soul, or spirit of Mary Roff vacated Lurancy Vennum and willingly returned to "heaven and angels." Lurancy was escorted back to the Vennum house, recovered in all her senses.

Thomas Binning had understood nothing. Lurancy's voice had boiled through him, leaving him empty of all but the most sedimentary opinion that spiritualists were deluded fools. He cared for Lurancy Vennum only as he knew her, present before his eyes. Ordinary.

Churned white butter, a sweaty caul over it, hung down the well. Two cakes, wrapped in cloth pale as cerements, lay like tiny mummies across the cookstove. Lurancy went out to cut oxeye sunflower, unrolling gaudy bunches of it from her apron, placing them in a stone crock on the kitchen windowsill and a pewter pitcher in the front parlor. The house otherwise stood plain, unsoftened by material prosperity.

(Lurancy's family had moved from Milford to Watseka the summer she turned seven, the same summer Martin Meara was hanged for tying his son across a hot stove because he had not, it was said by way of explanation, plowed his day's portion. Townspeople, mostly men and boys, had ridden out to see the hanging, brought back pieces of the hackberry tree. Hackberry branches, to be whittled by morbid hands, or thrillingly revolved down in dusty, worn pockets.)

Out on the porch steps Lurancy shook out her wavy black hair (*troughed as a washboard,* her mother would say), refastened it with the several tortoise combs her mother had given her on her wedding day. Lucia ran about on the planked porch, cradling the wood doll Thomas had fashioned for her. A wasp tagged near and Lurancy slapped at it with the hem of her gingham dress as she went past, joggling the baby, pacing restlessly from porch side to porch side, from road's edge to house and back, waiting for her friends. . . .

Pinned beneath a glary noon light, Lurancy held the baby in one arm, yanked the wooden wagon along with the other, Lucia bobbing in it, her sunbonnet hiding her diamond fleck of face, the picnic hamper rocking beside her. In the hamper Lurancy had put cold chicken, bread and butter slices, raspberries, and, in a conciliatory mood, one of the company cakes. The rift with Thomas had broken her peace, and she had no temperament to sustain any quarrel.

Scores of crows were raiding the white, blowing wheat. In turn, they would eat the grasshoppers. To everything a season and time. A solitary crow hopped boldly near them; Lucia cried out, afraid of the obsidian bird and its rapacious sideways eye.

The meadow was full-lit, porous and greenly translucent as a luna moth's wing. Clover was rampant, its puffy thick heads slewed like hail. The Iroquois River glittered behind a long shoulder of trees, a black collar tatted out of the trunks and shade running along its bottom. Dragonflies clicked, netted iridescence passing through a hot canvas of air. Lurancy stopped to pick some tickseed, the tattered gold ruffs and red eye. When Lucia complained, Lurancy set down the flowers, the baby, and lifted her from the wagon, helping her ruck up her skirts and squat. Sweet-smelling urine pooled into the seeding grasses.

Lurancy pulled the wagon toward a familiar break in the trees, the elms and maples, to the narrow path down which Thomas would have gone to fish.

His back was to them, standing by the dun, high-banked river, water both she and her brothers had been baptized in.

Thomas.

From his face, turned first on Lucia, then to herself, Lurancy perceived, and gratefully, that he had no stock in further argument.

They sat peaceably, ate what she had brought. She opened her dress to feed the baby. Thomas had caught a string of fish, shot two mallards, drakes.

The Roffs have not come.

Maybe they lost their way? He was teasing, yet so honestly hopeful that she laughed.

You should use the mallard or the fish if they'll be staying over for supper, Rancy.

Yes.

She knotted back her skirts, rinsed the pewter dishes in the river. Thomas stood nearby, holding the baby; when she lost a dish to the current, he retrieved it for her.

Thomas had begun, lately, to talk of homesteading. Selling the farm. Of Kansas. Moving to some treeless spot, worlds from anybody, living most likely in a sod hut. Where her life would ebb with the bearing of child upon child. With helping Thomas to tame a bit of tough prairie. Well, she had chosen him. Now he picked the course and rigor of their lives. The Roffs would come, stir up her old self, jog her longing for those wide, fertile talks about spirit worlds, angels, and spirit guides, all things which Thomas opposed, even cursed. *(What you cannot see, do you think you are to know, imagine that you know?)*

Lucia clasped the lank bouquet as the wagon rose and dipped through the meadow. The baby, shaded by the hamper, slept. Over where the farm lay, the sky was a massive block of gray-purple. By the river it would still be sunny and hot. Wind tossed like a wall of water over them. Lurancy's muslin apron buffeted fitfully. Lucia began to cry, covering her ears at the first crack of thunder. A blue skeletal jig of lightning flared. Lurancy dragged at the wagon as fast as she dared without throwing the baby. She could see the wash, make out her own dress and one of Lucia's a-skip on the line as if they were partnered at a town dance. Rain like a scatter of buckshot hit at her face. Pull up your bonnet, Lucia, she yelled over the wind, then pulled up her own.

The air was thick with a greenish, moldery light. Another heaving split of thunder, sounding like a house collapsed, with a crackle of husk beneath it. Trees blew, heeled in one direction, suddenly weak-seeming.

Lurancy strained to make out the shape of an unfamiliar object outside their house. The buggy, the Roffs' buggy, empty, stood outside their porch, the horses' heads dejected, rain stippling their reddish hides. It seemed the whole awash world of the dead had come with these people who would have cause to greet her, perhaps even to love her, then set about drawing their dead child's spirit like spittled thread through the blunt eye of able Lurancy Binning.

Lurancy willed her spirit to loft, untenant, so Mary Roff might enter, impetuously, this world.

> for all flesh is like
> grass
> and all its glory like the flower of
> grass
> but the grass withers, the flower falls
> but the word of the Lord will endure
> for ever

Lurancy picked up the baby, grabbed Lucia by the hand, and even with skirts nearly anchored by cold rain and hemmed by river clay, the near-empty vessel of Lurancy Binning pitched lightly up the wide solid steps her husband had built for her, to seek some short respite with those he refused to understand.

1889: Dr. Richard Hodgson, of the Society for Psychical Research, listens to
Minerva Alter, forty-six years old
and sister to Mary Roff

. . . Of us five Roff children, Mary stood forth, from the very beginning, as peculiar. Subject to fits, black pressing moods. Which grew increasingly worse, don't you see, to the point where Mother and Father tried a great many things to cure her. As a girl I can recall the house being overtaken by doctors, ministers, faith healers of all kinds. One remedy working,, then another, then nothing.

Mary, when she was well, had a great attachment to music. Solemn dreary tunes out of our Methodist hymnal pleased her most. We tried to tease her out of her preference for such dirges. "What sad, sobering music for a pretty child, Mary," our mother would say, but Mary would turn with her dark eyes from the piano, fix us with those impenetrable eyes. "But it is the exact pace and lyric which pleases me, Mother."

Would you like me to play one of Mary's hymns for you, Doctor? This is the exact piano she used to sit down to. Father gave it to Dr. Alter and myself when they moved out to Emporia. At the time Mary's spirit took up lodging in Miss Vennum, it was nearly the first object she recognized with affection when she stepped back into our family home. But it had been twelve years since her death, don't you see, so her fingers would not work over the keys with any of the grace they had once possessed, and for that she sweetly and, faintly troubled, apologized. . . .

Here, if I remember, is a favorite of Mary's before she died, aged eighteen years:

> *How blest is our brother bereft*
> *Of all that could burthen his mind!*
> *How easy the soul, that hath left*
> *The wearisome body behind!*

This languishing head is at rest,
Its thinking and aching are o'er,
This quiet immovable breast
Is heaved by affliction no more. . . .

For over a year Mary was sent off to Peoria, to the water cures. Again, it seemed to help, until the melancholia and fits returned. Most of our backwoods physicians still treated any overstimulation of the body by leeching. Mary herself took to placing leeches against her temples, to take away the "lump of pain," as she called it. There the leeches would lie, growing from cool to warm, flat to swollen, till they dropped off, all sated. And Mary would collect them into jars, treat them almost as her playthings (*rusty-black, wormy, eyeless creatures, like something the Devil might scheme to create*). Dr. Alter never held to the idea of cupping or leeching, thought it old-fashioned and dangerous to debilitate a weak person with fasting or draining of vital blood.

. . . Why yes, Dr. Hodgson, I do remember that one particular afternoon you refer to. Awful. Awful, discovering my sister in the backyard, just under some bushes. All bloody, nearly dead. She'd taken a kitchen knife and gone into the yard, deliberately cut into her arm. You must have heard then, Doctor, that part of the story where Mary's spirit, while in the bodily vehicle of Miss Vennum, went to show Dr. Stevens the knife scar along her arm, then remembered, saying, oh, this is not the one, that other arm is in the ground, then described to him her burial, named the mourners standing about her grave. . . .

Oh, stories did circulate and abound, details of Mary's spirit-return, her uncanny recall of old neighbors, past occasions, things no one but Mary Roff herself could have recalled.

Before passing back into the Borderland that May of 1878, Mary wanted Lurancy to be given certain small tokens, a few cards, some marbles, 25¢, Mary, you see, being grateful to Lurancy. This I did.

The first time I met my sister after her death? That would be February 1878: Mother and I were walking down Sixth Street to pay a visit to the Vennums, having heard about their oldest girl's strange seizures so much like

Mary's had been, her repeated claim to be Mary Roff. Before Mother, I noticed the girl leaning out from the top story of their small, rather shabby house, waving and calling "Nervie, Nervie!" Always Mary's nickname for me. The voice was exactly Mary's.

At our parents' house over those next three months, Mary and I spent many hours recalling childhood; or rather, Mary remembered while I affirmed. Pranks, for instance the time she and one of our younger cousins tried to rub a made-up ointment into the sore eyes of one of our hens. She remembered that.

Mary's spirit, at the beginning, refused food. At table she bowed her head, murmuring that she supped in heaven; but as the body of Miss Vennum regained its vigor, so did Mary begin to eat. That spring I accompanied Mother and Mary into many of our finest homes in Watseka. I was accustomed soon enough to being overlooked while all flocked to see the proof of Mary in young Lurancy Vennum . . . and rarely were disappointed.

In the years before her death, Mary was famous in Watseka and beyond for her fits and clairvoyances. Blindfolded, she read newspapers aloud, read sealed letters, then arranged boxes of letters alphabetically, things of that sort. Newspapermen, well-to-do townspeople, even Mayor Secrets and his wife, all paid ceaseless visits to our home, until our very lives revolved around Mary's peculiar orb, and by her reflection we were cast into that same unnatural light.

After she died, July the 5th, 1865, our lives took up some normalcy. I met Dr. Alter, we were married, I continued teaching Sunday school. He practiced the medicine he'd learned on the East Coast and in Boston. He was popular here in Watseka, with his new ideas and theories . . . yet these couldn't save our own children. When black diphtheria came through Milford, then Watseka, we watched our innocent children, six of our seven, sicken and succumb. Three taken in the span of one night. Dr. Alter made a slit in Ada's windpipe, trying to bring air to her lungs; without result he did the same for little Charles. Which of us was the more bereft by the loss in one week, of six of our children, myself still nursing Asa, who died in my arms, or my husband, being unable to save one of them? It was quick, beyond control; he was as helpless as I was.

If you would be so kind as to follow me, Dr. Hodgson, to the table over by the window, you can see what gives me peace at times. . . . This is hair from each one of our children. Ada's. Frederick's. Here is Maude's. Mary's. Charlie. Even little Asa, who had such a crop of it and so black. As they died in turn, Mother went into their rooms for me, cutting their hair. I plait and twist, like this, shaping the hair into patterns, bouquets. . . . When I finished that first time, pain welled up and so maddeningly that I was compelled to tear the bouquet apart, almost frantically, and begin again.

More often than Dr. Alter, I visit the grave beds at Oak Hill *(those pickets, a pale set of tongues swelling up from the earth).*

Yes. Well yes, he did. A seventh child, Robert, did survive. With his wife and five children he lives just outside Milford, a carpenter. Robert was left to raise, but I hadn't much heart for it. . . . Looking at him, I saw the others. Wondered why him spared, and not even my favorite. Many families lost children that winter; I suppose we were not singled out except in the extremity of our loss.

I have heard, as others have written it to me, that Lurancy Binning lives out in Kansas, Rawlins County, mother to six or seven. Those episodes in her early life nearly forgotten, occupied as she is with the obligations of rearing children, raising up living children . . .

As a physician, of course, my husband has slipped back into the lively stream of need and fulfillment of need. But since Mary, since my own children were taken, I savor so little. The spiritual cannot console me, perhaps from being overlong exposed to it. I am most content up at Oak Hill. Or in turning their hair to glinting shapes, vines.

I am removed from nature's lures, numb to its cruel trees, cruel birds, cruel river water, to its food, or to any fine thing. A bead-strand of monotony before my eyes. I have, as you see for yourself, been carted off by grief.

I would gain no benefit by lying to you or to anyone about my sister Mary. I care little what others beyond this place say of the case of Mary Roff or the "Watseka Wonder," as Miss Vennum is at times called. Mary's soul returned to us that one time, then briefly, twice more, when Mother and Father and I visited the Binning farm. Lurancy's husband, unaccustomed to our spiritualist beliefs, was neither welcoming nor hospitable; yet she seemed exceedingly joyful to see us. I remember that. How she pressed her children upon me, quite thoughtlessly (*agonizing, the sight of tiny, still-animate faces*).

I will walk with you over to our family home. You will want to talk with my brother and his family. No, I prefer not. I will go on to Oak Hill.

(*Where all one day will assemble in plain, purblind rows, under sober in eloquent stone, our lives reduced to that faint quaver of rumour . . . where some hundred years from now, we may persist, a source of curiosity and likely, some little disbelief . . .*)

Well now.

It has been nearly a lifting of some burden, to speak to you of these things.

MARY ROFF

> *I'm gonna take a trip on that old gospel ship*
> *I'm goin' far beyond the sky*
> *I'm gonna shout and sing, til the bell done ring*
> *When I bid this world good-bye*

What is a House but a hundred boards upended and smacked together, the ten hammers which plowed the humid air, the cracking of hammers, the thundering which resides in the air around the loosening nails, the dark fingerspaces between . . . ? And what is a town but fifty such buildings, lined up and stopping short . . . ending with my House, which goes only so far across the thickened ground to overlook the flat river . . . ? What is a town such as this but a hastily reassembled forest, trees felled, taken into measured pieces and put back together in such a way that they might move about in them secretly, sleep, fight, take supper, increase their poor numbers, instead of standing outside, looking up a solid, impenetrable trunk, awed and displaced?

* * *

And what is Bodily Flesh but a house so lightly mortised as to permit an occasional strike of soul to flash through like summer lightning? Mary Roff. I was that white, half-empty pitcher, born unwhole, unfinished, as a baby comes without its hearing or its proper sight, missing some symmetry of limb, so I did enter the clayey sphere of weights and dimensions, unfinished. No one saw that I was a soul not fixedly mortised. That older, swifter souls slid in and out of me, bats in an abandoned and shifting outbuilding. I was an incompleteness pouring like oil or watered wine between two vessels, a shiny arc rocking between one named assembly of flesh and another, and near the end, poured from Mary into Lurancy, and back from Lurancy poured yet again into Mary . . . a child's game, going in and out the windows. . . .

> If you are ashamed of me, you ought not to be
> And you'd better have a care,
> If too much fault you find, you'll sure be left behind
> When I'm sailing through the air

And what was Lurancy Vennum Binning but that vulnerable, slight growth latched on to by heavy, malevolent souls, then turned by me into a woman yoked to toil, to the magnetism of scraping her nourishment from dirt? I was glad for her to have husband-love and child-love, what I never knew, being encumbered by an oppression of spirits all crowding into the closet of one body as if it were some great vibrating hall.

And what, then, of Nervie, my sister Nervie, but a high-spirited woman, unable to tolerate either flesh or spirit, a woman possessed of no convictions but those passive ones of grief and loss—she grew attached to loss, dependent on sorrow, came to love them dearer than anything.

What is Soul or Spirit but Mystery, a Glory Ship, that Rumor founded by tales such as mine—Mad Mary Roff—tales bringing not confirmation but bare continuance of hope . . . instructing humanity in its keenest question: But if a man die, shall he live again?

154

I have good news to bring
And that is why I sing,
All my joys with you I'll share
I'm gonna take a trip on that old Gospel Ship
And go sailing through the air

PENELOPE LIVELY

Revenant as Typewriter

Muriel Rackham, reaching the penultimate page of her talk, spoke with one eye upon the public-library clock. The paper ("Ghosts: An Analysis of Their Fictional and Historic Function") lasted precisely fifty-one minutes, as she well knew, but the stamina of the Ilmington Literary and Philosophical Society was problematic; an elderly man in the back row had been asleep since page seven, and there was a certain amount of shuffle and fidget in the middle reaches of the thirty-odd seats occupied by the society's membership. Muriel skipped two paragraphs and moved into the concluding phase; it had perhaps been rash (not to say wasteful) to use on this occasion a paper that had had a considerable success at the English Studies Conference and with her colleagues at the College Senior Seminar, but she had nothing much else written up at the moment and had felt disinclined to produce a piece especially for the occasion. She paused (nothing like silence to induce attention) and went on: "So, leaving aside for the moment its literary role as vehicle for authorial comment in characters as diverse as Hamlet's father and Peter Quint, let us in conclusion try to summarize the historic function of the ghost—define as far as we can its social purpose, try to see why people needed ghosts and what they used them for. We've already paid tribute to that great source book for the student of the folkloric ghost—Dr. Katharine Briggs' *Dictionary of British Folk-Tales*—of which I think it was Bernard Levin who remarked in a review that a glance down its list of Tale-Types and Motifs disposes once and for all of the notion that the British are a phlegmatic and unfanciful people." (She paused at this point for the ripple of appreciative amusement that should run through the audience, but the Ilmington Lit. and Phil. sat unmoved; there were two sleepers now in the back row.) ". . . We've looked already at the repetitious nature of Motifs—Ghost follows its own corpse, reading the funeral service silently; Ghost laid when treasure is unearthed; Revenant as hare; Revenant in human form; Wraith appears to person in bedroom; Ghost haunts scene of former crime; Ghost exercises power through possessions of its lifetime—and so on and so forth. The subject matter of ghostly folklore, in fact, perfectly supports the thesis of Keith Thomas in his book *Religion and the Decline of Magic* that the historic ghost is no random or frivolous character but fulfills a particular social need—in a society where the arm of the law is short it serves to draw attention to the unpunished crime, to seek the rectification of wrongs, to act as a reminder of the past, to . . ."

She read on, the text familiar enough for the thoughts to wander: Bill Freeman, the chairman, had introduced her appallingly, neglecting to mention her publications and reducing her Senior Lectureship at Ilmington College of Education to a Lectureship—she felt again a flush of irritation, and wondered if it had been deliberate or merely obtuse. They were an undistinguished lot, the audience; surely that woman at the end of the third row was an assistant in W. H. Smith's? Muriel observed them with distaste, as she turned over to the last page; schoolteachers and librarians, for the most part, one was talking right above their heads, in all probability. A somewhat wasted evening—which could have usefully been spent doing things about the house, or going through students' essays, or looking at that article Paul had given her, in order to have some well-thought-out comments for the morning.

She concluded, and sat, with a wintry smile towards Bill Freeman, at her side, who, as one might have expected, rose to thank her with a sequence of remarks as inept as his introduction: ". . . our appreciation to Dr. Rackham for her fascinating talk and throw the meeting open to discussion."

Discussion could not have been said to flow. There was a man who had been to a production of *Macbeth* in which you actually saw Banquo and did the speaker think that was right or was it better if you just kind of guessed he was there . . . and a woman who thought *The Turn of the Screw* wasn't awfully good when they made it into an opera, and another who had been interested in the bit about people in historical times believing in ghosts and had the speaker ever visited Hampton Court because if you go there the guide tells you that . . .

Muriel dealt politely but briefly with the questioners. She glanced again at the clock, and then at Bill Freeman, who would do well to wind things up. There was a pause. Bill Freeman scanned the audience and said, "Well, if no one has anything more to ask Dr. Rackham I think perhaps . . ."

The small dark woman at the end of the front row leaned forward, looking at Muriel. "I thought what you said was quite interesting and I'd like to tell you about this thing that happened to a friend of mine. She was staying in this house, you see, where apparently . . ."

It went on for several minutes. It was very tedious, a long rigmarole about inexplicable creakings in the night, objects appearing and disappearing, ghostly footsteps and sounds and so on and so forth, all classifiable according to Tale-Type and Motif if one felt so inclined and hadn't in fact lost interest in the whole subject some time ago, now that one was doing this work on the metaphysical poets with Paul. . . . Muriel sat back and sighed. She eyed the woman with distaste; the face was vaguely familiar, someone local, presumably. An absurd little person with black, straight, short hair (dyed, by the look of it) fringing her face, those now unfashionable spectacles upswept at the corners and tinted a disagreeable mauve, long earrings of some cheap shiny stone. Earrings, Muriel noted, more suitable for a younger woman; this creature was her own age, at least. Her skirt was too short, also, and her shirt patterned with what looked like lotus flowers in a discordant pink.

". . . and my friend felt that it had come back to see about something, the ghost, something that had annoyed it. I just wondered what the speaker had to say about that, if she'd ever had any experiences of that kind." The woman stared at Muriel, almost aggressively.

Muriel gathered herself. "Well," she said briskly, "of course we've really been concerned this evening with the fictional and historical persona of the ghost, haven't we? As far as I'm concerned I would subscribe to what has been called the intellectual impossibility of ghosts—and of course experiences such as your friend's, if one stops to think about it, are open to all kinds of explanation, aren't they?"—she flashed a quick, placating smile—"And now, I feel perhaps that . . ."—she half turned toward the chairman—"if there are no more questions . . ."

Going home (after coffee and sandwiches in someone's house; the black-haired person, mercifully, had not been there) she shook off the dispiriting atmosphere of the evening with relief: the dingy room, the unresponsive audience. The paper had been far too academic for them, of course. She felt glad that Paul had not come. He had offered to, but she had insisted that he shouldn't. Turning the Mini out of the High Street and past the corner of his road, she allowed herself a glance at the lighted window of his house. The curtains were drawn; Sheila would be watching television, of course, Paul reading (the new Joyce book, probably, or maybe this week's *TLS*). Poor Paul. Poor, dear Paul. It was tragic, such a marriage. That dull, insensitive woman.

"Your friendship is of the greatest value to me, Muriel," he had said, one week ago exactly. He had said it looking out of the window, rather than at her—and she had understood at once. Understood the depth of his feeling, the necessity for understatement, for the avoidance of emotional display. Their position was of extreme delicacy—Paul's position. Head of Department, Vice-Principal of the College. She had nodded and murmured something, and they had gone on to discuss a student, some problems about the syllabus. . . .

At night, she had lain awake, thinking with complacency of their relationship, of its restraint and depth, in such contrast to the stridency of the times. Muriel considered herself—knew herself to be—a tolerant woman, but occasionally she observed her students with disgust; their behavior was coarse and vulgar, not to put too fine a point upon it. They brandished what should be kept private.

Occasionally, lying there, she was visited by other feelings, which she recognized and suppressed; a mature, balanced person is able to exercise self-control. The satisfaction of love takes more than one form.

She put the car in the garage and let herself into the house, experiencing the usual pleasure. It was delightful; white walls, bare boards sanded and polished, her choice and tasteful possessions—rugs, pictures, the few antique pieces, the comfortable sofa and armchairs, the William Morris curtains. It was so unlike, now, the dirty, cluttered, scruffy place she had bought five months ago as to be almost unrecognizable. Only its early-Victorian exterior remembered—and that too was now bright and trim under new paint, with a front door carefully reconstructed in keeping, to replace the appalling twenties porch some previous occupant had built on. The clearing-out process had been grueling—Muriel blenched even now at the thought of it: cupboards stacked with junk and rubbish that nobody had bothered to remove (there had been an executors' sale, the elderly owner having died some months before), the whole place filthy and in a state of horrid disrepair. She had done the bulk of the work herself, with the help of a local decorator and carpenter for the jobs she felt were beyond her. But alone she had emptied all those cavernous cupboards, carting the stuff down to a skip hired from a local firm. It had been a disagreeable job—not just because of the dirt and physical effort, but because of the nature of the junk, which hinted at an alien and unpleasing way of life. She felt that she wanted to scour the house of its past, make it truly hers, as she heaved bundle after bundle of musty rubbish down the stairs. There had been boxes of old clothes—too old and sour to interest either the salerooms or Oxfam—brash vulgar female clothes, shrill of color and pattern, in materials like sateen, chenille and rayon, the feel of which made Muriel shudder. They slithered from her hands, smelling of mold and mouse droppings, their touch so repellent that she took to wearing rubber gloves. And then there were shelves of old magazines and books—not the engrossing treasure-trove that such a hoard ought to be (secondhand bookshops, after all, were an addiction of hers) but dreary and dispiriting in what they suggested of whoever had owned them: pulp romantic fiction, stacks of the cheaper, shriller women's magazines (all sex and crime, not even that limited but wholesome stuff about cooking, children and health), some tattered booklets with pictures that made Muriel flush—she shoveled the beastly things into a supermarket carton and dumped the lot into the skip. This house had seen little or no literature that could even be called decent during its recent past, that was clear enough; with pleasure she had arranged her own books on the newly painted shelves at either side of the fireplace. They seemed to clinch her conquest of the place.

There had been other things, too. A dressmaker's dummy that she had found prone at the back of a cupboard (its murky shape had given her a hideous shock); she had scrubbed and kept it, occasionally she made herself a dress or skirt and it might conceivably be useful, though its torso was dumpier than her own. A tangle of hairnets and curlers in a drawer of the kitchen dresser, horribly scented of violets. Bits and pieces of broken and garish jewelry—all fake—that kept appearing from under floorboards or down crevices. Even now she came across things; it was as though the house would never have done with spewing out its tawdry memories. And of course the redecorating had been a major job—stripping away those fearful wallpapers that plastered every room, every conceivable misrepresentation of nature, loud and unnatural roses, poppies and less identifiable flowers that crawled and clustered up and down the walls. Sometimes two or three different ones had fought for survival in the same room; grimly, Muriel, aided by the decorator, tore and soaked and peeled. At last, every wall was crisply white, a background to her prints and lithographs, her Georgian mirror, the Khelim rug.

Now she felt at last that she had taken possession. There were one or two small things still that jarred—a cupboard in her bedroom from which, scrub as she might, she could not eradicate the sickly smell of some cheap perfume, a hideous Art Nouveau window (she gathered such things were once again in fashion—*chacun à son goût*) in the hall which she would eventually get around to replacing. Otherwise, all was hers; her quiet but distinctive taste in harmony with the house's original architectural grace.

It was just past nine; time for a look at that article before bed. Muriel went to her desk (which, by day, had a view of the small garden prettily framed in William Morris's *Honeysuckle*) and sat reading and taking notes for an hour or so. She remembered that Paul would be away all day tomorrow, at a meeting in London, and she would not be able to see him, so when she had finished reading she pulled her typewriter in front of her and made a résumé of her reflections on the article, to leave in his pigeonhole. She read them through, satisfied with what she felt to be some neatly put points. Then she got up, locked the back and front doors, checked the windows, and went to bed.

In the night, she woke; the room felt appallingly stuffy—she could even, from her bed, smell that disagreeable cupboard—and she assumed that she must have forgotten to open the window. Getting up to do so, she found the sash raised a couple of inches as usual. She returned to bed, and was visited by unwelcome yearnings which she drove out by a stern concentration on her second-year Shakespeare option.

She had left her page of notes on the article in the typewriter, and almost forgot it in the morning, remembering at the last moment as she was about to leave the house, and going back to twitch it hastily out and put it in her handbag. The day was busy with classes and a lecture, so that it was not until the afternoon that she had time to write a short note for Paul ("I entirely agree with you about the weaknesses in his argument; however, there are one or two points we might discuss, some thoughts on which I enclose. I do hope London was not too exhausting—MCR"), and glance again at the page of typescript.

It was not as satisfactory as Muriel remembered; in fact it was not satisfactory at all. She must have been a great deal more tired than she had realized last night—only in a stupor (and not even, one would have hoped, then) could she have written such muddled sentences, such hideous syntax, such illiteracies of style and spelling. "What I think is that he developed what he said about the character of Tess all wrong so what you ended up feeling was that . . ." she read in horror. ". . . if Hardy's descriptive passages are not always relevant then personally what I don't see is why . . ." And what was this note at the bottom—apparently added in haste? "What about meeting for a natter tomorrow—I was thinking about you last night—ssh! you aren't supposed to know that!" I must have been half asleep, she thought, how could I write such things?

Hot with discomfort (and relief—heavens! she might not have looked again at the thing), she crumpled the paper and threw it into the wastepaper basket. She wrote a second note to Paul saying that she had read the article but unfortunately had not the time now to say more, and hoped to discuss it with him at some point; she then canceled her late-afternoon class and went home early. I have been overdoing things, she thought—my work, the house—I need rest, a quiet evening.

She settled down to read, but could not concentrate; for almost the first time, she found herself wishing for the anodyne distraction of television. She polished and dusted the sitting room (finding, in the process, a disgusting matted hank of hairnets and ribbon that had got, quite inexplicably, into her Worcester teapot) and cleaned the windows. Then she did some washing, which led to an inspection of her wardrobe; it seemed sparse. A new dress, perhaps, would lift her spirits. On Saturday, she would buy one, and in the meantime, there was that nice length of tweed her sister had given her and which had lain untouched for months. Perhaps with the aid of the dressmaker's dummy it could be made into a useful skirt. She fetched the dummy and spent an hour or two with scissors and pins—a soothing activity, though the results were not quite as satisfactory as she could have wished. Eventually she left the roughly fashioned skirt pinned to the dummy and put it away in the spare-room cupboard before going to bed.

A few days later, to her pleasure, Paul accepted an invitation to call in at the house on his way home to pick up a book and have a drink. He had hesitated before accepting, and she understood his difficulties at once; such meetings were rare for them, and the reasons clear enough to her: the pressures of his busy life, Sheila. . . . "Well, yes, how kind, Muriel," he had said. "Yes, fine, then. I'll give Sheila a ring and tell her I'll be a little late."

Poor Paul; the strains of such a marriage did not bear contemplation. Of course, they always appeared harmonious enough in public, a further tribute to his wonderful patience and restraint. Nor did he ever hint or complain; one had be be perceptive to realize the tensions that must rise—a man of his intellectual stature fettered to someone without, so far as Muriel understood, so much as an A-level. His tolerance was amazing; Muriel had even heard him, once, join with well-simulated enthusiasm in a discussion of some trashy television series prompted by Sheila at a Staff Club party.

She was delayed at the College and only managed to arrive back at the house a few minutes before he arrived. Pouring the sherry, she heard him say, "What's this, then, Muriel—making a study of popular culture?" and turned round to see him smiling and holding up one of those scabrous women's magazines that—she thought—she had committed to the skip. Disconcerted, she found herself flushing, embarking on a defensive explanation of the rubbish that had been in the house. . . . (But she had cleared all that stuff out, every bit, how could that thing have been, apparently, lying on the little Victorian sewing table, from which Paul had taken it?)

The incident unnerved her, spoiled what should have been an idyllic hour.

Muriel woke the next day—Saturday—discontented and twitchy. She had slept badly, disturbed by the muffled sound of a woman's shrill laugh, coming presumably from the next house in the terrace; she had not realized before that noise could penetrate the walls.

Remembering her resolution of a few days before, she went shopping for a new dress. The facilities of Ilmington were hardly metropolitan, but adequate for a woman of her restrained tastes; she found, after some searching, a pleasant enough garment innocent of any of the nastier excesses of modern fashion, in a wholesome color and fabric, and took it home in a rather calmer frame of mind.

In the evening, there was the Principal's sherry party (Paul would be there; with any luck there would be the opportunity for a few quiet words). She went to take the dress from the wardrobe and indeed was about to put it on before the feel of it in her hands brought her up short; surely there was something wrong? She took it to the window, staring—this was never the dress she had chosen so carefully this morning? The remembered eau-de-nil was now, looked at again, in the light from the street, a harsh and unflattering apple-green; the coarse linen, so pleasant to the touch, a slimy artificial stuff. She had made the most disastrous mistake; tears of frustration and annoyance pricked her eyes. She threw the thing back in the cupboard and put on her old Jaeger print.

Sunday was a day that, normally, she enjoyed. This one got off to a bad start with the discovery of the *Sunday Mirror* sticking through the front door instead of the *Sunday Times*; after breakfast she rang the shop, knowing that they would be open till eleven, only to be told by a bewildered voice that surely that was what she had asked for, change it, you said on the phone, Thursday it was, for the *Sunday Mirror,* spicier, you said, good for a laugh. "There's been some mistake," said Muriel curtly. "I don't know what you can be thinking of." She slammed down the receiver and set about a massive cleaning of the house; it seemed the proper therapeutic thing to do.

After lunch she sat down at her desk to do some work; her article for *English Today* was coming along nicely. Soon it would be time to show a first draft to Paul. She took the lid off the typewriter and prepared to reread the page she had left in on Friday.

Two minutes later, her heart thumping, she was ripping out the paper, crumpling it into a ball. . . . I never wrote such stuff, she thought, it's impossible, words like that, expressions like—I don't even *know* such expressions.

She sat in horror, staring into the basilisk eye of a thrush on her garden wall. There is something wrong, she thought, I am not myself, am I going mad?

She took a sleeping pill, but even so woke in the depths of the night (again, those muffled peals of laughter), too hot, the room heavy around her so that she had to get up and open the window further; the house creaked. There must be a fault in the heating system, she thought, I'll have to get the man round. She lay in discomfort, her head aching.

In the days that followed it seemed to her that she suffered from continuous headaches. Headaches, and a kind of lightheadedness that made her feel sometimes that she had only a tenuous grip on reality; in the house, after work, she heard noises, saw things. There was that laughter again, which must be from next door, but when she enquired delicately of the milkman as to who her neighbors were (one didn't want actually to get involved with them) she learned that an elderly man lived there, alone, a retired doctor. And there were things that seemed hallucinatory, there was no other explanation; going to the cupboard where she had put the dummy, to have another go at that skirt, she had found the thing swathed not in her nice herringbone tweed but a revolting purple chenille. She slammed the cupboard closed (again, the lurking shape of the dummy had startled her, although she had expected to see it), and sat down on the bed, her chest pounding. I am not well, she thought, I am doing things and then forgetting that I have done them, there is something seriously wrong.

And then there was the wallpaper. She had come into the sitting room, one bright sunny morning—her spruce, white sitting room—and, glancing at her Dufy prints, had seen suddenly the shadowy presence of the old, hideous wallpaper behind them, those entwined violets and roses that she and the decorator had so laboriously scraped away. Two walls, she now saw, were scarred all over, behind the new emulsion paint, with the shadowy presence of the old paper; how can we have missed them, she thought angrily—that decorator, I should have kept a sharper eye on him—but surely, I *remember*, we did this room together, every bit was stripped, surely?

Her head spun.

She went to the doctor, unwillingly, disliking her list of neurotic symp-toms, envying the bronchitic coughs and bandaged legs in the waiting room. Stiffly, she submitted to the questions, wanting to say: I am not this kind of person at all, I am balanced, well adjusted, known for my good sense. With distaste, she listened to the diagnosis: yes, she wanted to say, impatiently, I have heard of menopausal problems but I am not the kind of woman to whom they happen, I keep things under better control than that, overwork is much more likely. She took his prescription and went away, feeling humiliated.

It was the examination season. She was faced, every evening, on returning home, with a stack of scripts and would sit up late marking, grateful for the distraction, though she was even more tired and prone to headaches. The tiredness was leading to confusion, also, she realized. On one occasion, giving a class, she had been aware of covert glances and giggles among her students, apparently prompted by her own appearance; later, in the staff cloakroom, she had looked in a mirror and been appalled to discover herself wearing a frightful low-cut pink blouse with some kind of flower pattern. It was vaguely familiar— I've seen it before, she thought, and realized it must be a relic of the rubbish in the house, left in the back of her cupboard and put on accidentally this morning, in her bleary awakening from a disturbed night. Condemned to wear it for the rest of the day, she felt taken over by its garishness, as though compelled to behave in character; she found herself joining a group of people at lunchtime with whom she would not normally have associated, the brash set among her colleagues, sharing jokes and a conversation that she found distasteful. In Paul's office, later, going over some application forms, she laid her hand on his sleeve, and felt him withdraw his arm; later, the memory of this made her shrivel. It was as though she had betrayed the delicacy of their relationship; never before had they made physical contact.

She decided to take a couple of days off from the College, and mark scripts at home.

The first day passed tranquilly enough; she worked throughout the morning and early afternoon. At around five she felt suddenly moved, against her better judgment, to telephone Paul with what she knew to be a trumped-up query about an exam problem. Talking to him, she was aware of her own voice, with a curious detachment; its tone surprised her, and the shrillness of her laugh. Do I always sound like that? she thought, have I always laughed in that way? It seemed to her that Paul was abrupt, that he deliberately ended the conversation.

She got up the next morning in a curious frame of mind. The scripts she had to mark filled her with irritation; not the irritation stemming from inadequacy in the candidates, but a petulant resentment of the whole thing. Sometimes, she did not seem able to follow the answers to questions. "Don't get you," she scribbled in the margin. "What are you on about?" At the bottom of one script she scrawled a series of doodles: indeterminate flowers, a face wearing upswept spectacles, a buxom female figure. At last, with the pile of scripts barely recorded, she abandoned her desk and wandered restlessly around the house.

Somehow, it displeased her. It was too stark, too bare, an unlived-in place. I like a bit of life, she thought, a bit of color, something to pep things up; rummaging in the scullery she found under the sink some gaily patterned curtaining that must have got overlooked when she cleared out those particular shelves. That's nice, she thought, nice and striking, I like that; as she hung it in place of the linen weave in the hall that now seemed so dowdy, it seemed to her that from somewhere in the house came a peal of laughter.

That day merged, somehow, into the next. She did not go to the College. Several times the telephone rang: mostly she ignored it. Once, answering, she heard the departmental secretary's voice, blathering on: "Dr. Rackham?" she kept saying, "Dr. Rackham? Professor Simons has been a bit worried, we wondered if . . . " Muriel laughed and hung up. The night, the intermediate night (or nights, it might have been, time was a bit confusing, not that it mattered at all) had been most extraordinary. She had had company of some kind; throughout the night, whenever she woke, she had been aware of a low murmuring. A voice. A voice of compulsive intimacy, coarse and insistent; it had repelled but at the same time fascinated her. She had lain there, silent and unresisting.

The house displeased her more and more. It's got no style, she thought, full of dreary old stuff. She took down the Dufy prints, and the Piper cathedral etchings, thinking: I don't like that kind of thing, I like a proper picture, where you can see what's what, don't know where I ever picked up these. She made a brief sortie to Boots round the corner and bought a couple of really nice things, not expensive either—a Chinese girl and a lovely painting of horses galloping by the sea. As she hung them in the sitting room, it seemed to her that someone clutched her arm, and for an instant she shuddered uncontrollably, but the sensation passed, though it left her feeling lightheaded, a little hysterical.

Her own appearance dissatisfied her, too. She sat looking at herself in her bedroom mirror and thought: "I've never made the best of myself, a woman's got to make use of what she's got, hasn't she? Where's that nice blouse I found the other day, it's flattering—a bit of décolleté, I'm not past that kind of thing yet. She put it on, and felt pleased. Downstairs, the telephone was ringing again, but she could not be bothered to answer it. Don't want to see anyone, she thought, fed up with people, if it's Paul he can come and find me, can't he? Play hard to get, that's what you should do with men, string them along a bit.

Anyway, she was not alone. She could feel, again, that presence in the room, though when she swung round suddenly—with a resurgence of that chill sensation—there was nothing but the dressmaker's dummy, standing in the corner. She must have brought it from the cupboard, and forgotten.

She wandered about the house, muttering to herself; from time to time, a person walked with her, not someone you could see, just a presence, its arm slipped through Muriel's, whispering intimacies, suggestions. All those old books of yours, it said, you don't want those, ring the newsagent, have them send round some mags, a good read, that's what we want. Muriel nodded.

Once, people hammered on the door. She could hear their voices; colleagues from the department. "Muriel?" they called. "Are you there, Muriel?" She went into the kitchen and shut herself in till they had gone. For a moment, sitting there, she felt clearer in her head, free of the confusion that had been dragging her down; something is happening, she thought wildly, something I cannot cope with, can't control. . . .

And then there came again that presence, with its insistent voice, and this time the voice was quite real, and she knew, too, that she had heard it before, somewhere, quite recently, not long ago. Where, where?

. . . I thought what you said was quite interesting, and I'd like to tell you about this thing that happened to a friend of mine . . .

Muriel held the banisters, to steady herself (she was on her way upstairs again, in her perpetual edgy drifting up and down the house): the Lit. and Phil., I remember now, that woman.

And it came to her too, with a horrid jolt, that she knew now, remembered suddenly, why, at the time, that evening, the face had been familiar, why she'd felt she'd seen it before.

It had been the face in a yellowed photograph that had tumbled from a tatty book when she had been clearing out the house: Violet Hanson, 1934, in faded ink on the back.

Sale by auction, by order of the Executors of Mrs. Violet Hanson, deceased, No. 27 Clarendon Terrace, a four-bedroomed house with scope for . . .

Someone was laughing, peals of shrill laughter that rang through the house, and as she reached the top floor, and turned into her bedroom, she knew that it was herself. She went into her bedroom and sat down at her dressing table and looked in the mirror. The face that looked back at her was haggard. I've got to do something about myself, she thought, I'm turning into an old frump. She groped on the table and found a pair of earrings, long, shiny ones that she had forgotten she had. She held them up against her face; yes, that's nice, stylish, and I'll dye my hair, have it cut short and dye it black, take years off me, that would. . . .

There was laughter again, but she no longer knew if it was hers or someone else's.

JACK MATTHEWS

Ghostly Populations

He first got in touch with me after I'd just had *Mansions of the Dead: Haunted Houses in the Ohio Valley* published, and there was considerable local interest in the subject of occult happenings, especially after my television appearance. I'd received a few phone calls and letters, including one from a probate judge in Clermont County who swore that he'd been visited by the ghost of his ex-girlfriend, dead for over thirty years.

Modest as it was, this whiff of fame was unsettling. I got the impression that people were throwing messages at me the way you throw popcorn into a lion cage. At odd moments, knowing such notions are not to be trusted, I fancied I could hear pages being flipped, and wondered if anything I knew was printed on them.

But Adler was in a class by himself. In his own cage. He neither wrote nor phoned, but simply appeared one day, abrupt as a sack of groceries that bursts and spills cans of peaches and salted peanuts onto your feet. Out of nowhere, right there in the parking lot, just as I was about to climb into my Plymouth Horizon and head for home.

I wasn't really alarmed. This was obviously not your average mugger, even though he had his hand in his pocket. A thin, wiry man in his sixties, with gray hair shaved close to his head and a broad-bridged nose between sad, wet, owlish eyes. He had the edgy moves of an old man fearful of rupturing himself.

There was strange traffic in his head, I could tell; and not all the street lamps were lit. The open collar of his maroon shirt revealed the wrinkled neck

171

of an aged rooster; and a glassy lump the size of a quarter glowed above his right eyebrow.

I knew his type: the steamy sort who idles his Mustang outside a Christian Science reading room, or gives you an unasked-for tip on a horse named Valdina Luster, or who tries to sell you a genuine blue-diamond ring he's just gotten from some cracked desperate millionaire in Newport, Kentucky. He was wearing a corduroy jacket so old and battered that some of the grooves were rubbed pale and smooth, the color of Adler's skin.

It was evident he'd been waiting for me. Briefly, I pictured him crouching between cars, chewing gum and idly tracing figures on the asphalt with his index finger, while horns blared in the street beyond the poplar trees. His first words seemed to continue an old harangue: "He's been keeping me under observation," he said.

Before I could ask what he was talking about, Adler shot his index finger slyly in the direction of the guard's station near the lot's entrance. I turned and saw the guard's shadow through the window of the kiosk, made of stone painted a liverish blood-red (close to the color of Adler's shirt). It was true: the guard was watching us.

"Adler," he said. "I know you, of course. I think we can talk business."

I glanced back at the kiosk and saw that the guard was now standing outside, his hands on his hips in that posture of tired appraisal that old cops have.

Adler twisted his mouth and shook his head. "God, how can they expect you to talk when it's like this?"

"Who?"

"Conditions," Adler said ambiguously. And then he nodded and told me we'd get together again, soon, and I told him I could hardly wait; but the irony was lost on him, because he was already edging away.

By the time I had climbed into my car, he was out of sight, and I was thinking good riddance. In another life, he'd been some kind of bird. The air was cool and damp and smelled of oil and a medley of carbons.

I eased the Horizon out of the lot and turned to a local radio station and was surprised to hear the music of an old-fashioned waltz, which I couldn't identify.

Shortly thereafter, I saw a car ahead that so help me appeared to be moving along the street without a driver inside. It was a strange sort of optical illusion, I thought at the time, composed by chance shadow and reflected sunlight. I didn't pay much attention to it, then; even though I can't help but remember it differently now, in view of subsequent events.

Being a veteran newspaperman, and recently something of a local celebrity, I should have strategies for coping with oddballs. I should either be able to shrug them off, inured by experience to the shock they bring, or I should be able to find them interesting, even instructive. Maybe even symptomatic of something out of whack in the social body.

And yet, there are a few you can't manage; and it appeared that Adler might be one of these. Moreover, the fact is, I was having problems with my health, diagnosis complicated, verging upon unknown, and I wasn't sure I could cope with some son of a bitch like Adler, coming forth to lay his hands on me with the curse of madness.

My wife, Una, was witness to the threat he might bring. Since I'd been ill, I seemed to have just enough strength to get through the day, with little margin or tolerance or energy left over for inscrutable games or the mumbling prophecies of cranks. Partly it had been that damned book on haunted houses: it seemed to have drained whatever surplus vitality I'd possessed.

It was a week later when the phone rang at a little after eleven at night.

"God, I hope it's not the paper," Una said. She was at her dressing table, putting her hair up, getting ready for bed. I was brushing my teeth.

She reached over and plucked the extension phone from its wall bracket, answered it, and then handed it to me, saying, "It's not the paper. I don't recognize the voice."

But I did, the instant I said hello and heard the single utterance: "Adler."

"What?"

"Adler. We've talked."

Silence. And then I remained silent, even after I remembered. I refused to say the next word, but Adler was not to be put off.

"We agreed to talk," he reminded me, somewhat inaccurately. "That day in the parking lot."

"What about?" I could tell that my voice was guarded, even though I could picture a smallmouth bass flopping under the seat of a rowboat. Not hostile, exactly; but certainly not friendly either.

"Reading your book," Adler went on, "and seeing you on television helped me make up my mind. I'm interested, and I'm going to trust you."

"Look," I said, "I don't know what in the hell you're after, but this is the second time you've approached me with the promise of some sort of mysterious message, and I think you'd better come right out with it, or else forget it. Okay?"

"Mystery is the word," Adler said. He really did sound like a gum-chewer. "And I'll come right out with it. Where can we talk?"

"We're talking *now!*" I said. "What is it you have to say?"

"It's the kind of thing we should have a cup of coffee over," Adler said. "It shouldn't take long. At least the first part. After you find out, though, I'm willing to bet you'll be *anxious* to talk about it. I won't have to do any begging then!"

"Who's begging?" I shouted, somewhat incoherently. And then I said, "Either you tell me right now what it is you want to talk about or I'm hanging up!"

"I didn't really think you'd get mad," Adler muttered. "At least so soon. Not at this stage."

Later, I was to think that this seemed to contradict what he'd just told me, but at the moment I simply slammed the receiver down, not taking the time to think about anything other than the irritation of Adler's call.

"Will he call right back?" Una asked.

"I don't think so," I said.

Una was worried. "With your health, you shouldn't be subjected to things like this. I wish you'd never written that book."

"I'm all right."

"You're always saying that, but you and I know better—not to mention Dr. Wallace. So why don't we stop pretending."

I made a face and thought of an old tricycle I'd had as a little boy. I wondered where its molecules had gotten to. I blew air through my mouth. "Don't start talking about Wallace! He doesn't know what's wrong."

"No, but that's just *it:* he knows *something's* wrong."

"Probably just nerves and overwork."

"Then why don't you let up a little?"

"By refusing to pick up the receiver when the phone rings?"

Una thought a minute, then she nodded and said, "I know. It isn't easy. But if you'd just let him know that you're not interested in what he has to tell you . . ."

"Maybe I am and don't know it."

"Now what's *that* supposed to mean?"

I cracked my knuckles and sighed. It was hard on Una, like poison ivy in the ear. I said, "Well, I don't know."

"I hope we're not going to have to have an unlisted number again."

Years before, when I'd been a reporter, I'd received enough uninvited phone calls that we'd changed our number, first, and then in exasperation had it unlisted.

"No," I said, winding an old alarm clock with angry twists of my hand, "I don't think he'll be calling again."

I have no idea what gave me such confidence.

One of the strangest things about Adler was his oblique wariness, the sense of waiting he conveyed. This came to me like the sound of an oboe, played by a talented woman with dim features. No matter how mysterious this revelation of his was, there was no clear reason he couldn't have told me that first day in the parking lot, or even over the phone. Why hadn't he?

Evidently, some chemistry of time and place was not right. Adler was hesitant. He was troubled by a delicate sensitivity that seemed at odds with everything else about him. It was as if a bleary-eyed wino, dressed in dark pants silvery with grime and wearing a torn and stinking cloth parka, showed a mandarin flair for protocol.

And yet, Adler was no bum. Not exactly. He was more of an apprentice. And this faint incongruity about him wasn't the oddest part, anyway: the oddest part was the elusive, faint air of familiarity I experienced when I thought about him. Somewhere, somehow (something kept telling me), I had seen Adler before; I had exchanged words with him, or someone like him. And yet, I had no idea where or when. It was all very puzzling. Mystery was the word: just as he'd said.

Customarily, I ate lunch in a small cafeteria, named the Calico Lion, half a block away; and almost always lunch was a continuation of work, with one of us pulling out a notepad and making notes while he or she kept on chewing and the others kept on talking.

But one day a week later, I happened to be having lunch alone, because Bill Tetlow had a noon-hour dental appointment and Charlotte Knoepfle was having a luncheon interview with the mayor. Usually, I took little notice of who was in the cafeteria line next to me, or who was seated nearby; but today, I happened to look up from my tomato soup and there was Adler, two tables away, disheveled, immobile, and ridiculously intense, hunched over a cup of coffee. A survivor of some minor-key catastrophe, you could tell. He was staring at me out of puffy eyes.

Before I could look away, he'd gotten up from his table and was coming over to join me. Walking like a deck hand on a rolling minesweeper.

"I knew that sooner or later we'd have a chance," he said, clattering his coffee cup onto the table. It was only half full and looked cold.

I told him I didn't have much time, and he said it wouldn't take much time. Then he narrowed his eyes and stirred his coffee meditatively, as if savoring the moment.

"I've never mentioned this to anyone else," he said.

"I gathered as much."

"The fact is, most people wouldn't understand. But you're getting to *be* somebody."

"Thanks for the compliment. That's what I've always wanted."

Adler was not listening. "I could see people noticing you. They know who you are."

"Big fish, little pond."

"Everybody starts somewhere."

"And stops somewhere," I said, rubbing my eyes. I had a hunch about this promised revelation of his, and I didn't like it. Somewhere, it was raining. "You say you've read the book?" I asked.

Adler nodded.

"Well," I said, "If you're going to start telling me about some sort of ESP experience you've had, or some kind of ghost story you've been wanting to tell, I suggest you go back and read my Introduction again. In case you don't remember, I make it quite clear in the Introduction that I don't believe a single thing that is reported in those ghost stories. What I did in the book was simply collect the tales and then have Cliff Dalbert take all the color photos of the twenty-three houses featured and . . . well, there you have a good coffee-table book. And I'm not *that* much of a celebrity, for God's sake!"

Adler blinked and appeared to listen, but I don't think he heard. Something in his expression bothered me, so that I was forced into the indecisiveness of repeating myself. I went into considerable detail, played variations on the theme, and elaborated upon my credentials as an old-fashioned, fundamentally anonymous, down-to-earth skeptic. In fact, my explicit cynicism in doing the book was part of its charm, a reviewer had said; however, others seemed to miss the cynicism (always conceived as good-natured and above-board, of course) and believed whatever they wanted to believe. I had written a book on "haunted houses," and, no matter what I said about them, or how cynically I exploited stories that revealed gullibility and superstition at their most spectacular, such readers were going to see their own ghosts somewhere beyond my stated intent.

Apparently, Adler was one of these. Because, when I finished, he nodded, as if in complete agreement with everything I'd said, and then—in a low voice, hunched over his cup half full of cold coffee, the lump over his eye shining like a metal knob—he told me something he claimed he'd never told anyone else.

And I want to tell you, it was something strange and unique, like the voice of a cricket coming out of the accumulated junk in an old shed—the woolen drawers of an old music-hall queen, perhaps, or a dead man's shoe.

In trying to remember that episode in the restaurant, my mind keeps sliding off to the next morning, when I had an appointment for additional tests at the clinic. I remember sitting in the waiting room, an open copy of *Field and Stream* in my lap, thinking back upon Adler's revelation. For some reason, I remember the remembering more than I remember the event itself. Somewhere in those hours there was a long climb up a long hill.

But what Adler had to say was astonishing. Let's acknowledge the fact. I have to admit it, and even admit that, in spite of everything, I would have missed out on something if Adler had not latched on to me, because the story he told was far more fantastic than any I had used in *Mansions of the Dead.*

Even now, I remember the way he began, and I remember it through the dull, numb apprehensiveness of that waiting room, the receptionist (dressed in white, like a nurse) talking on the phone and rolling her eyes upward as she listened. Soft music came out of the ceiling. Something was inscrutably wrong inside me; the bureaucracy of my body was not functioning as it should.

"Last month, I saw Roosevelt," Adler had said. "I can show you the exact spot, and I can tell you the exact time."

"Who?"

"Franklin Delano Roosevelt, FDR."

"Sure," I said.

Adler shook his head devoutly. He probably wasn't much older than I, but God, he looked ancient! He could talk with turtles, you could see that, just looking at him. My stomach flexed and I tasted bile in my throat. "Get him out of here," a voice said inside my mind.

"What do you think of that?" Adler asked, opening his eyes too wide.

"I think that's peachy goddamn keen," I said.

"You're not being serious."

"And you *are?*"

"Absolutely. He was walking out of the Sheraton along about ten o'clock. I was just passing by. Saw him plain as day."

"I would have thought he would be in a wheelchair," I said.

"Oh, he *limped* all right," Adler said, frowning and scratching his scalp in back. "I figured that wheelchair routine was just to gain sympathy and get votes."

"Sure."

"It's the solemn truth," Adler said.

"Sure."

"And there've been others. Churchill, Eisenhower, and even that damned Patton, riding in a limousine."

"You're sort of fixated on World War II, aren't you?"

"No, I saw Mark Twain, once. He'd shaved his mustache."

"Jesus Christ Almighty!" I whispered.

"The fact is," Adler went on, "they're all walking around, free as you please. But only in the big cities. I figure, because there they won't be noticed. At least by *most* people. And it's true: do you think people *notice?* Not at all. Big cities are where they hide. A perfect cover. Who would *look* at them, even? *Nobody* notices, except for me. I can spot them in a second. I don't miss a one. No sir! And I'll tell you something: there are *thousands* of them!"

"They're dead, but they're walking around: is that it?"

Adler nodded intensely. "That's it exactly. It sort of gives you the creeps that nobody else ever notices them. Especially when you realize how famous they all are."

"Famous?"

Adler nodded. "They have to be famous," he said. "That's what it takes."

"Well if they *weren't* famous," I said, "you wouldn't recognize them in the first place!"

But Adler paid no attention to that. "Famous," he repeated; and, at that instant, I was afraid of the operation that awaited me.

Adler was showed, pushed back, where he joined the crowd in the galleries inside my head, and they gave me my first injection and soon I wasn't thinking of anything very much, except for an occasional dwelling upon the appearance of huge wood doves standing in a row on the hood of a rusty old Autocar tractor. God knows where that scene came from, but it was there.

I won't bother trying to describe what it was like, except for the fact that one of the few things I can remember in that darkness (and you can remember more than you think you can, or allow yourself to remember, from something like that) is a moment of awesome oppression. I felt smothered by something as vast as a mound of earth, and I can remember struggling mightily for a while, and then suddenly finding myself out of it, as if I'd stepped through a door, and I was "outside" (whatever that meant, because it was just as dark) and the relief was enormous, as if I had been released from the most hateful of prisons.

I was also vaguely aware of great oceans of time compressed into that general darkness, but of course there was no clock that could measure it. Whatever its tides, they moved to other moons.

When I awoke, Una was there holding my hand; and then I was once more back inside something dark and vaguely uncomfortable. I was aware of a great surge of pain and nausea; and once again I went under, deeper than ever, deeper than possible. Then, the third time, I came out of it, more or less lucid, and had no real idea of how long I had been away.

The days of recovery were not desperately painful or uncomfortable. Filled with Demerol, I floated upon the hours. I couldn't lift my head to read; and watching television was something that couldn't hold my interest long, so there wasn't much left except to lie there in my bed and feel time move through me. And think about Adler.

Because I kept going over what he'd said, trying to see the world as he saw it out of his poor, screwed-up head. He was constantly running into the walking dead on the street . . . people who moved about and seemed as alive as anyone else; famous people, as he'd pointed out . . . but of course, as *I'd* pointed out, those were the only ones he would recognize.

Therefore, could one conclude that these were only a small minority, in Adler's thinking: the visible tip of an invisible iceberg of dead people, milling about the city streets at noon, or leaving the Sheraton at ten in the morning? No, he said you had to be famous. Fame was a precondition. The Elysian Fields, not Hades.

Without actually remembering that he'd said it, I seemed to recall that Adler was convinced that he was one in a billion, marked off to identify these people . . . even though they didn't actually look any different from their appearance in life, except for such details as Mark Twain's mustache being shaved off.

Then I remembered part of a conversation that I was certain had actually taken place, whose words I could remember verbatim.

"One thing is, they never talk or look up," Adler had told me. "You see them all of a sudden, pow, and they go right past. Maybe in a car. Oftentimes, in fact."

"Oftentimes?" I'd echoed.

Adler nodded. *"Very* oftentimes," he'd said.

Then he'd gone into an explanation of sundry details, including the fact that they were always in a hurry and never seemed to hear or see what was about them. Ingrid Bergman and Buffalo Bill; Bertrand Russell and Eva Perón.

"Folks who lived after the invention of the camera," I said, "so you can recognize them easily."

Adler said, "No, there are a lot of others, too."

"But all famous."

Adler nodded and said, "They're oftentimes jaywalkers."

"It's a wonder more of them don't get killed," I said.

Adler seemed to think about that for a moment, but said nothing.

Nevertheless, I recovered and gradually felt better, and increasingly lucid. During the next two weeks, I learned things. I realized that it was somewhat remarkable I was still around. My condition at one time had evidently been grave. Graver than grave. Still, I did feel a lot better, a little more secure, and I thought it had probably all been worth the pain and effort.

It was my second evening at home that Una came into my room and said she wanted to tell me something funny.

"Don't make me laugh too hard," I said. "I feel like Humpty Dumpty."

"Not that kind of funny," Una said. "Odd. Crazy."

When she said that, so help me, I knew it was Adler.

"It's about that oddball you met," she went on.

"Yes."

"I can't think of his name, though."

"Adler."

She nodded and swallowed. "Yes. He phoned the day after you had been operated on. You probably don't remember, but you'd sort of come around, but then you went out again. They said you'd be all right, so I came home.

I had to come here to get the phone numbers of everybody, so I could phone them from the hospital. I don't know why I forgot to take them with me."

"Get on with it," I said uneasily.

"I am," she said. "I just wanted to explain to you why I'd left the hospital. I wasn't gone over an hour and a half, and I don't suppose I was in the house over ten minutes . . ."

"But Adler called while you were here. Right?"

Una nodded. "That's exactly right. And when he answered, I knew it was him. I mean, I recognized his voice from that time he'd called late at night. Anyway, he wanted to know what you were doing at Sears the evening before, and why you didn't speak to him."

I laughed a little and threw my arm over my face.

"Are you all right?" Una asked.

"Yes. Go on."

"Well, I told him it couldn't have been you, because you had been operated on the day before, and were still under the anesthetic. But he didn't seem to want to take my word for it. He kept saying something, about, 'Seeing is believing,' and I asked him what difference it made, anyway, but he didn't answer me directly, but just said something about wanting to be sure you were going to tell his story."

"Sears," I whispered.

"He said you were riding in a car that turned out of the parking area, and you rode right past him without even turning your head."

I gave a little laugh. "Snubbed him, did I?"

Una nodded. "He didn't really put up much of an argument, but I could tell he didn't believe me. At least, he didn't act like it."

I closed my eyes and took a long breath.

"You *are* tired, aren't you?" Una said, and I thought a moment before admitting that I was.

After she left, I kept trying to think of how I must have looked to Adler . . . rather, how that man, whoever he was, or image, whatever it was, must have looked.

*   *   *

Perhaps the oddest part of this story I have to tell is the fact that I actually continued to believe that I'd died for exactly that moment when Adler claimed to have seen me in a passing car, and yet not for even as long as *that* instant believing Adler any more than I had from the beginning.

To say that his hallucination was coincidence is as sensible a conclusion as any other. And that hallucination itself did not (I reasoned) have to make any claim upon our capacity to believe in miracles. I am not sure the supernatural, however it may be said to exist, or however defined, has anything to do with the web of fact upon which our sensations are draped like so many pennants at a festival. To resort to something like that is to take refuge in a word, and I don't think Adler himself was ever tempted in this way, for his manner was always sturdily rational, in spite of the fundamental, radical madness of his conviction.

I've picked this idea apart, the way you disassemble an alarm clock, put it back together, and it still ticks. Don't argue with me: I don't want to hear argument. I'm listening to another kind of music these days.

I speak of Adler in the past tense, because I am convinced that Adler is dead. The realization has grown upon me gradually through the weeks and months of my convalescence. For one thing, he has not tried to get in touch with me.

Perhaps, I tell myself, he has been institutionalized by some long-worried wife or daughter. Or probated by a willful, balding son who likes to wear knit shirts and sells auto insurance for a living, and takes his own four daughters (Adler's grandchildren) to Sunday school and teaches them to be kind and prudent.

Or maybe Adler has come to his senses and now lives in a retirement village near Sarasota, where he sings tenor in a barbershop quartet, and goes shopping in the local K-Mart without ever once looking up to see who might be passing in the cars that glide to and fro before the entrances of such places.

But I think not. Powerfully so. Crows live in the high oaks behind our house, and Una is wistful.

And difficult as it may be for me to explain, and as it must be for another to understand, there is the fact that this assumption of mine has absolutely nothing to do with what happened the other evening while I was waiting to pull out of the neighborhood Exxon station, where I take my car for gas and normal maintenance. I was surprised to see Adler ride by in a long black limousine. He was not driving, nor was he looking about. No, his gaze was straight ahead, and the expression on his face was that of a man listening to his childhood. Even the bulge above his eyebrow was visible; even that look of needless intensity that was so ridiculous a part of him whenever he'd talked to me.

Never, I told myself, has he less need of that expression than now.

And when I arrived back home, and Una asked if I'd seen anyone I knew, I told her no, I had not; though I did point out that the world was so full of people, how could one ever really know?

And this, too, I have to admit: Adler was never famous; he was never conceivably even so much as that pathetic figure, "a local celebrity." Nobody knew him; he lived in everyone's absence, as he'd once lived in mine, before these adventures I've just recounted took place.

Full of people, indeed! The world is that, and great enough for all kinds of madness—Adler's and yours, and mine as well.

TIM O'BRIEN

The Ghost Soldiers

I was shot twice. The first time, out by Tri Binh, it knocked me against the pagoda wall, and I bounced and spun around and ended up on Teddy Thatcher's lap. Lucky thing, because Teddy was the medic. He tied on a compress and told me to get some sleep, then he ran off toward the fighting. For a long time I lay there all alone, listening to the battle, thinking, *I've been shot, I've been shot.* Winged, grazed, creased: all those Gene Autry movies I'd seen as a kid. In fact, I even laughed. Except then I started to think I might bleed to death. It was the fear, mostly, but I felt wobbly, and then I had a sinking sensation, ears all plugged up, as if I'd gone deep under water. Thank God for Teddy Thatcher. Every so often, maybe four times altogether, he trotted back to check me out. Which took guts. It was a wild fight, lots of noise, guys running and laying down fire, regrouping, running again, real chaos, but Teddy took the risks. "Easy does it," he said. "Just a side wound—no problem unless you're pregnant. You pregnant, buddy?" He ripped off the compress, applied a fresh one, and told me to clamp it in place with my fingers. "Press hard," he said. "Don't worry about the baby." Then he took off. It was almost dark before the fighting petered out and the chopper came to take me and two dead guys away. "Adios, amigo," Teddy said in his fake Mexican accent. I was barely up to it, but I said, "Oh, Cisco," and Teddy wrapped his arms around me and kissed my neck and said, "Oh, Pancho!" because we were buddies and that was how we did things.

On the ride in to Chu Lai, I kept waiting for the pain to come but actually I couldn't feel much. A throb, that's all. Even in the hospital it wasn't bad.

When I got back to Delta Company twenty-six days later, in mid-March, Teddy Thatcher was dead, and a new medic named Jorgenson had replaced him. Jorgenson was no Teddy. Incompetent and scared. So when I got shot the second time, in the butt, along the Song Tra Bong, it took the son of a bitch almost ten minutes to work up the courage to crawl over to me. By then I was gone with the pain. Later I found out I'd almost died of shock. Jorgenson didn't know about shock, or if he knew, the fear made him forget. To make it worse, the guy bungled the patch job, and a couple of weeks later my ass started to rot away. You could actually peel off chunks of butt with your fingernail.

It was borderline gangrene. I spent a month flat on my belly—couldn't play cards, couldn't sleep. I kept seeing Jorgenson's scared-green face. Those buggy eyes and the way his lips twitched and that silly excuse for a moustache. After the rot cleared up, once I could think straight, I devoted a lot of time to figuring ways to get back at him.

Getting shot should be an experience you can take some pride from. I'm not talking macho crap; I'm not saying you should strut around with your Purple Hearts on display. All I mean is that you should be able to *talk* about it: the stiff thump of the bullet and the way it knocks the air out of you and makes you cough, how the sound comes about ten decades later, the dizzy feeling, the smell of yourself, the stuff you think about and say and do right afterward, the way your eyes focus on a tiny pebble or a blade of grass and how you think, man, that's the last thing I'll ever see, *that* pebble, *that* blade of grass, which makes you want to cry. Pride isn't the right word; I don't know the right word. All I know is, you shouldn't feel embarrassed. Humiliation shouldn't be part of it.

Diaper rash, the nurses called it. Male nurses, too. That was the worst part. It made me hate Jorgenson the way some guys hated Charlie—the kind of hate you make atrocities out of.

I guess the higher-ups decided I'd been shot enough. In early May, when I was released from the Ninety-first Evac Hospital, they transferred me over to headquarters company—S-4, the battalion supply section. Compared with the boonies, of course, it was cushy duty. Regular hours, movies, floor shows, the blurry slow motion of the rear. Fairly safe, too. The battalion firebase was built into a big hill just off Highway One, surrounded on all sides by flat paddy land, and between us and the paddies there were plenty of bunkers and sandbags and rolls of razor-tipped barbed wire. Sure, you could still die there— once a month or so we'd get hit with some mortar fire—but you could die in the bleachers at Fenway Park, bases loaded, Yaz coming to the plate.

I wasn't complaining. Naturally there were times when I halfway wanted to head back to the field; I missed adventure, even the danger. A hard thing to explain to somebody who hasn't felt it. Danger, it makes things vivid. When you're afraid, really afraid, you see things you never saw before, you pay attention. On the other hand, I wasn't crazy. I'd already taken two bullets; the odds were deadly. So I just settled in, took it easy, counted myself lucky. I figured my war was over. If it hadn't been for the constant ache in my butt, I guess things would've worked out fine.

But Jesus, it *hurt*.

Pain, you know?

At night, for example, I had to sleep on my belly. That doesn't sound so terrible until you consider that I'd been a back-sleeper all my life. It got to where I was almost an insomniac. I'd lie there all fidgety and tight, then after a while I'd get angry. I'd squirm around on my cot, cussing, half nuts with hurt, then I'd start remembering stuff. Jorgenson, I'd think. Shock—how could the bastard forget to treat for shock? I'd remember how long it took him to get to me, how his fingers were all jerky and nervous, the way his lips kept twitching under that ridiculous mustache.

The nights were miserable.

Sometimes I'd roam around the base. I'd head down to the wire and stare out at the darkness, out where the war was, and I'd count ways to make Jorgenson suffer.

One thing for sure. You forget how much you use your butt until you can't use it any more.

* * *

In July, Delta Company came in for stand-down. I was there on the helipad to meet the choppers. Curtis and Lemon and Azar slapped hands with me, then I piled their gear in my jeep and drove them down to the Delta hootches. We partied until chow time. Afterward, we kept on partying. It was one of the rituals. Even if you weren't in the mood, you did it on principle.

By midnight it was story time.

"Morty Becker wasted his luck," said Lemon.

I smiled and waited. There was a tempo to how stories got told. Lemon peeled open a finger blister and sucked on it.

"Go on," Azar said. "Tell it."

"Becker used up his luck. Pissed it away."

"On *nothin'*," Azar said.

Lemon nodded, started to speak, then stopped and got up and moved to the cooler and shoved his hands deep into the ice. He was naked except for his socks and his dog tags. In a way, I envied him—all of them. Those deep bush tans, the jungle sores and blisters, the stories, the in-it-togetherness. I felt close to them, yes, but I also felt separate.

Bending forward, Lemon scooped ice up against his chest, pressing it there for a moment, eyes closed; then he fished out a beer and snapped it open.

"It was out by My Khe," he said. "Remember My Khe? Bad-ass country, right? A blister of a day, hot-hot, and we're just sort of groovin' it, lyin' around, nobody bustin' ass or anything. I mean, listen, it's *hot*. We're poppin' salt tabs just to stay conscious. Finally somebody says, 'Hey, where's Becker?' The captain does a head count, and guess what? No Becker."

"Gone," Azar said. "Vanished. *Poof*, no fuckin' Becker."

"We send out two patrols—no dice. Not a trace." Lemon poured beer on his open blister, slowly licked the foam off. "By then it's getting dark. Captain's about ready to have a fit—you know how he gets, right?—and then, guess what? Take a guess."

"Becker shows," I said.

"You got it, man. Becker shows. We've almost chalked him up as MIA, and then, bingo, he shows."

"Soaking wet," Azar said.

"Hey—"

"Okay, it's your story, but *tell* it."

Lemon frowned. "Soaking wet," he said.

"Ha!"

"Turns out he went for a swim. You believe that? All by himself, the moron just takes off, hikes a couple klicks, finds himself a river, strips, hops in, no security, no *nothin'*. Dig it? He goes swimming."

Azar giggled. "A hot day."

"Not that hot," said Curtis Young. "Not that fuckin' hot."

"Hot, though."

"Get the picture?" Lemon said. "I mean, this is fuckin' My Khe we're talking about. Doomsville, and the guy goes for a *swim.*"

"Yeah," I said. "Crazy."

I looked across the hootch. Thirty or forty guys were there, some drinking, some passed out, but I couldn't find Morty Becker among them.

Lemon grinned. He reached out and put his hand on my knee and squeezed.

"That's the kicker, man. No more Becker."

"No?"

"The kicker's this," Lemon said, "Morty Becker's luck gets all used up. See? On a lousy swim."

"And that's the truth. That's the truth," said Azar.

Lemon's hand still rested on my knee, very gently.

"What happened?"

"Ah, shit."

"Go on, tell."

"Fatality," Lemon said. "Couple days later, maybe a week, Becker gets real dizzy. Pukes a lot, temperature zooms way up. Out of sight, you know? Jorgenson says he must've swallowed bad water on that swim. Swallowed a virus or something."

"Jorgenson," I said. "Where is my good buddy Jorgenson?"

"Hey, look—"

"Just tell me where to find him."

Lemon made a quick clicking sound with his tongue. "You want to *hear* this? Yes or no?"

"Sure, but where's—"

"Listen up. Becker gets sick, right? Sick, sick, sick. Never seen nobody so bad off, *never*. Arms jerkin' all over hell, can't walk, can't talk, can't fart, can't nothin'. Like he's paralyzed. Can't move. Polio, maybe."

Curtis Young shook his head. "Not polio. You got it wrong."

"Maybe polio."

"No way," Curtis said. "Not polio."

"*Maybe*," Lemon said. "I'm just saying what Jorgenson says. Maybe fuckin' polio. Or that elephant disease. Elephantiasshole or whatever."

"But not polio."

Azar smiled and snapped his fingers. "Either way," he said, "it goes to show. Don't throw away luck on little stuff. Save it up."

"That's the lesson, all right."

"Becker was due."

"There it is. Overdue. Don't fritter away your luck."

"Fuckin' polio."

Lemon closed his eyes.

We sat quietly. No need to talk, because we were thinking about the same things: about Mort Becker, the way luck worked and didn't work, how it was impossible to gauge the odds. Maybe the disease was lucky. Who knows? Maybe it saved Morty from getting shot.

"Where's Jorgenson?" I said.

Another thing: Three times a day, no matter what, I had to stop whatever I was doing, go find a private place, drop my pants, bend over, and apply this antibacterial ointment to my ass. No choice—I had to do it. And the worst part was how the ointment left yellow stains on the seat of my trousers, big greasy splotches. Herbie's hemorrhoids, that was one of the jokes. There were plenty of other jokes, too—plenty.

During the first full day of Delta's stand-down, I didn't run into Jorgenson once. Not at chow, not at the flicks, not during our long booze sessions in the hootch.

I didn't hunt him down, though. I just waited.

"Forget it," Lemon said. "Granted, the man messed up bad, real bad, but you got to take into account how green he was. Brand new, remember?"

"I forget. Remind me."

"You survived."

I showed Lemon the yellow stain on my britches. "I'm in terrific shape. Really funny, right?"

"Not exactly," Lemon said.

But he was laughing. He started snapping a towel at my backside. I laughed—I couldn't help it—but I didn't see the big joke.

Later, after some dope, Lemon said: "The thing is, Jorgenson's doing all right. Better and better. People change, they adapt. I mean, okay, he's not a Teddy Thatcher, but the dude hangs in there, he knows his shit. Kept Becker alive."

"My sore ass."

Lemon nodded. He shrugged, leaned back, popped the hot roach into his mouth, chewed for a long time. "You've lost touch, man. Jorgenson . . . he's *with* us now."

"I'm not."

"No," he said. "I guess you're not."

"Good old loyalty."

Lemon shook his head. "We're friends, Herbie. You and me. But look, you're not *out* there anymore, and Jorgenson is. If you'd just seen him the past couple of weeks—the way he handled Becker, then when Pinko hit the mine—I mean, the kid did some good work. Ask anybody. So . . . I don't know. If it was me, Herbie, I'd say screw it. Leave it alone."

"I won't hurt him."

"Right."

"I won't. Show him some ghosts, that's all."

* * *

In the morning I spotted Jorgenson. I was up on the helipad, loading the resupply choppers, and then, when the last bird took off, while I was putting on my shirt, I looked up, and there he was. In a way, it was a shock. His size, I mean. Even smaller than I remembered—a little squirrel of a guy, five and a half feet tall, skinny and mousy and sad.

He was leaning against my jeep, waiting for me.

"Herb," he said, "can we talk?"

At first I just looked at his boots.

Those boots: I remembered them from when I got shot. Out along the Song Tra Bong, a bullet in my ass, all that pain, and the funny thing was that what I remembered, now, were those new boots—no scuffs; smooth, unblemished leather. One of those last details, Jorgenson's boots.

"Herb?"

I looked at his eyes—a long, straight-on stare—and he blinked and made a stabbing motion at his nose and backed off a step. Oddly, I felt some pity for him. The tiniest arms and wrists I'd ever seen—a sparrow's nervous system. He made me think of those sorry kids back in junior high who used to spend their time collecting stamps and butterflies, always off by themselves, no friends, no hope.

He took another half-step backward and said, very softly, "Look, I just wanted . . . I'm sorry, Herb."

I didn't move or look away or anything.

"Herb?"

"Talk, talk, talk."

"What can I say? It was—"

"Excuses?"

Jorgenson's tongue flicked out, then slipped away. He shook his head. "No, it was a bungle, and I don't . . . I was *scared.* All the noise and everything, the shooting, I'd never seen that before. I couldn't make myself move. After you got hit, I kept telling myself to move, move, but I couldn't *do* it. Like I was full of Novocaine or something. You ever feel like that? Like you can't even move?"

"Anyway," I said.

192

"And then I heard how you . . . the shock, the gangrene. Man, I felt like . . . couldn't sleep, couldn't eat. Nightmares, you know? Kept seeing you lying out there, heard you screaming, and . . . it was like my legs were filled up with cement. I *couldn't*."

His lip trembled, and he made a weird moaning sound—not quite a moan, feathery and high—and for a second I was afraid he might start crying. That would've ended it. I was a sucker for tears. I wouldn've patted his shoulder, told him to forget it. Thank God he tried to shake my hand. It gave me an excuse to spit.

"Kiss it," I said.

"Herb, I can't go back and do it over."

"Lick it, kiss it."

But Jorgenson just smiled. Very tentatively, like an invalid, he kept pushing his hand out at me. He looked so mournful and puppy-doggish, so damned hurt, that I made myself spit again. I didn't feel like spitting—my heart wasn't in it—but somehow I managed, and Jorgenson glanced away for a second, still smiling a weary little smile, resigned-looking, as if to show how generous he was, how bighearted and noble.

It almost made me feel guilty.

I got into the jeep, hit the ignition, left him standing there.

Guilty, for Chrissake. Why should it end up with *me* feeling the guilt? I hated him for making me stop hating him.

Thing is, it had been a vow. *I'll get him, I'll get him*—it was down inside me like a stone. Except now I couldn't generate the passion. Couldn't feel the anger. I still had to get back at him, but now it was a need, not a want. An obligation. To rev up some intensity, I started drinking a little—more than a little, a lot. I remembered the river, getting shot, the pain, how I kept calling out for a medic, waiting and waiting and waiting, passing out once, waking up, screaming, how the scream seemed to make new pain, the awful stink of myself, the sweating and shit and fear, Jorgenson's clumsy fingers when he finally got around to working on me. I remembered it all, every detail. *Shock*, I thought. *I'm dying of shock.* I tried to tell him that, but my tongue didn't connect with my brain. All I could do was go, "Ough! Ough!" I wanted to say, "You *jerk!* I'm *dying!* Treat for shock, treat for shock!" I remembered all that, and the hospital, and those giggling nurses. I even remembered the rage. Except I couldn't feel it anymore. Just a word—*rage*—spelled out in my head. No *feeling.* In the end, all I had were the facts. Number one: the guy had almost killed me. Number two: there had to be consequences. Only thing was, I wished I could've gotten some pleasure out of them.

I asked Lemon to give me a hand.

"No pain," I said. "Basic psy-ops, that's all. We'll just scare him. Mess with his head a little."

"Negative," Lemon said.

"Just spook the fucker."

"Sick, man."

Stiffly, like a stranger, Lemon looked at me for a long time. Then he moved across the hootch and lay down with a comic book and pretended to read. His lips were moving, but that didn't fool me a bit.

I had to get Azar in on it.

Azar didn't have Lemon's intelligence, but he had a better sense of justice.

"Tonight?" he said.

"Just don't get carried away."

"Me?"

Azar grinned and snapped his fingers. It was a tic. Snap, snap—whenever things got tight, whenever there was a prospect of action.

"Understand?"

"Roger-dodger," Azar said. "Only a game, right?"

We called the enemy "ghosts." "Bad night," we'd murmur. "Ghosts are out." To get spooked, in the lingo, meant not only to get scared but to get killed. "Don't get spooked," we'd say. "Stay cool, stay alive." The countryside was spooky; snipers, tunnels, ancestor worship, ancient papa-sans, incense. The land was haunted. We were fighting forces that didn't obey the laws of twentieth-century science. Deep in the night, on guard, it seemed that all of Nam was shimmering and swaying—odd shapes swirling in the dark; phantoms; apparitions; spirits in the abandoned pagodas; boogeymen in sandals.

When a guy named Olson was killed, in February, everybody started saying, "The Holy Ghost took him." And when Ron Ingo hit the booby trap, in April, somebody said he'd been made into a deviled egg—no arms, no legs, just a poor deviled egg.

It was ghost country, and Charlie was the main ghost. The way he came out at night. How you never really saw him, just thought you did. Almost magical—appearing, disappearing. He could levitate. He could pass through barbed wire. He was invisible, blending with the land, changing shape. He could fly. He could melt away like ice. He could creep up on you without sound or footsteps. He was scary.

In the daylight, maybe, you didn't believe in all this stuff. You laughed, you made jokes. But at night you turned into a believer: no skeptics in foxholes.

Azar was wound up tight. All afternoon, while we made preparations, he kept chanting, "Halloween, Halloween." That, plus the finger snapping, almost made me cancel the whole operation. I went hot and cold. Lemon wouldn't speak to me, which tended to cool it off, but then I'd start remembering things. The result was a kind of tepid numbness. No ice, no heat. I went through the motions like a sleepwalker—rigidly, by the numbers, no real emotion, no heart. I rigged up my special effects, checked out the battle terrain, measured distances, gathered the ordnance and gear we'd need. I was professional enough about it, I didn't miss a thing, but somehow it felt as if I were gearing up to fight somebody else's war. I didn't have that patriotic zeal.

Who knows? If there'd been a dignified way out, I might've taken it.

During evening chow, in fact, I kept staring across the mess hall at Jorgenson, and when he finally looked up at me, a puzzled frown on his face, I came very close to smiling. Very, very close. Maybe I was fishing for something. A nod, one last apology—anything. But Jorgenson only gazed back at me. In a strange way, too. As if he didn't *need* to apologize again. Just a straight, unafraid gaze. No humility at all.

To top it off, my ex-buddy Lemon was sitting with him, and they were having this chummy-chummy conversation, all smiles and sweetness.

That's probably what cinched it.

I went back to my hootch, showered, shaved, threw my helmet against the wall, lay down awhile, fidgeted, got up, prowled around, applied some fresh ointment, then headed off to find Azar.

Just before dusk, Delta Company stood for roll call. Afterward the men separated into two groups. Some went off to drink or sleep or catch a movie; the others trooped down to the base perimeter, where, for the next eleven hours, they would pull night guard duty. It was SOP—one night on, one night off.

This was Jorgenson's night on.

I knew that in advance, of course. And I knew his bunker assignment: number six, a pile of sandbags at the southwest corner of the perimeter. That morning I'd scouted every inch of his position; I knew the blind spots, the ripples of land, the places where he'd take cover in case of trouble. I was ready. To guard against freak screwups, though, Azar and I tailed him down to the wire. We watched him lay out his bedroll, connect the Claymores to their firing devices, test the radio, light up a cigarette, yawn, then sit back with his rifle cradled to his chest like a teddy bear.

"A pigeon," Azar whispered. "Roast pigeon on a spit. I smell it cookin'."

"Remember, though. This isn't for real."

Azar shrugged. He touched me on the shoulder, not roughly but not gently either. "What's real?" he said. "Eight months in Fantasyland, it tends to blur the line. Honest to God, I sometimes can't remember what real *is*."

Psychology—that was one thing I knew. I never went to college, and I wasn't exactly a whiz in high school either, but all my life I've paid attention to how things operate inside the skull. Example: You don't try to scare people in broad daylight. You wait. Why? Because the darkness squeezes you inside yourself, you get cut off from the outside world, the imagination takes over. That's basic psychology. I'd pulled enough night guard to know how the fear factor gets multiplied as you sit there hour after hour, nobody to talk to, nothing to do but stare blank-eyed into the Big Black Hole. The hours pile up. You drift; your brain starts to roam. You think about dark closets, madmen, murderers hiding under the bed, all those childhood fears. Fairy tales with gremlins and trolls and one-eyed giants. You try to block it out but you can't. You see ghosts. You blink and laugh and shake your head. Bullshit, you say. But then you remember the guys who died: Teddy, Olson, Ingo, maybe Becker, a dozen others whose faces you can't see anymore. Pretty soon you begin to think about the stories you've heard about Charlie's magic. The time some guys cornered two VC in a dead-end tunnel, no way out, but how, when the tunnel was fragged and searched, nothing was found but dead rats. A hundred stories. A whole bookful: ghosts swinging from the trees, ghosts wiping out a whole Marine platoon in twenty seconds flat, ghosts rising from the dead, ghosts behind you and in front of you and inside you. Your ears get ticklish. Tiny sounds get heightened and distorted, crickets become monsters, the hum of the night takes on a weird electronic tingle. You try not to breathe. You coil and tighten up and listen. Your knuckles ache, and your pulse ticks like an alarm clock. What's *that?* You jerk up. Nothing, you say, nothing. You check to be sure your weapon is loaded. Put it on full automatic. Count your grenades, make sure the pins are bent for quick throwing. Crouch lower. Listen, listen. And then, after enough time passes, things start to get bad.

"Come on, man," Azar said. "Let's *do* it." But I told him to be patient. "Waiting, that's half the trick," I said. So we went to the movies, *Barbarella* again, the sixth straight night. But it kept Azar happy—he was crazy about Jane Fonda. "Sweet Janie," he kept saying, over and over. "Sweet Janie boosts a man's morale." Then, with his hand, he showed me which part of his morale got boosted. An old joke. Everything was old. The movie, the heat, the booze, the war. I fell asleep during the second reel—a hot, angry sleep—and forty minutes later I woke up to a sore ass and a foul temper.

It wasn't yet midnight.

We hiked over to the EM club and worked our way through a six-pack. Lemon was there, at another table, but he pretended not to see me.

Around closing time, I made a fist and showed it to Azar. He smiled like a little boy. "Goody," he said. We picked up the gear, smeared charcoal on our faces, then moved down to the wire.

Azar lifted his thumb. Then he grinned and peeled away from me and began circling behind Bunker Six. For a second I couldn't move. Not fear, exactly; I don't know what it was. My boots felt heavy.

In a way, it was purely mechanical. I didn't think. I just shouldered the gear and crossed quietly over to a heap of boulders that overlooked Jorgenson's bunker.

I was directly behind him. Thirty-two meters away, exactly. My measurements were precise.

Even in the heavy darkness, no moon yet, I could make out Jorgenson's silhouette: a helmet, his shoulders, the rifle barrel. His back was to me. That was the heart of the psychology. He'd be looking out at the wire, the paddies, where the danger was; he'd figure his back was safe.

Quiet, quiet.

I knelt down, took out the flares, lined them up in front of me, unscrewed the caps, then checked my wristwatch. Still five minutes to go. Edging over to my left, I groped for the ropes, found them wedged in the crotch of two boulders. I separated them and tested the tension and checked the time again. One minute.

My head was light. Fluttery and taut at the same time. It was the feeling I remembered from the boonies, on ambush or marching at night through ghost country. Peril and doubt and awe, all those things and a million more. You wonder if you're dreaming. It's like you're in a movie. There's a camera on you, so you begin acting, following the script: "Oh, Cisco!" You think of all the flicks you've seen, Audie Murphy and Gary Cooper and Van Johnson and Roy Rogers, all of them, and certain lines of dialogue come back to you—"I been plugged!"—and then, when you get shot, you can't help falling back on them. "Jesus, Jesus," you say, half to yourself, half to the camera. "I been fuckin' *plugged!*" You expect it of yourself. On ambush, poised in the dark, you fight to control yourself. Not too much fidgeting; it wouldn't look good. You try to grin. Eyes open, be alert—old lines, old movies. It all swirls together, clichés mixing with your own emotions, and in the end you can't distinguish. . . .

I fingered one of the ropes, took a breath, then gave it a sharp jerk.

Instantly there was a clatter outside the wire.

I expected the noise, I was even tensed for it, but still my heart took a funny little hop. I winced and ducked down.

"Now," I murmured. "Now it starts." Eight ropes altogether. I had four, Azar had four. Each rope was hooked up to a homemade noisemaker out in front of Jorgenson's bunker—eight tin cans filled with rifle cartridges. Simple devices, but they worked.

I waited a moment, and then, very gently, I gave all four of my ropes a little tug. Delicate—nothing loud. If you weren't listening, listening hard, you might've missed it. But Jorgenson was listening. Immediately, at the first low rattle, his silhouette seemed to freeze. Then he ducked down and blended in with the dark.

There—another rattle. Azar this time.

We kept at it for ten minutes. Noise, silence, noise, silence. Stagger the rhythm. Start slowly, gradually build the tension.

Crouched in my pile of boulders, squinting down at Jorgenson's position, I felt a swell of immense power. It was the feeling Charlie must have. Like a puppeteer. Yank on the ropes, watch the silly wooden puppet jump and twitch. It made me want to giggle. One by one, in sequence, I pulled on each of the ropes, and the sound came bouncing back at me with an eerie, indefinite formlessness: a rattlesnake, maybe, or the creak of a closet door or footsteps in the attic—whatever you made of it.

"There now," I whispered, or thought. "There, there."

Jorgenson wasn't moving. Not yet. He'd be coiled up in his circle of sandbags, listening.

Again I tugged on my ropes.

I smiled. Eyes closed, I could almost *see* what was happening down there.

Bang. Jorgenson would jerk up. Rub his eyes, and bend forward. Muscles hard, brains like Jell-O. I could *see* it. Right now, at this instant, he'd glance up at the sky, hoping for a moon, a few stars. But no moon, no stars. He'd start talking to himself: "Relax, relax." He'd try to bring the night into focus, but the effort would only cause distortions: objects would seem to pick themselves up and twist and wiggle; trees would creep forward; the earth itself would begin to sway. Funhouse country. Trick mirrors and trapdoors and pop-up monsters. I could *see* it. It was as if I were down there *with* him, *beside* him. "Easy," he was muttering, "easy, easy, easy," but it didn't get easier.

"Creepy," Azar cackled. "Wet pants, goose bumps. Ghost town!" He held a beer out to me, but I shook my head.

We sat in the dim quiet of my hootch, boots off, smoking, listening to Mary Hopkin.

"So what next?"

"Wait," I said. "More of the same."

"Well, sure, but—"

"Shut up and *listen.*"

That high elegant voice. That melody. Someday, when the war was over, I'd go to London and ask Mary Hopkin to marry me. Nostalgic and crazy, but so what? That's what Nam does to you. Turns you sentimental, makes you want to marry girls like Mary Hopkin. You learn, finally, that you'll die. That's what war does to you.

Azar switched off the tape.

"Shit, man," he said. "Don't you got some *music?*"

And now, finally, the moon was out. We slipped back to our positions and went to work again with the ropes. Louder now, more insistently. The moon added resonance. Starlight shimmied in the barbed-wire reflections, layerings of shadow. Slowly, we dragged the tin cans closer to Jorgenson's bunker, and this, plus the moon, gave a sense of creeping peril, the slow tightening of a noose.

At 0300 hours, the very deepest part of the night, Azar set off the first trip flare.

There was a light popping sound out in front of Bunker Six. Then a sizzle. And then the night seemed to snap itself in half. The flare burned ten paces from the bunker.

I fired three more and it was instant daylight.

Then Jorgenson moved. There was a short, squeaky cry—not even a cry, really, just a sound of terror—and then a blurred motion as he jumped up and ran a few paces and rolled and lay still. His silhouette was framed like a cardboard cutout against the burning flares.

In the dark outside my hootch, even though I bent toward him, nose to nose, all I could see were Azar's white eyes.

"Enough," I told him.

"Oh, sure."

"Seriously."

"Serious?" he said. "That's too serious for me. I'm a fun lover."

When Azar smiled I saw the quick glitter of teeth, but then the smile went away, and I knew it was hopeless. I tried, though. I told him the score was even—no need to rub it in.

Azar just peered at me, almost dumbly.

"Poor Herbie," he said.

Nothing dramatic. The rest was inflection and those white eyes.

An hour before dawn he moved up for the last phase. Azar was in command now. I tagged after him, thinking maybe I could keep a lid on.

"Don't take this personal," Azar whispered. "You know? It's just that I like to finish things."

I didn't look at him; I looked at my fingernails, at the moon. When we got down near the wire, Azar gently put his hand on my shoulder, guiding me over toward the boulder pile. He knelt down and inspected the ropes and flares, nodded, peered out at Jorgenson's bunker, nodded again, removed his helmet and sat on it.

He was smiling again.

"Herbie?" he whispered.

I ignored him. My lips had a waxy, cold feel, like polished rock. I kept running my tongue over them. I told myself to stop it, and I did, but then a second later I was doing it again.

"You know something?" Azar said, almost to himself. "Sometimes I feel like a little kid again. Playing war, you know? I get into it. I mean, wow, I *love* this shit."

"Look, why don't we—"

"Shhhh."

Smiling, Azar put a finger to his lips, partly as a warning, partly as a nifty gesture.

We waited another twenty minutes. It was cold now, and damp. I had a weird feeling of brittleness, as if somebody could reach out and crush me like a Christmas-tree ornament. It was the same feeling out along the Song Tra Bong, when I got shot: I tried to grin wryly, like Bogie or Gable, and I thought about all the zingers Teddy Thatcher and I would use—except now Teddy was dead. Except when I called out for a medic, loud, nobody came. I started whimpering. The blood was warm, like dishwater, and I could feel my pants filling up with it. God, I thought, all this blood; I'll be *hollow.* Then the brittle feeling came over me. I passed out, woke up, screamed, tried to crawl but couldn't. I felt alone. All around me there was rifle fire, voices yelling, and yet for a moment I thought I'd gone deaf: the sounds were in my head, they weren't real. I smelled myself. The bullet had smashed through the colon, and the stink of my own shit made me afraid. I was crying. Leaking to death, I thought—blood and crap leaking out—and I couldn't quit crying. When Jorgenson got to me, all I could do was go "Ough! Ough!" I tightened up and pressed and grunted, trying to stop the leak, but that only made it worse, and Jorgenson punched me and told me to cut it out, ease off. *Shock,* I thought. I tried to tell him that: "Shock, man! Treat for shock!" I was lucid, things were clear, but my tongue wouldn't make the right words. And I was squirming. Jorgenson had to put his knee on my chest, turn me over, and when he did that, when he ripped my pants open, I shouted something and tried to wiggle away. I was hollowed out and cold. It was the *smell* that scared me. He was pressing down on my back—sitting on me, maybe, holding me down—and I kept trying to buck him off, rocking and moaning, even when he stuck me with morphine, even when he used his shirt to wipe my ass, and tried to plug up the hole. Shock, I kept thinking. And then, like magic, things suddenly clicked into slow motion. The morphine, maybe: I focused on those brand-new black boots of his, then on a pebble, then on a single wisp of dried grass—the last things I'd ever see. I couldn't look away, I didn't dare, and I couldn't stop crying.

Even now, in the dark, I felt the sting in my eyes.

Azar said, "Herbie."

"Sure, man, I'm solid."

Down below, the bunker was silent. Nothing moved. The place looked almost abandoned, but I knew Jorgenson was there, wide awake, and I knew he was waiting.

Azar went to work on the ropes.

It began like a breeze: a soft, lush, sighing sound. I was hugging myself. You can *die* of fright; it's possible, it can happen. I'd heard stories about it, about guys so afraid of dying that they died. You freeze up, your muscles snap, the heart starts fluttering, the brain floats away. It can *happen*.

"Enough," I whispered. "Stop it."

Azar looked at me and winked. Then he yanked sharply on all four ropes, and the sound made me squeal and jerk up.

"Call it quits, right now. Please, man."

Azar wasn't listening. His white eyes glowed as he shot off the first flare. "Please," I said, but then I watched the flare arc up over Jorgenson's bunker, very slowly, pinwheeling, exploding almost without noise, just a sudden red flash.

There was a short whimper in the dark. At first I thought it was Jorgenson, or maybe a bird, but then I knew it was my own voice. I bit down and folded my hands and squeezed.

Twice more, rapidly, Azar fired off red flares, and then he turned and looked at me and lifted his eyebrows.

"Herbie," he said softly, "you're a sad case."

"Look, can't we—"

"Sad."

I was frightened—of him, of us—and though I wanted to do something, wanted to stop him, I crouched back and watched him pick up the tear-gas grenade, pull the pin, stand up, smile, pause, and throw. Then the gas puffed up in a smoky cloud that partly obscured the bunker. Even from thirty meters away, upwind, I could smell it: not really *smell* it, though. I could *feel* it, like breathing razor blades.

"Jesus," I said, but Azar lobbed over another one, waited for the hiss, then scrambled over to the rope we hadn't used yet.

It was my idea. That morning I'd rigged it up: a sandbag painted white, a pulley system, a rope.

Show him a ghost.

Azar pulled, and out in front of Bunker Six, the white sandbag lifted itself up and hovered in the misty swirl of gas.

Jorgenson began firing. Just one round at first—a single red tracer that thumped into the sandbag and burned.

"Ooooooh!" Azar murmured. "Star light, star bright . . ."

Quickly, talking to himself, Azar hurled the last gas grenade, shot up another flare, then snatched the rope and made the white sandbag dance.

Jorgenson did not go nuts. Quietly, almost with dignity, he stood up and took aim and fired at the sandbag. I could see his profile against the red flares. His face seemed oddly relaxed. No twitching, no screams. He gazed out at the sandbag for several seconds, as if deciding something, and then he shook his head and smiled. Very slowly, he began marching out toward the wire. He did not crouch or run or crawl. He walked. When he reached the sandbag he stopped and turned, then he shouted my name, then he placed his rifle muzzle directly against the bag.

"Herbie!" he hollered, and he fired.

Azar dropped the rope.

"Show's over," he said. He looked down at me with pity. "Sad, sad, sad."

I was weeping.

"Disgusting," Azar said. "Herbie, you're the saddest fuckin' case I ever seen."

Azar smiled. He looked out at Jorgenson, then at me. Those eyes—falcon eyes, ghost eyes. He moved toward me as if to help me up, but then, almost as an afterthought, he kicked me hard in the knee.

"Sad," he murmured, then he turned and headed off to bed.

* * *

"No big deal," I told Jorgenson. "Leave it alone."

But he hooked my arm over his shoulder and helped me down to the bunker. My knee was hurting bad, but I didn't say anything.

It was almost full dawn now, a hazy silver dawn. For a while we didn't speak.

"So," he finally said.

"Right."

We shook hands. Neither of us put much emotion in it and we didn't look at each other's eyes.

Jorgenson pointed out at the shot-up sandbag.

"That was a nice touch," he said. "No kidding, it had me . . . a nice touch. You've got a real sense of drama, Herbie. Someday maybe you should go into the movies or something."

I nodded and said, "Sure I've thought about that."

"Another Hitchcock. *The Birds.* You ever see it?"

"Scary shit, eh," I said.

We sat for a while longer, then I started to get up, except my knee wasn't working right. Jorgenson had to give me a hand.

"Even?" he asked.

"Pretty much."

We almost shook hands again but we didn't. Jorgenson picked up his helmet, brushed it off, touched his funny little mustache, and looked out at the sandbag. His face was filthy.

Up at the medic's hootch, he cleaned and bandaged my knee, then we went to chow. We didn't have much to say. Afterward, in an awkward moment, I said, "Let's kill Azar."

Jorgenson smiled. "Scare him to death, right?"

"Right," I said.

"What a movie!"

I shrugged. "Sure. Or just kill him."

LANCE OLSEN

Family

Zach had been splitting wood most of the morning down by the shed when he first sniffed the familiar scent of his father, who had died five years ago in a mining accident. It was early spring. Pale green buds fuzzed the birches along Amos Ridge and the ground was soggy and almost black with runoff. Zach straightened and let the axe swing down by his side. He sniffed the air again like a cat suddenly aware of chicken livers on the kitchen counter. The intimate aroma was hard to pin down. Some honey was in it. And some salt. Cinnamon was there. And maybe some sourdough and pine needles. Beyond that, precise words didn't work well. Something sweet. Something acrid. Something like rum and something gamy and musty and earthy and clean all at the same time. He hadn't smelled anything like it for half a decade but he knew it right away, down behind his stomach, down behind his knees. It didn't frighten him and it didn't gladden him. It was more interest that he felt.

He turned and squinted a little into the intense sunshine fanning through the branches around him and saw his father standing with his hands in his pockets in a misty golden nimbus of light near a wild dogwood. He looked just as he had on the day he left the cabin for the last time, wearing overalls and olive-green rubber tie-up boots and a stained undershirt and yesterday's bread. They stood there eyeing each other for several heartbeats. Then Zach nodded slightly in a gesture of acknowledgment and his father's ghost nodded back slightly in a gesture of acknowledgment and Zach turned and picked up his axe and picked up a foot-and-a-half pine log and set it upright on the stump before him and started splitting wood once more because there was still a good part of an hour left until lunchtime.

Strip mining had peaked outside of Frenchburg, Kentucky, in the late sixties and early seventies and then it began falling off. Houses went up for sale. Ken's Market, one of the two grocery stores in town, shut down. The lone car dealership burned to the ground one night and for nearly two years no one seemed to have enough money to clean up the charred remains. But Zach's father didn't have much else that he felt comfortable doing so he decided to stick with mining as long as mining would stick with him. The company had brought in a mechanical monster called Little Egypt to make the job of digging more cost-efficient. Little Egypt was a machine the size of a small hotel. It was several stories tall and several stories wide and it was covered with gears the size of most men and it looked more like something people would use on Mars for space exploration than it did like something people would use in Menifee County for mining. Its sole purpose was to dig into the earth, slowly, cumbersomely, relentlessly, twenty-four hours a day, seven days a week, three hundred sixty-five days a year, processing coal as it went, eating, gnawing, wheezing and clanking away with a deafening sound. Zach's father, who was fifty-seven at the time, was part of a team of men responsible for keeping the huge gears of Little Egypt clear from crushed stone and grit and keeping them oiled and running smoothly. One day in late summer during his lunch break Zach's father sampled a swig too much of shine a buddy of his offered him, turned tipsy, and tripped as he was shinnying among the intricate workings of the behemoth. Instantly he was pulled into the innards of the creaking, banging, raucous colossus, kicking and screaming, and was never seen in one piece again. Until, of course, that spring day.

At noon Zach's wife, Amelia, called him for lunch. She had made bean soup and black bread and apple cobbler. He washed his hands at the spigot outside and walked around his dark blue Ford pickup truck and went in and sat at the table near the stove and began to eat. Amelia told him how she was going to Frenchburg to pick up some things and Zach told her how he was going to start patching the aluminum roof on the shed that had blown off during a big storm last November. Amelia told Zach how she had phoned

Madge at the next farm over and how Madge and Opal's dog Mork had been bitten by the first copperhead of the season and how the dog's snout had grown a lump that made it appear as if it were raising a plum under the flesh. As Zach listened he became aware of another presence in the kitchen. He glanced up and saw his father standing by the refrigerator, hands in the pockets of his overalls, watching the couple talk and eat. Zach's father wasn't smiling and he wasn't frowning but his eyes seemed a little more yellowish than usual and they seemed infinitely sad. He didn't speak and he didn't move. He just looked on as Zach raised a forkful of apple cobbler to his mouth and then washed it down with a gulp of water. Amelia noticed Zach was staring hard and long at the refrigerator and turned to see what he was looking at.

"Your father's here," she said after a moment.

"Yep," Zach said, cutting himself another bite of cobbler. "I reckon he is."

And that's how it started. Zach's father just appeared one beautiful spring day in a misty golden nimbus of light and Zach and Amelia acknowledged his appearance and then they didn't say a whole bunch else about it. After all, they had a lot of other things to think about. The field down the road needed plowing and planting. The shed needed mending. The winter wood needed tending to. And if they knew anything about Zach's father they knew he could take care of himself.

In the beginning Zach had the impression his father had come to tell him something he didn't already know. Maybe some secret about life that fathers come back from the dead to tell their sons because it's so important. Maybe some word of wisdom that would suddenly illuminate the world for him and release some vise that had been clamping his head so he could see things in a way he had never seen them before. But Zach's father never spoke. In fact he never made any sort of sound, not even when he walked across the wooden kitchen floor in his olive-green rubber tie-up boots. Zach waited two weeks, thinking his father might be trying to find the right words in which to stick his wisdom. And when at the end of that time Zach figured maybe his father could use some coaxing, he prompted him one rainy night by asking, "So what do you have to say for yourself?"

His father had nothing to say for himself. His facial expression didn't change. His eyes continued to look more yellowish than usual and infinitely sad and they focused on Zach's moving lips and then on Zach's blue eyes and then it occurred to Zach that the problem was that his father couldn't hear a word he was saying. There must have been some kind of interference between this world and the next. So he went and got a slip of paper and a pencil and he came back and wrote down his question and tried to give it to his father but the paper just passed through his father's extended hand as though it were no more than colored air and it fluttered to the floor.

When Zach told this to his wife, she told him she was convinced his father had come back to visit them because death was such a lonely place.

"Death isn't a lonely place at all," Zach said. "Lots of people are dead. He should have lots of company where he's at."

"That's all you know, Zach Ingram," she said.

Amelia smiled a considerate smile at Zach's father as you might at any infirm elderly parent or parent-in-law and let him accompany her from room to room and when she went outside to hang clothes and clean the outhouse. The ghost followed her at a respectful distance and took what seemed an exquisite interest in the simple chores of daily life: baking muffins, boiling pot roast, frying potatoes, scrubbing the skillet, folding down the quilt on the bed, hanging the winter coats in the back of the closet until next fall. She set a place for him at dinner and even put scraps on his plate although he couldn't sit at the table without falling through the chair and although when he bent down and tried to pick up a crumb with his tongue the crumb passed right through his jaw. She lit a candle for him at night and put it on the kitchen table and bought a newspaper for him to read every Sunday when she headed into church even though she knew he wouldn't be able to hold it. Every night he stood in their bedroom door when they were ready to go to sleep until they said good night to him and turned off the lights and then he would wander into the living room and stand by the window and wait for the first gray glow of dawn. Sometimes Zach would come upon him standing at the end of Amos Ridge on Whippoorwill Point amid wild-blueberry bushes and sassafras shrubs, looking out over the limestone cliffs and pines and cedars below, or kneeling by the thousands of large amazing jelly-bubble sacks of frog eggs in puddles that collected in ruts along the dirt road that lead up to the cabin.

They had no idea how good his presence made them feel until one morning in July Amelia went into the kitchen at six o'clock to grind some coffee and discovered he was gone. She thought he must be in the living room at the window watching the orange sun roll up behind the trees but when she checked no one was there. She stuck her head into all the closets and then she went outside and searched the shed and the outhouse and the area around the woodpile. She woke Zach and told him what had happened and he immediately dressed and headed down to Whippoorwill Point and called out his father's name and when he didn't see him there he walked all the way to Madge and Opal's farm before understanding somewhere under his lungs that he had lost his father a second time. It hurt Zach terribly, like a hole in the heart hurts, like a hammer in the head hurts. He slowly walked back into the cabin and told Amelia what he hadn't found and then sat down in a foldup chair on the porch and didn't get up for three weeks.

He sat there with his left ankle on his right knee and his hands in his lap and he looked out over the ridge and waited for his father to return. The hot hazy sky purpled at twilight. Crickets chirruped. Stars blinked on in the sky. And after a while he put his chin on his chest and fell asleep. In the morning he didn't eat his breakfast. In the afternoon he didn't eat his lunch. In the evening he didn't eat his dinner. Gradually he became as quiet as his father had been. Amelia told him he was getting thinner and more pathetic every day and when he didn't respond to her she began to eat his meals in addition to her own. First it was simply a way not to let the food go to waste. Then it was a way to express her own grief, her own pain, her own sense of absence. She gained five pounds the first week. She gained eight pounds the second. She gained ten the third.

Late in August as Zach watched the burning ball of the sun dip behind the treeline he noticed two figures walking up the road toward him. Through half-closed eyes he took them to be Madge and Opal coming over to check on them. But the closer the couple came the easier it was to tell they couldn't be Madge and Opal: the man was too old and the woman too short. Zach squinted and then he cocked his head to one side and then he shut one eye and then the other and then he opened both of them and then it struck him that he was looking at his parents, both of his parents, walking arm in arm up the road as they often did after dinner. His father was still wearing the same clothes he had on the day he fell into Little Egypt. His mother was still wearing the nightshirt she wore the day she said living without her husband was a stupid foolish thing and crawled into her bed and pulled up the quilt and turned her face to the wall. The couple mounted the porch and walked by Zach and he rose and followed them and saw them halt in the bedroom door, watching Amelia, chubby, soft, round, and wide-eyed, watch them back from the bed.

Zach's parents were extremely considerate. They always stood in corners, out of the way, arm in arm, or, at night, by the window in the living room from which they could see the first gray glow of dawn. They never asked for anything, never offered advice, and never nagged. They took obvious delight in the woodgrain rippling through the kitchen table; the black-and-white patterns on the wings of the willet that magically appeared on the roof of the shed one cold autumn afternoon; the yellow-green leaves of tobacco ready for harvest in the field down the road; the five-inch-long acorn-brown lizard that perched every morning on the top step, head raised with dignity and alertness, reptilian grin frozen on its face; the short stubby ocher squiggle near the woodpile, looking at them with its black glassbead eyes. Sometimes at dusk they craned their heads slightly and closed their eyes and sniffed at the cool evening air filled with honeysuckle, jasmine, wet grass, endive, pine, moist soil, leafy mulch, a hint of cantaloupe rinds. Sometimes in the afternoon they bent over near a tall curl of wild grass and studied the shiny blue body of the dragonfly arched just above it.

Zach and Amelia barely noticed it when his mother disappeared for two nights, returning with Cousin Virgil, who had died at thirty-one when his sleak black Toyota pickup skidded off Route 641 one rainy night in 1984 and smashed into a tree at eighty miles an hour. Or when Zach's father disappeared for nearly twenty-four hours, showing up cradling a baby in his arms, the Armstids' little girl, who had died last year when she was two weeks old because she had been born with some of her insides backward. Amelia was startled to see her uncle Ferrell, who'd been killed in 1968 somewhere in Cambodia although the government had always said it had been in Vietnam, and her aunt Helen, who'd taken her own life in 1963 when she caught her husband Tom fooling around with that cheap blond Bobbie Ann Stills. Zach tried to shake hands with his nephew Billy, whose spine had snapped during an accident on his Honda three-wheeler RV in 1987, and he tried to hug his mother's friend Mildred, who'd been bitten by a rattler while picking raspberries in 1956 on Madge and Opal's farm. Zeb, whose tractor engine fell on him two years ago while he was trying to tighten a bolt under it, showed up after all the leaves had dropped off the trees on Amos Ridge, and Abel, who choked on a chicken bone while watching the 1979 World Series Game, appeared just as the skies turned the color of a field mouse's neck and the first light snow began to fall.

"House sure is gettin' mighty cramped," Zach said when he stayed in on Thanksgiving to watch the Macy's parade on television.

"Family's family," Amelia said.

Her voice was simple, kind, and firm.

Somewhere in his chest around where hope is kept Zach knew she was right and didn't say anything else. He felt good. He felt complete. He felt a system of networks, harmonies, symmetries forming around him and had a tremendous sense of being somewhere, and knowing where that place was, and knowing what he should be doing and why and how. Only he had to confess at the same time that it was hard to see the TV set, what with little Dinamarie playing tag with Hazel and Gladys and Grace and Gary Bob and Johnny Jim in front of it and Angie smooching with George over at the kitchen table and Susie and Flinn bopping each other over the heads because Flinn had decided to appropriate Susie's favorite rhinestone pinky ring which he wouldn't give back and Aunt Beryl was trying unsuccessfully to bake and Uncle Gus was trying unsuccessfully to clean his 38-gauge shotgun on the living-room floor.

Sleeping was difficult too because the children wanted to be in bed between Zach and Amelia and many of the adults felt the need to stretch out on the floor nearby. Zach couldn't turn over or get up to visit the outhouse and he could never show his affection for Amelia, who had never stopped eating two portions of each meal every day and was now the size of a large flaccid dolphin. Little Ainsley and Harlan and Jake and Remus wanted to help with all the chores but they continually got under foot. More than once Zach bruised an ankle or knocked a knee, tripping because he didn't see one of the children waiting right behind him like a shadow. Amelia fared no better in the kitchen, where her mother-in-law and aunts supervised all her cooking, which she now performed nearly fourteen hours a day. Although no one except Zach and herself could eat, Amelia felt it only courteous to make enough for everyone. Sometimes at three in the morning she would rise and begin cooking breakfast and sometimes after midnight she would still be cleaning dishes. Over time she turned big as a baby elephant with wrinkled skin. She turned big as a bear whose stubby arms could no longer touch its sides. She turned big as a small whale which plowed through the cabin, shaking the foundation, moving ponderously yet carefully because she had lost sensation in her extremities and could no longer feel whether or not she might be bumping into things or people. Her neck disappeared and she forgot what it was like to bend from the waist and she only vaguely remembered what her once beautiful red-painted toenails had looked like.

By February the food supply had run down and Zach felt more tired than ever before in his life and Amelia could no longer walk. She could no longer fit through the bedroom door. Zach arranged pillows and blankets for her to lie in on the living-room floor and he began feeding her through a funnel because she could no longer lift her hands to help herself. The voluminous flesh of her face tugged at her tiny miraculous brown eyes and made her look a little oriental. Fat from her arms and legs puddled near her on the rug and made it appear as though she were melting. All the ghosts were fascinated by her lying there gazing at the ceiling, unable to speak just as they were unable to speak, unable to partake of the world just as they were unable to partake of the world. They seemed to understand that Amelia was eating for all of them now, that her metabolism was lovingly digesting for the whole family. The adults solemnly kneeled by her. The children frolicked on her body as though it were an astonishingly soft playground. They burrowed under her breasts and they slid down the wonderful smoothness of her thighs and they curled by her massive head to nap.

Every day more relatives appeared: Samuella, who had fallen down a well when she was three; Rachel, who had cooked up some bad mushrooms when she was twenty-seven; Ferris, who lived until he was ninety-four and would have lived until he was ninety-seven if he hadn't strained trying to pick up those logs in the autumn of 1934; Selby, who shot Seaton because Seaton had knifed Seldon because Seldon had got Leanne with child when she was four-teen. More relatives than Zach could count. More relatives than he could squeeze into the space of his imagination. More relatives than he could squeeze into the space of his cabin. They spilled out onto the porch and they spilled out into the shed and by the middle of March they were sleeping in the woods all the way down to Whippoorwill Point and Zach couldn't go anywhere without stumbling over them, being surprised by their faces, finding them staring back at him from around a corner or under a bush or behind a birch. He gave up all chores except feeding Amelia and he gave up all food except Amelia's food and he went out of the cabin less and less and he stayed in his bed more and more. The hot weather settled down and he realized he should have planted months ago. The cool weather came and he realized he had nothing more for Amelia to eat and nothing more to grow next year and no more firewood for next fall and winter.

In September as the sky blanched Zach walked down to Madge and Opal's and borrowed some tools and supplies and began to construct a mobile pulley near his dark blue Ford pickup truck. At first the gizmo looked like an eight-foot-tall oil well. Then it looked like an eight-foot-tall oil well on a sturdy wooden base with wheels under it. When it was done Zach removed the skeletal braces and rolled the contraption over to the sliding doors that led off the living room. He padded the sturdy wooden base with pillows and blankets and then went to the shed and got his snow shovel. He returned to the living room and gingerly navigated among the ghosts until he reached Amelia sprawled in the middle of the floor. He shoved his snow shovel under a lump of fat that he took to be her flank and heaved. Haltingly, falteringly, agonizingly, he began to roll his gigantic doughy wife across the floor. She could not move herself and she could not speak, but each time she found herself on her back she looked up at Zach with her exquisite brown oriental eyes, which were infinitely sad. Zach avoided her gaze and put his back into the work. He rolled her through the sliding doors and rolled her onto the porch and, having removed the banisters there, he rolled her over the edge and onto the padded mobile pulley, which groaned and wheezed and shook under Amelia's enormous weight. Then he struggled and pushed and heaved the mobile pulley around toward the front of the cabin.

Half an hour later Amelia flooded the back of his mud-spattered dark blue Ford pickup. Her rubbery arms and squelchy legs draped over the sides. Whitish flubber oozed all around her. She stared up at the trees above her. Zach climbed into the cab and turned on the engine and eased down the pedal. The shock absorbers creaked and swayed. The pickup lurched and began to crawl down the dirt road. When it tapped the first bump the metal belly scraped sand and gravel. But Zach didn't pay any attention to the bump and he didn't pay any attention to the sound. He already felt his heart expanding. He already felt a lightness entering his stomach. He blinked and smiled and looked up into the rearview mirror. All the dead people had collected outside the cabin behind him. They were watching the mud-spattered dark blue pickup creep down the driveway, winding its way toward Madge and Opal's and beyond. Zach saw them all raising their hands and waving goodbye. And, as he turned the corner, Zach caught a glimpse of them begin to follow.

PADGETT POWELL

Letter from a Dogfighter's Aunt, Deceased

*H*umpy, *the stuck-up librarian, ruined little Brody.* There is a certain truth down in there allowing them a purchase, at least, upon what happened. For I must say that if I had not read so many books, I could only have seen Brody as a runaway and so would probably not have helped him. This is not to say, of course, that a more legitimate member of the family might not have come along, spotted him making his break, and helped him out of another motive: to teach him a lesson, let us say. His father would have done that, moral waste dump that he is.

Humpy'd turn over in her grave. They say that when a family member uses incorrect grammar—grammar so out of form, that is, that they, its chief torturers on earth, can recognize something awry. *Don't say aint, your Aunt Humpy she'd turn over in her grave if she couldn't hardly hear you.* The remonstrated child, if he has some spirit, will sneak outside and put his mouth to the ground and yell *aint* into the dirt, blowing ants and debris away from his dirty face. They have one of these, Brody's wife's sister's child, for whom I am performing unbid the services of guardian angel, endeared more and more to the little delinquent with each lip-to-ground utterance he calls me with.

What does happen in heaven—heaven or hell, it is purely a matter of choice, and I have ever preferred, no matter the situation, the happier name for it—what does happen when one is alleged to turn in a grave, is generally that one does spin, but in a kind of spiritual pirouette. *Aint, yestiddy, spose to,* and all precocious profanity comes shouted into the dirt and I do my tickled dance and love that child the more for daring to torture the dead.

You needn't believe me, but that—a high quotient of daring—is what heaven (again, call it hell if you will) is all about, if I may speak in earthly parlance. Here we are the children we were born as, without the myriad prejudices and passions and myopias that made us the human beings we mortally became. And when you can see, from the vantage of correct vision restored, a young child yet unoccupied by teachings human, it will make you dance. All guardian angels are secured in the first six days of human life.

This is a bit specious-looking for you. You do not want to buy it. You wonder, I hope you do, how I inform you of Brody's thoughts on picking damp bolls, the cruelty of having to pick damp cotton, the day he decided to run away. I tell you. Humpy, the dead egghead spinster librarian, tells you all they think and know on earth.

One night my special child, Lonnie, was involved in some ghost-story telling in a tent in the backyard. He went outside and squatted close and yelled *haint.* No one had corrected him against the word (or will); it was to him clearly guilty of association with *aint.* Inches from his straining face a startled copperhead drew back. I possessed that snake to simply smile.

While it occurs to me, Brody did not become a dogfighter, any more than I was a queer librarian, despite his acknowledged associations with real dogfighters and despite my developed habit of looking over reading glasses at ill-bred men.

Here's Brody: I was going to be a *big dogfighter.* It's something. The *defenses.* The *dogs* is still good. But . . . it's not for me. It's the people. The trash. It's just not for me.

His old man, the preacher: My boy, I don't know *what* he is, come specifically to it. I know he's *not* a preacher. I know he's got a hundred monsters on chains in a piece of swamp he bought. You tell me. I don't know what he is. What does a man do with monsters on chains in a swamp comes by in a new Buick or new panel truck all the time? To talk about *nothing.* Any old kid can just trying things out run away once, even leave his own mother picking cotton alone—me, I was at the Bible convention. But to turn out a common man, that tries me, that almost tries my *faith.*

A dogfighter: Ho! Dogfight'll take ten *years* off your life. God the yelling and swearing and . . . niggers! Nigger don't know how to act no matter *where* you put him. And they aint all of it. I just go to cockfights now. *Gentlemen* still run a cockfight.

And dear Lonnie: My Aunt Humpy she is not buried very deep. She can hear talk. I think they don't even know where she is buried, because if you say certain things, anywhere, like even in Darlington under the canopy for a race, they say she can hear it even though you can't hear it yourself what your own self says. I want to be sure she hears it if she can get to turn over when she does.

My dear sister Cecelia: It's hard to say your own sister was a queer, but I have to admit it. That's the worst thing. Rescuing Brody from the brier patch with his tied-up suitcase was a drop in the bucket next to the main crimes, though that was about the first of the big ones. She was an intellectual. They say the Library over at Pembert is still ahead of its time, even though they stopped spending money on it when she died. She had nothing to do with Brody *staying* gone four years, coming home married to a Mormon girl of all things. They rolled up in a newish pickup, all sheepish looks at the ground, one sofa and about five of them dogs tied in the back, the dogs sitting on the sofa smiling at everything, like what a joke it all was.

Brody on the dogs: These dogs you read about eating babies don't have a thing to do with it. I've sold three thousand dogs in ten years and not one of them has bit a child or I'd know. I'd know about it *quick,* buddyro. I sell these dogs to people who pay $300, and when they pay $300 they don't expect something to eat their children. I don't think most of my dogs would bite a man without proper training, to tell the truth. They don't have to.

Ceece even says it: my picking up Brody and setting him on the road to ruin is minuscule. Queer. Ha. Or, Ho!

It is funny how folk can extrapolate aberrations ultimately all to the sexual: to say, the first child in a family of heathen to receive an education—to refine himself in virtually any way—will be sooner or later alleged homosexual. And naturally my relatives, my living relatives, were no different. Let me essay to classify us our clan directly, lest anyone waste energy on the very simplest of human taxonomy by my failure to state the obvious. We are white North Carolina Baptist—not the absolute worst run of trash on earth only because of a strange rubbing-off of the otherwise bogus FIRST IN FREEDOM presumptions wafting out of the Research Triangle.

I am grateful to be able now to take the long view, as we say here. We see the earth many ways, time in its various dimensions—one of my favorites is the micrometer slice of a living life. It is possible to see Brody that day as if he is on a thin transparency cut from the waxen log that his whole life, and all lives around him, have come to be. The nice light of one pure moment shines easily through him as he stands, nervous, courage-screwed, hugging his suitcase, in the wet briers. He looks rather like an overgrown, beaten child. We can place a slice of a later Brody over this same setting: today, for example, he stands there waiting for me (not for me, for anyone) in blue polyester pants the color of the sky and an olive duck shirt he cannot keep tucked in, his crew cut a little shaggy, looking diffidently off to the ground near one of his hard shoes, still looking a little beat-up. That quality remains: though he did not become a dogfighter, he did come close enough to share the common mark of the fraternity—the beaten-up. Dogfighters look, to a man (not to mention the ladies), beaten-up, despite brave cosmetics against it: buntline pistols, leather sport jackets, fancy boots, contractors' jewelry, full bellies and pomaded hair, and many, many Mickey Gilley smiles. This is partly why they take the pleasure they do in watching a thoroughbred dog, conditioned to a point suggesting piano wires and marble, reduced by another sculpted cat to a soft red lump resembling bloody terry cloth.

There is Brody, his nose suggesting a broken nose, his slightly wet eyes, looking mystified by nothing in particular, looking up the road at someone (me) coming, taking a deep breath to step out into view to discover if it is someone who will help or hinder him run away, to discover it is me and that he will need to compound the crime of escaping with that of lying. Yesm, he says, almost before I ask, Ceece knows I'm going. Of course she knows.

Well, I guess she would, I say, smiling, touching his knee, which he has pressed hard into his suitcase, as though he would if he could compress the thing into nothing so that no more suspicion might be raised. This was the moment I first knew I was going to die. I do not mean to sound so melodramatic—I was to live yet for years.

I mean to say that when I saw Brody running, and when I saw myself aiding and abetting, I saw myself fully defined as the black sheep I was, and for once I was legitimate (I had *company*—with Brody there we were a conspiracy of two black-wool fools), and in a complex surge of emotion I loved little Brody, loved him much more than any queer aunt could confess, and I saw at the same time, as one truly does very few times in a normal life, that I was actually going to die someday, go to a funeral as the lead, and I considered seducing Brody and dismissed seducing Brody. He would hoot to hear that today, but *that* day he would not have chuckled, and I could have had my way with him, if a queer forty-year-old librarian popping out of a girdle did not scare the priapic wits out of him, which I presumed at the time not unlikely. And so I put Brody out on a corner in Lumberton, helped him become in his attempted escape the only other member of this clan to attend college (one of several accidents that befell him), and stand accused of—not merely accused, am held responsible for—his low living today, the very thing his escape was to have been from, and I the only one who helped him go.

Brody has come to ignore the church, crime one, and make money without holding a job, crime two. At this minute he is talking to a man he cannot understand in Taiwan who wants ten grown bulldogs. The Oriental cannot understand Brody either, because the English he knows is not the English Brody practices. And Brody is not altogether fluent in some Charlie Chan English that seems to parody the *r/l* problem.

Brody says: Imone sin you time *young* dawgs.

Mr. Ho says: They rast rong time we purchase rots burrdog to you, Mista Blode.

Brody: No sir, iss not the wrong time. I just caint keep puppies till they grown dawgs.

Ho: Rots.

Brody: Rots?

Ho: Yes!

Brody: What do you *mean?*

Ho: Satisfactly.
Brody: *What* is?
Ho: You, Mista Blode.
Brody: Send me a check for five thousand dollars.
Ho: Thank you.

How did Brody's escape fail? Or did it fail? Perhaps it did not. He came back with full intention of becoming a dogfighter. He fell, or stopped, short. He decided to make the dogs but not make them fight. Which is an inaccurately cute way of putting it: one doesn't need to make these dogs fight. They volunteer.

I couldn, you know, stand to knock so many dawgs in the head. That's what you have to do. He is talking about culling, culling the cowards and the inept from the brave and the strong, which in practice means shooting beautiful year-old dogs because they do not measure up. It is a point of pride with a dogfighter to allow a dog to *live* on his yard. This blood courage in dogs (parlance; I mean *in dogfighting,* but one commonly says *in dogs*) is an outrigger courage, a pontoon of vicarious guts running beside your own tipsy, slender, sinkable soul, your soul which accepts bad teeth, bad jobs, bad diet, which purports to refuse all injustice done you since and because of the Civil War, purports to accept no slight or slander and yet must take all and every and so locates one accidental day, or night, a *dog,* two dogs, with jaw muscles like golf balls addressing each other *like men*—not taking no for an answer. Your trod-down my-daddy's-daddy's-daddy-was-whipped-and-lost-his-cotton soul, now eating Cheetos instead of smothered quail and oysters hauled up from Charleston, standing there in blue jeans with a pistol in your armpit, sees an answer to all the daily failures of a failing late-trailer-payment life, and a dogfighter is born.

The real item: I tookeem home and tiedeem up in a inner tube and hungeem and beateem with a hammer. I coottn killeem acause he was swinging and bouncin like iss, springy, the rubber, you know, leteem git away. But I gotteem the quittin bastard, quit on me like that, I never been so embairsed in my life.

—If a dog fight for me an hour good as that—

—And you a fool, too.

—Well, tell you what, Jackie. Meet me ahine my house with your tube and your hammer, and I get me a rig, and we get up in a tree and go at it. I want to see *you* go an hour.

—You don't have the *least* notion what a good dog *is*.

—Yes I do. You had one.

—That's fuckin right. I had one. And I git rid of the next one I git like it the damned straight same way.

Alive, I never went to a dogfight, but I have been since. I did also go one night looking for Brody in his kennel, the first time I went there, and found myself suddenly ringed by what seemed large big cats axled to the ground on chains begging me with bloody wags to pet them.

His old man: If his Aunt Humpy had known what she was setting in motion that morning she'd of killed herself, I hope. We are not fancy people, airs and all, but we are not common. She might have even knowed he was lying, that Cecelia would of never let him go to Lumberton or anywhere else during cotton. But even so she could not have knowed that that little lift would have created our largest disgrace. It defies my logic. It defies my logic.

Brody: She wouldn't let it wait to dry out, and when you pull you know on the bolls, when they wet, they *pool* back, and you get this—it hurts.

My fine living relatives say that, in general, my problem was reading too many books. What they cannot guess is that when I saw Brody step out of the briers on the Lumberton road I thought, There's Brody, making his move, as wild and plenary *as a character in a book.* I knew Ceece wasn't letting him go anywhere. He had on these huge, hard shoes and brilliant white socks, and he was pigeon-toed. His suitcase had straw on it. He even tried while standing to hide the suitcase between his legs, which made him more pigeon-toed.

I bought a beanfield, if fifty acres can be called a field, and Land Banked it, let it fallow, and took to walking the regenerating scrub in my after-work dress: pantsuit and parasol. For the first years I could be seen, of course, so the people were able to graft on one more badge of idiosyncrasy to the already highly decorated spinster librarian. The parasol contributed more to this, I think, than simply walking one's field (indeed, walking banked land out here is regarded a normal if unfortunate substitute for farming it), the parasol that carried with it—last seen bobbing over the tops of three-year pines—a suggestion of spinsterism that I believe included in local mythos not only elements Southern but New England as well. I was a kind of Scarlett-Emily, witch and Poppins, gathering beggar weeds. The truth was I carried the umbrella less from a concern with image or sun than from a concern with lizards, of which I had an inordinate fear and an equally misinformed notion of parrying the assaults of with said rapier.

This field was a curious purchase for anyone, let alone a woman seen swordfighting lizards at dusk in it. It was worthless as cropland. But I had decided at some point to own some earth, and it did not matter to me which part, and that scrubby squat is what I took. Brody sweet himself put the idea in my head when he bought the adjacent fifteen acres that were even less desirable by farming standards. He got his dog stock chained down to it and managed thereby to depress even further the local values. So I took an adjacent fifty. You do things like that in life, and the less readily the act can be made to seem sensible the more gratifying it is. I was proud, daft owner of my useless spread, and in five years of strolling it I had intimate trails, trails pressed into the weeds by a combination of my random prowling and the more purposed prowling of rabbits and rodents and I think in the end even deer. I was happy with that sorry field.

I will confess to having lived finally a hungry, hollow life. I never left Pembroke and I had the stuff to have been anywhere. Yet whether my life was a failure or not is not the large matter, I hope: for I look at all the people who for one reason or another do not rise but remain routine and routinely small, and their failure as a class does not seem to amount to anything.

I took my pleasure then and now in small things—watching Brody run away one day, years later listening to him explain why he could not be a dogfighter, he there on the edge of his worthless plot and I on mine, his wild-eyed cat-dogs wagging at us. Brody excitedly telling me of his discovery of a new food concentrate calculated to save money and back, and of two puppies to be certified for international shipping—to Australia this time, where a man wants to see what they can do to kangaroos.

"Kangaroos?" I say. "Why hurt kangaroos?"

"I don't know, Humpy."

We must both have pictured our private, limited visions of kangaroo—gloved in carnivals, hopping the veld—and I remember thinking this is life, my life, standing at dusk speculating about the fate of a dimly known marsupial with my dimly known nephew I once rescued from pulling damp bolls and maybe from more, and Brody no doubt was thinking a bit less heavily, with refreshingly less profundity, about sending the *red-and-white male or the larger washed-out gray dog, who might do better* against the down-under foe he's heard can disembowel a man.

"Good night, Brody."

"Night, Humpy."

He stands there a minute more, as I do, he in his slippery, hard dress shoes which he perversely insists on wearing instead of practical boots. He is yet escaping that original, damp field, dressed for travel. The moon glints off these large, shiny wingtips, which trod uncertain across the sloping dirt to the jumping dogs.

ANNE SEXTON

The Ghost

I was born in Maine, Bath, Maine, Down East, in the United States of America, in the year of 1851. I was one of twelve (though only eight lasted beyond the age of three) and within the confines of that state we lived at various times in our six houses, four of which were scattered on a small island off Boothbay Harbor. They were not called houses on that island for they are summering places and thus entitled cottages. My father, at one time Governor, was actually a frustrated builder and would often say to the carpenters, "another story upwards, please." One house had five stories, and although ugly to look upon, stood almost at the edge of the rocks that the sea locked in and out of.

I was, of course, a Victorian lady, however I among my brothers and sisters was well educated and women were thought, by my father, to be as *interesting* as men, or as capable. My education culminated at Wellesley College, and I was well versed in languages, both the ancient and unusable as well as the practical, for the years after Wellesley College I spent abroad perfecting the accent and the idiomatic twists. Later I held a job on a newspaper. But it was not entirely fulfilling and made no use of these foreign languages but only of the mother tongue. I was fortunately a maiden lady all my life, and I do say *fortunate* because it allowed me to adopt to maiden heart the nieces and nephews, the grandnieces, the grandnephews. And there was one in particular, my sister's grandchild, who was named after me. And as she wore my name, I wore hers, and at the end of my life she and her mother and an officious practical nurse stood their ground beside me as I went out. Death taking place twice. Once at sixty-four when my ears died and the most ignominious madness overtook me. Next the half-death of sixty shock treatments and then still deaf as a haddock—a half-life until seventy-seven spent in a variety of places called nursing homes. Dying on a hot day in a crib with diapers on. To die like a baby is not desirable and just barely tolerable, for there is fear spooned into you and radios playing in your head. I, the suffragette, I of the violet sachets, I who always changed my dress for dinner and kept my pride, died like a baby with my breasts bared, my corset, my camisole, tucked away, and every other covering that was my custom. I would have preferred the huntsman stalking me like a moose to that drooling away.

There is more to say of my lifetime, but my interest at this point, my main thrust, is to tell you of my life as a ghost. Life? Well, if there is action and a few high kicks, is that not similar to what is called life? At any rate, I *bother* the living, act up a bit, slip like a radio into their brains or a sharp torchlight going on suddenly to blind and then reveal myself. (With no explanation!) I can put a moan into my namesake's dog if I wish to make a point. (I have always liked to make my point!) It is *her* life I linger over, for she is wearing my name and that gives a ghost a certain right that no one knows when they present the newborn with a name. She is somewhat aware—but of course denies it as best she can—that there are any ghosts at all. However, it can be noted that she is unwilling to move into a house that is not newly made, she is unwilling to live within the walls that might whisper and tell stories of other lives. It is her ghost theory. But like many, she has made the perfect mistake; the mistake being that a ghost belongs to a house, a former room, whereas this ghost (and I can only speak for myself for we ghosts are not allowed to converse about how we go about practicing our trade) belongs to my remaining human, to bother her, to enter the human her, who once was given my name. I could surmise that there are ghosts of houses wading through the attics where once they hoarded their hoard, throwing dishes off shelves, but I am not sure of it. I think the English believe it because their castles were passed on from generation to generation. Indeed, perhaps an American ghost does something quite different, because the people of the present are very mobile, the executives are constantly thrown from city to city, dragging their families with them. But I

do not know for I haunt namesake's, and she lives in the suburbs of Boston—
despite a few moves from new house to new house. I follow her as a hunting
dog follows the scent, and as long as she breathes, I will peer in her window
at noon and watch her sip the vodka, and if I so desire, can place one drop
of an ailment into it to teach her a little lesson about such indulgence and
imperfection. I gave her five years ago a broken hip. I immobilized her flat on
the operating table as I peered over his shoulder, the surgeon said as he did
a final X-ray before slicing in with his knife, "shattered," and there was
namesake, her hip broken like a crystal goblet and later with two four-inch
screws in her hip she lay in a pain that had only been an intimation of pain
during the birth of two children. A longing for morphine dominated her hours
and her conscience rang in her head like a bell tolling for the dead. She had
at the time been committing a major sin, and I found it so abhorrent that it
was necessary to make my ailment decisive and sharp. When the morphine was
working, she was perfectly lucid, but as it wore off, she sipped a hint of madness
and that too was an intimation of things to come. Later, I tried lingering fevers
that were quite undiagnosable and then when the world became summer and
the green leaves whispered, I sat upon leaf by leaf and called out with a voice
of my youth and cried, "Come to us, come to us" until she finally pulled down
each shade of the house to keep the leaves out of it—as best she could. Then
there are the small things that I can do. I can tear the pillow from under her
head at night and leave her as flat as I was when I lay dying and thus crawl
into her dream and remind her of my death, lest it be her death. I do not in
any way consider myself evil but rather a good presence, trying to remind her
of the Yankee heritage, back to the *Mayflower* and William Brewster, or back
to kings and queens of the Continent who married and intermarried. She is
becoming altogether too modern, and when a man enters her, I am constantly
standing at the bedside to observe and call forth a child to be named my name.
I do not actually *watch* the copulation because it is an alien act to me, but I
know full well what it should mean and have often plucked out a few of her
birth-control pills in hopes. But I fear it is a vain hope. She is perhaps too old
to conceive, or if she should, the result might be imperfect. As I stand there
at that bedside while this man enters her, I hum a little song into her head

that we made up, she and I, when she was eight and we sang each year thereafter for years. We had kissed thirteen lucky times over the mistletoe that hung under a large chandelier and two door frames. This mistletoe was *our* custom and *our* act and tied the knot more surely year by year. The song that she sang haunted me in the madness of old age and now I let it enter her ear and at first she feels a strange buzzing as if a fly has been caught in her brain and then the song fills her head and I am at ease.

She senses my presence when she cooks things that are not to my liking, or drives beyond the speed limit, or makes a left turn when it says NO LEFT TURN. For I play in her head the song called "The Stanley Steamer" for Mr. Stanley's wife was my close friend and we took a memorable ride from Boston to Portland and the horses were not happy, but we disobeyed nothing and were cautious—though I must add, a bit dusty and a little worse for wear at the end of the trip.

It is unfortunate that she did not inherit my felicity with the foreign tongue. But not all can be passed on, the genes carry some but not all. As a matter of fact, it is far *more* unfortunate that she did not inherit my gift with the English language. But here I do interfere the most, for I put *my* words onto her page, and when she observes them, she wonders how it came about and calls it "a gift from the muse." Oh how sweet it is! How adorable! How the song of the mistletoe rips through the metal of death and plays on, singing from two mouths, making me a loyal ghost. Loyal though I am I have felt for a long time something missing from her life that she must experience to be whole, to be truly alive. Although one might say it be the work of the devil, I think that it is not (the devil lurks among the living and she must push him out day by day, but first he must enter her as he entered me in my years of deafness and lunacy). Thus I felt it quite proper and fitting to drop such a malady onto a slice of lemon that floated in her tea at 4 P.M. last August. It started immediately and became in the end immoderate. First the teacup became two teacups, then three, then four. Her cigarettes as she lit them in confusion tasted like dung and she stamped them out. Then she turned on the radio and all it would give at every station on the dial were the names and the dates of the dead. She turned it off quickly, but it would not stop playing.

The dog chased her tail and then attacked the woodwork; baying at the moon as if their two bodies had gone awry. At that point, she sat very still. She kept telling herself to dial "O" for operator but could not. She shut her eyes, but they kept popping open to see the objects of the kitchen multiply, widen, stretch like rubber and their colors changing and becoming ugly and the lemon floated in the multiplying and dividing teacups like something made of neon.

When her husband returned home, she was as if frozen and could not speak, though I had put many words in her head they were like a game and were mixed and had lost their meaning. He shook her, she wobbled side to side. He spoke, he spoke. For an hour at least he tried for response, then dialed the doctor, and she went into Mass. General, half carried, half walking like a drunk, feet numb as erasers, legs melting and stiffening and was given the proper modern physical and neurological exams, EEG, EKG, etc., but the fly in her head still buzzed and the obituaries of the radio played on, and when they took her in an ambulance to a mental hospital, she could not sign her name on the commitment papers but spoke at last, "no name." They could not, those psychiatrists, nurses' aides, diagnose exactly and most days she is not able to swallow. The tranquilizers they shot into her, variety after variety, have no power over *this*. I will give her a year of it, an exact to the moment year of it, and during that time, I will be constantly at her side to push the devil from her although there was no one in my time to push him from me. She is at this point enduring a great fear, but I am with her, I am holding her hand and she senses this despite her conviction that each needle is filled with Novocain, for that is the effect on her limbs and parts. Still, the slight pressure of my hand, the sound of the song of the mistletoe must comfort her. Right now they scream to her and fill her with an extraordinary terror. But somehow, I know full well she is indubitably pleased that I have not left. Nor do I plan to.

FAY WELDON

Angel, All Innocence

There is a certain kind of unhappiness, experienced by a certain kind of woman married to a certain kind of man, which is timeless: outrunning centuries, interweaving generations, perpetuating itself from mother to daughter, feeding off the wet eyes of the puzzled girl, gaining fresh strength from the dry eyes of the old woman she will become—who, looking back on her past, remembers nothing of love except tears and the pain in the heart which must be endured, in silence, in case the heart stops altogether.

Better for it to stop, now.

Angel, waking in the night, hears sharp footsteps in the empty attic above and wants to wake Edward. She moves her hand to do so, but then stills it for fear of making him angry. Easier to endure in the night the nightmare terror of ghosts than the day-long silence of Edward's anger.

The footsteps, little and sharp, run from a point above the double bed in which Angel and Edward lie, she awake, he sleeping, to a point somewhere above the chest of drawers by the door; they pause briefly, then run back again, tap-tap, clickety-click. There comes another pause and the sound of pulling and shuffling across the floor; and then the sequence repeats itself, once, twice. Silence. The proper unbroken silence of the night.

Too real, too clear, for ghosts. The universe is not magic. Everything has an explanation. Rain, perhaps? Hardly. Angel can see the moon shine through the drawn blind, and rain does not fall on moonlit nights. Perhaps, then, the rain of past days collected in some blocked gutter, to finally splash through

230

onto the rolls of wallpaper and pots of paint on the attic floor, sounding like footsteps through some trick of domestic acoustics. Surely! Angel and Edward have not been living in the house for long. The attic is still unpainted, and old plaster drops from disintegrating laths. Edward will get round to it sooner or later. He prides himself on his craftsman's skills, and Angel, a year married, has learned to wait and admire, subduing impatience in herself. Edward is a painter—of pictures, not houses—and not long out of art school, where he won many prizes. Angel is the lucky girl he has loved and married. Angel's father paid for the remote country house, where now they live in solitude and where Edward can develop his talents, undisturbed by the ugliness of the city, with Angel, his inspiration, at his side. Edward, as it happened, consented to the gift unwillingly, and for Angel's sake rather than his own. Angel's father Terry writes thrillers and settled a large sum upon his daughter in her child-hood, thus avoiding death duties and the anticipated gift tax. Angel kept the fact hidden from Edward until after they were married. He'd thought her an ordinary girl about Chelsea, sometime secretary, sometime barmaid, sometime artist's model.

Angel, between jobs, did indeed take work as an artist's model. That was how Edward first clapped eyes upon her; Angel, all innocence, sitting nude upon her plinth, fair curly hair glinting under strong lights, large eyes closed beneath stretched blue-veined lids, strong breasts pointed upwards, stubby pale bush irritatingly and coyly hidden behind an angle of thigh that both gave Angel cramps and spoiled the pose for the students. So they said.

"If you're going to be an exhibitionist," as Edward complained to her later in the coffee bar, "at least don't be coy about it." He took her home to his pad, that handsome, dark-eyed, smiling young man, and wooed her with a nostalgic Sinatra record left behind by its previous occupant; half mocking, half sincere, he sang love words into her pearly ear, his warm breath therein stirring her imagination, and the gentle occasional nip of his strong teeth in her flesh promising passion and pain beyond belief. Angel would not take off her clothes for him: he became angry and sent her home in a taxi without her fare. She borrowed from her flatmate at the other end. She cried all night, and the next day, sitting naked on her plinth, had such swollen eyelids as to set a student or two scratching away to amend the previous day's work. But she lowered her thigh, as a gesture of submission, and felt a change in the studio ambience from chilly spite to warm approval, and she knew Edward had forgiven her. Though she offered herself to multitudes, Edward had forgiven her.

"I don't mind you being an exhibitionist," Edward said to her in the coffee bar, "in fact that rather turns me on, but I do mind you being coy. You have a lot to learn, Angel." By that time Angel's senses were so aroused, her limbs so languid with desire, her mind so besotted with his image, that she would have done whatever Edward wished, in public or in private. But he rose and left the coffee bar, leaving her to pay the bill.

Angel cried a little, and was comforted by and went home with Edward's friend Tom, and even went to bed with him, which made her feel temporarily better, but which she was to regret forever.

"I don't mind you being a whore," Edward said before the next studio session, "but can't you leave my friends alone?"

It was a whole seven days of erotic torment for Angel before Edward finally spent the night with her: by that time her thigh hung loosely open in the studio. Let anyone see. Anyone. She did not care. The job was coming to an end anyway. Her new one as secretary in a solicitor's office began on the following Monday. In the nick of time, just as she began to think that life and love were over, Edward brought her back to their remembrance. "I love you," he murmured in Angel's ear. "Exhibitionist slut, typist, I don't care. I still love you."

Tap-tap, go the footsteps above, staring off again: clickety-click. Realer than real. No, water never sounded like that. What then? Rats? No. Rats scutter and scamper and scrape. There were rats in the barn in which Angel and Edward spent a camping holiday together. Their tent had blown away: they'd been forced to take refuge in the barn. All four of them. Edward, Angel, Tom and his new girlfriend Ray. Angel missed Edward one night after they all stumbled back from the pub to the barn, and searching for him in the long grass beneath an oak tree, found him in tight embrace with Ray.

"Don't tell me you're hysterical as well as everything else," complained

Edward. "You're certainly irrational. You went to bed with Tom, after all."

"But that was before."

Ah, before, so much before. Before the declarations of love, the abandoning of all defense, all prudence, the surrendering of common sense to faith, the parceling up and handing over of the soul into apparent safekeeping. And if the receiving hands part, the trusted fingers lose their grip, by accident or by design, why then, one's better dead.

Edward tossed his Angel's soul into the air and caught it with his casual hands.

"But if it makes you jealous," he said, "why I won't . . . Do you want to marry me? Is that it? Would it make you happier?"

What would it look like when they came to write his biography? Edward Holst, the famous painter, married at the age of twenty-four—to what? Artist's model, barmaid, secretary, crime-writer's daughter? Or exhibitionist, whore, hysteric? Take your choice. Whatever makes the reader happiest, explains the artist in the simplest terms, makes the most successful version of a life. Crude strokes and all.

"Edward likes to keep his options open," said Tom, but would not explain his remark any further. He and Ray were witnesses at the secular wedding ceremony. Angel thought she saw Edward nip Ray's ear as they all formally kissed afterwards, then thought she must have imagined it.

This was his overture of love: turning to Angel in the dark warmth of the marriage bed, Edward's teeth would seek her ear and nibble the tender flesh, while his hand traveled down to open her thighs. Angel never initiated their lovemaking. No. Angel waited, patiently. She had tried once or twice, in the early days, letting her hand roam over his sleeping body, but Edward not only failed to respond, but was thereafter cold to her for days on end, sleeping carefully on his side of the bed, until her penance was paid and he lay warm against her again.

Edward's love made flowers bloom, made the house rich and warm, made water taste like wine. Edward, happy, surrounded Angel with smiles and soft encouragement. He held her soul with steady hands. Edward's anger came unexpectedly, out of nowhere, or nowhere that Angel could see. Yesterday's permitted remark, forgiven fault, was today's outrage. To remark on the weather to break an uneasy silence, might be seen as evidence of a complaining nature: to be reduced to tears by his first unexpected biting remark, further fuel for his grievance.

Edward, in such moods, would go to his studio and lock the door, and though Angel (soon learning that to weep outside the door or beat against it, moaning and crying and protesting, would merely prolong his anger and her torment) would go out to the garden and weed or dig or plant as if nothing were happening, would feel Edward's anger seeping out from under the door, darkening the sun, poisoning the earth; or at any rate spoiling her fingers in relation to the earth, so that they trembled and made mistakes and nothing grew.

The blind shakes. The moon goes behind a cloud. Tap, tap, overhead. Back and forth. The wind? No. Don't delude yourself. Nothing of this world. A ghost. A haunting. A woman. A small, desperate, busy woman, here and not here, back and forth, out of her time, back from the grave, ill-omened, bringing grief and ruin: a message that nothing is what it seems, that God is dead and the forces of evil abroad and unstoppable. Does Angel hear, or not hear?

Angel, through her fear, wants to go to the bathroom. She is three months pregnant. Her bladder is weak. It wakes her in the night, crying out its need, and Angel, obeying, will slip cautiously out of bed, trying not to wake Edward. Edward needs unbroken sleep if he is to paint well the next day. Edward, even at the best of times, suspects that Angel tossing and turning, and moaning in her sleep, as she will, wakes him on purpose to annoy.

Angel has not yet told Edward that she is pregnant. She keeps putting it off. She has no real reason to believe he does not want babies: but he has not said he does want them, and to assume that Edward wants what other people want is dangerous.

Angel moans aloud: afraid to move, afraid not to move, afraid to hear, afraid not to hear. So the child Angel lay awake in her little white bed, listening to her mother moaning, afraid to move, afraid not to move, to hear or not to hear. Angel's mother was a shoe-shop girl who married the new assistant manager after a six-week courtship. That her husband went on to make a fortune, writing thrillers that sold by the million, was both Dora's good fortune and tragedy. She lived comfortably enough on alimony, after all, in a way she could never have expected, until dying by mistake from an overdose of sleeping pills. After that Angel was brought up by a succession of her father's mistresses and au-pairs. Her father Terry liked Edward, that was something, or at any rate he had been relieved at his appearance on the scene. He had feared an element of caution in Angel's soul: that she might end up married to a solicitor or stockbroker. And artists were at least creative, and an artist such as Edward Holst might well end up rich and famous. Terry had six Holst canvases on his walls to hasten the process. Two were of his daughter, nude, thigh slackly falling away from her stubby fair bush. Angel, defeated—as her mother had been defeated. "I love you, Dora, but you must understand. I am not *in* love with you." As I'm in love with Helen, Audrey, Rita, whoever it was: off to meetings, parties, off on his literary travels, looking for fresh copy and new backgrounds, encountering always someone more exciting, more interesting, than an ageing ex–shoe-shop assistant. Why couldn't Dora understand? Unreasonable of her to suffer, clutching the wretched Angel to her alarmingly slack bosom. Could he, Terry, really be the only animation of her flesh? There was a sickness in her love, clearly; unaccompanied as it was by the beauty which lends grace to importunity.

Angel had her mother's large, sad eyes. The reproach in them was inbuilt. Better Dora's heart had stopped (she'd thought it would: six months pregnant, she found Terry in the housemaid's bed. She, Dora, mistress of servants! What bliss!) and the embryo Angel never emerged to the light of day.

The noise above Angel stops. Ghosts! What nonsense! A fallen lath grating and rattling in the wind. What else? Angel regains her courage, slips her hand out from beneath Edward's thigh preparatory to leaving the bed for the bathroom. She will turn on all the lights and run. Edward wakes; sits up.

"What's that? What in God's name's that?"

"I can't hear anything," says Angel, all innocence. Nor can she, not now. Edward's displeasure to contend with now; worse than the universe rattling its chains.

"Footsteps, in the attic. Are you deaf? Why didn't you wake me?"

"I thought I imagined it."

But she can hear them, once again, as if with his ears. The same pattern across the floor and back. Footsteps or heartbeats. Quicker and quicker now, hastening with the terror and tension of escape.

Edward, unimaginably brave, puts on his slippers, grabs a broken banister (five of these on the landing—one day soon, someday, he'll get round to mending them—he doesn't want some builder, paid by Angel, bungling the job) and goes on up to the attic. Angel follows behind. He will not let her cower in bed. Her bladder aches. She says nothing about that. How can she? Not yet. Not quite yet. Soon. "Edward, I'm pregnant." She can't believe it's true, herself. She feels a child, not a woman.

"Is there someone there?"

Edward's voice echoes through the three dark attic rooms. Silence. He gropes for and switches on the light. Empty, derelict rooms: plaster falling, laths hanging, wallpaper peeling. Floorboards broken. A few cans of paint, a pile of wallpaper rolls, old newspapers. Nothing else.

"It could have been mice," says Edward, doubtfully.

"Can't you hear it?" asks Angel, terrified. The sound echoes in her ears: footsteps clattering over a pounding heart. But Edward can't, not any more.

"Don't start playing games," he murmurs, turning back to warmth and bed. Angel scuttles down before him, into the bathroom; the noise in her head fades. A few drops of urine tinkle into the bowl.

Edward lies awake in bed: Angel can feel his wakefulness, his increasing hostility towards her, before she is so much as back in the bedroom.

"Your bladder's very weak, Angel," he complains. "Something else you inherited from your mother?"

Something else, along with what? Suicidal tendencies, alcoholism, a drooping bosom, a capacity for being betrayed, deserted and forgotten?

Not forgotten by me, Mother. I don't forget, I love you. Even when my body cries out beneath the embraces of this man, this lover, this husband, and my mouth forms words of love, promises of eternity, still I don't forget. I love you, Mother.

"I don't know about my mother's bladder," murmurs Angel rashly.

"Now you're going to keep me awake all night," says Edward. "I can feel it coming. You know I've nearly finished a picture."

"I'm not going to say a word," she says, and then, fulfilling his prophesy, sees fit to add, "I'm pregnant."

Silence. Stillness. Sleep?

No, a slap across nostrils, eyes, mouth. Edward has never hit Angel before. It is not a hard slap: it contains the elements of a caress.

"Don't even joke about it," says Edward, softly.

"But I am pregnant."

Silence. He believes her. Her voice made doubt impossible.

"How far?" Edward seldom asks for information. It is an act which implies ignorance, and Edward likes to know more than anyone else in the entire world.

"Three and a half months."

He repeats the words, incredulous.

"Too far gone to do anything," says Angel, knowing now why she did not tell Edward earlier, and the knowledge making her voice cold and hard. Too far gone for the abortion he will most certainly want her to have. So much for the fruits of love. Love? What's love? Sex, ah, that's another thing. Love has babies: sex has abortions.

But Angel will turn sex into love—yes, she will—seizing it by the neck, throttling it till it gives up and takes the weaker path. Love! Edward is right to be frightened, right to hate her.

"I hate you," he says, and means it. "You mean to destroy me."

"I'll make sure it doesn't disturb your nights," says Angel, Angel of the bristly fair bush, "if that's what you're worrying about. And you won't have to support it. I do that, anyway. Or my father does."

Well, how dare she! Angel, not nearly as nice as she thought. Soft-eyed, vicious Angel.

Slap, comes the hand again, harder. Angel screams, he shouts; she collapses, crawls about the floor—he spurns her, she begs forgiveness; he spits his hatred, fear, and she her misery. If the noise above continues, certainly no one hears it, there is so much going on below. The rustlings of the night erupting into madness. Angel is suddenly quiet, whimpering, lying on the floor; she squirms. At first Edward thinks she is acting, but her white lips and taloned fingers convince him that something is wrong with her body and not just her mind. He gets her back on the bed and rings the doctor. Within an hour Angel finds herself in a hospital with a suspected ectopic pregnancy. They delay the operation and the pain subsides; just one of those things, they shrug. Edward has to interrupt his painting the next afternoon to collect her from the hospital.

"What was it? Hysteria?" he inquires.

"I dare say!"

"Well, you had a bad beginning, what with your mother and all," he concedes, kissing her nose, nibbling her earlobe. It is forgiveness; but Angel's eyes remain unusually cold. She stays in bed, after Edward has left it and gone back to his studio, although the floors remain unswept and the dishes unwashed.

Angel does not say what is in her mind, what she knows to be true. That he is disappointed to see both her and the baby back, safe and sound. He had hoped the baby would die, or failing that, the mother would die and the baby with her. He is pretending forgiveness, while he works out what to do next.

In the evening the doctor comes to see Angel. He is a slight man with a sad face: his eyes, she thinks, are kind behind his pebble glasses. His voice is slow and gentle. I expect his wife is happy, thinks Angel, and actually envies her. Some middle-aged, dowdy, provincial doctor's wife, envied by Angel! Rich, sweet, young and pretty Angel. The efficient secretary, lovable barmaid, and now the famous artist's wife! Once, for two rash weeks, even an art school model.

The doctor examines her, then discreetly pulls down her nightie to cover her breasts and moves the sheet up to cover her crotch. If he were my father, thinks Angel, he would not hang my naked portrait on his wall for the entertainment of his friends. Angel had not known until this moment that she minded.

"Everything's doing nicely in there," says the doctor. "Sorry to rush you off like that, but we can't take chances."

Ah, to be looked after. Love. That's love. The doctor shows no inclination to go.

"Perhaps I should have a word with your husband," he suggests. He stands at the window gazing over daffodils and green fields. "Or is he very busy?"

"He's painting," says Angel. "Better not disturb him now. He's had so many interruptions lately, poor man."

"I read about him in the Sunday supplement," says the doctor.

"Well, don't tell him so. He thought it vulgarized his work."

"Did you think that?"

Me? Does what I think have anything to do with anything?

"I thought it was quite perceptive, actually," says Angel, and feels a surge of good humor. She sits up in bed.

"Lie down," he says. "Take things easy. This is a large house. Do you have any help? Can't afford it?"

"It's not that. It's just why should I expect some other woman to do my dirty work?"

"Because she might like doing it and you're pregnant, and if you can afford it, why not?"

"Because Edward doesn't like strangers in the house. And what else have I got to do with my life? I might as well clean as anything else."

"It's isolated out here," he goes on. "Do you drive?"

"Edward needs peace to paint," says Angel. "I do drive but Edward has a thing about women drivers."

"You don't miss your friends?"

"After you're married," says Angel, "you seem to lose contact. It's the same for everyone, isn't it?"

"Um," says the doctor. And then, "I haven't been in this house for fifteen years. It's in a better state now than it was then. The house was divided into flats, in those days. I used to visit a nice young woman who had the attic floor. Just above this. Four children, and the roof leaked; a husband who spent his time drinking cider in the local pub and only came home to beat her."

"Why did she stay?"

"How can such women leave? How do they afford it? Where do they go? What happens to the children?" His voice is sad.

"I suppose it's money that makes the difference. With money, a woman's free," says Angel, trying to believe it.

"Of course," says the doctor. "But she loved her husband. She couldn't bring herself to see him for what he was. Well, it's hard. For a certain kind of woman, at any rate."

Hard, indeed, if he has your soul in his safekeeping, to be left behind at the bar, in the pub, or in some other woman's bed, or in a seat in the train on his literary travels. Careless!

"But it's not like that for you, is it?" says the doctor calmly. "You have money of your own, after all."

Now how does he know that? Of course, the Sunday supplement article.

"No one will read it," wept Angel, when Edward looked up, stony-faced from his first perusal of the fashionable columns. "No one will notice. It's tucked away at the very bottom."

So it was. "Edward's angelic wife, Angel, daughter of best-selling crime-writer Terry Toms, has smoothed the path upwards, not just with the soft smiles our cameraman has recorded, but by enabling the emergent genius to forswear the cramped and inconvenient, if traditional, artist's garret for a sixteenth-century farmhouse in greenest Gloucestershire. It is interesting, moreover, to ponder whether a poor man would have been able to develop the white-on-white techniques which have made Holst's work so noticeable: or whether the sheer price of paint these days would not have deterred him."

"Edward, I didn't say a word to that reporter, not a word," she said, when the ice showed signs of cracking, days later.

"What are you talking about?" he asked, turning slow, unfriendly eyes upon her.

"The article. I know it's upset you. But it wasn't my fault."

"Why should a vulgar article in a vulgar newspaper upset me?"

And the ice formed over again, thicker than ever. But he went to London for two days, presumably to arrange his next show, and on his return casually mentioned that he'd seen Ray while he was there.

Angel had cleaned, baked, and sewed curtains in his absence, hoping to soften his heart towards her on his return: and lay awake all the night he was away, the fear of his infidelity so agonizing as to make her contemplate suicide, if only to put an end to it. She could not ask for reassurance. He would throw the fears so neatly back at her. "Why do you think I should want to sleep with anyone else? Why are you so guilty? Because that's what you'd do if you were away from me?"

Ask for bread and be given stones. Learn self-sufficiency: never show need. Little, tough Angel of the soft smiles, hearing some other woman's footsteps in the night, crying for another's grief. Well, who wants a soul, tossed here and there by teasing hands, overbruised and overhandled. Do without it!

Edward came home from London in a worse mood than he'd left, shook his head in wondering stupefaction at his wife's baking—"I thought you said we were cutting down on carbohydrates"—and shut himself into his studio for twelve hours, emerging just once to say—"Only a madwoman would hang curtains in an artist's studio, or else a silly rich girl playing at artist's wife, and in public at that"—and thrusting the new curtains back into her arms, vanished inside again.

Angel felt that her mind was slowing up, and puzzled over the last remark for some time before realizing that Edward was still harking back to the Sunday supplement article.

"I'll give away the money if you like," she pleaded through the keyhole. "If you'd rather. And if you want not to be married to me I don't mind." That was before she was pregnant.

Silence.

Then Edward emerged laughing, telling her not to be so ridiculous, bearing her off to bed, and the good times were restored. Angel sang about the house, forgot her pill, and got pregnant.

"You have money of your own, after all," says the doctor. "You're perfectly free to come and go."

"I'm pregnant," says Angel. "The baby has to have a father."

"And your husband's happy about the baby?"

"Oh yes!" says Angel. "Isn't it a wonderful day!"

And indeed today the daffodils nod brightly under a clear sky. So far, since first they budded and bloomed, they have been obliged to droop beneath the weight of rain and mist. A disappointing spring. Angel had hoped to see the countryside leap into energy and color, but life returned only slowly, it seemed, struggling to surmount the damage of the past: cold winds and hard frosts, unseasonably late. "Or at any rate," adds Angel, softly, unheard, as the doctor goes, "he *will* be happy about the baby."

Angel hears no more noises in the night for a week or so. There had been misery in the attic rooms, and the misery had ceased. Good times can wipe out bad. Surely!

Edward sleeps soundly and serenely: she creeps from bed to bathroom without waking him. He is kind to her and even talkative, on any subject, that is, except that of her pregnancy. If it were not for the doctor and her stay in the hospital, she might almost think she was imagining the whole thing. Edward complains that Angel is getting fat, as if he could imagine no other cause for it but greed. She wants to talk to someone about hospitals, confinements, layettes, names—but to whom?

She tells her father on the telephone—"I'm pregnant."

"What does Edward say?" asks Terry, cautiously.

"Nothing much," admits Angel.

"I don't suppose he does."

"There's no reason *not* to have a baby," ventures Angel.

"I expect he rather likes to be the center of attention." It is the nearest Terry has ever got to a criticism of Edward.

Angel laughs. She is beyond believing that Edward could ever be jealous of her, ever be dependent upon her.

"Nice to hear you happy, at any rate," says her father wistfully. His twenty-year-old girlfriend has become engaged to a salesman of agricultural machinery, and although she has offered to continue the relationship the other side of marriage, Terry feels debased and used, and was obliged to break off the liaison. He has come to regard his daughter's marriage to Edward in a romantic light. The young bohemians!

"My daughter was an art school model before she married Edward Holst . . . you've heard of him? It's a real Rembrandt and Saskia affair." He even thinks lovingly of Dora: if only she'd understood, waited for youth to wear itself out. Now he's feeling old and perfectly capable of being faithful to an ex–shoe-shop assistant. If only she weren't dead and gone!

An art school model. Those two weeks! Why had she done it? What devil wound up her works and set poor Angel walking in the wrong direction? It was in her nature, surely, as it was in her mother's to follow the paths to righteousness, fully clothed.

Nightly, Edward studied her naked body, kissing her here, kissing her there, parting her legs. Well, marriage! But now I'm pregnant, now I'm pregnant. Oh, be careful. That hard lump where my soft belly used to be. Be careful! Silence, Angel. Don't speak of it. It will be the worse for you and your baby if you do.

Angel knows it.

Now Angel hears the sound of lovemaking up in the empty attic, as she might hear it in hotels in foreign lands. The couplings of strangers in an unknown tongue—only the cries and breathings universal, recognizable anywhere.

The sounds chill her: they do not excite her. She thinks of the mother of four who lived in this house with her drunken, violent husband. Was that what kept you by his side? The chains of fleshly desire? Was it the thought of the night that got you through the perils of the day?

What indignity, if it were so.

Oh, I imagine it. I, Angel, half mad in my unacknowledged pregnancy, my mind feverish, and the doctor's anecdotes feeding the fever—I imagine it! I must!

Edward wakes.

"What's that noise?"

"What noise?"

"Upstairs."

"I don't hear anything."

"You're deaf."

"What sort of noise?"

But Edward sleeps again. The noise fades, dimly. Angel hears the sound of children's voices. Let it be a girl, dear Lord, let it be a girl.

"Why do you want a girl?" asks the doctor, on Angel's fourth monthly visit to the clinic.

"I'd love to dress a girl," says Angel vaguely, but what she means is, if it's a girl, Edward will not be so—what is the word?—hardly jealous, difficult perhaps. Dreadful. Yes, dreadful.

Bright-eyed Edward: he walks with Angel now—long walks up and over stiles, jumping streams, leaping stones. Young Edward. She has begun to feel rather old, herself.

"I am a bit tired," she says, as they set off one night for their moonlit walk. He stops, puzzled.

"Why are you tired?"

"Because I'm pregnant," she says, in spite of herself.

"Don't start that again," he says, as if it were hysteria on her part. Perhaps it is.

That night, he opens her legs so wide she thinks she will burst. "I love you," he murmurs in her nibbled ear, "Angel, I love you. I do love you." Angel feels the familiar surge of response, the holy gratitude, the willingness to die, to be torn apart if that's what's required. And then it stops. It's gone. Evaporated! And in its place, a new strength. A chilly icicle of nonresponse, wonderful, cheerful. No. It isn't right; it isn't what's required: on the contrary. "I love you," she says in return, as usual; but crossing her fingers in her mind, forgiveness for a lie. Please God, dear God, save me, help me save my baby. It is not me he loves, but my baby he hates: not me he delights in, but the pain he causes me, and knows he does. He does not wish to take root in me: all he wants to do is root my baby out. I don't love him. I never have. It is sickness. I must get well. Quickly.

"Not like that," says Angel, struggling free—bold, unkind, prudish Angel—rescuing her legs. "I'm pregnant. I'm sorry, but I am pregnant."

Edward rolls off her, withdraws.

"Christ, you can be a monster. A real ball-breaker."

"Where are you going?" asks Angel, calm and curious. Edward is dressing. Clean shirt; cologne. Cologne!

"To London."

"Why?"

"Where I'm appreciated."

"Don't leave me alone. Please." But she doesn't mean it.

"Why not?"

"I'm frightened. Here alone at night."

"Nothing ever frightened you." Perhaps he is right.

Off he goes; the car breaking open the silence of the night. It closes again. Angel is alone.

Tap, tap, tap, up above. Starting up as if on signal. Back and forward. To the attic bed which used to be, to the wardrobe which once was; the scuffle of the suitcase on the floor. Goodbye. I'm going. I'm frightened here. The house is haunted. Someone upstairs, downstairs. Oh, women everywhere, don't think your misery doesn't seep into walls, creep downstairs, and then upstairs again. Don't think it will ever be done with, or that the good times wipe it out. They don't.

Angel feels her heart stop and start again. A neurotic symptom, her father's doctor had once said. It will get better, he said, when she's married and has babies. Everything gets better for women when they're married with babies. It's their natural state. Angel's heart stops all the same, and starts again, for good or bad.

Angel gets out of bed, slips on her mules with their sharp little heels, and goes up the attic stairs. Where does she find the courage? The light, reflected up from the hallway, is dim. The noise from the attic stops. Angel hears only—what?—the rustling noise of old newspapers in a fresh wind. That stops, too. As if a film were now running without sound. And coming down towards Angel, a small, tired woman in a nightie, slippers silent on the stairs, stopping to stare at Angel as Angel stares at her. Her face marked by bruises.

"How can I see that," wonders Angel, now unafraid, "since there isn't any light?"

She turns on the switch, hand trembling, and in the light, as she'd known, there is nothing to be seen except the empty stairs and the unmarked dust upon them.

Angel goes back to the bedroom and sits on the bed.

"I saw a ghost," she tells herself, calmly enough. Then fear reasserts itself: panic at the way the universe plays tricks. Quick, quick! Angel pulls her suitcase out from under the bed—there are still traces of wedding confetti within—and tap-tap she goes, with sharp little footsteps, from the wardrobe to the bed, from the chest of drawers and back again, not so much packing as retrieving, salvaging. Something out of nothing!

Angel and her predecessor, rescuing each other, since each was incapable of rescuing herself, and rescue always comes, somehow. Or else death.

Tap, tap, back and forth, into the suitcase, out of the house.

The garden gate swings behind her.

Angel, bearing love to a safer place.

CYNTHIA KADOHATA

Jack's Girl

I talked to a ghost once, but he didn't talk back. I asked the ghost questions and then I told him I hated him. The ghost was my father, who had died a month earlier. We sat on a curb and ate candy bars together. I ate the real thing; he ate candy that you couldn't exactly see through but that wavered whenever the wind blew. By the time we parted, I no longer hated him. Or I realized it wasn't as simple as that. He was standing next to his rose-colored convertible—he'd always liked racy cars. The top was open. It was a lovely night—hazy, but the sort of haze that makes the air itself seem to be all different colors.

This happened in Arizona about ten years ago, when I was twenty. My father—whom I called Jack—had died in Barstow, California. That's where he'd been living, with his wife and kids, when he met my mother, the year before I was born. I lived only a few hours' drive away, in Los Angeles, but Jack and I hardly ever saw each other.

When my father was alive, he was "in vending machines," as my mother used to say, when she said anything about him at all. He owned and serviced a vending-machine route, and when he died his wife, whom I knew even less well, asked me to take over the route until she could sell it. A vending-machine route had to be kept alive, she said. If the machines stayed empty too long, the customers—gas stations, bus stops, offices, and schools—might let new venders move in. Even if that didn't happen, the route would shrivel and die without constant servicing. Jack and his wife had two sons, but neither of them could get away just then, and his wife was in bad health. For helping her, she promised me a very small percentage of the profits from the sale of the business. The route was in California, Arizona, and Nevada, and it was while I was servicing it that I saw the ghost. The last time I'd seen Jack alive was five years earlier. I'd always lived with my mother and stepfather—whom I called Dad—and my three younger brothers.

A year before Jack died, I left college and moved in with a boy I loved. Of course, my parents wanted me to stay in school, and it felt strange to go against their wishes about something so important. But it also felt good. My boyfriend and I lived in a stucco apartment house near downtown Los Angeles. Music ruled that building, in an insane sort of way. The man in the adjoining apartment used to practice throwing knives into the wall while listening to loud classical music. He was a former child movie star.

Below our apartment lived a girl who couldn't have been more than eighteen years old, and she played disco music constantly. She didn't always close the curtains, so if you were outside you could see into her place. She would be sitting in front of her tape player and turntable changing songs. She'd play a song from an album and just as it was ending she would start a tape. On weekends she would play disk jockey like that for hours, from when she woke up to when she went to bed.

Jack's wife sent all of his business papers, maps, keys, and files to me in Los Angeles, and I tried to figure everything out. Jack used codes that I couldn't always understand for the machines' keys. I'd planned to organize for a couple of days before I left to service the route, but it took me nearly a week. As I sat at my desk and started decoding, I felt surreptitious and secretive, like a spy, but that illusion was destroyed by the din of the disco from below and the knives thumping alongside.

I had written my mother about all this, and she called me one night while I was decoding. "Honey, your dad says he would be glad to go with you on the route," she said.

I could hear his voice in the background saying, "Tell her things aren't that busy at work for me right now." He owned a garage, a good one, and I had never known him not to be busy.

"I can do it myself," I said. Actually, I had some doubts about that, but I didn't want to admit them to my parents.

I heard my dad, closer to the phone now, saying, "What did she say?"

My mother said, "Well, your dad just thought maybe you wouldn't want to be alone."

I asked whether he would come just until I felt comfortable, and he agreed. I didn't doubt that he wanted to help me, but I also thought he was curious about the man he had perceived as a rival: when he married my mother, she still loved Jack. She had married my dad because she was pregnant with me, and though she later claimed that she loved him, I was never really sure. The first time my mother saw me with my boyfriend, she'd kept staring at us in a funny way. Later, when I asked her what had made her stare, she said we'd both had the same look on our faces, as if we'd been washed over with the same water. I used to try to picture her with Jack, both of them washed over with the same water.

My dad and I left Los Angeles on one of those hot, ashy days when the surrounding hills are burning with brushfires and a feeling of siege has settled on the whole city. The fires filled me with languor and restlessness, so it was a good time to leave.

Since the time I went to college, when I was eighteen, I had seen little of my family; it took me by surprise how naturally and quickly new people covered the surface of my life. My dad and I didn't talk much on the phone, and though my mother and I wrote, my dad and I never did any more. We had at first, but one of my brothers told me that whenever my dad received a letter from me he got a weary look on his face, the way he did when he had to do a chore like filling out tax forms. He always wrote me back, but I knew it was a burden. "It's almost as bad as having to read a book," my brother told me he'd said.

I had worked out a logical route, to cover the territory in the most efficient way. The first day our stops were mainly gas stations, plus a couple of offices. Mostly small stuff. Our last stop, in the evening, was a Chinese-Italian restaurant. The restaurant had live entertainment—a man in a bow tie singing ballads. Signs hanging inside and out said that if you bought two entrées you'd get the second free.

"Let's eat here," said my dad. "A free meal." Bargains always delighted him in ways that were embarrassing or that seemed to me out of proportion to the amount of money saved. Once when I was younger, my dad took us over to the house of a friend of his to pick up some spare car parts for his garage. Our own car was being fixed at the time. On our way back, we walked through town, one of my brothers carrying a carburetor, another brother, my father, and I carrying a blue car door, and my youngest brother carrying two hubcaps that he kept trying to balance on his head.

"It's not really a free meal," I said. He mumbled something I couldn't quite make out, but it sounded like "Killjoy." "Oh, all right," I said.

My dad ordered sweet-and-sour pork with spaghetti for twelve ninety-five, and I wanted to order a vegetable plate.

"That's only five ninety-five," said my dad. "Besides, didn't you tell me when you were in high school that eating too many vegetables would make your complexion orange?"

"It's what I feel like eating."

"You had a date with that Scott guy, or Trott, or whatever his name was, and you wouldn't eat any carrots all week."

The waitress came and I asked for the vegetable plate. My dad looked crestfallen: "Don't you feel like shrimp? Look, here's some great shrimp for fourteen ninety-five." His face, always changeable, looked hopeful now. I gave in, which didn't seem to surprise him.

The shrimp was supposed to be marinated in ginger sauce; it arrived bathed in ketchup, but my dad didn't want me to return it. "We got a free meal!" he said.

When we were finished, we went into the foyer, where I had to climb on the cigarette machine to reach the lock on the candy machine. I smiled to myself when I realized that Jack must have done the same thing. 'Can you hand me a screwdriver?" I said. "The lock is stuck." My dad didn't answer and when I looked down he was staring glassy-eyed out a window into the parking lot.

"You know, sometimes I have thoughts so big they scare me," he said.

A couple of customers walked by and gave each other a look on the way out. "The screwdriver?" I said. My dad kept staring. "What was the big thought?"

"I don't know. I can't explain it. It's gone now anyway."

"About Mom?"

"Maybe."

My dad handed me the screwdriver. "So have you thought any more about going back to school?" he said. He spoke tentatively, as if he were afraid I would lose my temper and say once again that it was *my* life. "No" was all I said.

His face took on a sad aspect and I wondered whether he was having a different kind of thought now—a practical, unhappy one. He had never finished high school himself, and I think he felt that going to college would guarantee me my place in the world. Maybe he worried I might end up unhappy, the way he thought my mother was.

Many of the machines we filled were in small towns, clusters of one-story buildings surrounded by yellowed weeds. The buildings had cracked stucco walls of pale pink, pale yellow, or white, and nearly all the windows in all the buildings were open, the curtains behind them shivering in the breeze. The children I saw always appeared to me tan and curious without being either healthy or alert, and the houses, as if they were organic, seemed to blend into the fields. In the background there were water towers, silver globes protecting the towns from the surrounding desert. At night the scenery was bare but not barren. There were no lights along the highway, and sometimes it was hard to tell we were in a real car, because the scenery on either side changed hardly at all. It was like one of those pretend cars in arcades, where you have a seat and a steering wheel and the road moves on a screen in front of the wheel. When trucks passed us, their emblems hung surreally in the blackness between the headlights.

One day in the car my dad said that he'd already stayed away from the garage longer than he'd planned to. But he quickly added that he would be glad to continue the route with me. Who knows what he really wanted to do? I told him I thought I could handle things by myself now. There was a machine in an Arizona bus-stop restaurant that we'd reach in a few more hours, and my dad decided to catch a bus back to his home from there. When we got to the restaurant's address, I asked a passerby where the place was, and he pointed to a white frame house and said, "Second floor." I hesitated, because there was no sign anywhere, and he said again, this time irritably, "Second floor." We followed his directions and found a small, quiet, dark restaurant up a flight of squeaky stairs. A young girl served us. She lingered at our table, eager to talk. She wanted to know where we were from and what we did. Ordinarily my dad was the talkative one, but this time I answered. He had been looking more tired each day.

"So you're only halfway done with the route," he said, after the girl left. "Think you can hold out?"

"I'm fine. I kind of like it." And in fact I did—I realized it was the first time I'd ever had any genuine responsibility.

My dad was quiet again. A little boy at the next table dropped a container of milk and knocked over his chair as he caught it. His mother told him to sit still, and he smiled at me, sly and angelic.

When the bus came we went downstairs. My dad idly leaned over and knocked on one of the wheels of the bus. He examined the tread, nodded approvingly, then got that glassy-eyed look again.

"What are you thinking about?" I said.

"To tell the truth, I was thinking did you know your mother had an affair once?"

I hesitated, then said, "I know."

"Did you know I almost had one, too, a couple of years ago?"

I shook my head, though his back was to me now. I felt sick and sad inside to hear this, and I was glad he didn't turn to look at me.

He shrugged. "It doesn't matter. We went out to dinner a couple of times. See, I wanted to tell you because nothing happened. See, your mother told me once how she ended with Jack. She said he took her to his house one day and on the wall was this thing called a Wish List. It had writing all over it, like 'toy truck' and 'stuffed animal' and Jack's wife had written 'a new couch for my birthday.' Your mother was about seventeen years old. A few weeks later he took her there again and a new couch was sitting in the living room. His wife

252

had wanted this thing for the house and he'd gotten it for her, and that made your mother see for the first time the way his wife was connected to him and the way he was connected to her. She and Jack went into the bedroom then, but the whole time she just lay there feeling sad. So I kept thinking about that when I met this other lady, and somehow that stuff your mother had told me meant more to me than the other things, the things she did to me." He turned to me and became energized for the first time in days. "It's wrong!" he said. "Two people get married! They get married. Period."

There had always been something primitive about his morality; it was as if his need for a moral order were as strong as the need for food and water. When I was growing up, I'd always felt sheltered by his convictions, and by his belief that all his children would grow up "good." Whenever we did something "bad" or "wrong," he wasn't so much disappointed as confused and disbelieving.

As my dad was about to get on the bus, he reached into his wallet and took out all the money in there: twelve dollars. "Here, you might need some cash."

"Dad, I'm grown up, I work, I have money—remember?" I said. "Plus, I've got all the change from the machines."

"Don't worry, I have credit cards," he said, handing me the bills. As he was going up the bus steps, he paused and turned and said plaintively, "Now, don't you write me." Then he took his seat.

After the bus left, I walked back upstairs to the restaurant. I felt greasy and ragged, and I noticed spots on my blouse, and bruises on my hands from working.

The girl from the restaurant talked with me while I filled the candy machines. She said her town was bigger than it looked, maybe ten thousand people. She said she was fifteen, then seemed to be studying my face to see whether I believed her. Before I left I gave her a bottle of clear nail polish and she gave me a few breakfast rolls she sneaked out of the kitchen.

Work grew less complex as time passed, because the more machines I serviced the fewer keys remained that I hadn't matched with a machine. I worked harder, but I also felt relaxed. I would sit on the car in the sun eating candy bars and figuring things out—working on adjustments to my route, computing how much money I'd spent. Jack's wife was going to reimburse me for my expenses. Using Jack's notebooks, I saw that his neat handwriting had changed over time, the slant moving from left to right. Occasionally, there was a note in the margins: "Need new lock for C-24. . . . New man trying to take over territory, A-5." I wondered what *he* had written on the Wish List.

I knew I didn't have to service all the machines. I had originally planned to leave some, doing only enough to keep the route salable. But then I decided to do them all anyway, just for the obsession of it. A couple of the most out-of-the-way places were tiny offices for which Jack had simply laid out candy on shelves, with no machines, and the office workers paid on the honor system. He'd gotten to know the people in those offices better than the people at his more profitable locations. I thought maybe he'd told some of those smaller customers about me, maybe showed them pictures if he had any. In any case, "Jack's girl" is what a couple of them called me.

I saw my father's ghost when I was almost finished with the route, at one of those out-of-the-way places I had considered not servicing. Earlier that night someone had been tailgating me, though the road was empty and he could easily have passed. I slowed, he slowed, I pulled over, and he stopped rather than pass. Finally, I turned onto a side road and he sped on.

It was very late, but I had only two more stops for the night. The next-to-last one was a gas station; it had two machines, one with snacks like potato chips and cookies, and one with candy bars and gum. I was testing keys when I suddenly noticed Jack standing next to me, at a third vending machine that had appeared out of nowhere. I think I screamed and ran a few steps toward my car, but something made me stop and turn. Jack was shaking his keys, but I heard no jingling. "Jack?" I called. I walked back. His image was not quite right. I realized he was a ghost when the wind came up but didn't muss his hair, just made his whole body flow to the side and back. His personality seemed to flow back and forth as well: at first, with his cagey glances to one side, he reminded me of a weasel; then he smiled to himself and seemed almost innocent. I looked around and behind me and saw nothing, no one.

I had that same relaxed feeling I'd had a lot lately, a hypnotized feeling. "Do you always come out here to service this machine, even though it's so out of the way?" I said. Like me, he had probably been tempted to skip it. But I bet he never did. He needed to be diligent for a business like this to work, I realized. I'd never thought about that before. The first time I remember seeing him, he was driving a convertible, and I guessed he didn't need to worry much about money. It had probably been important for him to appear that way to people.

He began putting coins into the machine and checking each candy slot to make sure nothing was out of order. Before he put his key into the lock he studied the key, blew on the metal, shined it with his shirt. He paused for a split second, and I realized it was to see whether he could catch a piece of his reflection in the key.

"I see your car over there," I said. "You were following me earlier." My voice sounded the way it always did, but it also sounded strange, because I was basically talking to myself. We worked silently together.

When he was finished, he sat on the gas-station curb, and I joined him. Across the road the ground was so flat it exhilarated me, the way it went on and on. We both tore open a candy-bar wrapper. I had never eaten so much candy in my life. For the last couple of weeks, I'd been living mostly on candy bars and milk.

Jack ate appreciatively, as if chocolate were his favorite food. I reached out and ran my hand through him, only it didn't go through, exactly, it just stretched him out in the middle, as if he were elastic. I asked him about my mother, what she had been like and how much he had loved her, and when he didn't answer I told him I hated him for putting a curse on my dad's life. He tore the wrapper on his candy bar lower and wiped his mouth with his shirt. It seemed like such a lonely life suddenly—before he died he had sat out here in the middle of this nowhere or another again and again for twenty years.

"Well, if you're just going to be sitting there we ought to talk," I said. "Do you have any questions? Shall I tell you about my brothers? Do you want to hear about my boyfriend?"

He nodded at an appropriate moment, but I guess it was just coincidence. "My boyfriend's name is Andy Chin. He's twenty, like me. He's moody, but

I wouldn't say he has a bad temper. Sometimes we talk about having a baby and about what kind of house we'd like. But the thing is, we'd rather get a really nice apartment than a house. A condo is more our ideal." Jack sneezed soundlessly. "Bless you," I said. "Did I ever show you any pictures of my brothers? Walker's really quiet, but he's not really shy, the way he used to be. He just doesn't like to talk to people if they don't interest him. Ben's the opposite. He has too many friends. Walker and Ben are in high school. Peter's in grammar school. He skipped a grade because he's so smart." I couldn't help adding, "I bet neither of your sons skipped a grade."

I took a breath. I noticed for the first time that Jack was quite young, maybe about my age or a few years older. He was younger than I could remember ever having seen him. That meant he'd probably just bought the candy route. I think he met my mother around that time. But perhaps that was still in the future for him, a few months or years away. I hadn't been born yet as he sat there. When my mother fell in love with Jack, she must have realized how young they were and that things wouldn't turn out well.

Jack got up and went to his car, brushed it with his hand, admired it. He took out a small notebook and started writing. I wondered where he was going now. Down the highway past the gas station sat a couple of small signs, the back of a billboard, another gas station, and then the highway curved into the night. In the other direction there were no signs and no buildings, just the highway cutting through the fields of yellowed grass. The grass was so pale with dryness it looked almost snow-covered.

Jack started scribbling in a bigger notebook, probably one that I later read. I got angry again, because he wouldn't or couldn't pay attention to me. "If it weren't for you, maybe my mother would have loved my dad more," I said. But that didn't quite make sense. I tried to figure why not: I was at Max's Texaco, but Jack wasn't, although in a way he was, and I wouldn't be there if it weren't for him, even though he . . . What time was it? I was getting sleepy. The dry air smelled faintly of gasoline. I still had another stop, and for a moment I began to worry about my work and forgot about Jack. I tried to calculate from the night sky what time it was, but then I gave up. It didn't matter; it was high time I left.

A. S. BYATT

The Next Room

The two young men in the front of the hearse had rolled up their shirtsleeves, very neatly, and opened the windows. They were basking a little, parked on the tarmac. You couldn't blame them. It was so hot out there, incandescent you might say, if that were not an unfortunate choice of word. Joanna Hope, stepping out of the dark chapel into the bright sun, blinked tearlessly and looked at them with approval. They were sleekly and pleasantly alive. They had brought her mother to that place safely and would not be wanted to take her anywhere else. Behind her Mrs. Stillingfleet plucked at her sleeve and said they must wait for the smoke. Mrs. Stillingfleet's eyes were wet and screwed-up, though not flowing. Behind Mrs. Stillingfleet Nurse Dawes and the minister were both solemn and dry-eyed. They constituted the whole party.

"The smoke," echoed Joanna, not at first understanding, and then, catching up, affirmatively, "of course, the smoke." The garden of remembrance stretched away enticingly in the bright light, still under arching boughs, bright with roses, crimson, gold and white. She had chosen Pink Perpetue to commemorate her mother, who had been very fond of pink, who had lain only ten minutes ago inside her satin casing clothed in a soft pink silk nightdress Joanna had once bought for her in Hong Kong, which she had always declared too good to wear. Joanna looked up at the sky above the chimney: a 1920s brick chimney, slightly cottagey. The sky was a hot dark blue and the air danced a little, reminding Joanna, inappositely, of the simmering heat on the North African desert where she had sat, by the hour, in a jeep, counting the intermittent traffic, six camels, two mules, three lorries, two land-rovers, six-teen tramping, burdened women. She remembered Mike's wrist next to hers, holding the clipboard, gold hairs and sweat round the canvas strap of his watch. The smoke, creamy and dense, began to stain the still dancing blue. Joanna fancied she saw fine filaments of papery black in it. Her body shook with an emotion to which, firmly and with shame, she put a name. It was elation. It had been sweeping across her, intermittently and more and more strongly, ever since Nurse Dawes had woken her in the small hours to break the sad news. Her mother was free carbon molecules and potash. It was the end. She had dutifully given her mother a large part of her life, for which she had been castigated and thanked. Now it was over. It was the end. "She's in a better place now, I know it," said Mrs. Stillingfleet, looking round at the silent rosy alleys. "She's at peace." Joanna nodded, not wanting to contradict. For herself, she was absolutely sure that there was no *better* place, that the end was the end. She thought Mrs. Stillingfleet, who had borne her mother's mocks and scorn and disparagement with almost saintly patience, might have been glad to think so too. She had told Mrs. Stillingfleet that Molly Hope had left her £500, which was not true; Joanna had suggested it and Molly had replied tartly that she hardly did enough to earn the very generous wages she received, let alone any posthumous bonus. Without Mrs. Stillingfleet, and latterly Nurse Dawes, Joanna herself could not have gone on. She was also beholden to the Economic Development Survey, who had kept her on, during all the years of Molly's immobility, without insisting that she did any foreign tours or fieldwork. She had mastered the computer, and processed other people's statistics. She coordinated. Now at last the world was all before her, as she had intended, when choosing her profession. Except that now, she was fifty-nine.

The house, now her house, was still full of her mother's presence. Little sounds, scratchings and rattles, were automatically translated by Joanna as her mother putting down teacups on the Russian metal tray, or rearranging the tooth mugs in the bathroom. She went into her own bedroom, the bedroom of her early days at the Survey, of her father's precipitate and still unexplained retirement from the Ministry of Defence. Her own eyes met her steadily from the mirror. A handsome, tall, thin woman in white-spotted navy-blue pleated silk, her well-cut hair heavily flecked with silver. The room was north-facing, and outside was the road. Her parents' bedroom, and her mother's later downstairs room, once the breakfast room, faced south onto the garden for which the house had been bought. I shall sell this house, she thought, safely inside this admittedly chilly room. I shall start again. Not precipitately: I need to think things out. The room had no character, and dark green silk hangings. Stairs creaked under no foot. Joanna went out and toured all the empty rooms. They were instinct with her mother's presence and absence in about equal proportions. The presence was worst inside the wardrobe—some of the small pastel crimplene dresses still held Molly's increasingly angular shape. In a dark depth she saw her father's burberry and his gardening jacket. He had been dead twelve years. A tweed hat of his, pale blue herringbone, gathered dust on a shelf. She herself, over the years, had given away most things, driving down to the Salvation Army with dark suits folded into black plastic bin-liners. Dark suits were particularly useful to the Salvation Army. They rendered the unemployed respectable for interviews for jobs. They gave them a chance. Joanna had never understood the indifference with which Molly had accepted Donald's persisting presence, in the shape of his things, after he was gone. She had never even moved his empty twin bed out from beside her own: she lay there at night, under her fringed, clip-on reading lamp, receiving her Benger's Food from Joanna, sometimes carping, sometimes gracious, and beyond her in the shadows was the square outline of his mattress, naked under a shot-silk counterpane, and an identical reading lamp, dangling its egg-shaped switch, extinguished.

Both these beds were now empty; so was Molly's more recent downstairs bed, in the most pleasant room, with its bay overlooking the lawn, and hung with wisteria and summer jasmine. Her dressing gown was still across the foot of this bed: her alarm clock still ticked beside it. Joanna, moved by grief and a ferocious need to clear all this away, dropped both of them into the woven cane linen-basket, pale green, braid-trimmed. She heard the clock cluck in protest, and felt an absence of outrage, in which she felt herself expand, as though she could skip in this room, or shout, or whirl around, and no one would hear to condemn. She added the hairbrush. There was something terrible and pathetic in the last shining white hairs in its thick, real bristles. She listened to the empty silence. Outside on the lawn, a thrush churred. She stood in the bay and looked at the bird, strutting busily, staring arrogantly about it. The lawn was white with daisies and pink with fallen petals from the rose pergola. The garden was at its loveliest, in the summer sun. Her father's ashes had been scattered at the feet of these climbing roses; she and Molly had done it together, in silence and disaccord. Molly objected to the pergola, which she called "your father's folly." She was right that it was too large and obtrusive for the space it occupied. But he had loved it, had loved Albertine, and Madame Alfred Carrière and Madame Grégoire Staechelin. Joanna liked to think that he now, perhaps, was indissolubly part of these vegetable beauties, climbing and tumbling and breathing over the wooden arch. She had not known him very well and had not understood him at all: he was mediated for her by Molly's disappointment, disapproval, wrath and disgust. Now in Molly's empty room she looked out at his pergola and thought of him in peace.

She made herself a sort of supper on a tray, intending to sit down with a good book, not to watch the television—Molly's last years, and perforce her own, had been increasingly dominated by long serial dramas Molly had initially condemned as vulgar, and had later, contradictory and unapologetic, become obsessed by. *Dallas, Dynasty*, Wimbledon. The World Cup, *Eastenders*, Embassy Snooker, *The Edge of Darkness*. Not now dear, it's time for my serial. Always "my," as though the television companies planned with Molly's interests foremost in their mind. The opaque, gray, lightless screen was the sharpest reminder yet of Molly's absolute absence: reflected in it Joanna saw her parents' drawing-room furniture, bulging slightly, and the color of a photograph from her childhood. I shall sell the house, she said to herself, tapping her egg. As soon as possible, but not without some sort of sensible thought about how I want to live now. Nothing precipitate and silly. The screen reflected Molly's knitting bag, a tapestry sack on wooden handles. It had pathos. Joanna rose in the middle of her egg to close it into a bureau drawer before sitting down again. What do I do with one and a half sides of a manically complicated fair-isle pullover?

She became aware of two quite different aspects of her sense of her mother who was not here. The first was an expectation of her imminent arrival, querulous or ready with a piece of witty self-deprecation, to take up her seat in her chair and ask for this and that to be fetched or taken away. This almost comfortable expectation was uncanny only because Molly would never come again; it was usual, and would not be switched off to order, or for reason's sake. The second was not expectation, but reminiscence and later came to constitute itself in Joanna's thought as "the jigsaw." She had had such a jigsaw during the long and tedious years at boarding school—a set of images, strip-cartoon pictures, patches of color, she seemed to snip out with mental scissors and fit together awkwardly and with overlaps or gaps, labeling this for reference "my mother," an entity which had little or nothing to do with the living, slippered creature who would not again patter between Cliff Thorburn and the toaster, or take up the knitting needles and count stitches. "My mother" in Joanna's school days had, like most people's mothers, worn embarrassing and strident hats. She was frozen forever in Joanna's playroom doorway like an avenging angel crying out against powder paint on the carpet fifty-four years ago. A comforting corner of the jigsaw held a kitchen mother with a wooden spoon, dripping cochineal into birthday icing: she was good at cakes, and enjoyed Joanna's pleasure. Joanna turned the finished jigsaw in her mind like a kaleidoscope; there were things now, that constituted sharp corners and jagged edges, that she had never brought out to look at in those long flickering evenings in case Molly overlooked or overheard her thoughts. Many of these pieces were to do with her vanished father, who had begun to vanish long before he had in fact choked gently to death, who had begun to vanish at precisely the moment when he had become perpetually present, when his premature retirement, or whatever it had been, had confined him to Molly's territory and its margins, the far reaches of the garden, the bonfire, the compost heap, the battle with ground elder from next door. Molly had been a great requirer: she had expected much from life, and had not had it, and had made her disappointment vociferous. Joanna was not, and now never would be, quite sure *what* she had wanted—it was not particularly to do anything, but to be something, the wife of an influential and successful man. (Joanna's own life, a career devoted to useful work for underdeveloped societies, had been conceived in direct opposition to this want.) Joanna sometimes suspected that her mother had married her father simply because he represented the nearest thing she knew to this vicarious influence and success. He had been clever, shy, and formal, a step up the social scale for the daughter of a subpostmistress. He might have become an Under-Secretary or even better. He never talked about his work, and then, suddenly, there was trouble—"the silly mess your father got into"—Joanna would never know what—and it was at an end.

He had become ill, almost immediately, within a year at most. A wasting disease had attacked him. Joanna had heard him say once, in the conservatory, "I wasted time, and now doth time waste me," but he had been saying it into the trumpets of his lilies, not to her. He said nothing to Molly, who said a great deal to him, and Joanna had always bitterly felt that he saw Joanna herself as an extension of his wife. He had had fine, cobwebby gray hair, that when he worked he sleeked, briefly, with water. As he wasted away he became all gray; his face grew thinner, and ashen, and developed long fine downward pleats and incisions, and then a crazy crisscross of cracks as he diminished steadily. His eyes had always been a pale, smoky gray. He wandered among the smoke of his bonfires in a grey V-necked pullover, carrying increasingly small forkfuls of twigs and dried weeds, ghost-gray. Joanna had been very startled that the ashes which she sifted onto the roots of Madame Alfred Carriére, at the last, had been creamy-white.

The stages of his slow decline were marked on the whole by jigsaw pieces depicting, not him, but Molly's dealings with him. Molly declaring, after the fateful interview with the specialist, "There's nothing really wrong with him: he just needs to pull himself together, you'll see." Molly's distaste for his bodily presence and all his activities. He had tried, in the early days, to have a glass of beer in the early evenings. Molly had taken exception to this. The smell, she said, disgusted her. Beer was a sickening smell. (The fact that Joanna also disliked its smell had rendered her icily neutral in this dispute.) Molly had pounced on his beer glass the moment it was emptied, when the air still lingered in the fringe of froth at its brim, and had washed and washed it, her mouth set. Later, she had commented to Joanna on every small eructation.

Your father's tummy grumbles all the time. He makes awful belching noises. It's the beer. It's disgusting. Towards the end, when the discreet belches were an inevitable function of his failing body, she had not even waited for his absence to comment. He appeared not to hear. He gave up the beer. The plant dispute had been harder and longer. The plants were his great love, and he was good with them. The conservatory was ranged with brave and brilliant exotics. If he could have had his way, every windowsill would have been fringed with leafage, every table scented with its own perfume. He brought things in from the conservatory, tentatively, in ones and twos, and Molly, decisively, swiftly, returned these intruders to where, she seemed to believe, they belonged, often balancing them dangerously on the edge of shelves, or breaking off delicate new growth in the process. "Earth is poisonous," she would say. "You know that. Things have their proper places." The windowsills were airless inside the double glazing. Joanna's jigsaw mother brandished a pot in her hand, her face blazing. But she was an ambiguous figure. After his death, though with no hint, before it, of this extraordinary turnabout, she had tended the plants herself, clumsily and diligently, keeping alive what she could, practicing propagation by layering and leaf-cuttings. Donald's pride had been a collection of Christmas cactuses, which flower in the dark days, brief and brilliant at the end of their fleshy segments. He had bred a new variety of this plant, and had asked Molly whether it should be called "Molly Hope" or "Mrs Donald Hope." Molly had replied that this was a matter of indifference to her. The plant, called in the event "Joanna Hope," a deep salmon-pink bloom when it came, now occupied, in various exemplars, many windowsills and whatnots about the place. Even in Molly's own room.

Joanna's jigsaw mother was densest at the points of medical crisis. It was during Joanna's last African tour that her father had become finally bedridden. Molly had been wonderful about this for just long enough, a prop and a stay admired and trusted by her GPs and neighbors, coping brilliantly, turning to. On Joanna's return, her own spectacular collapse had set in. The blood pressure—"I just *sensed* it was unnatural, dear, but I was really shocked when Dr. Highet told me just *how* high it was, and when I was doing so much for your unfortunate father, which really can't have done it any good, now can it?'' The palpitations, the blue lips, the partially paralyzed shoulder muscles, the unstable legs, culminating in a collapse into unconsciousness at Joanna's feet when the daughter had been preparing to announce that she was setting off on a road-feasibility study in Burma. We shall not be with you long, now, Molly had declared on that occasion, twenty years ago, putting out a tremulous hand from under a crocheted bed-jacket. It's a lot to ask, but it won't be for long, and then you will be free as the wind. The illnesses were real: Joanna had asked. They gave serenity and dignity to Molly Hope. Pain was an occupation. They won't want to employ me any longer, Joanna had said, the terms of my contract don't allow it. But they had been so generous. So accommodating. This was civilized society: a series of accommodations to need and helplessness. After Donald's death, Molly had recovered a little, enough to take holidays with her daughter in the Trossachs and once in Paris. On that occasion Molly had had her handbag snatched by a crowd of vehement dancing gypsy children, who had flapped at her face with sheets of newspaper and irregular slabs of cardboard, keeping up a shrill mesmeric cry. Joanna saw her now as she had been then, bewildered, turning her little face from side to side, all tremulous, weeping slow tears of impotent rage. At home, a woolly chrysalis between sheets, she was threatening. Out there she had been pathetic, little and lost, and Joanna's own feelings unbearable. Oh I am *sorry*, Joanna had cried, as though it was all her fault, and her mother had recovered her look of disapproval and her vitality.

Joanna noticed that she had toothache. Psychosomatic, she told herself briskly, thinking of Molly's endlessly discriminated neuralgias and fibrositis. She was a little rattled by the image of her mother in the dusty Paris street, mocked by the wild children. She felt cruel. She turned on the television, a final concession to the silence. A Red Indian chief was talking, fully feathered, black and white, his ancient face lined and thoughtfully set. "My people," he said, "can hear the voices of the creatures; we love the earth, which you white men tear up with your railroads and level for your agriculture. We can hear the spirit voices of our ancestors, close to us, not gone away, in the grass and trees and stones we know and love. You send your ancestors away in closed boxes to your faraway Heaven. We leave our people in the spirit hunting-grounds, open to the air we know. We do not go very far away. You may not notice, as you hunt amongst our trees with your cracking guns, but behind you press a whole company of our people, invisible but present, inhabiting our land." He was, the credits informed Joanna, a real chief, filmed in 1934, a lasting, mouthing, echoing, mobile ghost-face of a defeated alien, long crumbled. Ghosts too of trembling trees and chuckling icy water flickered in Joanna's drawing room; a white hunter penetrated silence, crunching twigs, and behind him crowded a greater silence. Joanna did not like this, though foreign faces and unravaged lands were her desire and hope. In black Africa, spirits came to drink blood and strangle children; in South America they were propitiated, at crossroads, in building sites, with bunches of bloody feathers and ears of corn. In a home-counties drawing room, what buzzed was the electric circuit, what tapped at the casement the long tendrils of the creeper, looking for a place to adhere to. Where had her mother gone, particles and smoke? The twinge in her jaw became a gimlet-boring, intermittent enough to be shocking every time it began again.

The toothache was no better at the Survey the next day. Joanna's colleagues confused its effects with those of grief, and tried to persuade her that she should have stayed at home and looked after herself, that they could easily have managed without her, which was what she feared. "I'm not upset, I have toothache," she told Mike, at the end of the morning. Mike spent much less time in England than on tour; it might have been seen as Joanna's luck that he was here, at the time of Molly's death, for three months. Mike, her only lover, and now for many years her limited but real and only friend, might be relied on to see that she meant exactly what she said. "Then you must go to the dentist," he said. "Though you can't expect not to be upset at all, Joanna." Joanna wanted to speak to him in a rush, about her limited but important future, about the possibility of other work, of seeing other parts of the world, but was inhibited by the presence of his latest assistant, Bridget Connolly, dark and pretty and just back from a course in Japan. She said, for Bridget's benefit, "Of course I miss Mother. It hasn't yet at all sunk in that she isn't there. I hear her rummaging in the cupboards and moving things in the conservatory, you know, things like that. But I did what I could, I consider, and now it's all over, there is some relief, I must admit. That part of my life is finished, now. I shall sell the house. When I've thought what to do next."

Bridget spoke. She spoke with disproportionate urgency, as though saying something she needed to say, that was not quite called for now, but could be inserted in their talk. "In Tokyo," she said, "I had breakfast every day with the family's grandfather, who was dead. He was present at every meal—his picture, anyway, in the middle of the table—we all bowed to it, and he had his own little servings of meals. They all went off to work at some unearthly hour so by the time I ate there was only me and him—and the maid brought tea for both of us, and asked him respectfully if he'd enjoyed it. He was a terribly fierce-looking old man. It was his house. They consulted him about everything."

There was a little silence. Then Bridget and Joanna spoke simultaneously. Bridget said, "I'm sorry: it was all rather a culture shock: I was quite frightened, actually: I just wanted to say . . ."

Joanna said, "I'm quite sure death is the end. I'm sure one just goes nowhere, as one came from nowhere. I'm sure."

Mike said, "I think I'll ring my dentist and make you an emergency appointment, Joanna. I shall charge it to the Survey. I've done it before. In the interests of efficiency, I shall say. You look a bit washed-out." He touched both their arms. The young woman looked up at him, quick, electric, wanting contact and reassurance. Joanna looked down at her desk, remembering. She was embarrassed—yes, that was the exact word—to feel Mike moving into a place that had always been cramped by the exigencies of her parents. She supposed she had loved him, though she had never for a moment doubted that he preferred his wife to her—both in and out of bed—and this certainty had made her morally comfortable, not guilty about his wife, not desirous of supplanting her. Now she thought, watching him telephone, that although she had ancestors, she would not be one, she was the end of some genetic string. Was she unnatural not to have wanted him—or someone—more? What she wanted, was the time back. The empty desert and her own young eyes, watching for signs of life, out of a young face in a young body. Her tooth shrilled. Mike put down the phone. "Mr. Kestelman will see you right away," he said. "He's got another emergency patient there. He'll manage to help you both as quickly as possible. I'll order you a cab, Joanna."

The dentist's waiting room was white and streamlined, somewhere between the modernist and the clinical. Its walls were white and its tables spotless and unscratched white melamine; its lighting came from huge opaque white bowls, suspended or supported on chrome. It was like a time capsule in a science-fiction film, colorless, and therefore about equally soothing and alarming. No flowers, not a speck of dust. It was already inhabited by a restless woman when Joanna arrived. The other emergency case. Joanna sat on a white tweed sofa, slung on chrome with leather bands, and put her feet together on an off-white Berber rug. The other woman, sitting opposite, leafed through and again through a heap of glossy magazines. She had pure white hair arranged in curls round her face and in a longer fall to her shoulders: this white had a spun-silk, glossy quality, full of vitality. Her skin was, by contrast, darkish, moist though, not desiccated. She was difficult to put an age to. She wore a puce angora sweater, with a low scoop neckline, embroidered with iridescent bugles and beads: the perceivable edge of her breasts seemed rounded and lively, with a few freckles. She was made up, lavishly but not grotesquely, a fuchsia lipstick to match the angora, huge hoops of violet shadow between black lashes and silver eyebrows. She wore gypsyish hooped earrings, silver, not gold. Joanna put a hand to her own jaw and gave the other an opening.

"Does it hurt? Does it hurt badly?"

"Pretty bad."

"I'm a coward about pain. Or I used to be, I should say, before things changed. Mr. Kestelman thinks I've got an abscess. I only came here as a last resort. I'm ashamed, really. I tried healing by other means, but it didn't work."

"Other means?"

"What you might call faith healing. Spiritual healing. I have the gift. It is a marvelous gift, I don't know if you know anything about it, I developed it only fairly recently. I've achieved extraordinary things, marvelous cures, *mysterious* things, but for some reason I can't soothe away this pain. Physician, heal thyself, and all that. My theory is, the pain distracts me from the necessary concentration. My husband said I should give conventional medicine a go, it also exists in the world for a reason, and has helped many, don't you agree, so here I am."

"How did you discover you had the gift?" asked Joanna, politely and with some curiosity.

"It's a fairly frequent consequence of an NDE. I didn't know that at the time, naturally. But it turns out, many of those who experience NDEs have these gifts."

"NDE?"

"Near Death Experience. I was clinically dead, and brought back. Really." She laughed, and Joanna laughed, and both put their hands to their painful faces. "I had a heart attack, two years ago now—you wouldn't think it to look at me, would you?—and I was clinically dead, stopped breathing, everything, and then they brought me back. And when I was dead, I had this wonderful experience. It changed my life. Changed absolutely."

"Tell me," said Joanna, who would have been told anyway, who had encountered her own Ancient Mariner, in this antechamber. The other swung into a well-polished narration, impeded by twinges of dental agony.

"I didn't mention it for ages, I thought I wouldn't be believed. But I knew all along it was true, truer than most things, if you see what I mean, *more* true. There I was, swimming as it were, up and up, away from myself—I could see myself lying there, it was in an underpass at Pimlico tube station actually—I could see this body lying there like a banana skin someone had dropped—and there was I, moving away quite fast *up* a kind of tunnel—or funnel-thing—and at the other end was a sort of opening and an indescribable light, ever so bright. And more than anything I wanted to go through that door. It was bliss. Bliss. I can't describe it. When I got near, there were Figures, who Opened, and I came out into a kind of green place—a *clean* green place, all washed clean, it made me see how polluted our poor earth is—you've never dreamed such green—and there across a field was a little bungalow, ever such a lovely bungalow, with a garden *brimming* with every kind of peony, and I thought: Mum would have *loved* that, she always said her idea of heaven was a labor-saving bungalow and a garden full of peonies—and when I came to the door, there they all were, inside, Mum and Dad, and Uncle Charlie I never liked much, and my auntie Beryl, and a quietish lady who I knew was my grandmother, though I'd never set eyes on her, she died before I was born, I proved it later from photographs. They were all sort of young and healthy-looking. The *scent* of those peonies. Mum was baking cakes, and I stood in the doorway and said, "Oh Mum, can I come in, oh can I come in, how good it all looks." And Mum said, "No, you can't come now. This cake is for your uncle Jack. Not you. It's not your time. You must go back. You are needed back there." And a shining kind of person, dark-skinned like a Red Indian maybe, came up the path, and said—he didn't exactly speak but I *heard* him tell me, no, Bonnie, you've got to go back, it isn't your time, there are things for you to do, and people who need you. And then I was back in my body in intensive care in St. George's and I heard them cry out, she's breathing. Ever since then, I've *known*. I've *known* death was good and not frightening. But all the rest—the healing and the clairvoyance and all that—I discovered when I joined the Academy."

"The Academy?"

"The Academy of the Return. We're a research group and a therapeutic community. You see, it turns out that my experience wasn't unusual really, not in terms of the other experiences of NDE. The experience seems to be the same—in all cultures and religions—the tunnel and the light and the figures, and seeing your parents again—"

"I've just lost my mother," said Joanna, involuntarily.

"Well, there you are. We were brought together, because of your need to know what I have to impart. Our two toothaches were brought about with a purpose, and that's why I couldn't cure mine, of course it is, our meeting was *meant*."

"But," said Joanna, her face furiously stabbing. How can you say, I don't want heaven, I want . . .

A white-clothed figure beckoned from the inner room. "Mr. Kestelman will see you now, Mrs. Roote."

Mrs. Roote rose, a little tremulously, looked to Joanna for reassurance, and crossed the threshold.

Joanna remembered Molly, in her last few months, complaining of noises. Joanna did not wish to remember the exact nature of these complaints, but they rose in her mind, with a difference. It was Molly's habit to wake herself with an automatic radio-teamaker, so that the voices of the world's news and the chatter and gossip of the BBC's presenters mingled with the vanishing veils of her uneasy sleep and the half-apprehended creatures of dream and nightmare. Or so Joanna now imagined, having tried out the device herself once and found her mind slipping in and out of what she vaguely felt were Molly's apprehensions and not her own. Anyway, she had thought Molly's last visions, if they could be dignified with that name, were functions of that domestic machinery. Molly, it was fair to admit, had insisted that they were not. She had asked for sympathy which Joanna had failed to offer. "I don't know often," she had said, trying to characterize these experiences, "if I'm waking or sleeping, I don't know where I am, either, but I do hear your grandparents, dear, quarreling dreadfully in the next room, ever so close, and it's as though I can't quite be heard or seen yet, but I might be at any minute, they might turn on me and draw me into it at any minute, and I always tried so hard not to be drawn in. . . ."

And once, "Oh, Joanna, they are waiting for me—I almost said, lying in wait, but that would be an awful thing to say, about one's own parents, wouldn't it? I don't want you to miss me, dear, when I'm gone, I want you to have a good time and know I was grateful for all you did, even if I'm a cantankerous old bitch a lot of the time. I've had my time, and that's it, and if it wasn't much of a time, it's no good crying over spilt milk, is it?"

And the next day, "I can hear more and more of what they're saying, in the next room. Just as it always was, nothing changed. Ma feels neglected and Pa feels nagged and put-upon, *just* the same. . . ."

"Old memories are reactivated in your brain, Mother. It's usual. People remember things in their seventies they haven't thought of for thirty years."

"I know. But I can't sleep for their wrangling. And I can't wake up enough to stop hearing it."

Bonnie Roote came out of the surgery, clutching a wad of tissues to her face, like a huge peony, the edges of its petals stained with bright pink lipstick and scarlet threads of blood. The attendant told Joanna Mr. Kestelman would be ready in a moment. Bonnie Roote sat on the sofa, the side of her lively face swollen and awkward.

"Was it bad?" said Joanna.

Bonnie shook her head, indicating no. She mopped at her mouth. She opened her handbag, and held out a card to Joanna. She said, carefully, slurring, "We were destined to meet, dear, that's the meaning of it. Here is the address—come when you need us, if you need us."

The card said, "The Academy of the Return. Thanatology and the study of the Afterlife. Therapeutic groups: spiritual and physical health alike our concern. We may have the answers to the questions you have always been asking. Try us."

Mr. Kestelman, taciturn and scientific in his sterile workplace, removed one of Joanna's teeth, which, he explained, had had a mosaic of tiny cracks and had finally crumbled altogether. Joanna must not, on any account, he said, disturb the blood clot, which would eventually form the new gum in the gap. Joanna tasted blood, iron and gravy combined, and felt the temporary absence of a huge segment of her head. She nodded with heavy gravity to his instructions, which included going home immediately and lying down, trying to have a sleep, to get over the shock. Munificent in small things, he filled her handbag with paper tissues and little strips of encapsulated painkillers in foil. "You'll feel queasy when it comes back to life, at first," he told her. "But don't worry. It doesn't last." He told her not to explore with her tongue and she withdrew its tip guiltily from what felt like a huge soft cabbage of congealing flabby matter, replacing the lost grinder, the shining citadel of the toothpaste advertisements of her childhood. Under lost childish teeth, fringed and rootless, had been the purposeful saw-ridge of the mature, the real thing. She remembered the taste and the intricacy. It was a shock that there would, this time, be no replacement.

The house was unwelcoming, rebarbative and reproachful. She hurried through it, ignoring it, to her bedroom, and drew the curtains for the prescribed lying-down. Then she got up again and opened them. Closed curtains in daylight meant death. The good weather persisted: let the sun shine in. It didn't shine in, much: Joanna's room was not on the sunny side of the house. She got into the bed, in her petticoat, and closed her eyes; her inner vision immediately projected, on a screen, a terrible horse head, a stripped skull long in the tooth, its empty sockets and gaunt jaws running with pale carnation-colored blood, the color of the inside of her eyelid no doubt, crawling on the ivory bones, long, long in the tooth. Joanna said to herself, precisely, that loss of a tooth aroused all sorts of primitive fears and opened her eyes waterily focusing on the pelmet, the dressing table, the silk lampshade. When she closed her eyes again all she could see was the carnation color, turbulent in tossing waves. She sighed, and slept.

There were voices in the next room. Aggrieved voices, running on in little dashes like a thwarted beck clucking against pebble beds and rooted impediments. They had the ease of long custom and the abrasiveness of new rage. Joanna could not put words together, only the tone, which pricked the skin of her shoulders, primeval hackles shaved away by centuries of civilization. She could hear other sounds: the clink of teacups and once, surely, the angry smack of iron on ironing board. Sleep and throbbing washes of toothache insulated her for a while but she had in the end to acknowledge that she was awake and that the yammer persisted; it could not be extinguished, as she had extinguished the horse head, by appeal to daylight. She got up and walked to and fro in her bedroom, and the voices in the next room sharpened and faded as she approached and retreated. She could see this nonexistent room very clearly, a dusty place, with a table, two chairs, a gas cooker and a high, inaccessible closed window. The room next to hers was in fact an airing cupboard; she went to open its door, where its innocent shelves held her innocent nightdresses, tidily folded. The voices spoke beyond their flimsy wall. "I shall put the house on the market," Joanna told the airing cupboard, to see if her live voice would banish these dusty ones. They rustled furiously. Phrases came through. "*No* consideration . . . *No* imagination . . ." And then, "Out of sight, out of mind, I see." And then, silence. She could not see why silence should ever have supervened. Or for how long it might last.

She put the house on the market. The estate agent, Mr. Maw, called, and Joanna showed him over it, room by room, and lastly the garden, early one morning before she left for the Survey. In the garden, swifts swooped and a blackbird sang, and the pergola roses breathed soft and sweet. In the house Mr. Maw was effusive. A delightful property, he said, entering its vital statistics on a kind of abstract map on yellow paper, as Mr. Kestelman had earlier entered Joanna's ravaged or vanished teeth on some archetypal mouth-plan. He paced the rooms, measuring them with his bright black shoes, toe to heel. In parts of the house, even while he was there, the voices hissed and jangled. It was as though these brick walls were interwoven with some other tough, flexible, indestructible structure, containing other rooms, other vistas, other jammed doors. Like a dress and its lining, with the slimmest space between. He should have no trouble selling this lovely residence, Mr. Maw told Joanna, in such good repair and so tastefully done up. Anyone could see it had been lived in very happily. It was *homely*, it had good vibrations, you came to recognize them in his business. It must be a real wrench for Miss Hope, leaving this pleasant spot. Could he recognize *bad* vibrations, Joanna asked him? Oh yes, he assured her. Like the smell of unattended drains, on very rare occasions. He had had a client once who had had to resort to an exorcist. The property had been brimful of rage and hatred. You could feel it like a temperature change, like a damp chill, coming over the threshold. Now here, you can feel love and consideration, like the polish on good furniture. Joanna said, I mean to travel. I never meant to settle down in this way. This was my mother's house, my mother's idea of. She could not say, of what. Nor did Mr. Maw want to know. He said he was sure she would find a nice holiday abroad very restorative, and then he could perhaps help her to find a labor-saving little maisonette.

Mike found her crying amongst the filing cabinets in the Survey Record Room. She did not say that she had been looking up their official report on the North African desert road, which had concluded in fact that it need never be built, that there was not enough demand. She had been thinking of the close bright stars, the bargaining in the bazaar, the heat in the jeep. Mike made her a plastic beaker of nasty but welcome coffee and put his arm round her shoulder. "Poor old Jo," he said, and she did not take offense, for that was what he had said then, when the mosquitoes bit her and her feet blistered. "Poor old Jo. What's up exactly?"

"I put the house on the market."

"Isn't that a bit precipitate?"

"I don't want it. And I keep hearing my parents quarreling in the next room."

She did not expect him to believe her, but there was relief in the statement.

"You did them proud. They're gone now. You can get a place of your own."

And if I had had, once, a place of my own . . . we should not now be sitting companionably here. She persisted.

"I keep feeling they're not gone. I hear them."

"You need a change."

"I know. I was going to ask. I wondered. I've lived all these years hoping—believing I could travel again, do another tour, get away—I suppose it's hopeless."

"On the whole," said Mike gently, "the foreign tours are saved for the tough young men, the single ones at that. You know how it is. But I did have an idea. If it appeals. It isn't glamorous. It's a change, though. Would you want to go to Durham? We've got a project on, on the feasibility of new small industries in mining villages. You know, the Survey always did a little local work, as well as the international. Nowadays, that's on the increase. You'd be talking to skilled men, interviewing local planners. What do you think?"

The African moon faded and the horizon contracted like a brace. All the same.

"It's a challenge."

"Right. Exercise the old fieldwork techniques even if not exactly breaking new ground? Get you away from the voices in the next room."

"They won't like that."

"Now you're being silly. I'll fix you up with a lunch with Protheroe, who's liaising with the finance companies, and we'll get you off next week."

The night before she left for Durham, Joanna spent a considerable time in the conservatory. The plants were silent, living their own lives. Mrs. Stillingfleet would come in and attend to them until the house was sold. Mr. Maw had had one or two tempting nibbles, he said, but nothing definite yet. It was early days, he said. He could get in touch if Miss Hope was needed. Durham wasn't the end of the earth. The conservatory had a harsh pool of light in its center, and a peripheral population of ghostly plants, reflected amongst harsh slivers of glitter off dark glass squares. The sky was very close; a black layer on black walls and roof, apparently solid above the solid glass. Tendrils hung softly from invisible struts, feathery fronds of jasmine, corkscrew curls of passion flowers, a contained little jungle, neatly trained and tied. The potted plants were banked on trays of sandy gravel on benches, smelling paradoxically of cold, moonlit steam. Joanna moved amongst them, breaking off a dead leaf here, removing a spent bloom there. Several of these had blushed unseen; she had not visited them since Molly's death. Now she looked at the cactuses and their pups, Molly's favorites. "I must see to my pups," she had said, the week after Donald's scattering, though she had mocked him when he boasted of their health and multiplicity. Pups, indeed, Molly had then said. Anyone would think they were sentient creatures, the way you go on. Looking at the major cactus, now, swollen and furry, sprouting cobwebs of silvery hairs, and surrounded by little, fat, arachnoid replicas of itself, Joanna more or less felt its discomfort in her own blood. It was unbalanced, sprawling heavily over the rim of its container. Carefully she broke off and repotted some of the younger tumuli, digging with Molly's little brass shovel in Molly's little tub of gritty, arid potting compost. Not a creak, not a whisper. The Christmas cactus,

Joanna Hope, was not a true cactus. It needed watering and feeding freely, it needed a good loam, like any other flowering plant. It did not of course flower in summer, but it did put on new growth. Joanna picked one up. It had strange, gawkily bent arms, made of segments at slight angles to each other. The lower segments were dark green and ridged. The higher ones were paler green. The newest, perhaps the size of Joanna's little fingernail, were glossy with health and were flushed with a roseate glow that hinted at the pure salmon-flesh pink the improbable bloom would be, in midwinter. This pink color, and the hooked, serrated end of the segment, gave it a resemblance to the claw of some marine creature; this was enhanced by the little fringe of hairy feelers that sprouted where the new segment joined the old, and so, repeated and invariable, down all the joints of the awkward stem or arm. These feelers were of course roots. If you broke off one of these segments, delicately, roots and all, and planted it firmly in a new pot of new earth, it would expand into another plant, darken and lose its translucent pinkness, sprout more segments. Some of these plants must be parts of other plants her father himself had teased into shape, fed and watered. They represented a sort of eternity, predictable, cyclical, unchanging in form and color. The roseate segments with their very new crenellated edges reminder her of her baby teeth: but after the baby teeth had come the rooted teeth, and after the rooted teeth this fleshed and shrinking hole. Joanna picked up a small, unassuming "Joanna Hope" stuck, by Molly no doubt, into a pale blue plastic plant pot, and took it up to bed with her. It was quiet, and alive. It might be possible to take it out of this house, up to Durham.

In the next room, the voices had acquired a certain ruggedness and clarity. Why not irises, said one, an iris bed, a raised iris bed, is a splendid feature. Not for most of the year, said the other, querulous granite, just a mass of ugly old leaves, taking up space, you want something serviceable and adaptable. You never give any credit to the larger things of the imagination, said the first voice, never. It's worth the old leaves for its time of glory. You never could see that, you never could see glory. You could have one or two at the back, said the ungiving voice, by the cistern there, one or two. What use are one or two, said the sad voice, and was answered, you never understand the proper *scale* of things, a bed of that size is just silly, just presumptuous, in the space you've got. One or two by the cistern. The roots need sun, said the other, you fool, the roots need sun, they must be baked in sun, soaked in light, you never understood that, never, you never admitted how much light they needed, you moved that bronze bearded one I had under the laurels where it rotted. . . .

There must, Joanna thought, be endless quarreling singing voices attached to this piece of earth: why do I hear only these? Are the happy silent? Bonnie Roote's relatives were in suburban bliss. The Academy of the Return might explain this anger, but I will not go there. I will go north and leave the field to them, the garden and the next room both, and they can call on Mr. Maw to arbitrate, who will not hear them, who experiences them, if he senses them at all, as, what was it, full of love and consideration. Be quiet, she said to them, aloud or not, she hardly knew, and she heard them hear her protest and ignore it. Impossible to come to any civilized arrangement with you, one said to the other, impossible, impossible.

County Durham was full of ancient things that had once been powerful new beginnings. The cathedral, slipping slightly into the river down its craggy steep, houses the bones of St. Cuthbert and the black slab under which rests the Venerable Bede, who changed the shape of the English sense of the English and their history. The mining villages are scattered in pockets amongst purple and gray moorland, not strung in a black chain as they are further south in Yorkshire. Ancient mills have become industrial archaeological sites, as Roman camps became before them, where the wind whistles in over heather and soughing bracken. New steel mills stand, silent, empty and cold; colliery wheels above their conical slag heaps are rusty and forever still. Joanna for some reason noticed the dead, though her work was with the living and despondent. Legionnaires from Scythia and Mesopotamia and the sunlit Provincia Romana lay under that heather. Undernourished girls and boys haunted the mills and the old workings, perhaps still lacerated by the straps with which they had hauled loads of ore. Joanna listened for them and could not hear them. She herself was housed in the splendid Mitre Hotel in Durham, where the assize judges had slept when not housed in the Castle, where they still slept, feeding well, laughing sonorously, going out to admonish sinners, release the innocent, and command the confinement of the guilty in the fortresslike jail where other dead lay in quicklime and where the sheriff's hair had gone white with horror at a hanging. The hotel was, it claimed in its parchmentlike, tasteful brochure, quite possibly haunted by a wrongfully hanged highwayman and a distraught Jacobite widow who had ridden vainly to save her beloved from his terrible march to the Tower. Their presence, the brochure said, announced itself respectively by a feeling of great coldness and panic, or by a kind of sighing noise and unbearable apprehension. Joanna liked the hotel, which had ancient uneven floors and romantically low and heavy doorways, newly embellished with heavy firedoors. She dined in the dining room among warm smells of good cooking, brandy *flambé,* crisp hot pastry, garlic-simmered sauces, a long and splendid way away from poached eggs on toast and Benger's Food. Her terror of the presences in the next room in her own house, she thought, over apple pie and crumbly Wensleydale and fresh cream, was not a gut terror such as that evoked by highwayman and mourning lady. Her ghosts only grumbled, they did not threaten, nor did they bear with them any searing experience of unbearable pain. No, the truth was, they were simply *theoretically* frightening. She did not wish to believe the revenant of the Academy of the Return. She did not wish to spend eternity, or even an indefinable future life or lives, in the company of Donald and Molly, the iron and the kettle. She had formed the hypothesis, for want of a better one, that her parents did indeed persist in death, much as they had been in life. She might conceivably be schizophrenic and hallucinating, of course, but she believed she was not, and was by no means going to waste her valuable and abbreviated future on discussion of raised iris beds with an expensive psychiatrist. She had formed the further hypothesis, or hope, that these spirits, or presences, were attached to the earth where they had lived and died, as the Red Indian so providentially revealed to her had suggested. They were there, and she was here. Mr. Maw would sell them, and their husks of housing, with the bricks and mortar they had been previously confined by. This view was encouraged by the *local* nature of their disputes, insofar as she had heard them.

There was another hypothesis, a worse one, which she refused to entertain. She slept soundly the first night in her brown and gold hotel room, enjoying everything, a dark blood-red bathroom *en suite,* a marvelous tray full of instant teas, coffees, little sugar biscuits, a television, a radio, everything anonymous, user-friendly, you might say, or simply indifferent to its users, who were not inhabitants, who were rootless passengers on the earth, as Joanna had always wished to be. She slept one night in silence. Two. Three. She went into Durham and met the team of economists and market researchers and computer experts who were testing out various job-creation plans. She met also the local unemployed, the skilled men, whose predicament funded her own precarious livelihood. She sat in Job Centres across scarred formica tables on hard leatherette chairs and discussed retraining. She had some hopes. Joanna had always been a believer in human ingenuity. Also in progress. It is hard to become a development economist if you do not believe in those things. She had supposed human ingenuity would find ways round food shortages and overpopulation, round scarcity of fossil fuels and the joblessness initially caused by the second industrial revolution, round third-world hunger and starvation wages battling with first-world standards of living and normal requirements for a decent day's work. Beyond that she had more vaguely believed in men becoming wiser, cleverer, healthier, more adaptable and accommodating, outgrowing war and anger as childish things. It was hard to maintain these beliefs in the face of the kind of cultural and personal vertigo experienced by whole communities of men with complex crafts which would never be needed again, never again be a guarantee of wit, or pride or marvel. The ones who distressed her were those a little younger than herself, who had invested a life in this form of activity, whose bodies and brain cells were excited functions of cutting *this* tool, gauging *this* kind of coal face, wiring *this* kind of digger. One she talked to, a large man who had been foreman of a specialized tube-making team in the steel mills, turned on her with a kind of personal accusation. "Me father worked in t'mill, and his father before him, and I wanted nowt for me son, nowt but that he should do an honest day's wek in t'mill, the same as I did. We have us pride, you know, we have us sense of community, we know who and what we are, and now they come along and say no, you're not economic, you're not competitive, we don't want to know. But we have *the skills.* . . ."

"You could acquire other skills."

"Oh yes. To do what? What skills? Young men might learn to operate them computers, but us as are set in our ways, we're dead men, and you know it, you've written us off, a whole generation, you can't wait for us to be tidied away. Come on, admit it."

"I'm not here for that reason."

"No. O'course you aren't. But you're not here to help men like me, are you? Th'young, maybe. Th'bright ones. I'd give up investigating us and let us die wi decency as fast as we can, Miss. Honest I would."

Later, in her hotel room again, Joanna felt despondent after this conversation with a self-styled dead man. The mass of men, she thought, are disappointed and angry. Why should the dead be any different, why should we suppose that it isn't our absolute nature to want more than we can have and yet to cling like limpets to what we know and have made of ourselves? Why not bungalows with peonies, why not a department of the afterlife full of fine steel tubing? Why should not the worst and most tenacious aspects of our characters persist longest? Why should I suppose that I have any right to hope either to change the world or to be quietly annihilated: those hopes are just part of what I am, which goes on and on within certain clearly defined and very narrow limits. As if in answer to her thoughts on disappointment and anger the voices started up, muttering behind the bathroom door, indistinguishable but furious, furious, purely enraged. Joanna's second hypothesis had been that it is indeed our ancestors who form our eternity, the time before and the time after our short time on earth, like the Japanese grandfather who presided at breakfast, like Bonnie Roote's happy family gathering. For an individual man or woman was an object not unlike the Christmas cactus, "Joanna Hope," bearing its eternal genes which dictate its form and future forever and forever. The voices were attached, not to the vacated garden, but to her own blood and presence. She could go to the Academy of the Return and inquire what quality in her it was that enabled her to hear them, or she could close her mind to them, confront and ignore them. She went to the bathroom door. She imagined the alternatives behind it: shower curtain, nonslip rubber bathmat, glistening red porcelain, or the dusty garret the voices inhabited. There was a susurration: shifting plastic, dripping tap, monotonous plaint.

"Please be quiet," she said. "I can hear you. I can't help you, and I don't want to hear you. You must make things better yourselves. . . . Please, I beg of you, leave me alone. Now."

Silence. More silence. Courage, Joanna thought, turning back towards the delightful anonymous bed, with its strip of discreet lighting, with its warm gold sheets.

As she raised her knee to get into it, the voice said, "Of course, if you'd treated her a bit better, she wouldn't be so spiteful, she'd show more understanding, more consideration, she was often lacking in feeling but I put some of it down to your mismanagement. . . ."

"She'll learn, in the fullness of time."

In the fullness of time, the fine barrier would indeed be opened, Joanna concluded, and she would in her turn pass, none too quietly, into that next room.

BARRY YOURGRAU

Grass

I go to the graveyard after dinner. My mother's ghost stoops beside my parents' headstone, pulling a weed. "Hello, dear," she says. "Just tidying up a bit. I don't know why they bother to pay the people here, they don't do a thing. How are you, my darling?" I give her a kiss, pressing my lips to her flickering cheek. "Looks very nice," I tell her, indicating the paired graves. "It's a handsome site, and a handsome marker," she says. She considers the gravestone. "It's what a gravestone should look like: simple lettering, very elegant and plain. You chose well," she says. "You did right for your poor departed mom and dad." "Thanks," I tell her. I look about. "Where is he? I brought him some pickles, at least to sniff." "Oh how sweet of you," she says. "He's turned in already. But you can leave that right over there, he'll be sure to pounce on it when he wakes." I put the jar down in the grass. "Yes, that worm is still giving him hell in his ear, poor thing," she says. "You don't think we could get a doctor to come and look at it?" "Mom, doctors don't really like to make house calls to cemeteries," I point out. "I suppose you're right," she says. "I'm afraid there's nothing for him to do but put up with it," I tell her. I shrug. "I'm sorry. It just goes with the general condition." "Is that so?" she sighs. "My, what a knowledgeable young man you are. Well, just wait, one day you'll be buried six feet under with the worms gnawing away at you, and we'll see what wise things you have to say then." "I won't say a thing, because I'll have myself cremated and stored away in a silver urn," I tell her. "My, what a clever lad you are too," she says. I give a smile at all this bantering. "So tell me, how are you, Mom?" I ask gently.

"Are you getting used to this?" "Oh, you know me, I'm fine," she says. "Fine. Very peaceful. The worms don't seem to like me at all, which offends me greatly. Oh, it's a bit startling now and then," she says, looking down at a flickering hand, "to be able to see right through one's moldering body. But we have to take things as they come, and make the best of them." I nod, contemplating her bare, crooked feet, which never did have the hammer-toe operation they needed. I can make out the darkness of the grass through them. "I'm sorry," I say quietly. "Nothing to be sorry about," she replies. "All part of the grand scheme." We fall silent. I look off at the graveyard, and then up into the night. The night sky is shot through with the benevolent plentitude of the stars. "When I get low," my mother says beside me, "I just lift up my eyes." She indicates the expanse of the heavens. "I gaze up there for a long, long time every night," she says. "The stars are my friends. Each one of them has a soul, you know. I've given them names." "I believe they already have names," I murmur. "Not my names," she replies. "That one over there, shining for all it's worth, that's you. That big gleaming greenish thing near it, that's your father. . . ." "And which one are you?" I ask. "Oh, I haven't quite made up my mind," she says. "I'm up there all right. But it's a very special one, my particular star. Very special indeed, you can bet your boots on it." Together we scan the constellations. My mother exhibits a hand, wavering and pale. "I'm a star already, just look at me," she says.

STEVEN MILLHAUSER

Eisenheim the Illusionist

In the last years of the nineteenth century, when the Empire of the Hapsburgs was nearing the end of its long dissolution, the art of magic flourished as never before. In obscure villages of Moravia and Galicia, from the Istrian Peninsula to the mists of Bukovina, bearded and black-caped magicians in market squares astonished townspeople by drawing streams of dazzling silk handkerchiefs from empty paper cones, removing billiard balls from children's ears, and throwing into the air decks of cards that assumed the shapes of fountains, snakes, and angels before returning to the hand. In cities and larger towns, from Zagreb to Lvov, from Budapest to Vienna, on the stages of opera houses, town halls, and magic theaters, traveling conjurers equipped with the latest apparatus enchanted sophisticated audiences with elaborate stage illusions. It was the age of levitations and decapitations, of ghostly apparitions and sudden vanishings, as if the tottering Empire were revealing through the medium of its magicians its secret desire for annihilation. Among the remarkable conjurers of that time, none achieved the heights of illusion attained by Eisenheim, whose enigmatic final performance was viewed by some as a triumph of the magician's art, by others as a fateful sign.

Eisenheim, né Eduard Abramowitz, was born in Bratislava in 1859 or 1860. Little is known of his early years, or indeed of his entire life outside the realm of illusion. For the scant facts we are obliged to rely on the dubious memoirs of magicians, on comments in contemporary newspaper stories and trade periodicals, on promotional material and brochures for magic acts; here and there the diary entry of a countess or ambassador records attendance at a performance in Paris, Cracow, Vienna. Eisenheim's father was a highly respected cabinetmaker, whose ornamental gilt cupboards and skillfully carved lowboys with lion-paw feet and brass handles shaped like snarling lions graced the halls of the gentry of Bratislava. The boy was the eldest of four children; like many Bratislavan Jews, the family spoke German and called their city Pressburg, although they understood as much Slovak and Magyar as was necessary for the proper conduct of business. Eduard went to work early in his father's shop. For the rest of his life he would retain a fondness for smooth pieces of wood joined seamlessly by mortise and tenon. By the age of seventeen he was himself a skilled cabinetmaker, a fact noted more than once by fellow magicians who admired Eisenheim's skill in constructing trick cabinets of breathtaking ingenuity. The young craftsman was already a passionate amateur magician, who is said to have entertained family and friends with card sleights and a disappearing-ring trick that required a small beechwood box of his own construction. He would place a borrowed ring inside, fasten the box tightly with twine, and quietly remove the ring as he handed the box to a spectator. The beechwood box, with its secret panel, was able to withstand the most minute examination.

A chance encounter with a traveling magician is said to have been the cause of Eisenheim's lifelong passion for magic. The story goes that one day, returning from school, the boy saw a man in black sitting under a plane tree. The man called him over and lazily, indifferently, removed from the boy's ear first one coin and then another, and then a third, coin after coin, a whole handful of coins, which suddenly turned into a bunch of red roses. From the roses the man in black drew out a white billiard ball, which turned into a wooden flute that suddenly vanished. One version of the story adds that the man himself then vanished, along with the plane tree. Stories, like conjuring tricks, are invented because history is inadequate to our dreams, but in this case it is reasonable to suppose that the future master had been profoundly affected by some early experience of conjuring. Eduard had once seen a magic shop, without much interest; he now returned with passion. On dark winter mornings on the way to school he would remove his gloves to practice manipulating balls and coins with chilled fingers in the pockets of his coat. He enchanted his three sisters with intricate shadowgraphs representing Rumpelstiltskin and Rapunzel, American buffaloes and Indians, the golem of Prague. Later a local conjurer called Ignazc Molnar taught him juggling for the sake of coordinating movements of the eye and hand. Once, on a dare, the thirteen-year-old boy carried an egg on a soda straw all the way to Bratislava Castle and back. Much later, when all this was far behind him, the Master would be sitting gloomily in the corner of a Viennese apartment where a party was being held in his honor, and reaching up wearily he would startle his hostess by producing from the air five billiard balls that he proceeded to juggle flawlessly.

But who can unravel the mystery of the passion that infects an entire life, bending it away from its former course in one irrevocable swerve? Abramowitz seems to have accepted his fate slowly. It was as if he kept trying to evade the disturbing knowledge of his difference. At the age of twenty-four he was still an expert cabinetmaker who did occasional parlor tricks.

As if suddenly, Eisenheim appeared at a theater in Vienna and began his exhilarating and fatal career. The brilliant newcomer was twenty-eight years old. In fact, contemporary records show that the cabinetmaker from Bratislava had appeared in private performances for at least a year before moving to the Austrian capital. Although the years preceding the first private performances remain mysterious, it is clear that Abramowitz gradually shifted his attention more and more fully to magic, by way of the trick chests and cabinets that he had begun to supply to local magicians. Eisenheim's nature was like that: he proceeded slowly and cautiously, step by step, and then, as if he had earned the right to be daring, he would take a sudden leap.

The first public performances were noted less for their daring than for their subtle mastery of the stage illusions of the day, although even then there were artful twists and variations. One of Eisenheim's early successes was The Mysterious Orange Tree, a feat made famous by Robert-Houdin. A borrowed handkerchief was placed in a small box and handed to a member of the audience. An assistant strode onto the stage, bearing in his arms a small green orange tree in a box. He placed the box on the magician's table and stepped away. At a word from Eisenheim, accompanied by a pass of his wand, blossoms began to appear on the tree. A moment later, oranges began to emerge;

Eisenheim plucked several and handed them to members of the audience. Suddenly two butterflies rose from the leaves, carrying a handkerchief. The spectator, opening his box, discovered that his handkerchief had disappeared; somehow the butterflies had found it in the tree. The illusion depended on two separate deceptions: the mechanical tree itself, which produced real flowers, real fruit, and mechanical butterflies by means of concealed mechanisms; and the removal of the handkerchief from the trick box as it was handed to the spectator. Eisenheim quickly developed a variation that proved popular: the tree grew larger each time he covered it with a red silk cloth, the branches produced oranges, apples, pears, and plums, at the end a whole flock of colorful, real butterflies rose up and fluttered over the audience, where children screamed with delight as they reached up to snatch the delicate silken shapes, and at last, under a black velvet cloth that was suddenly lifted, the tree was transformed into a bird-cage containing the missing handkerchief.

At this period, Eisenheim wore the traditional silk hat, frock coat, and cape and performed with an ebony wand tipped with ivory. The one distinctive note was his pair of black gloves. He began each performance by stepping swiftly through the closed curtains onto the stage apron, removing the gloves, and tossing them into the air, where they turned into a pair of sleek ravens.

Early critics were quick to note the young magician's interest in uncanny effects, as in his popular Phantom Portrait. On a darkened stage, a large blank canvas was illuminated by limelight. As Eisenheim made passes with his right hand, the white canvas gradually and mysteriously gave birth to a brighter and brighter painting. Now, it is well known among magicians and mediums that a canvas of unbleached muslin may be painted with chemical solutions that appear invisible when dry; if sulphate of iron is used for blue, nitrate of bismuth for yellow, and copper sulphate for brown, the picture will appear if sprayed with a weak solution of prussiate of potash. An atomizer, concealed in the conjurer's sleeve, gradually brings out the invisible portrait. Eisenheim increased the mysterious effect by producing full-length portraits that began to exhibit lifelike movements of the eyes and lips. The fiendish portrait of an archduke, or a devil, or Eisenheim himself would then read the contents of sealed envelopes, before vanishing at a pass of the magician's wand.

However skillful, a conjurer cannot earn and sustain a major reputation without producing original feats of his own devising. It was clear that the restless young magician would not be content with producing clever variations of familiar tricks, and by 1890 his performances regularly concluded with an illusion of striking originality. A large mirror in a carved frame stood on the stage, facing the audience. A spectator was invited onto the stage, where he was asked to walk around the mirror and examine it to his satisfaction. Eisenheim then asked the spectator to don a hooded red robe and positioned him some ten feet from the mirror, where the vivid red reflection was clearly visible to the audience; the theater was darkened, except for a brightening light that came from within the mirror itself. As the spectator waved his robed arms about, and bowed to his bowing reflection, and leaned from side to side, his reflection began to show signs of disobedience—it crossed its arms over its chest instead of waving them about, it refused to bow. Suddenly the reflection grimaced, removed a knife, and stabbed itself in the chest. The reflection collapsed onto the reflected floor. Now a ghostlike white form rose from the dead reflection and hovered in the mirror; all at once the ghost emerged from the glass, floated toward the startled and sometimes terrified spectator, and at the bidding of Eisenheim rose into the dark and vanished. This masterful illusion mystified even professional magicians, who agreed only that the mirror was a trick cabinet with black-lined doors at the rear and a hidden assistant. The lights were probably concealed in the frame between the glass and the lightly silvered back; as the lights grew brighter the mirror became transparent and a red-robed assistant showed himself in the glass. The ghost was more difficult to explain, despite a long tradition of stage ghosts; it was said that concealed magic lanterns produced the phantom, but no other magician was able to imitate the effect. Even in these early years, before Eisenheim achieved disturbing effects unheard of in the history of stage magic, there was a touch of the uncanny about his illusions; and some said even then that Eisenheim was not a showman at all, but a wizard who had sold his soul to the devil in return for unholy powers.

Eisenheim was a man of medium height, with broad shoulders and large, long-fingered hands. His most striking feature was his powerful head: the black intense eyes in the austerely pale face, the broad black beard, the thrusting forehead with its receding hairline, all lent an appearance of unusual mental force. The newspaper accounts mention a minor trait that must have been highly effective: when he leaned his head forward, in intense concentration, there appeared over his right eyebrow a large vein shaped like an inverted Y.

As the last decade of the old century wore on, Eisenheim gradually came to be acknowledged as the foremost magician of his day. These were the years of the great European tours, which brought him to Egyptian Hall in London and the Théâtre Robert-Houdin in Paris, to royal courts and ducal palaces, to halls in Berlin and Milan, Zurich and Salamanca. Although his repertoire continued to include perfected variations of popular illusions like The Vanishing Lady, The Blue Room, The Flying Watch, The Spirit Cabinet (or Specters of the Inner Sanctum), The Enchanted House, The Magic Kettle, and The Arabian Sack Mystery, he appeared to grow increasingly impatient with known effects and began rapidly replacing them with striking inventions of his own. Among the most notable illusions of those years were The Tower of Babel, in which a small black cone mysteriously grew until it filled the entire stage; The Satanic Crystal Ball, in which a ghostly form summoned from hell smashed through the glass globe and rushed out onto the stage with unearthly cries; and The Book of Demons, in which black smoke rose from an ancient book, which suddenly burst into flames that released hideous dwarfs in hairy jerkins who ran howling across the stage. In 1898 he opened his own theater in Vienna, called simply Eisenheimhaus, or The House of Eisenheim, as if that were his real home and all other dwellings illusory. It was here that he presented The Pied Piper of Hamelin. Holding his wand like a flute, Eisenheim led children from the audience into a misty hill with a cavelike opening and then, with a pass of his wand, caused the entire hill to vanish into thin air. Moments later a black chest materialized, from which the children emerged and looked around in bewilderment before running back to their parents. The children told their parents they had been in a wondrous mountain, with golden tables and chairs and white angels flying in the air; they had no idea how they had gotten into the box, or what had happened to them. A few complaints were made; and when, in another performance, a frightened child told his mother that he had been in hell and seen the devil, who was green and breathed fire, the chief of the Viennese police, one Walther Uhl, paid Eisenheim a visit. The Pied Piper of Hamelin never appeared again, but two results had emerged: a certain disturbing quality in Eisenheim's art was now officially acknowledged, and it was rumored that the stern master was being closely watched by Franz Josef's secret police. This last was unlikely, for the Emperor, unlike his notorious grandfather, took little interest in police espionage; but the rumor surrounded Eisenheim like a mist, blurring his sharp outline, darkening his features, and enhancing his formidable reputation.

Eisenheim was not without rivals, whose challenges he invariably met with a decisiveness, some would say ferocity, that left no doubt of his self-esteem. Two incidents of the last years of the century left a deep impression among contemporaries. In Vienna in 1898 a magician called Benedetti had appeared. Benedetti, whose real name was Paul Henri Cortot, of Lyon, was a master illusionist of extraordinary smoothness and skill; his mistake was to challenge Eisenheim by presenting imitations of original Eisenheim illusions, with clever variations, much as Eisenheim had once alluded to his predecessors in order to outdo them. Eisenheim learned of his rival's presumption and let it be known through the speaking portrait of a devil that ruin awaits the proud. The very next night, on Benedetti's stage, a speaking portrait of Eisenheim intoned in comic accents that ruin awaits the proud. Eisenheim, a proud and brooding man, did not allude to the insult during his Sunday night performance. On Monday night, Benedetti's act went awry: the wand leaped from his fingers and rolled across the stage; two fishbowls with watertight lids came crashing to the floor from beneath Benedetti's cloak; the speaking portrait remained mute; the levitating lady was seen to be resting on black wires. The excitable Benedetti, vowing revenge, accused Eisenheim of criminal tampering; two nights later, before a packed house, Benedetti stepped into a black cabinet, drew a curtain, and was never seen again. The investigation by Herr Uhl failed to produce a trace of foul play. Some said the unfortunate Benedetti had simply chosen the most convenient way of escaping to another city, under a new name, far from the scene of his notorious debacle; others were convinced that Eisenheim had somehow spirited him off, perhaps to hell. Viennese society was enchanted by the scandal, which made the round of the cafés; and

Herr Uhl was seen more than once in a stall of the theater, nodding his head appreciatively at some particularly striking effect.

If Benedetti proved too easy a rival, a far more formidable challenge was posed by the mysterious Passauer. Ernst Passauer was said to be Bavarian; his first Viennese performance was watched closely by the Austrians, who were forced to admit that the German was a master of striking originality. Passauer took the city by storm; and for the first time there was talk that Eisenheim had met his match, perhaps even—was it possible?—his master. Unlike the impetuous and foolhardy Benedetti, Passauer made no allusion to the Viennese wizard; some saw in this less a sign of professional decorum than an assertion of arrogant indifference, as if the German refused to acknowledge the possibility of a rival. But the pattern of their performances, that autumn, was the very rhythm of rivalry: Eisenheim played on Sunday, Wednesday, and Friday nights, and Passauer on Tuesday, Thursday, and Saturday nights. It was noted that as his rival presented illusions of bold originality, Eisenheim's own illusions became more daring and dangerous; it was as if the two of them had outsoared the confines of the magician's art and existed in some new realm of dextrous wonder, of sinister beauty. In this high but by no means innocent realm, the two masters vied for supremacy before audiences that were increasingly the same. Some said that Eisenheim appeared to be struggling or straining against the relentless pressure of his brilliant rival; others argued that Eisenheim had never displayed such mastery; and as the heavy century lumbered to its close, all awaited the decisive event that would release them from the tension of an unresolved battle.

And it came: One night in mid-December, after a particularly daring illusion, in which Passauer caused first his right arm to vanish, then his left arm, then his feet, until nothing was left of him but his disembodied head floating before a black velvet curtain, the head permitted itself to wonder whether Herr "Eisenzeit," or Iron Age, had ever seen a trick of that kind. The mocking allusion caused the audience to gasp. The limelight went out; when it came on, the stage contained nothing but a heap of black cloth, which began to flutter and billow until it gradually assumed the shape of Passauer, who bowed coolly to tumultuous applause; but the ring of a quiet challenge was not lost in the general uproar. The following night Eisenheim played to a packed, expectant house. He ignored the challenge while performing a series of new illusions that in no way resembled Passauer's act. As he took his final bow, he remarked casually that Passauer's hour had passed. The fate of the unfortunate Benedetti had not been forgotten, and it was said that if the demand for Passauer's next performance had been met, the entire city of Vienna would have become a magic theater.

Passauer's final performance was one of frightening brilliance; it was well attended by professional magicians, who agreed later that as a single performance it outshone the greatest of Eisenheim's evenings. Passauer began by flinging into the air a handful of coins that assumed the shape of a bird and flew out over the heads of the audience, flapping its jingling wings of coins; from a silver thimble held in the flat of his hand he removed a tablecloth, a small mahogany table, and a silver salver on which sat a steaming roast duck. At the climax of the evening, he caused the properties of the stage to vanish one by one: the magician's table, the beautiful assistant, the far wall, the curtain. Standing alone in a vanished world, he looked at the audience with an expression that grew more and more fierce. Suddenly he burst into a demonic laugh, and reaching up to his face he tore off a rubber mask and revealed himself to be Eisenheim. The collective gasp sounded like a great furnace igniting; someone burst into hysterical sobs. The audience, understanding at last, rose to its feet and cheered the great master of illusion, who himself had been his own greatest rival and had at the end unmasked himself. In his box, Herr Uhl rose to his feet and joined in the applause. He had enjoyed the performance immensely.

Perhaps it was the strain of that sustained deception, perhaps it was the sense of being alone, utterly alone, in any case Eisenheim did not give another performance in the last weeks of the fading century. As the new century came in with a fireworks display in the Prater and a hundred-gun salute from the grounds of the Imperial Palace, Eisenheim remained in his Vienna apartment, with its distant view of the same river that flowed through his childhood city. The unexplained period of rest continued, developing into a temporary withdrawal from performance, some said a retirement; Eisenheim himself said nothing. In late January he returned to Bratislava to attend to details of his father's business; a week later he was in Linz; within a month he had purchased a three-story villa in the famous wooded hills on the outskirts of Vienna. He was forty or forty-one, an age when a man takes a hard look at his life. He had never married, although romantic rumors occasionally united him with one or another of his assistants; he was handsome in a stern way, wealthy, and said to be so strong that he could do thirty knee-bends on a single leg. Not long after his move to the Wienerwald he began to court Sophie Ritter, the twenty-six-year-old daughter of a local landowner who disapproved of Eisenheim's profession and was a staunch supporter of Lueger's anti-Semitic Christian Social party; the girl appears to have been in love with Eisenheim, but at the last moment something went wrong, she withdrew abruptly, and a month later married a grain merchant from Graz. For a year Eisenheim lived like a reclusive country squire. He took riding lessons in the mornings, in the afternoons practiced with pistols at his private shooting range, planted a spring garden, stocked his ponds, designed a new orchard. In a meadow at the back of his house he supervised the building of a long low shedlike structure that became known as the Teufelsfabrik, or Devil's Factory, for it housed his collection of trick cabinets, deceptive mirrors, haunted portraits, and magic caskets. The walls were lined with cupboards that had sliding glass doors and held Eisenheim's formidable collection of magical apparatus: vanishing bird-cages, inexhaustible punch bowls, devil's targets, Schiller's bells, watch-spring flowers, trick bouquets, and an array of secret devices used in sleight-of-hand feats: ball shells, coin droppers, elastic handkerchief-pulls for making handkerchiefs vanish, dummy cigars, color-changing tubes for handkerchief tricks, hollow thumb-tips, miniature spirit lamps for the magical lighting of candles, false fingers, black silk ball-tubes. In the basement of the factory was a large room in which he conducted chemical and electrical experiments, and a curtained darkroom; Eisenheim was a close student of photography and the new art of cinematography. Often he was seen working late at night, and some said that ghostly forms appeared in the dim-lit windows.

On the first of January, 1901, Eisenheim suddenly returned to his city apartment with its view of the Danube and the Vienna hills. Three days later he reappeared on stage. A local wit remarked that the master of illusion had simply omitted the year 1900, which with its two zeros no doubt struck him as illusory. The yearlong absence of the Master had sharpened expectations, and the standing-room-only crowd was tensely quiet as the curtains parted on a stage strikingly bare except for a plain wooden chair before a small glass table. For some in that audience, the table already signaled a revolution; others were puzzled or disappointed. From the right wing Eisenheim strode onto the stage. A flurry of whispers was quickly hushed. The Master wore a plain dark suit and had shaved off his beard. Without a word he sat down on the wooden chair behind the table and faced the audience. He placed his hands lightly on the tabletop, where they remained during the entire performance. He stared directly before him, leaning forward slightly and appearing to concentrate with terrific force.

In the middle of the eighteenth century the magician's table was a large table draped to the floor; beneath the cloth an assistant reached through a hole in the tabletop to remove objects concealed by a large cone. The modern table of Eisenheim's day had a short cloth that exposed the table legs, but the disappearance of the hidden assistant and the general simplification of design in no sense changed the nature of the table, which remained an ingenious machine equipped with innumerable contrivances to aid the magician in the art of deception: hidden receptacles or *servantes* into which disappearing objects secretly dropped, invisible wells and traps, concealed pistons, built-in spring-pulls for effecting the disappearance of silk handkerchiefs. Eisenheim's transparent glass table announced the end of the magician's table as it had been known throughout the history of stage magic. This radical simplification was not only esthetic: it meant the refusal of certain kinds of mechanical aid, the elimination of certain effects.

And the audience grew restless: nothing much appeared to be happening. A balding man in a business suit sat at a table, frowning. After fifteen minutes a slight disturbance or darkening in the air was noticeable near the surface of the table. Eisenheim concentrated fiercely; over his right eyebrow the famous vein, shaped like an inverted Y, pressed through the skin of his forehead. The air seemed to tremble and thicken—and before him, on the glass table, a dark shape slowly formed. It appeared to be a small box, about the size of a jewel box. For a while its edges quivered slightly, as if it were made of black smoke. Suddenly Eisenheim raised his eyes, which one witness described as black mirrors that reflected nothing; he looked drained and weary. A moment later he pushed back his chair, stood up, and bowed. The applause was uncertain; people did not know what they had seen.

Eisenheim next invited spectators to come onto the stage and examine the box on the table. One woman, reaching for the box and feeling nothing, nothing at all, stepped back and raised a hand to her throat. A girl of sixteen, sweeping her hand through the black box, cried out as if in pain.

The rest of the performance consisted of two more "materializations": a sphere and a wand. After members of the audience had satisfied themselves of the immaterial nature of the objects, Eisenheim picked up the wand and waved it over the box. He next lifted the lid of the box, placed the sphere inside, and closed the lid. When he invited spectators onto the stage, their hands passed through empty air. Eisenheim opened the box, removed the sphere, and laid it on the table between the box and the wand. He bowed, and the curtain closed.

Despite a hesitant, perplexed, and somewhat disappointed response from that first audience, the reviews were enthusiastic; one critic called it a major event in the history of stage illusions. He connected Eisenheim's phantom objects with the larger tradition of stage ghosts, which he traced back to Robertson's Phantasmagoria at the end of the eighteenth century. From concealed magic lanterns Robertson had projected images onto smoke rising from braziers to create eerie effects. By the middle of the nineteenth century magicians were terrifying spectators with a far more striking technique: a hidden assistant, dressed like a ghost and standing in a pit between the stage and the auditorium, was reflected onto the stage through a tilted sheet of glass invisible to the audience. Modern ghosts were based on the technique of the black velvet backdrop: overhead lights were directed toward the front of the stage, and black-covered white objects appeared to materialize when the covers were pulled away by invisible black-hooded assistants dressed in black. But Eisenheim's phantoms, those immaterial materializations, made use of no machinery at all—they appeared to emerge from the mind of the magician. The effect was startling, the unknown device ingenious. The writer considered and rejected the possibility of hidden magic lanterns and mirrors; discussed the properties of the cinematograph recently developed by the Lumière brothers and used by contemporary magicians to produce unusual effects of a different kind; and speculated on possible scientific techniques whereby Eisenheim might have caused the air literally to thicken and darken. Was it possible that one of the Lumière machines, directed onto slightly misted air above the table, might have produced the phantom objects? But no one had detected any mist, no one had seen the necessary beam of light. However Eisenheim had accomplished the illusion, the effect was incomparable; it appeared that he was summoning objects into existence by the sheer effort of his mind. In this the master illusionist was rejecting the modern conjurer's increasing reliance on machinery and returning the spectator to the troubled heart of magic, which yearned beyond the constricting world of ingenuity and artifice toward the dark realm of transgression.

The long review, heavy with *fin de siècle* portentousness and shot through with a secret restlessness or longing, was the first of several that placed Eisenheim beyond the world of conjuring and saw in him an expression of spiritual striving, as if his art could no longer be talked about in the old way.

During the next performance Eisenheim sat for thirty-five minutes at his glass table in front of a respectful but increasingly restless audience before the darkening was observed. When he sat back, evidently spent from his exertions, there stood on the table the head and shoulders of a young woman. The details of witnesses differ, but all reports agree that the head was of a young woman of perhaps eighteen or twenty with short dark hair and heavy-lidded eyes. She faced the audience calmly, a little dreamily, as if she had just wakened from sleep, and spoke her name: Greta. Fraülein Greta answered questions from the audience. She said she came from Brünn, she was seventeen years old; her father was a lens grinder; she did not know how she had come here. Behind her, Eisenheim sat slumped in his seat, his broad face pale as marble, his eyes staring as if sightlessly. After a while Fraülein Greta appeared to grow tired. Eisenheim gathered himself up and fixed her with his stare; gradually she wavered and grew dim, and slowly vanished.

With Fraülein Greta, Eisenheim triumphed over the doubters. As word of the new illusion spread, and audiences waited with a kind of fearful patience for the darkening of the air above the glass table, it became clear that Eisenheim had touched a nerve. Greta-fever was in the air. It was said that Fraülein Greta was really Marie Vetsera, who had died with Crown Prince Rudolf in the bedroom of his hunting lodge at Mayerling; it was said that Fraülein Greta, with her dark, sad eyes, was the girlhood spirit of the Empress Elizabeth, who at the age of sixty had been stabbed to death in Geneva by an Italian anarchist. It was said that Fraülein Greta knew things, all sorts of things, and could tell secrets about the other world. For a while Eisenheim was taken up by the spiritualists, who claimed him for one of their own: here at last was absolute proof of the materialization of spirit forms. A society of disaffected Blavatsky-ites called the Daughters of Dawn elected Eisenheim to an honorary member-ship, and three bearded members of a Salzburg Institute for Psychic Research began attending performances with black notebooks in hand. Magicians heaped scorn on the mediumistic confraternity but could not explain or duplicate the illusion; a shrewd group of mediums, realizing they could not reproduce the Eisenheim phenomena, accused him of fraud while defending themselves against the magicians' charges. Eisenheim's rigorous silence was taken by all sides as a sign of approval. The "manifestations," as they began to be called, soon included the head of a dark-haired man of about thirty, who called himself Frankel and demonstrated conventional tricks of mind reading and telepathy before fading away. What puzzled the professionals was not the mind reading but the production of Frankel himself. The possibility of exert-ing a physical influence on air was repeatedly argued; it was suggested in some quarters that Eisenheim had prepared the air in advance with a thickening agent and treated it with invisible chemical solutions, but this allusion to the timeworn trick of the muslin canvas convinced no one.

In late March Eisenheim left Vienna on an Imperial tour that included bookings in Ljubljana, Prague, Teplitz, Budapest, Kolozsvár, Czernowitz, Tar-nopol, Uzhgorod. In Vienna, the return of the Master was awaited with an impatience bordering on frenzy. A much-publicized case was that of Anna Scherer, the dark-eyed sixteen-year-old daughter of a Vienna banker, who declared that she felt a deep spiritual bond with Greta and could not bear life without her. The troubled girl ran away from home and was discovered by the police two days later wandering disheveled in the wooded hills northeast of the city; when she returned home she shut herself in her room and wept violently and uncontrollably for six hours a day. An eighteen-year-old youth was arrested at night on the grounds of Eisenheim's villa and later confessed that he had planned to break into the Devil's Factory and learn the secret of raising the dead. Devotees of Greta and Frankel met in small groups to discuss the Master, and it was rumored that in a remote village in Carinthia he had demonstrated magical powers of a still more thrilling and disturbing kind.

And the Master returned, and the curtains opened, and fingers tightened on the blue velvet chair-arms. On a bare stage stood nothing but a simple chair. Eisenheim, looking pale and tired, with shadowy hollows in his temples, walked to the chair and sat down with his large, long hands resting on his knees. He fixed his stare at the air and sat rigidly for forty minutes, while rivulets of sweat trickled along his high-boned cheeks and a thick vein pressed through the skin of his forehead. Gradually a darkening of the air was discernible and a shape slowly emerged. At first it seemed a wavering and indistinct form, like shimmers above a radiator on a wintry day, but soon there was a thickening, and before the slumped form of Eisenheim stood a beautiful boy. His large brown eyes, fringed with dark lashes, looked out trustingly, if a little dreamily; he had a profusion of thick hay-colored curls and wore a school uniform with dark green shorts and high gray socks. He seemed surprised and shy, uncomfortable before the audience, but as he began to walk about he became more animated and told his name: Elis. Many commented on the striking contrast between the angelic boy and the dark, brooding magician. The sweetness of the creature cast a spell over the audience, broken only when a woman was invited onto the stage. As she bent over to run her fingers through Elis's hair, her hand passed through empty air. She gave a cry that sounded like a moan and hurried from the stage in confusion. Later she said that the air had felt cold, very cold.

Greta and Frankel were forgotten in an outbreak of Elis-fever. The immaterial boy was said to be the most enchanting illusion ever created by a magician; the spiritualist camp maintained that Elis was the spirit of a boy who had died in Helgoland in 1787. Elis-fever grew to such a pitch that often sobs and screams would erupt from tense, constricted throats as the air before Eisenheim slowly began to darken and the beautiful boy took shape. Elis did not engage in the conventions of magic, but simply walked about on the stage, answering questions put to him by the audience or asking questions of his own. He said that his parents were dead; he seemed uncertain of many things, and grew confused when asked how he had come to be there. Sometimes he left the stage and walked slowly along the aisle, while hands reached out and grasped empty air. After half an hour Eisenheim would cause him to waver and grow dim, and Elis would vanish away. Screams often accompanied the disappearance of the beautiful boy; and after a particularly troubling episode, in which a young woman leaped onto the stage and began clawing the vanishing form, Herr Uhl was once again seen in attendance at the theater, watching with an expression of keen interest.

He was in attendance when Eisenheim stunned the house by producing a companion for Elis, a girl who called herself Rosa. She had long dark hair and black, dreamy eyes and Slavic cheekbones; she spoke slowly and seriously, often pausing to think of the exact word. Elis seemed shy of her and at first refused to speak in her presence. Rosa said she was twelve years old; she said she knew the secrets of the past and future, and offered to predict the death of anyone present. A young man with thin cheeks, evidently a student, raised his hand. Rosa stepped to the edge of the stage and stared at him for a long while with her earnest eyes; when she turned away she said that he would cough up blood in November and would die of tuberculosis before the end of the following summer. Pale, visibly shaken, the young man began to protest angrily, then sat down suddenly and covered his face with his hands.

Rosa and Elis were soon fast friends. It was touching to observe Elis's gradual overcoming of shyness and the growth of his intense attachment to her. Immediately after his appearance he would begin to look around sweetly, with his large, anxious eyes, as if searching for his Rosa. As Eisenheim stared with rigid intensity, Elis would play by himself but steal secret glances at the air in front of the magician. The boy would grow more and more agitated as the air began to darken; and a look of almost painful rapture would glow on his face as Rosa appeared with her high cheekbones and her black, dreamy eyes. Often the children would play by themselves onstage, as if oblivious of an audience. They would hold hands and walk along imaginary paths, swinging their arms back and forth, or they would water invisible flowers with an invisible watering can; and the exquisite charm of their gestures was noted by more than one witness. During these games Rosa would sing songs of haunting, melancholy beauty in an unfamiliar Low German dialect.

It remains unclear precisely when the rumor arose that Eisenheim would be arrested and his theater closed. Some said that Uhl had intended it from the beginning and had simply been waiting for the opportune moment; others pointed to particular incidents. One such incident occurred in late summer, when a disturbance took place in the audience not long after the appearance of Elis and Rosa. At first there were sharp whispers, and angry shushes, and suddenly a woman began to rise and then leaned violently away as a child rose from the aisle seat beside her. The child, a boy of about six, walked down the aisle and climbed the stairs to the stage, where he stood smiling at the audience, who immediately recognized that he was of the race of Elis and Rosa. Although the mysterious child never appeared again, spectators now began to look nervously at their neighbors; and it was in this charged atmosphere that the rumor of impending arrest sprang up and would not go away. The mere sight of Herr Uhl in his box each night caused tense whispers. It began to seem as if the policeman and the magician were engaged in a secret battle: it was said that Herr Uhl was planning a dramatic arrest, and Eisenheim a brilliant escape. Eisenheim for his part ignored the whispers and did nothing to modify the disturbing effects that Elis and Rosa had on his audience; and as if to defy the forces gathering against him, one evening he brought forth another figure, an ugly old woman in a black dress who frightened Elis and Rosa and caused fearful cries from the audience before she melted away.

The official reason given for the arrest of the Master, and the seizure of his theater, was the disturbance of public order; the police reports, in preparation for more than a year, listed more than one hundred incidents. But Herr Uhl's private papers reveal a deeper cause. The chief of police was an intelligent and well-read man who was himself an amateur conjurer, and he was not unduly troubled by the occasional extreme public responses to Eisenheim's illusions, although he recorded each instance scrupulously and asked himself whether such effects were consonant with public safety and decorum. No, what disturbed Herr Uhl was something else, something for which he had difficulty finding a name. The phrase "crossing of boundaries" occurs pejoratively more than once in his notebooks; by it he appears to mean that certain distinctions must be strictly maintained. Art and life constituted one such distinction; illusion and reality, another. Eisenheim deliberately crossed boundaries and therefore disturbed the essence of things. In effect, Herr Uhl was accusing Eisenheim of shaking the foundations of the universe, of undermining reality, and in consequence of doing something far worse: subverting the Empire. For where would the Empire be, once the idea of boundaries became blurred and uncertain?

On the night of February 14, 1902—a cold, clear night, when horseshoes rang sharply on the avenues, and fashionable women in chin-high black boas plunged their forearms into heavy, furry muffs—twelve uniformed policemen took their seats in the audience of Eisenheimhaus. The decision to arrest the Master during a performance was later disputed; the public arrest was apparently intended to send a warning to devotees of Eisenheim, and perhaps to other magicians as well. Immediately after the appearance of Rosa, Herr Uhl left his box. Moments later he strode through a side door onto the stage and announced the arrest of Eisenheim in the name of His Imperial Majesty and the City of Vienna. Twelve officers stepped into the aisles and stood at attention. Eisenheim turned his head wearily toward the intruding figure and did not move. Elis and Rosa, who had been standing at the edge of the stage, began to look about fearfully: the lovely boy shook his head and murmured "No" in his angelic voice, while Rosa hugged herself tightly and began to hum a low melody that sounded like a drawn-out moan or keen. Herr Uhl, who had paused some ten feet from Eisenheim in order to permit the grave Master to rise unaided, saw at once that things were getting out of hand—someone in the audience began murmuring "No," the chant was taken up. Swiftly Uhl strode to the seated magician and placed a hand on his shoulder. That was when it happened: his hand fell through Eisenheim's shoulder, he appeared to stumble, and in a fury he began striking at the magician, who remained seated calmly through the paroxysm of meaningless blows. At last the officer drew his sword and sliced through Eisenheim, who at this point rose with great dignity and turned to Elis and Rosa. They looked at him imploringly as they wavered and grew dim. The Master then turned to the audience; and slowly, gravely, he bowed. The applause began in scattered sections and grew louder and wilder until the curtains were seen to tremble. Six officers leaped onto the stage and attempted to seize Eisenheim, who looked at them with an expression of such melancholy that one policeman felt a shadow pass over his heart. And now a nervousness rippled through the crowd as the Master seemed to gather himself for some final effort: his face became rigid with concentration, the famous vein pressed through his forehead, the unseeing eyes were dark autumn nights when the wind picks up and branches creak. A shudder was seen to pass along his arms. It spread to his legs, and from the crowd rose the sound of a great inrush of breath as Eisenheim began his unthinkable final act: bending the black flame of his gaze inward, locked in savage concentration, he began to unknit the threads of his being. Wavering, slowly fading, he stood dark and unmoving there. In the Master's face some claimed to see, as he dissolved before their eyes, a look of fearful exaltation. Others said that at the end he raised his face and uttered a cry of icy desolation. When it was over the audience rose to its feet. Herr Uhl promptly arrested a young man in the front row, and a precarious order was maintained. On a drab stage, empty except for a single wooden chair, policemen in uniform looked tensely about.

Later that night the police ransacked the apartment with a distant view of the Danube, but Eisenheim was not there. The failed arrest was in one respect highly successful: the Master was never seen again. In the Devil's Factory trick mirrors were found, exquisite cabinets with secret panels, ingenious chests and boxes representing high instances of the art of deception, but not a clue about the famous illusions, not one, nothing. Some said that Eisenheim had created an illusory Eisenheim from the first day of the new century; others said that the Master had gradually grown illusory from trafficking with illusions. Someone suggested that Herr Uhl was himself an illusion, a carefully staged part of the final performance. Arguments arose over whether it was all done with lenses and mirrors, or whether the Jew from Bratislava had sold his soul to the devil for the dark gift of magic. All agreed that it was a sign of the times; and as precise memories faded, and the everyday world of coffee cups, doctors' visits, and war rumors returned, a secret relief penetrated the souls of the faithful, who knew that the Master had passed safely out of the crumbling order of history into the indestructible realm of mystery and dream.

WILLIAM GOYEN

Ghost and Flesh, Water and Dirt

Was somebody here while ago acallin for you. . . .

O don't say that, don't tell me who . . . was he fair and had a wrinkle in his chin? I wonder was he the one . . . describe me his look, whether the eyes were pale light-colored and swimmin and wild and shifty; did he bend a little at the shoulders was his face agrievin what did he say where did he go, whichaway, hush don't tell me; wish I could keep him but I can't, so go, go (but come back).

Cause you know honey there's a time to go roun and tell and there's a time to set still (and let a ghost grieve ya); so listen to me while I tell, cause I'm in my time a tellin and you better run fast if you don wanna hear what I tell, cause I'm goin ta tell. . . .

Dreamt last night again I saw pore Raymon Emmons, all last night seen im plain as day. There uz tears in iz glassy eyes and iz face uz all meltin away. O I was broken of my sleep and of my night disturbed, for I dreamt of pore Raymond Emmons live as ever.

He came on the sleepin porch where I was sleepin (and he's there to stay) riding a purple horse (like King was), and then he got off and tied im to the bedstead and come and stood over me and commenced iz talkin. All night long he uz talking and talkin, his speech (whatever he uz sayin) uz like steam streamin outa the mouth of a kettle, streaming and streamin and streamin. At first I said in my dream, "Will you do me the favor of tellin me just who in the world you can be, will you please show the kindness to tell me who you can be, breaking my sleep and disturbin my rest?" "I'm Raymon Emmons," the steamin voice said, "and I'm here to stay; putt out my things that you've putt away, putt out my oatmeal bowl and putt hot oatmeal in it, get out my rubber boots when it rains, iron my clothes and fix my supper. . . . I never died and I'm here to stay."

(Oh go way ole ghost of Raymon Emmons, whisperin in my ear on the pilla at night; go way ole ghost and lemme be! Quit standing over me like that, all night standin there saying something to me . . . behave ghost of Raymon Emmons, behave yoself and lemme be! Lemme get out and go roun, lemme put on those big ole rubberboots and go clompin. . . .)

Now, you shoulda known that Raymon Emmons. *There* was *somebody,* I'm tellin you. Oh he uz a bright thang, quick 'n fair, tall, about six feet, real lean and a devlish face full of snappin eyes, he had eyes all over his face, didn't miss a thang, that man, saw everthang; and a clean brow. He was a rayroad man, worked for the Guff Coast Lines all iz life, our house always smelt like a train.

When I first knew of him he was livin at the Boardinhouse acrost from the depot (oh that uz years and years ago), and I uz in town and wearin my first pumps when he stopped me on the corner and ast me to do him the favor of tellin him the size a my foot. I was not afraid atall to look at him and say the size a my foot uz my own affair and would he show the kindness to not be so fresh. But when he said I only want to know because there's somebody livin up in New Waverley about your size and age and I want to send a birthday present of some houseshoes to, I said that's different; and we went into Richardson's store, to the back where the shoes were, and tried on shoes till he found the kind and size to fit me and this person in New Waverley. I didn't tell im that the pumps I'uz wearin were Sistah's and not my size (when I got home and Mama said why'd it take you so long? I said it uz because I had to walk so slow in Sistah's pumps).

Next time I saw im in town (and I made it a point to look for im, was why I come to town), I went up to im and said do you want to measure my foot again Raymon Emmons, ha! And he said any day in the week I'd measure that pretty foot; and we went into Richardson's and he bought *me* a pair of white summer pumps with a pink tie (and I gave Sistah's pumps back to her).

Miz Richardson said my lands Margy you buyin lotsa shoes lately, are you going to take a trip (O I took a trip, and one I come back from, too).

We had other meetins and was plainly in love; and when we married, runnin off to Groveton to do it, everybody in town said things about the marriage because he uz thirty and I uz seventeen.

We moved to this house owned by the Picketts, with a good big clothes-yard and a swing on the porch, and I made it real nice for me and Raymond Emmons, made curtains with fringe, putt jardinears on the front banisters and painted the fern buckets. We furnished those unfurnished rooms with our brand-new lives, and started goin along.

Between those years and this one I'm telling about them in, there seems a space as wide and vacant and silent as the Neches River, with my life *then* standin on one bank and my life *now* standin on the other, looking acrost at each other like two diffrent people wonderin who the other can really be.

How did Raymon Emmons die? Walked right through a winda and tore hisself all to smithereens. Walked right through a second-story winda at the depot and fell broken on the tracks—nothin much left a Raymon Emmons after he walked through that winda—broken his crown, hon, broken his crown. But he lingered for three days in Victry Hospital and then passed, sayin just before he passed away, turning toward me, "I hope you're satisfied. . . ."

Why did he die? From grievin over his daughter and mine, Chitta was her name, that fell off a horse they uz both ridin on the Emmonses' farm. Horse's name was King and we had im shot.

Buried im next to Chitta's grave with iz insurance, two funerals in as many weeks, then set aroun blue in our house, cryin all day and crying half the night, sleep all broken and disturbed of my rest, thinkin oh if he'd come knockin at that door right now I'd let him in, oh I'd let Raymon Emmons in! After he died, I set aroun sayin "who's gonna meet all the hours in a day with me, whatever is in each one—*all those hours*—who's gonna be with me in the morning, in the ashy afternoons that we always have here, in the nights of lightnin who's goan be lying there, seen in the flashes and making me feel as safe as if he uz a lightnin rod (and honey he *wuz*); who's gonna be like a light turned on in a dark room when I go in, who's gonna be at the door when I open it, who's goin to be there when I wake up or when I go to sleep, who's goin to call my name? I cain't stand a life of just me and our furniture in a room, who's gonna *be* with me?" Honey it's true that you never miss water till the well runs dry, tiz truly true.

Went to talk to the preacher, but he uz no earthly help, regalin me with iz pretty talk, he's got a tongue that will trill out a story pretty as a bird on a bobwire fence—but meanin what?—sayin "the wicked walk on every hand when the vilest men are exalted"—now what uz that mean?—; went to set and talk with Fursta Evans in her Millinary Shop (who's had her share of tumult in her sad life, but never shows it) but she uz no good, sayin "Girl pick up the pieces and go on . . . here try on this real cute hat" (that woman had nothing but hats on her mind—even though she taught me *my* life, grant cha *that*—for brains she's got hats). Went to the graves on Sundays carryin pot-plants and cryin over the mounds, one long wide one and one little un—how sad are the little graves a childrun, childrun ought not to have to die it's not right to bring death to childrun, they're just little toys grownups play with or neglect (thas how some of em die, too, honey, but won't say no more bout that); but all childrun go to Heaven so guess it's best—the grasshoppers flyin all roun me (they say graveyard grasshoppers spit tobacco juice and if it gets in your eye it'll putt your eye out) and an armadilla diggin in the crepemyrtle bushes—sayin "dirt lay light on Raymon Emmons and iz child," and thinkin "all my life is dirt I've got a famly of dirt." And then I come back to set and scratch aroun like an armadilla myself in these rooms, alone; but honey that uz no good either.

And then one day, I guess it uz a year after my famly died, there uz a knock on my door and it uz Fursta Evans knockin when I opened it to see. And she said "honey now listen I've come to visit with you and to try to tell you somethin: why are you so glued to Raymon Emmonses memry when you never cared a hoot bout him while he was on earth, you despised all the Emmonses, said they was just trash, wouldn't go to the farm on Christmas or Thanksgivin, wouldn't set next to em in church, broke pore Raymon Emmons' heart because you'd never let Chitta stay with her grandparents and when you finely did the Lord purnished you for bein so hateful by takin Chitta. Then you blamed it on Raymon Emmons, hounded im night and day, said he killed Chitta, drove im stark ravin mad. While Raymon Emmons was live you'd never even given him the time a day, wouldn't lift a hand for im, you never would cross the street for im, to you he uz just a dog in the yard, and you know it, and now that he's dead you grieve yo life away and suddenly fall in love with im." Oh she tole me good and proper—said, "you never loved im till you lost im, till it uz too late," said, "now set up and listen to me and get some brains in yo head, chile." Said, "cause listen honey, I've had four husbands in my time, two of em died and two of em quit me, but each one of em I thought was going to be the *only* one, and I took each one for that, then let im go when he uz gone, kept goin roun, kept ready, we got to honey, left the gate wide open for anybody to come through, friend or stranger, ran with the hare and hunted with the hound, honey we got to *greet* life not grieve life," is what she said.

"Well," I said, "I guess that's the way life is, you don't know what you have till you don't have it any longer, till you've lost it, till it's too late."

"Anyway," Fursta said, "little cattle little care—you're beginnin again now, fresh and empty-handed, it's later and it's shorter, yo life, but go on from *here* not *there*," she said. "You've had one kind of a life, had a husband, putt im in iz grave (now leave im there!), had a child and putt her away, too; start over, hon, the world don't know it, the world's fresh as ever—it's a new day, putt some powder on yo face and start goin round. Get you a job, and try that; or take you a trip. . . ."

"But I got to stay in this house," I said. "Feel like I cain't budge. Raymon Emmons is here, live as ever, and I cain't get away from im. He keeps me fastened to this house."

"Oh poot," Fursta said, lightin a cigarette. "Honey you're losin ya mine. Now listen here, put on those big ole rubberboots and go clompin, go steppin high and wide—cause listen here, if ya don't they'll have ya up in the Asylum at Rusk sure's as shootin, specially if you go on talkin about this ghost of Raymon Emmons the way you do."

"But if I started goin roun, what would people say?"

"You can tell em it's none of their beeswax. Cause listen honey, the years uv passed and are passin and you in ever one of em, passin too, and not gettin any younger—yo hairs gettin bunchy and the lines clawed roun yo mouth and eyes by the glassy claws of cryin sharp tears. We got to paint ourselves up and go on, young *outside,* anyway—cause listen honey the sun comes up and the sun crosses over and *goes down*—and while the sun's up we got to get on that fence and crow. Cause night muss fall—and then thas all. Come on, les go roun; have us a Sataday-night weddin ever Sataday night; forget this ole patched-faced ghost I hear you talkin about. . . ."

"In this town?" I said. "I hate this ole town, always rain fallin—'cept this ain't rain it's rainin, Fursta, it's rainin mildew. . . ."

"O deliver me!" Fursta shouted out, and putt out her cigarette, "you won't do. Are you afraid you'll *melt?*"

"I wish I'd melt—and run down the drains. Wish I uz rain, fallin on the dirt of certain graves I know and seepin down into the dirt, could lie in the dirt with Raymon Emmons on one side and Chitta on the other. Wish I uz dirt. . . ."

"I wish you are just crazy," Fursta said. "Come on, you're gonna take a trip. You're gonna get on a train and take a nonstop trip and get off at the end a the line and start all over again new as a New Year's Baby, baby. I'm gonna see to that."

"Not on no train, all the king's men couldn't get me to ride a train again, no siree. . . ."

"Oh no train my foot," said Fursta.

"But what'll I use for money please tell me," I said.

"With Raymon Emmons' insurance of course—it didn't take all of it to bury im, I know. Put some acreage tween you and yo past life, and maybe some new friends and scenery, too, and pull down the shade on all the water that's gone under the bridge; and come back here a new woman. Then if ya want tew you can come into my millinary shop with me."

"Oh," I said, "is the world still there? Since Raymon Emmons walked through that winda seems the whole world's gone, the whole world went out through that winda when he walked through it."

* * *

309

Closed the house, sayin "goodbye ghost of Raymon Emmons," bought my ticket at the depot, deafenin my ears to the sound of the tickin telegraph machine, got on a train and headed west to California. Day and night the trainwheels on the train tracks said *Raymon Emmons Raymon Emmons Raymon Emmons,* and I looked through the winda at dirt and desert, miles and miles of dirt, thinkin I wish I uz dirt I wish I uz dirt. O I us vile with grief.

In California the sun was out, wide, and everybody and everthing lighted up; and oh honey the world *was* still there. I decided to stay a while. I started my new life with Raymon Emmons' insurance money. It uz in San Diego, by the ocean and with mountains of dirt standin gold in the blue waters. A war had come. I was alone for a while, but not for long. Got me a job in an airplane factory, met a lotta girls, met a lotta men. I worked in fusilodges.

There uz this Nick Natowski, a brown clean Pollock from Chicago, real wile, real Satanish. What kind of a life did he start me into? I don't know how it started, but it did, and in a flash we uz everwhere together, dancin and swimming and *everthing.* He uz in the war and in the U.S. Navy, but we didn't think of the war or of water. I just liked him tight as a glove in iz uniform, I just liked him laughin, honey, I just liked him *ever* way he was, and that uz all I knew. And then one night he said, "Margy I'm going to tell you somethin, goin on a boat, be gone a long long time, goin in a week." Oh I cried and had a nervous fit and said, "Why do you have to go when there's these thousands of others all aroun San Diego that could go?" and he said, "We're going away to Coronada for that week, you and me, and what happens there will be enough to keep and save for the whole time we're apart." We went, honey, Nick and me, to Coronada, I mean we really *went.* Lived like a king and queen—where uz my life behind me that I thought of once and a while like a story somebody was whisperin to me?—laughed and loved and I cried; and after that week at Coronada, Nick left for sea on his boat, to the war, saying I want you to know baby I'm leavin you my allotment.

I was blue, so blue, all over again, but this time it uz diffrent someway, guess cause I uz blue for somethin live this time and not dead under dirt, I don't know; anyway I kept goin roun, kept my job in fusilodges and kept going roun. There was this friend of Nick Natowski's called George, and we went together some. "But why doesn't Nick Natowski write me, George?" I said. "Because he cain't yet," George said, "but just wait and he'll write." I kept waitin but no letter ever came, and the reason he didn't write when he could of, finely, was because his boat was sunk and Nick Natowski in it.

Oh what have I ever done in this world, I said, to send my soul to torment? Lost one to dirt and one to water, makes my life a life of mud, why was I ever put to such a test as this O Lord, I said. I'm goin back home to where I started, gonna get on that train and backtrack to where I started from, want to look at dirt a while, can't stand to look at water. I rode the train back. Somethin drew me back like I'd been pastured on a rope in California.

Come back to this house, opened it up and aired it all out, and when I got back you know who was there in that house? That ole faithful ghost of Raymon Emmons. He'd been there, waitin, while I went around, in my going-roun time, and was there to have me back. While I uz gone he'd covered everythin in our house with the breath a ghosts, fine ghost dust over the tables and chairs and a curtain of ghost lace over my bed on the sleepin-porch.

Took me this job in Richardson's Shoe Shop (this town's big now and got money in it, the war 'n oil made it rich, ud never know it as the same if you hadn't known it before; and Fursta Evans married to a rich widower), set there fittin shoes on measured feet all day—it all started in a shoestore measurin feet and it ended that way—can you feature that? Went home at night to my you-know-what.

Comes riding onto the sleepinporch ever night regular as clockwork, ties iz horse to the bedstead and I say hello Raymon Emmons and we start our conversation. Don't ask me what he says or what I say, but ever night is a night full of talkin, and it last the whole night through. Oh onct in a while I get real blue and want to hide away and just set with Raymon Emmons in my house, cain't budge, don't see daylight nor dark, putt away my wearin clothes, couldn't walk outa that door if my life depended on it. But I set real still and let it all be, claimed by that ghost until he unclaims me—and then I get up and go roun, free, and that's why I'm here, setting with you here in the Pass Time Club, drinkin this beer and tellin you all I've told.

* * *

Honey, why am I tellin all this? Oh all our lives! So many things to tell. And I keep em to myself a long long time, tight as a drum, won't open my mouth, just set in my blue house with that ole ghost agrievin me, until there comes a time of tellin, a time to tell, a time to putt on those big ole rubber-boots.

Now I believe in *tellin,* while we're live and goin round; when the tellin time comes I say spew it out, we just got to tell things, things in our lives, things that've happened, things we've fancied and things we dream about or are haunted by. Cause you know honey the time to shut yo mouth and set moltin and mildewed in yo room, grieved by a ghost and fastened to a chair, comes back roun again, don't worry honey, it comes roun again. There's a time ta tell and a time ta set still ta let a ghost grieve ya. So listen to me while I tell, cause I'm in my time atellin, and you better run fast if you don wanna hear what I tell, cause I'm goin ta tell. . . .

The world is changed, let's drink ower beer and have us a time, tell and tell and tell, let's get that hot bird in a cole bottle tonight. Cause next time you think you'll see me and hear me tell, you won't: I'll be flat where I cain't budge again, like I wuz all that year, settin and hidin way . . . until the time comes roun again when I can say oh go way ole ghost of Raymon Emmons, go way ole ghost and lemme be!

Cause I've learned this and I'm gonna tell ya: there's a time for live things and a time for dead, for ghosts and for flesh 'n bones: all life is just a sharin of ghost and flesh. Us humans are part ghost and part flesh—part fire and part ash—but I think maybe the ghost part is the longest lastin, the fire blazes but the ashes last forever. I had fire in California (and water putt it out) and ash in Texis (and it went to dirt); but I say now, while I'm tellin you, there's a world both places, a world where there's ghosts and a world where there's flesh, and I believe the real right way is to take our worlds, of ghosts or of flesh, take each one as they come and take what comes in em: take a ghost and grieve with im, settin still; and take the flesh 'n bones and go roun; and even run out to meet what worlds come into our lives, strangers (like you), and ghosts (like Raymon Emmons) and lovers (like Nick Natowski) . . . and be what each world wants us to be.

312

And I think that ghosts, if you set still with em long enough, can give you over to flesh 'n bones; and that flesh 'n bones, if you go roun when it's time, can send you back to a faithful ghost. One provides the other.

Saw pore Raymon Emmons all last night, all last night seen im plain as day.

NADINE GORDIMER

Letter from His Father

My dear son,

  You wrote me a letter you never sent.

  It wasn't for me—it was for the whole world to read. (You and your instructions that everything should be burned. Hah!) You were never open and frank with me—that's one of the complaints you say I was always making against you. You write it in the letter you didn't want me to read; so what does *that* sound like, eh? But I've read the letter now, I've read it anyway, I've read everything, although you said I put your books on the night table and never touched them. You know how it is, here where I am: not something that can be explained to anyone who isn't here—they used to talk about secrets going to the grave, but the funny thing is there are no secrets here at all. If there was something you wanted to know, you should have known, if it doesn't let you lie quiet, then you can *have knowledge of it,* from here. Yes, you gave me that much credit, you said I was a true Kafka in "strength . . . eloquence, endurance, a certain way of doing things on a grand scale" and I've not been content just to rot. In that way, I'm still the man I was, the go-getter. Restless. Restless. Taking whatever opportunity I can. There isn't anything, now, you can regard as hidden from me. Whether you say I left it unread on the night table or whether you weren't man enough, even at the age of thirty-six, to show me a letter that was supposed to be for me.

  I write to you after we are both dead. Whereas you don't stir. There won't be any response from you, I know that. You began that letter by saying you were afraid of me—and then you were afraid to let me read it. And now you've

314

escaped altogether. Because without the Kafka willpower you can't reach out from nothing and nowhere. I was going to call it a desert, but where's the sand, where're the camels, where's the sun—I'm still *mensch* enough to crack a joke—you see? Oh excuse me, I forgot—you didn't like my jokes, my fooling around with kids. My poor boy, unfortunately you had no life in you, in all those books and diaries and letters (the ones you posted, to strangers, to women) you said it a hundred times before you put the words in my mouth, in your literary way, in that letter: you yourself were "unfit for life." So death comes, how would you say, quite naturally to you. It's not like that for a man of vigor like I was, I can tell you, and so here I am writing, talking. . . . I don't know if there is a word for what this is. Anyway, it's *Hermann Kafka.* I've outlived you here, same as in Prague.

That is what you really accuse me of, you know, for sixty or so pages (I notice the length of that letter varies a bit from language to language, of course it's been translated into everything—I don't know what—Hottentot and Ice-landic, Chinese, although you wrote it "for me" in German). I *outlived* you, not for seven years, as an old sick man, after you died, but while you were young and alive. Clear as daylight, from the examples you give of being afraid of me, from the time you were a little boy: you were not afraid, you were envious. At first, when I took you swimming and you say you felt yourself a nothing, puny and weak beside my big, strong, naked body in the change-house—all right, you also say you were proud of such a father, a father with a fine physique. . . . And may I remind you that father was taking the trouble and time, the few hours he could get away from the business, to try and make something of that *nebbish,* develop his muscles, put some flesh on those poor little bones so he would grow up sturdy? But even before your bar mitzvah the normal pride every boy has in his father changed to jealousy, with you. You couldn't be like me, so you decided I wasn't good enough for you: coarse, loud-mouthed, ate "like a pig" (your very words), cut my fingernails at table, cleaned my ears with a toothpick. Oh yes, you can't hide anything from me, now, I've read it all, all the thousands and thousands of words you've used to shame your own family, your own father, before the whole world. And with your gift for words you turn everything inside out and prove, like a circus

315

magician, it's love, the piece of dirty paper's a beautiful silk flag, you *loved your father too much,* and so—what? *You* tell me. You couldn't be like him? You wanted to be like *him?* The *ghasa,* the shouter, the gobbler? Yes, my son, these "insignificant details" you write down and quickly dismiss—these details hurt. Eternally. After all, you've become immortal through writing, as you insist you did, only about me, "everything was about you, father"; a hundred years after your birth, the Czech Jew, son of Hermann and Julie Kafka, is supposed to be one of the greatest writers who ever lived. Your work will be read as long as there are people to read it. That's what they say everywhere, even the Germans who burned your sisters and my grandchildren in incinerators. Some say you were also some kind of prophet (God knows what you were thinking, shut away in your room while the rest of the family was having a game of cards in the evening); after you died, some countries built camps where the things you made up for that story "In the Penal Colony" were practiced, and ever since then there have been countries in different parts of the world where the devil's work that came into your mind is still carried out—I don't want to think about it.

You were not blessed to bring any happiness to this world with your genius, my son. Not at home, either. Well, we had to accept what God gave. Do you ever stop to think whether it wasn't a sorrow for me (never mind—for once—how you felt) that your two brothers, who might have grown up to bring your mother and me joy, died as babies? And you sitting there at meals always with a pale, miserable, glum face, not a word to say for yourself, picking at your food . . . You haven't forgotten that I used to hold up the newspaper so as not to have to see that. You bear a grudge. You've told everybody. But you don't think about what there was in a father's heart. From the beginning. I had to hide it behind a newspaper—anything. For your sake.

Because you were never like any other child. You admit it: however we had tried to bring you up, you say you would have become a "weakly, timid, hesitant person." What small boy doesn't enjoy a bit of a roughhouse with his father? But writing at thirty-six years old, you can only remember being frightened when I chased you, in fun, round the table, and your mother, joining in, would snatch you up out of my way while you shrieked. For God's sake, what's so terrible about that? I should have such memories of my childhood! I know you never liked to hear about it, it bored you, you don't spare me the written information that it "wore grooves in your brain," but when *I* was seven years old I had to push my father's barrow from village to village, with open sores on my legs in winter. Nobody gave me delicacies to mess about on my plate; we were glad when we got potatoes. You make a show of me, mimicking how I used to say these things. But wasn't I right when I told you and your sisters—provided for by me, living like fighting cocks because I stood in the business twelve hours a day—what did you know of such things? What did anyone know, what I suffered as a child? And then it's a sin if I wanted to give my own son a little pleasure I never had.

And that other business you *schlepped* up out of the past—the night I'm supposed to have shut you out on the *pavlatche*. Because of you the whole world knows the Czech word for the kind of balcony we had in Prague! Yes, the whole world knows that story, too. I am famous, too. You made me famous as the father who frightened his child once and for all: for life. Thank you very much. I want to tell you that I don't even remember that incident. I'm not saying it didn't happen, although you always had an imagination such as nobody ever had before or since, eh? But it could only have been the last resort your mother and I turned to—you know that your mother spoilt you, *over-protected* they would call it, now. You couldn't possibly remember how naughty you were at night, what a little tyrant you were, how you thought of every excuse to keep us sleepless. It was all right for you, you could nap during the day, a small child. But I had my business, I had to earn the living, I needed some rest. Pieces of bread, a particular toy you fancied, make wee-wee, another blanket on, a blanket taken off, drinks of water—there was no end to your tricks and whining. I suppose I couldn't stand it any longer. I feared to do you some harm. (You admit I never beat you, only scared you a little by taking off my braces in preparation to use them on you.) So I put you out of harm's way. That night. Just for a few minutes. It couldn't have been more than a minute. As if your mother would have let you catch cold! God forbid! And you've held it against me all your life. I'm sorry, I have to say it again, that old expression of mine that irritated you so much: I wish I had your worries.

Everything that went wrong for you is my fault. You write it down for sixty pages or so and at the same time you say to me "I believe you are entirely blameless in the matter of our estrangement." I was a "true Kafka," you took after your mother's, the Löwy side, etc.—all you inherited from me, according to you, were your bad traits, without having the benefit of my vitality. I was "too strong" for you. You could not help it; I could not help it. So? All you wanted was *for me to admit that,* and we could have lived in peace. You were judge, you were jury, you were accused; you sentenced yourself, first. "At my desk, that is my place. My head in my hands—that is my attitude." (And that's what your poor mother and I had to look at, that was our pride and joy, our only surviving son!) But I was accused, too; you were judge, you were jury in my case, too. Right? By what right? Fancy goods—you despised the family business that fed us all, that paid for your education. What concern was it of yours, the way I treated the shop assistants? You only took an interest so you could judge, judge. It was a mistake to have let you study law. You did nothing with your qualification, your expensive education that I slaved and ruined my health for. Nothing but sentence me.—Now what did I want to say? Oh yes. Look what you wanted me to admit, under the great writer's beautiful words. If something goes wrong, somebody must be to blame, eh? We were not straw dolls, pulled about from above on strings. One of *us* must be to blame. And don't tell me you think it could be you. The stronger is always to blame, isn't that so? I'm not a deep thinker like you, only a dealer in retail fancy goods, but isn't that a law of life? "The effect you had on me was the effect you could not help having." You think I'll believe you're paying me a compliment, forgiving me, when you hand me the worst insult any father could receive? If it's what I am that's to blame, then I'm to blame, to the last drop of my heart's blood and whatever this is that's survived my body, for what *I am,* for being alive and begetting a son! You! Is that it? Because of you *I* should never have lived at all!

You always had a fine genius (never mind your literary one) for working me up. And you knew it was bad for my heart condition. Now, what does it matter . . . but, as God's my witness, you aggravate me . . . you make me . . .

Well.

All I know is that I am to blame forever. You've seen to that. It's written, and not alone by you. There are plenty of people writing books about Kafka, Franz Kafka. I'm even blamed for the name I handed down, our family name. *Kavka* is Czech for jackdaw, so that's maybe the reason for your animal obsession. *Dafke!* Insect, ape, dog, mouse, stag, what didn't you imagine yourself. They say the beetle story is a great masterpiece, thanks to me—I'm the one who treated you like an inferior species, gave you the inspiration. . . . You wake up as a bug, you give a lecture as an ape. Do any of these wonderful scholars think what this meant to me, having a son who didn't have enough self-respect to feel himself a man?

You have such a craze for animals, but may I remind you, when you were staying with Ottla at Zürau you wouldn't even undress in front of a cat she'd brought in to get rid of the mice. . . .

Yet you imagined a dragon coming into your room. It said (an educated dragon, *noch*): "Drawn hitherto by your longing . . . I offer myself to you." Your longing, Franz: ugh, for monsters, for perversion. You describe a person (yourself, of course) in some crazy fantasy of living with a horse. Just listen to you, ". . . for a year I lived together with a horse in such ways as, say, a man would live with a girl whom he respects, but by whom he is rejected." You even gave the horse a girl's name, Eleanor. I ask you, is that the kind of story made up by a normal young man? Is it decent that people should read such things, long after you are gone? But it's published, everything is published.

And worst of all, what about the animal in the synagogue. Some sort of rat, weasel, a marten you call it. You tell how it ran all over during prayers, running along the lattice of the women's section and even climbing down to the curtain in front of the Ark of the Covenant. A *schande*, an animal running about during divine service. Even if it's only a story—only you would imagine it. No respect.

You go on for several pages (in that secret letter) about my use of vulgar Yiddish expressions, about my "insignificant scrap of Judaism," which was "purely social" and so meant we couldn't "find each other in Judaism" if in nothing else. This, from you! When you were a youngster and I had to drag you to the Yom Kippur services once a year you were sitting there making up stories about unclean animals approaching the Ark, the most holy object of the Jewish faith. Once you were grown up, you went exactly once to the Altneu synagogue. The people who write books about you say it must have been to please me. I'd be surprised. When you suddenly discovered you were a Jew, after all, of course your Judaism was highly intellectual, nothing in common with the Jewish customs I was taught to observe in my father's *shtetl,* pushing the barrow at the age of seven. Your Judaism was learned at the Yiddish Theater. That's a *nice* crowd! Those dirty-living traveling players you took up with at the Savoy Café. Your friend the actor Jizchak Löwy. No relation to your mother's family, thank God. I wouldn't let such a man even meet her. You had the disrespect to bring him into your parents' home, and I saw it was my duty to speak to him in such a way that he wouldn't ever dare to come back again. (Hah! I used to look down from the window and watch him, hanging around in the cold, outside the building, waiting for you.) And the Tschissik woman, that *nafke,* one of his actresses—I've found out you thought you were in love with her, a married woman (if you can call the way those people live a marriage). Apart from Fräulein Bauer you never fancied anything but a low type of woman. I say it again as I did then: if you lie down with dogs, you get up with fleas. You lost your temper (yes, you, this time), you flew into a rage at your father when he told you that. And when I reminded you of my heart condition, you put yourself in the right again, as usual, you said (I remember like it was yesterday) "I make great efforts to restrain myself." But now I've read your diaries, the dead don't need to creep into your bedroom and read them behind your back (which you accused your mother and me of doing), I've read what you wrote afterwards, that you sensed in me, your father, "as always at such moments of extremity, the existence of a wisdom which I can no more than scent." So you *knew,* while you were defying me, you knew I was right!

The fact is that you were anti-Semitic, Franz. You were never interested in what was happening to your own people. The hooligans' attacks on Jews in the streets, on houses and shops, that took place while you were growing up—I don't see a word about them in your diaries, your notebooks. You were only *imagining* Jews. Imagining them tortured in places like your "Penal Colony," maybe. I don't want to think about what that means.

Right, towards the end you studied Hebrew, you and your sister Ottla had some wild dream about going to Palestine. You, hardly able to breathe by then, digging potatoes on a kibbutz! The latest book about you says you were in revolt against the "shopkeeper mentality" of your father's class of Jew; but it was the shopkeeper father, the buttons and buckles, braid, ribbons, ornamental combs, press studs, hooks-and-eyes, bootlaces, photo frames, shoe horns, novelties and notions that earned the bread for you to dream by. You were anti-Semitic, Franz; if such a thing is possible as for a Jew to cut himself in half. (For you, I suppose, anything is possible.) You told Ottla that to marry that goy Josef Davis was better than marrying ten Jews. When your great friend Brod wrote a book called *The Jewesses* you wrote there were too many of them in it. You saw them like lizards. (Animals again, low animals.) "However happy we are to watch a single lizard on a footpath in Italy, we would be horrified to see hundreds of them crawling over each other in a pickle jar." From where did you get such ideas? Not from your home, that I know.

And look how Jewish you are, in spite of the way you despised us—Jews, your Jewish family! You answer questions with questions. I've discovered that's your style, your famous literary style: your Jewishness. Did you or did you not write the following story, playlet, wha'd'you-call-it, your friend Brod kept every scribble and you knew he wouldn't burn even a scrap. "Once at a spiritualist seance a new spirit announced its presence, and the following conversation with it took place. The spirit: Excuse me. The spokesman: Who are you? The spirit: Excuse me. The spokesman: What do you want? The spirit: To go away. The spokesman: But you've only just come. The spirit: It's a mistake. The spokesman: No, it isn't a mistake. You've come and you'll stay. The spirit: I've just begun to feel ill. The spokesman: Badly? The spirit: Badly? The spokesman: Physically? The spirit: Physically? The spokesman: You answer with questions. That will not do. We have ways of punishing you, so I advise you to answer, for then we shall soon dismiss you. The spirit: Soon? The spokesman: Soon. The spirit: In one minute? The spokesman: Don't go on in this miserable way. . . ."

Questions without answers. Riddles. You wrote "It is always only in contradiction that I can live. But this doubtless applies to everyone; for living, one dies, dying, one lives." Speak for yourself! So who did you think you were when that whim took you—their prophet, Jesus Christ? What did you *want*? The *goyishe* heavenly hereafter? What did you mean when a lost man, far from his native country, says to someone he meets "I am in your hands" and the other says, "No. You are free and that is why you are lost"? What's the sense in writing about a woman "I lie in wait for her in order not to meet her"? There's only one of your riddles I think I understand, and then only because for forty-two years, God help me, I had to deal with you myself. "A cage went in search of a bird." That's you. The cage, not the bird. I don't know why. Maybe it will come to me. As I say, if a person wants to, he can know everything, here.

All that talk about going away. You called your home (more riddles) "My prison—my fortress." You grumbled—in print, everything ended up in print, my son—that your room was only a passage, a thoroughfare between the living room and your parents' bedroom. You complained you had to write in pencil because we took away your ink to stop you writing. It was for your own good, your health—already you were a grown man, a qualified lawyer, but you know you couldn't look after yourself. Scribbling away half the night, you'd have been too tired to work properly in the mornings, you'd have lost your position at the Assicurazioni Generali (or was it by then the Arbeiter-Unfall-Versicher-ungs-Anstalt für das Königreich Böhmen, my memory doesn't get any better, here). And I wasn't made of money. I couldn't go on supporting everybody forever.

You've published every petty disagreement in the family. It was a terrible thing, according to you, we didn't want you to go out in bad weather, your poor mother wanted you to wrap up. You with your delicate health, always sickly—you didn't inherit my constitution, it was only a lifetime of hard work, the business, the family worries that got me, in the end! You recorded that you couldn't go for a walk without your parents making a fuss, but at twenty-eight you were still living at home. Going away. My poor boy. You could hardly get yourself to the next room. You shut yourself up when people came to visit. Always crawling off to bed, sleeping in the day (oh yes, you couldn't sleep at night, not like anybody else), sleeping your life away. You invented *Amerika* instead of having the guts to emigrate, get up off the bed, pack up and go there, make a new life! Even that girl you jilted twice managed it. Did you know Felice is still alive somewhere, there now, in America? She's an old, old woman with great-grandchildren. They didn't get her into the death camps those highly educated people say you knew about before they happened. America you never went to, Spain you dreamt about . . . your Uncle Alfred was going to find you jobs there, in Madeira, the Azores . . . God knows where else. Grandson of a ritual slaughterer, a *schochet*, that was why you couldn't bear to eat meat, they say, and that made you weak and undecided. So that was my fault, too, because my poor father had to earn a living. When your mother was away from the flat, you'd have starved yourself to death if it hadn't been for me. And what was the result? You resented so much what I provided for you, you went and had your stomach pumped out! Like someone who's been poisoned! And you didn't forget to write it down, either: "My feeling is that disgusting things will come out."

Whatever I did for you was *dreck*. You felt "despised, condemned, beaten down" by me. But you despised *me*; the only difference, I wasn't so easy to beat down, eh? How many times did you try to leave home, and you couldn't go? It's all there in your diaries, in the books they write about you. What about that other masterpiece of yours, "The Judgment." A father and son quarreling, and then the son goes and drowns himself, saying "Dear parents, I have always loved you, all the same." The wonderful discovery about that story, you might like to hear, it proves Hermann Kafka most likely didn't want his son to grow up and be a man, any more than his son wanted to manage without his parents' protection. The *meshuggener* who wrote that, may he get rich on it! I wouldn't wish it on him to try living with you, that's all, the way we had to. When your hunchback friend secretly showed your mother a complaining letter of yours, to get you out of your duty of going to the asbestos factory to help your own sister's husband, Brod kept back one thing you wrote. But now it's all published, all, all, all the terrible things you thought about your own flesh and blood. "I hate them all": father, mother, sisters.

You couldn't do without us—without me. You only moved away from us when you were nearly thirty-two, a time when every *man* has a wife and children already, a home of his own.

You were always dependent on someone. Your friend Brod, poor devil. If it hadn't been for the little hunchback, who would know of your existence today? Between the incinerators that finished your sisters and the fire you wanted to burn up your manuscripts, nothing would be left. The kind of men you invented, the Gestapo, confiscated whatever papers of yours there were in Berlin, and no trace of them has ever been found, even by the great Kafka experts who stick their noses into everything. You said you loved Max Brod more than yourself. I can see that. You liked the idea he had of you, that you knew wasn't yourself (you see, sometimes I'm not so *grob*, uneducated, knowing nothing but fancy goods, maybe I got from you some "insights"). Certainly, I wouldn't recognize my own son the way Brod described you: "the aura Kafka gave out of extraordinary strength, something I've never encountered elsewhere, even in meetings with great and famous men. . . . The infallible solidity of his insights never tolerated a single lacuna, nor did he ever speak an insignificant word . . . He was life-affirming, ironically tolerant towards the idiocies of the world, and therefore full of sad humor."

I must say, your mother who put up with your faddiness when she came back from a day standing in the business, your sisters who acted in your plays to please you, your father who worked his heart out for his family—we never got the benefit of your tolerance. Your sisters (except Ottla, the one you admit you were a bad influence on, encouraging her to leave the shop and work on a farm like a peasant, to starve herself with you on rabbit food, to marry that goy) were giggling idiots, so far as you were concerned. Your mother never felt the comfort of her son's strength. You never gave us anything to laugh at, sad or otherwise. And you hardly spoke to me at all, even an insignificant word. Whose fault was it you were that person you describe "strolling about on the island in the pool, where there are neither books nor bridges, hearing the music, but not being heard." You wouldn't cross a road, never mind a bridge, to pass the time of day, to be pleasant to other people, you shut yourself in your room and stuffed your ears with Oropax against the music of life, yes, the sounds of cooking, people coming and going (what were we supposed to do, pass through closed doors?), even the singing of the pet canaries annoyed you, laughter, the occasional family tiff, the bed squeaking where normal married people made love.

What I've just said may surprise. That last bit, I mean. But since I died in 1931 I know the world has changed a lot. People, even fathers and sons, are talking about things that shouldn't be talked about. People aren't ashamed to read anything, even private diaries, even letters. There's no shame, anywhere. With that, too, you were ahead of your time, Franz. You were not ashamed to write in your diary, which your friend Brod would publish—you must have known he would publish everything, make a living out of us—things that have led one of the famous Kafka scholars to *study* the noises in our family flat in Prague. Writing about me: "It would have been out of character for Hermann Kafka to restrain any noises he felt like making during coupling; it would have been out of character for Kafka, who was ultra-sensitive to noise and had grown up with these noises, to mention the suffering they caused him."

You left behind you for everyone to read that the sight of your parents' pajamas and nightdress on the bed disgusted you. Let me also speak freely like everyone else. You were made in that bed. That disgusts me: your disgust over a place that should have been holy to you, a place to hold in the highest respect. Yet you are the one who complained about my coarseness when I suggested you ought to find yourself a woman—buy one, hire one—rather than try to prove yourself a man at last, at thirty-six, by marrying some Prague Jewish tart who shook her tits in a thin blouse. Yes, I'm speaking of that Julie Wohryzek, the shoemaker's daughter, your second fiancée. You even had the insolence to throw the remark in my face, in that letter you didn't send, but I've read it anyway, I've read everything now, although you said I put "In the Penal Colony" on the bedside table and never mentioned it again.

I have to talk about another matter we didn't discuss, father and son, while we were both alive—all right, it was my fault, maybe you're right, as I've said, times were different. . . . Women. I must bring this up because—my poor boy—marriage was "the greatest terror" of your life. You write that. You say your attempts to explain why you couldn't marry—on these depends the "success" of the whole letter you didn't send. According to you, marrying, founding a family was "the utmost a human being can succeed in doing at all." Yet you couldn't marry. How is any ordinary human being to understand that? You wrote more than a quarter of a million words to Felice Bauer, but you couldn't be a husband to her. You put your parents through the farce of traveling all the way to Berlin for an engagement party (there's the photograph you had taken, the happy couple, in the books they write about you, by the way). The engagement was broken, was on again, off again. Can you wonder? Anyone who goes into a bookshop or library can read what you wrote to your fiancée when your sister Elli gave birth to our first granddaughter. You felt nothing but nastiness, envy against your brother-in-law because "I'll never have a child." No, not with the Bauer girl, not in a decent marriage, like anybody else's son; but I've found out you had a child, Brod says so, by a woman, Grete Bloch, who was supposed to be the Bauer girl's best friend, who even acted as matchmaker between you! What do you say to that? Maybe it's news to you. I don't know. (That's how irresponsible you were.) They say she went away. Perhaps she never told you.

As for the next one you tried to marry, the one you make such a song and dance over because of my remark about Prague Jewesses and the blouse, etc.—for once you came to your senses, and you called off the wedding only two days before it was supposed to take place. Not that I could have influenced you. Since when did you take into consideration what your parents thought? When you told me you wanted to marry the shoemaker's daughter—naturally I was upset. At least the Bauer girl came from a nice family. What I said about the blouse just came out, I'm human, after all. But I was frank with you, man to man. You weren't a youngster any more. A man doesn't have to marry a nothing who will go with anybody.

I saw what that marriage was about, my poor son. You wanted a woman. Nobody understood that better than I did, believe me, I was normal man enough, eh! There were places in Prague where one could get a woman. (I suppose whatever's happened, there still are, always will be.) I tried to help you; I offered to go along with you myself. I said it in front of your mother, who—yes, as you write you were so shocked to see, was in agreement with me. We wanted so much to help you, even your own mother would go so far as that.

But in that letter you didn't think I'd ever see, you accuse me of humiliating you and I don't know what else. You wanted to marry a tart, but you were insulted at the idea of buying one?

Writing that letter only a few days after you yourself called off your second try at getting married, aged thirty-six, you find that your father, as a man-of-the-world, not only showed "contempt" for you on that occasion, but that when he had spoken to you as a broad-minded father when you were a youngster, he had given you information that set off the whole ridiculous business of your never being able to marry, ever. Already, twenty years before the Julie Wohryzek row, with "a few frank words" (as you put it) your father made you incapable of taking a wife and pushed you down "into the filth as if it were my destiny." You remember some walk with your mother and me on the Josefsplatz when you showed curiosity about, well, men's feelings and women, and I was open and honest with you and told you I could give you advice about where to go so that these things could be done quite safely, without bringing home any disease. You were sixteen years old, physically a man, not a child, eh? Wasn't it time to talk about such things?

Shall I tell you what *I* remember? Once you picked a quarrel with your mother and me because we hadn't educated you sexually—your words. Now you complain because I tried to guide you in these matters. I did—I didn't. Make up your mind. Have it your own way. Whatever I did, you believed it was *because of what I did* that you couldn't bring yourself to marry. When you thought you wanted the Bauer girl, didn't I give in, to please you? Although you were in no financial position to marry, although I had to give your two married sisters financial help, although I had worries enough, a sick man, you'd caused me enough trouble by persuading me to invest in a *mechulah* asbestos factory? Didn't I give in? And when the girl came to Prague to meet your parents and sisters, you wrote, "My family likes her almost more than I'd like it to." So it went as far as that: you couldn't like anything we liked, was that why you couldn't marry her?

A long time ago, a long way . . . Ah, it all moves away, it's getting faint. . . . But I haven't finished. Wait.

You say you wrote your letter because you wanted to explain why you couldn't marry. I'm writing this letter because you tried to write it for me. *You would take even that away from your father.* You answered your own letter, before I could. You made what you imagine as my reply part of the letter you wrote me. To save me the trouble . . . Brilliant, like they say. With your great gifts

327

as a famous writer, you express it all better than I could. You are there, quickly, with an answer, before I can be. You take the words out of my mouth: while you are accusing yourself, in my name, of being "too clever, obsequious, parasitic and insincere" in blaming your life on me, you are—yet again, one last time!—finally being too clever, obsequious, parasitic and insincere in the trick of stealing your father's chance to defend himself. A genius. What is left to say about you if—how well you know yourself, my boy, it's terrible—you call yourself the kind of vermin that doesn't only sting, but at the same time sucks blood to keep itself alive? And even that isn't the end of the twisting, the cheating. You then confess that this whole "correction," "rejoinder," as you, an expensively educated man, call it, "does not originate" in your father but in yourself, Franz Kafka. So you see, here's the proof, something *I* know you, with all your brains, can't know *for me:* you say you always wrote about me, it was all about me, your father; but it was all about you. The beetle. The bug that lay on its back waving its legs in the air and couldn't get up to go and see America or the Great Wall of China. You, you, self, self. And in your letter, after you have defended me against yourself, when you finally make the confession—right again, in the right again, always—you take the last word, in proof of your saintliness I could know nothing about, never understand, a businessman, a shopkeeper. That is your "truth" about us you hoped might be able to "make our living and our dying easier."

The way you ended up, Franz. The last woman you found yourself. It wasn't our wish, God knows. Living with that Eastern Jewess, and in sin. We sent you money; that was all we could do. If we'd come to see you, if we'd swallowed our pride, meeting that woman, our presence would only have made you worse. It's there in everything you've written, everything they write about you: everything connected with us made you depressed and ill. We knew she was giving you the wrong food, cooking like a gypsy on a spirit stove. She kept you in an unheated hovel in Berlin. . . . May God forgive me (Brod has told the world), I had to turn my back on her at your funeral.

Franz . . . When you received copies of your book *In the Penal Colony* from Kurt Wolff Verlag that time . . . You gave me one and I said "Put it on the night table." You say I never mentioned it again. Well, don't you understand—I'm not a literary man. I'm telling you now. I read a little bit, a page or two at a time. If you had seen that book, there was a pencil mark every two, three pages, so I would know next time where I left off. It wasn't like the books I knew—I hadn't much time for reading, working like a slave since I was a small boy, I wasn't like you, I couldn't shut myself up in a room with books, when I was young. I would have starved. But you know that. Can't you understand that I was—yes—not too proud—ashamed to let you know I didn't find it easy to understand your kind of writing, it was all strange to me.

Hah! I know I'm no intellectual, but I knew how to live!

Just a moment . . . give me time . . . there's a fading . . . Yes—can you imagine how we felt when Ottla told us you had tuberculosis? Oh how could you bring it over your heart to remind me I once said, in a temper, to a useless assistant coughing all over the shop (you should have had to deal with those lazy *goyim*), he ought to die, the sick dog. Did I know you would get tuberculosis, too? It wasn't our fault your lungs rotted. I tried to expand your chest when you were little, teaching you to swim; you should never have moved out of your own home, the care of your parents, to that rat hole in the Schönbornpalais. And the hovel in Berlin . . . We had some good times, didn't we? Franz? When we had beer and sausages after the swimming lessons? At least you remembered the beer and sausages, when you were dying.

One more thing. It chokes me, I have to say it. I know you'll never answer. You once wrote "Speech is possible only where one wants to lie." You were too ultra-sensitive to speak to us, Franz. You kept silence, with the truth; those playing a game of cards, turning in bed on the other side of the wall—it was the sound of live people you didn't like. Your revenge, that you were too cowardly to take in life, you've taken here. We can't lie peacefully in our graves; dug up, unwrapped from our shrouds by your fame. To desecrate your parents' grave as well as their bed, aren't you ashamed? Aren't you ashamed—now? Well, what's the use of quarreling. We lie together in the same grave—you, your mother and I. We've ended up as we always should have been, united. Rest in peace, my son. I wish you had let me.

Your father,
Hermann Kafka

R. K. NARAYAN

Old Man of the Temple

The Talkative Man said:

It was some years ago that this happened. I don't know if you can make anything of it. If you do, I shall be glad to hear what you have to say; but personally I don't understand it at all. It has always mystified me. Perhaps the driver was drunk; perhaps he wasn't.

I had engaged a taxi for going to Kumbum, which, as you may already know, is fifty miles from Malgudi. I went there one morning and it was past nine in the evening when I finished my business and started back for the town. Doss, the driver, was a young fellow of about twenty-five. He had often brought his car for me and I liked him. He was a well-behaved, obedient fellow, with a capacity to sit and wait at the wheel, which is really a rare quality in a taxi driver. He drove the car smoothly, seldom swore at passersby, and exhibited perfect judgment, good sense, and sobriety; and so I preferred him to any other driver whenever I had to go out on business.

It was about eleven when we passed the village Koopal, which is on the way down. It was the dark half of the month and the surrounding country was swallowed up in the night. The village street was deserted. Everyone had gone to sleep; hardly any light was to be seen. The stars overhead sparkled brightly. Sitting in the back seat and listening to the continuous noise of the running wheels, I was half lulled into a drowse.

All of a sudden Doss swerved the car and shouted: "You old fool! Do you want to kill yourself?"

I was shaken out of my drowse and asked: "What is the matter?"

330

Doss stopped the car and said, "You see that old fellow, sir. He is trying to kill himself. I can't understand what he is up to."

I looked in the direction he pointed and asked, "Which old man?"

"There, there. He is coming towards us again. As soon as I saw him open that temple door and come out I had a feeling, somehow, that I must keep an eye on him."

I took out my torch, got down, and walked about, but could see no one. There was an old temple on the roadside. It was utterly in ruins; most portions of it were mere mounds of old brick; the walls were awry; the doors were shut to the main doorway, and brambles and thickets grew over and covered them. It was difficult to guess with the aid of the torch alone what temple it was and to what period it belonged.

"The doors are shut and sealed and don't look as if they had been opened for centuries now," I cried.

"No, sir," Doss said, coming nearer. "I saw the old man open the doors and come out. He is standing there; shall we ask him to open them again if you want to go in and see?"

I said to Doss, "Let us be going. We are wasting our time here."

We went back to the car. Doss sat in his seat, pressed the self-starter, and asked without turning his head, "Are you permitting this fellow to come with us, sir? He says he will get down at the next milestone."

"Which fellow?" I asked.

Doss indicated the space next to him.

"What is the matter with you, Doss? Have you had a drop of drink or something?"

"I have never tasted any drink in my life, sir," he said, and added, "Get down, old boy. Master says he can't take you."

"Are you talking to yourself?"

"After all, I think we needn't care for these unknown fellows on the road," he said.

"Doss," I pleaded. "Do you feel confident you can drive? If you feel dizzy don't drive."

"Thank you, sir," said Doss. "I would rather not start the car now. I am feeling a little out of sorts." I looked at him anxiously. He closed his eyes, his breathing became heavy and noisy, and gradually his head sank.

"Doss, Doss," I cried desperately. I got down, walked to the front seat, opened the door, and shook him vigorously. He opened his eyes, assumed a hunched-up position, and rubbed his eyes with his hands, which trembled like an old man's.

"Do you feel better?" I asked.

"Better! Better! Hi! Hi!" he said in a thin, piping voice.

"What has happened to your voice? You sound like someone else," I said.

"Nothing. My voice is as good as it was. When a man is eighty he is bound to feel a few changes coming on."

"You aren't eighty, surely," I said.

"Not a day less," he said. "Is nobody going to move this vehicle? If not, there is no sense in sitting here all day. I will get down and go back to my temple."

"I don't know how to drive," I said. "And unless you do it, I don't see how it can move."

"Me!" exclaimed Doss. "These new chariots! God knows what they are drawn by, I never understand, though I could handle a pair of bullocks in my time. May I ask a question?"

"Go on," I said.

"Where is everybody?"

"Who?"

"Lots of people I knew are not to be seen at all. All sorts of new fellows everywhere, and nobody seems to care. Not a soul comes near the temple. All sorts of people go about but not one who cares to stop and talk. Why doesn't the king ever come this way? He used to go this way at least once a year before."

"Which king?" I asked.

"Let me go, you idiot," said Doss, edging towards the door on which I was leaning. "You don't seem to know anything." He pushed me aside, and got down from the car. He stooped as if he had a big hump on his back, and hobbled along towards the temple. I followed him, hardly knowing what to do. He turned and snarled at me: "Go away, leave me alone. I have had enough of you."

"What has come over you, Doss?" I asked.

"Who is Doss, anyway? Doss, Doss, Doss. What an absurd name! Call me by my name or leave me alone. Don't follow me calling 'Doss, Doss.' "

"What is your name?" I asked.

"Krishna Battar, and if you mention my name people will know for a hundred miles around. I built a temple where there was only a cactus field before. I dug the earth, burnt every brick, and put them one upon another, all single-handed. And on the day the temple held up its tower over the surrounding country, what a crowd gathered! The king sent his chief minister...."

"Who was the king?"

"Where do you come from?" he asked.

"I belong to these parts certainly, but as far as I know there has been only a collector at the head of the district. I have never heard of any king."

"Hi! Hi! Hi!" he cackled, and his voice rang through the gloomy silent village. "Fancy never knowing the king! He will behead you if he hears it."

"What is his name?" I asked.

This tickled him so much that he sat down on the ground, literally unable to stand the joke any more. He laughed and coughed uncontrollably.

"I am sorry to admit," I said, "that my parents have brought me up in such utter ignorance of worldly affairs that I don't know even my king. But won't you enlighten me? What is his name?"

"Vishnu Varma, the emperor of emperors . . ."

I cast my mind up and down the range of my historical knowledge but there was no one by that name. Perhaps a local chief of pre-British days, I thought.

"What a king! He often visited my temple or sent his minister for the Annual Festival of the temple. But now nobody cares."

"People are becoming less godly nowadays," I said. There was silence for a moment. An idea occurred to me, I can't say why. "Listen to me," I said. "You ought not to be here any more."

"What do you mean?" he asked, drawing himself up, proudly.

"Don't feel hurt; I say you shouldn't be here any more because you are dead."

"Dead! Dead!" he said. "Don't talk nonsense. How can I be dead when you see me before you now? If I am dead how can I be saying this and that?"

"I don't know all that," I said. I argued and pointed out that according to his own story he was more than five hundred years old, and didn't he know that man's longevity was only a hundred? He constantly interrupted me, but considered deeply what I said.

He said: "It is like this. . . . I was coming through the jungle one night after visiting my sister in the next village. I had on me some money and gold ornaments. A gang of robbers set upon me. I gave them as good a fight as any man could, but they were too many for me. They beat me down and knifed me; they took away all that I had on me and left thinking they had killed me. But soon I got up and tried to follow them. They were gone. And I returned to the temple and have been here since. . . ."

I told him, "Krishna Battar, you are dead, absolutely dead. You must try and go away from here."

"What is to happen to the temple?" he asked.

"Others will look after it."

"Where am I to go? Where am I to go?"

"Have you no one who cares for you?" I asked.

"None except my wife. I loved her very much."

"You can go to her."

"Oh, no. She died four years ago. . . ."

Four years! It was very puzzling. "Do you say four years back from now?" I asked.

"Yes, four years ago from now." He was clearly without any sense of time.

So I asked, "Was she alive when you were attacked by thieves?"

"Certainly not. If she had been alive she would never have allowed me to go through the jungle after nightfall. She took very good care of me."

"See here," I said. "It is imperative you should go away from here. If she comes and calls you, will you go?"

"How can she when I tell you that she is dead?"

I thought for a moment. Presently I found myself saying, "Think of her, and only of her, for a while and see what happens. What was her name?"

"Seetha, a wonderful girl . . ."

"Come on, think of her." He remained in deep thought for a while. He suddenly screamed, "Seetha is coming! Am I dreaming or what? I will go with her. . . ." He stood up, very erect; he appeared to have lost all the humps and twists he had on his body. He drew himself up, made a dash forward, and fell down in a heap.

Doss lay on the rough ground. The only sign of life in him was his faint breathing. I shook him and called him. He would not open his eyes. I walked across and knocked on the door of the first cottage. I banged on the door violently.

Someone moaned inside, "Ah, it is come!"

Someone else whispered, "You just cover your ears and sleep. It will knock for a while and go away." I banged on the door and shouted who I was and where I came from.

I walked back to the car and sounded the horn. Then the door opened, and a whole family crowded out with lamps. "We thought it was the usual knocking and we wouldn't have opened if you hadn't spoken."

"When was this knocking first heard?" I asked.

"We can't say," said one. "The first time I heard it was when my grandfather was living; he used to say he had even seen it once or twice. It doesn't harm anyone, as far as I know. The only thing it does is bother the bullock carts passing the temple and knock on the doors at night. . . ."

I said as a venture, "It is unlikely you will be troubled any more."

It proved correct. When I passed that way again months later I was told that the bullocks passing the temple after dusk never shied now and no knocking on the doors was heard at nights. So I felt that the old fellow had really gone away with his good wife.

GRAHAM GREENE

A Little Place off the Edgware Road

Craven came up past the Achilles statue in the thin summer rain. It was only just after lighting-up time, but already the cars were lined up all the way to the Marble Arch, and the sharp acquisitive faces peered out ready for a good time with anything possible which came along. Craven went bitterly by with the collar of his mackintosh tight round his throat: it was one of his bad days.

All the way up the park he was reminded of passion, but you needed money for love. All that a poor man could get was lust. Love needed a good suit, a car, a flat somewhere, or a good hotel. It needed to be wrapped in cellophane. He was aware all the time of the stringy tie beneath the mackintosh, and the frayed sleeves: he carried his body about with him like something he hated. (There were moments of happiness in the British Museum reading room, but the body called him back.) He bore, as his only sentiment, the memory of ugly deeds committed on park chairs. People talked as if the body died too soon—that wasn't the trouble, to Craven, at all. The body kept alive—and through the glittering tinselly rain, on his way to a rostrum, he passed a little man in a black suit carrying a banner, "The Body shall rise again." He remembered a dream from which three times he had woken trembling: he had been alone in the huge dark cavernous burying ground of all the world. Every grave was connected to another under the ground: the globe was honeycombed for the sake of the dead, and on each occasion of dreaming he had discovered anew the horrifying fact that the body doesn't decay. There are no worms and dissolution. Under the ground the world was littered with masses of dead flesh ready to rise again with their warts and boils and eruptions. He had lain in bed and remembered—as "tidings of great joy"—that the body after all was corrupt.

He came up into the Edgware Road walking fast—the Guardsmen were out in couples, great languid elongated beasts—the bodies like worms in their tight trousers. He hated them, and hated his hatred because he knew what it was, envy. He was aware that every one of them had a better body than himself: indigestion creased his stomach: he felt sure that his breath was foul—but who could he ask? Sometimes he secretly touched himself here and there with scent: it was one of his ugliest secrets. Why should he be asked to believe in the resurrection of this body he wanted to forget? Sometimes he prayed at night (a hint of religious belief was lodged in his breast like a worm in a nut) that *his* body at any rate should never rise again.

He knew all the side streets round the Edgware Road only too well: when a mood was on, he simply walked until he tired, squinting at his own image in the windows of Salmon & Gluckstein and the ABCs. So he noticed at once the posters outside the disused theater in Culpar Road. They were not unusual, for sometimes Barclays Bank Dramatic Society would hire the place for an evening—or an obscure film would be trade-shown there. The theater had been built in 1920 by an optimist who thought the cheapness of the site would more than counterbalance its disadvantage of lying a mile outside the conventional theater zone. But no play had ever succeeded, and it was soon left to gather rat holes and spiderwebs. The covering of the seats was never renewed, and all that ever happened to the place was the temporary false life of an amateur play or a trade show.

Craven stopped and read—there were still optimists it appeared, even in 1939, for nobody but the blindest optimist could hope to make money out of the place as "The Home of the Silent Film." The first season of "primitives" was announced (a highbrow phrase): there would never be a second. Well, the seats were cheap, and it was perhaps worth a shilling to him, now that he was tired, to get in somewhere out of the rain. Craven bought a ticket and went in to the darkness of the stalls.

In the dead darkness a piano tinkled something monotonous recalling

Mendelssohn: he sat down in a gangway seat, and could immediately feel the emptiness all round him. No, there would never be another season. On the screen a large woman in a kind of toga wrung her hands, then wobbled with curious jerky movements towards a couch. There she sat and stared out like a sheepdog distractedly through her loose and black and stringy hair. Sometimes she seemed to dissolve altogether into dots and flashes and wiggly lines. A subtitle said, "Pompilia betrayed by her beloved Augustus seeks an end to her troubles."

Craven began at last to see—a dim waste of stalls. There were not twenty people in the place—a few couples whispering with their heads touching, and a number of lonely men like himself, wearing the same uniform of the cheap mackintosh. They lay about at intervals like corpses—and again Craven's obsession returned: the toothache of horror. He thought miserably—I am going mad: other people don't feel like this. Even a disused theater reminded him of those interminable caverns where the bodies were waiting for resurrection.

"A slave to his passion Augustus calls for yet more wine."

A gross middle-aged Teutonic actor lay on an elbow with his arm round a large woman in a shift. "The Spring Song" tinkled ineptly on, and the screen flickered like indigestion. Somebody felt his way through the darkness, scrabbling past Craven's knees—a small man: Craven experienced the unpleasant feeling of a large beard brushing his mouth. Then there was a long sigh as the newcomer found the next chair, and on the screen events had moved with such rapidity that Pompilia had already stabbed herself—or so Craven supposed—and lay still and buxom among her weeping slaves.

A low breathless voice sighed out close to Craven's ear, "What's happened? Is she asleep?"

"No. Dead."

"Murdered?" the voice asked with a keen interest.

"I don't think so. Stabbed herself."

Nobody said "Hush": nobody was enough interested to object to a voice. They drooped among the empty chairs in attitudes of weary inattention.

The film wasn't nearly over yet: there were children somehow to be considered: was it all going on to a second generation? But the small bearded man in the next seat seemed to be interested only in Pompilia's death. The fact that he had come in at that moment apparently fascinated him. Craven heard the word "coincidence" twice, and he went on talking to himself about it in low out-of-breath tones. "Absurd when you come to think of it," and then "no blood at all." Craven didn't listen: he sat with his hands clasped between his knees, facing the fact as he had faced it so often before, that he was in danger of going mad. He had to pull himself up, take a holiday, see a doctor (God knew what infection moved in his veins). He became aware that his bearded neighbor had addressed him directly. "What?" he asked impatiently, "what did you say?"

"There would be more blood than you can imagine."

"What are you talking about?"

When the man spoke to him, he sprayed him with damp breath. There was a little bubble in his speech like an impediment. He said, "When you murder a man . . ."

"This was a woman," Craven said impatiently.

"That wouldn't make any difference."

"And it's got nothing to do with murder anyway."

"That doesn't signify." They seemed to have got into an absurd and meaningless wrangle in the dark.

"I know, you see," the little bearded man said in a tone of enormous conceit.

"Know what?"

"About such things," he said with guarded ambiguity.

Craven turned and tried to see him clearly. Was he mad? Was this a warning of what he might become—babbling incomprehensibly to strangers in cinemas? He thought, By God, no, trying to see: I'll be sane yet. I *will* be sane. He could make out nothing but a small black hump of body. The man was talking to himself again. He said, "Talk. Such talk. They'll say it was all for fifty pounds. But that's a lie. Reasons and reasons. They always take the first reason. Never look behind. Thirty years of reasons. Such simpletons," he added again in that tone of breathlessness and unbounded conceit. So this was madness. So long as he could realize that, he must be sane himself—relatively speaking. Not so sane perhaps as the seekers in the park or the Guardsmen in the Edgware Road, but saner than this. It was like a message of encouragement as the piano tinkled on.

Then again the little man turned and sprayed him. "Killed herself, you say? But who's to know that? It's not a mere question of what hand holds the knife." He laid a hand suddenly and confidingly on Craven's: it was damp and sticky: Craven said with horror as a possible meaning came to him, "What are you talking about?"

"I know," the little man said. "A man in my position gets to know almost everything."

"What is your position?" Craven asked, feeling the sticky hand on his, trying to make up his mind whether he was being hysterical or not—after all, there were a dozen explanations—it might be treacle.

"A pretty desperate one *you'd* say." Sometimes the voice almost died in the throat altogether. Something incomprehensible had happened on the screen—take your eyes from these early pictures for a moment and the plot had proceeded on at such a pace . . . Only the actors moved slowly and jerkily. A young woman in a nightdress seemed to be weeping in the arms of a Roman centurion: Craven hadn't seen either of them before. *"I am not afraid of death, Lucius—in your arms."*

The little man began to titter—knowingly. He was talking to himself again. It would have been easy to ignore him altogether if it had not been for those sticky hands which he now removed: he seemed to be fumbling at the seat in front of him. His head had a habit of lolling sideways—like an idiot child's. He said distinctly and irrelevantly: "Bayswater Tragedy."

"What was that?" Craven said. He had seen those words on a poster before he entered the park.

"What?"

"About the tragedy."

"To think they call Cullen Mews Bayswater." Suddenly the little man began to cough—turning his face toward Craven and coughing right at him: it was like vindictiveness. The voice said, "Let me see. My umbrella." He was getting up.

"You didn't have an umbrella."

"My umbrella," he repeated. "My—" and seemed to lose the word altogether. He went scrabbling out past Craven's knees.

Craven let him go, but before he had reached the billowy dusty curtains of the Exit the screen went blank and bright—the film had broken, and somebody immediately turned up one dirt-choked chandelier above the circle. It shone down just enough for Craven to see the smear on his hands. This wasn't hysteria: this was a fact. He wasn't mad: he had sat next to a madman who in some mews—what was the name, Colon, Collin . . . Craven jumped up and made his own way out: the black curtain flapped in his mouth. But he was too late: the man had gone and there were three turnings to choose from. He chose instead a telephone box and dialed with a sense odd for him of sanity and decision 999.

It didn't take two minutes to get the right department. They were interested and very kind. Yes, there had been a murder in a mews—Cullen Mews. A man's neck had been cut from ear to ear with a bread knife—a horrid crime. He began to tell them how he had sat next the murderer in a cinema: it couldn't be anyone else: there was blood on his hands—and he remembered with repulsion as he spoke the damp beard. There must have been a terrible lot of blood. But the voice from the Yard interrupted him. "Oh no," it was saying, "we have the murderer—no doubt of it at all. It's the body that's disappeared."

Craven put down the receiver. He said to himself aloud, "Why should this happen to *me*? Why to *me*?" He was back in the horror of his dream—the squalid darkening street outside was only one of the innumerable tunnels connecting grave to grave where the imperishable bodies lay. He said, "It was a dream, a dream," and leaning forward he saw in the mirror above the telephone his own face sprinkled by tiny drops of blood like dew from a scent spray. He began to scream, "I won't go mad. I won't go mad. I'm sane. I won't go mad." Presently a little crowd began to collect, and soon a policeman came.

ISAAC BASHEVIS SINGER

A Crown of Feathers

Reb Naftali Holishitzer, the community leader in Krasnobród, was left in his old age with no children. One daughter had died in childbirth and the other in a cholera epidemic. A son had drowned when he tried to cross the San River on horseback. Reb Naftali had only one grandchild—a girl, Akhsa, an orphan. It was not the custom for a female to study at a yeshiva, because "the King's daughter is all glorious within" and Jewish daughters are all the daughters of kings. But Akhsa studied at home. She dazzled everyone with her beauty, wisdom, and diligence. She had white skin and black hair; her eyes were blue.

Reb Naftali managed an estate that had belonged to the Prince Czartoryski. Since he owed Reb Naftali twenty thousand guldens, the prince's property was a permanent pawn, and Reb Naftali had built for himself a water mill and a brewery and had sown hundreds of acres with hops. His wife, Nesha, came from a wealthy family in Prague. They could afford to hire the finest tutors for Akhsa. One taught her the Bible, another French, still another the pianoforte, and a fourth dancing. She learned everything quickly. At eight, she was playing chess with her grandfather. Reb Naftali didn't need to offer a dowry for her marriage, since she was heir to his entire fortune.

Matches were sought for her early, but her grandmother was hard to please. She would look at a boy proposed by the marriage brokers and say, "He has the shoulders of a fool," or, "He has the narrow forehead of an ignoramus."

One day Nesha died unexpectedly. Reb Naftali was in his late seventies and it was unthinkable that he remarry. Half his day he devoted to religion, the other half to business. He rose at daybreak and pored over the Talmud and the Commentaries and wrote letters to community elders. When a man was sick, Reb Naftali went to comfort him. Twice a week he visited the poorhouse with Akhsa, who carried a contribution of soup and groats herself. More than once, Akhsa, the pampered and scholarly, rolled up her sleeves and made beds there.

In the summer, after midday sleep, Reb Naftali ordered his britska harnessed and he rode around the fields and village with Akhsa. While they rode, he discussed business, and it was known that he listened to her advice just as he had listened to her grandmother's.

But there was one thing that Akhsa didn't have—a friend. Her grandmother had tried to find friends for her; she had even lowered her standards and invited girls from Krasnobród. But Akhsa had no patience with their chatter about clothes and household matters. Since the tutors were all men, Akhsa was kept away from them, except for lessons. Now her grandfather became her only companion. Reb Naftali had met famous noblemen in his lifetime. He had been to fairs in Warsaw, Kraków, Danzig, and Koenigsberg. He would sit for hours with Akhsa and tell her about rabbis and miracle workers, about the disciples of the false messiah Sabbatai Zevi, quarrels in the Sejm, the caprices of the Zamojskis, the Radziwills, and the Czartoryskis—their wives, lovers, courtiers. Sometimes Akhsa would cry out, "I wish you were my fiancé, not my grandfather!" and kiss his eyes and his white beard.

Reb Naftali would answer, "I'm not the only man in Poland. There are plenty like me, and young to boot."

"Where, Grandfather? Where?"

After her grandmother's death, Akhsa refused to rely on anyone else's judgment in the choice of a husband—not even her grandfather's. Just as her grandmother saw only bad, Reb Naftali saw only good. Akhsa demanded that the matchmakers allow her to meet her suitor, and Reb Naftali finally consented. The young pair would be brought together in a room, the door would be left open, and a deaf old woman servant would stand at the threshold to watch that the meeting be brief and without frivolity. As a rule, Akhsa stayed with the young man not more than a few minutes. Most of the suitors seemed dull and silly. Others tried to be clever and made undignified jokes. Akhsa dismissed them abruptly. How strange, but her grandmother still expressed her opinion. Once, Akhsa heard her say clearly, "He has the snout of a pig." Another time, she said, "He talks like the standard letter book."

Akhsa knew quite well that it was not her grandmother speaking. The dead don't return from the other world to comment on prospective fiancés. Just the same, it was her grandmother's voice, her style. Akhsa wanted to talk to her grandfather about it, but she was afraid he would think her crazy. Besides, her grandfather longed for his wife, and Akhsa didn't want to stir up his grief.

When Reb Naftali Holishitzer realized that his granddaughter was driving away the matchmakers, he was troubled. Akhsa was now past her eighteenth year. The people in Krasnobród had begun to gossip—she was demanding a knight on a white horse or the moon in heaven; she would stay a spinster. Reb Naftali decided not to give in to her whims any more but to marry her off. He went to a yeshiva and brought back with him a young man named Zemach, an orphan and a devout scholar. He was dark as a gypsy, small, with broad shoulders. His sidelocks were thick. He was nearsighted and studied eighteen hours a day. The moment he reached Krasnobród, he went to the study house and began to sway in front of an open volume of the Talmud. His sidelocks swayed, too. Students came to talk with him, and he spoke without lifting his gaze from the book. He seemed to know the Talmud by heart, since he caught everyone misquoting.

Akhsa demanded a meeting, but Reb Naftali replied that this was conduct befitting tailors and shoemakers, not a girl of good breeding. He warned Akhsa that if she drove Zemach away he would disinherit her. Since men and women were in separate rooms during the engagement party, Akhsa had no chance of seeing Zemach until the marriage contract was to be signed. She looked at him and heard her grandmother say, "They've sold you shoddy goods."

Her words were so clear it seemed to Akhsa that everyone should have heard them, but no one had. The girls and women crowded around her, congratulating her and praising her beauty, her dress, her jewelry. Her grandfather passed her the contract and a quill, and her grandmother cried out, "Don't sign!" She grabbed Akhsa's elbow and a blot formed on the paper.

Reb Naftali shouted, "What have you done!"

Akhsa tried to sign, but the pen fell from her hand. She burst into tears. "Grandfather, I can't."

"Akhsa, you shame me."

"Grandfather, forgive me." Akhsa covered her face with her hands. There was an outcry. Men hissed and women laughed and wept. Akhsa cried silently. They half led, half carried her to her room and put her on her bed.

Zemach exclaimed, "I don't want to be married to this shrew!"

He pushed through the crowd and ran to get a wagon back to the yeshiva. Reb Naftali went after him, trying to pacify him with words and money, but Zemach threw Reb Naftali's banknotes to the ground. Someone brought his wicker trunk from the inn where he had stayed. Before the wagon pulled away, Zemach cried out, "I don't forgive her, and God won't, either."

For days after that, Akhsa was ill. Reb Naftali Holishitzer, who had been successful all his life, was not accustomed to failure. He became sick; his face took on a yellow pallor. Women and girls tried to comfort Akhsa. Rabbis and elders came to visit Reb Naftali, but he got weaker as the days passed. After a while, Akhsa gained back her strength and left her sickbed. She went to her grandfather's room, bolting the door behind her. The maid who listened and spied through the keyhole reported that she had heard him say, "You are mad!"

Akhsa nursed her grandfather, brought him his medicine and bathed him with a sponge, but the old man developed an inflammation of the lungs. Blood ran from his nose. His urine stopped. Soon he died. He had written his will years before and left one-third of his estate to charity and the rest to Akhsa.

According to the law, one does not sit shivah in mourning after the death of a grandfather, but Akhsa went through the ceremony anyway. She sat on a low stool and read the book of Job. She ordered that no one be let in. She had shamed an orphan—a scholar—and caused the death of her grandfather. She became melancholy. Since she had read the story of Job before, she began

345

to search in her grandfather's library for another book to read. To her amazement, she found a Bible translated into Polish—the New Testament as well as the Old. Akhsa knew it was a forbidden book, but she turned the pages anyway. Had her grandfather read it, Akhsa wondered. No, it couldn't be. She remembered that on the Gentile feast days, when holy icons and pictures were carried in processions near the house, she was not allowed to look out of the window. Her grandfather told her it was idolatry. She wondered if her grandmother had read this Bible. Among the pages she found some pressed cornflowers—a flower her grandmother had often picked. Grandmother came from Bohemia; it was said that her father had belonged to the Sabbatai Zevi sect. Akhsa recalled that Prince Czartoryski used to spend time with her grandmother when he visited the estate, and praised the way she spoke Polish. If she hadn't been a Jewish girl, he said, he would have married her—a great compliment.

That night Akhsa read the New Testament to the last page. It was difficult for her to accept that Jesus was God's only begotten son and that He rose from the grave, but she found this book more comforting to her tortured spirit than the castigating words of the prophets, who never mentioned the Kingdom of Heaven or the resurrection of the dead. All they promised was a good harvest for good deeds and starvation and plague for bad ones.

On the seventh night of shivah, Akhsa went to bed. The light was out and she was dozing when she heard footsteps that she recognized as her grandfather's. In the darkness, her grandfather's figure emerged: the light face, the white beard, the mild features, even the skullcap on his high forehead. He said in a quiet voice, "Akhsa, you have committed an injustice."

Akhsa began to cry. "Grandfather, what should I do?"

"Everything can be corrected."

"How?"

"Apologize to Zemach. Become his wife."

"Grandfather, I hate him."

"He is your destined one."

He lingered for a moment, and Akhsa could smell his snuff, which he used to mix with cloves and smelling salts. Then he vanished and an empty space

346

remained in the darkness. She was too amazed to be frightened. She leaned against the headboard, and after some time she slept.

She woke with a start. She heard her grandmother's voice. This was not a murmuring like Grandfather's but the strong voice of a living person. "Akhsa, my daughter."

Akhsa burst into tears. "Grandmother, where are you?"

"I'm here."

"What should I do?"

"Whatever your heart desires."

"What, Grandmother?"

"Go to the priest. He will advise you."

Akhsa became numb. Fear constricted her throat. She managed to say, "You're not my grandmother. You're a demon."

"I am your grandmother. Do you remember how we went wading in the pond that summer night near the flat hill and you found a gulden in the water?"

"Yes, Grandmother."

"I could give you other proof. Be it known that the Gentiles are right. Jesus of Nazareth is the Son of God. He was born of the Holy Spirit as prophesied. The rebellious Jews refused to accept the truth and therefore they are punished. The Messiah will not come to them because He is here already."

"Grandmother, I'm afraid."

"Akhsa, don't listen!" her grandfather suddenly shouted into her right ear. "This isn't your grandmother. It's an evil spirit disguised to trick you. Don't give in to his blasphemies. He will drag you into perdition."

"Akhsa, that is not your grandfather but a goblin from behind the bathhouse," Grandmother interrupted. "Zemach is a ne'er-do-well, and vengeful to boot. He will torment you, and the children he begets will be vermin like him. Save yourself while there is time. God is with the Gentiles."

"Lilith! She-demon! Daughter of Ketev M'riri!" Grandfather growled. "Liar!"

Grandfather became silent, but Grandmother continued to talk, although her voice faded. She said, "Your real grandfather learned the truth in

Heaven and converted. They baptized him with heavenly water and he rests in Paradise. The saints are all bishops and cardinals. Those who remain stubborn are roasted in the fires of Gehenna. If you don't believe me, ask for a sign."

"What sign?"

"Unbutton your pillowcase, rip open the seams of the pillow, and there you will find a crown of feathers. No human hand could make a crown like this."

Her grandmother disappeared, and Akhsa fell into a heavy sleep. At dawn, she awoke and lit a candle. She remembered her grandmother's words, unbuttoned the pillowcase, and ripped open the pillow. What she saw was so extraordinary she could scarcely believe her eyes: down and feathers entwined into a crown, with little ornaments and complex designs no worldly master could have duplicated. On the top of the crown was a tiny cross. It was all so airy that Akhsa's breath made it flutter. Akhsa gasped. Whoever had made this crown—an angel or a demon—had done his work in darkness, in the inside of a pillow. She was beholding a miracle. She extinguished the candle and stretched out on the bed. For a long time she lay without any thoughts. Then she went back to sleep.

In the morning when she awoke, Akhsa thought she had had a dream, but on the night table she saw the crown of feathers. The sun made it sparkle with the colors of the rainbow. It looked as if it were set with the smallest of gems. She sat and contemplated the wonder. Then she put on a black dress and a black shawl and asked that the carriage be brought round for her. She rode to the house where Koscik, the priest, resided. The housekeeper answered her knock. The priest was nearing seventy and he knew Akhsa. He had often come to the estate to bless the peasants' bread at Eastertime and to give rites to the dying and conduct weddings and funerals. One of Akhsa's teachers had borrowed a Latin-Polish dictionary from him. Whenever the priest visited, Akhsa's grandmother invited him to her parlor and they conversed over cake and vishniak.

The priest offered Akhsa a chair. She sat down and told him everything. He said, "Don't go back to the Jews. Come to us. We will see to it that your fortune remains intact."

"I forgot to take the crown. I want to have it with me."

"Yes, my daughter, go and bring it."

Akhsa went home, but a maid had cleaned her bedroom and dusted the night table; the crown had vanished. Akhsa searched in the garbage ditch, in the slops, but not a trace could she find.

Soon after that, the terrible news was abroad in Krasnobród that Akhsa had converted.

Six years passed. Akhsa married and became the Squiress Maria Malkowska. The old squire, Wladyslaw Malkowski, had died without direct heir and had left his estate to his nephew Ludwik. Ludwik had remained a bachelor until he was forty-five, and it seemed he would never marry. He lived in his uncle's castle with his spinster sister, Gloria. His love affairs were with peasant girls, and he had sired a number of bastards. He was small and light, with a blond goatee. Ludwik kept to himself, reading old books of history, religion, and genealogy. He smoked a porcelain pipe, drank alone, hunted by himself, and avoided the noblemen's dances. The business of the estate he handled with a strong hand, and he made sure his bailiff never stole from him. His neighbors thought he was a pedant, and some considered him half mad. When Akhsa accepted the Christian faith, he asked her—now Maria—to marry him. Gossips said that Ludwik, the miser, had fallen in love with Maria's inheritance. The priests and others persuaded Akhsa to accept Ludwik's proposal. He was a descendant of the Polish king Leszczyński. Gloria, who was ten years older than Ludwik, opposed the match, but Ludwik for once did not listen to her.

The Jews of Krasnobród were afraid that Akhsa would become their enemy and instigate Ludwik against them, as happened with so many converts, but Ludwik continued to trade with the Jews, selling them fish, grain, and cattle. Zelig Frampoler, a court Jew, delivered all kinds of merchandise to the estate. Gloria remained the lady of the castle.

In the first weeks of their marriage, Akhsa and Ludwik took trips together in a surrey. Ludwik even began to pay visits to neighboring squires, and he talked of giving a ball. He confessed all his past adventures with women to Maria and promised to behave like a God-fearing Christian. But before long he fell back into his old ways; he withdrew from his neighbors, started up his affairs with peasant girls, and began to drink again. An angry silence hung between man and wife. Ludwik ceased coming to Maria's bedroom, and she did not conceive. In time, they stopped dining at the same table, and when Ludwik needed to tell Maria something he sent a note with a servant. Gloria, who managed the finances, allowed her sister-in-law a gulden a week; Maria's fortune now belonged to her husband. It became clear to Akhsa that God was punishing her and that nothing remained but to wait for death. But what would happen to her after she died? Would she be roasted on a bed of needles and be thrown into the waste of the netherworld? Would she be reincarnated as a dog, a mouse, a millstone?

Because she had nothing to occupy her time with, Akhsa spent all day and part of the night in her husband's library. Ludwik had not added to it, and the books were old, bound in leather, in wood, or in moth-eaten velvet and silk. The pages were yellow and foxed. Akhsa read stories of ancient kings, faraway countries, of all sorts of battles and intrigues among princes, cardinals, dukes. She pored over tales of the Crusades and the Black Plague. The world crawled with wickedness, but it was also full of wonders. Stars in the sky warred and swallowed one another. Comets foretold catastrophes. A child was born with a tail; a woman grew scales and fins. In India, fakirs stepped barefooted on red-hot coals without being burned. Others let themselves be buried alive, and then rose from their graves.

It was strange, but after the night Akhsa found the crown of feathers in her pillow she was not given another sign from the powers that rule the universe. She never heard from her grandfather or grandmother. There were times when Akhsa desired to call out to her grandfather, but she did not dare mention his name with her unclean lips. She had betrayed the Jewish God and she no longer believed in the Gentile one, so she refrained from praying. Often when Zelig Frampoler came to the estate and Akhsa saw him from the window, she wanted to ask him about the Jewish community, but she was afraid that he might hold it a sin to speak to her, and that Gloria would denounce her for associating with Jews.

* * *

Years rolled by. Gloria's hair turned white and her head shook. Ludwik's goatee became gray. The servants grew old, deaf, and half blind. Akhsa, or Maria, was in her thirties, but she often imagined herself an old woman. With the years she became more and more convinced that it was the Devil who had persuaded her to convert and that it was he who had fashioned the crown of feathers. But the road back was blocked. The Russian law forbade a convert to return to his faith. The bit of information that reached her about the Jews was bad: the synagogue in Krasnobród had burned down, as well as the stores in the marketplace. Dignified householders and community elders hung bags on their shoulders and went begging. Every few months there was an epidemic. There was nowhere to return to. She often contemplated suicide, but how? She lacked the courage to hang herself or cut her veins; she had no poison.

Slowly, Akhsa came to the conclusion that the universe was ruled by the black powers. It was not God holding dominion but Satan. She found a thick book about witchcraft that contained detailed descriptions of spells and incantations, talismans, the conjuring up of demons and goblins, the sacrifices to Asmodeus, Lucifer, and Beelzebub. There were accounts of the Black Mass; and of how the witches anointed their bodies, gathered in the forest, partook of human flesh, and flew in the air riding on brooms, shovels, and hoops, accompanied by bevies of devils and other creatures of the night that had horns and tails, bat's wings, and the snouts of pigs. Often these monsters lay with the witches, who gave birth to freaks.

Akhsa reminded herself of the Yiddish proverb "If you cannot go over, go under." She had lost the world to come; therefore, she decided to enjoy some revelry while she had this life. At night she began to call the Devil, prepared to make a covenant with him as many neglected women had done before.

Once in the middle of the night, after Akhsa had swallowed a potion of mead, spittle, human blood, crow's egg spiced with galbanum and mandrake, she felt a cold kiss on her lips. In the shine of the late-night moon she saw a naked male figure—tall and black, with long elflocks, the horns of a buck, and two protruding teeth, like a boar's. He bent down over her, whispering, "What is your command, my mistress? You may ask for half my kingdom."

His body was as translucent as a spiderweb. He stank of pitch. Akhsa had been about to reply, "You, my slave, come and have me." Instead, she murmured, "My grandparents."

The Devil burst into laughter. "They are dust!"

"Did you braid the crown of feathers?" Akhsa asked.

"Who else?"

"You deceived me?"

"I am a deceiver," the Devil answered with a giggle.

"Where is the truth?" Akhsa asked.

"The truth is that there is no truth."

The Devil lingered for a while and then disappeared. For the remainder of the night, Akhsa was neither asleep nor awake. Voices spoke to her. Her breasts became swollen, her nipples hard, her belly distended. Pain bored into her skull. Her teeth were on edge, and her tongue enlarged so that she feared it would split her palate. Her eyes bulged from their sockets. There was a knocking in her ears as loud as a hammer on an anvil. Then she felt as if she were in the throes of labor. "I'm giving birth to a demon!" Akhsa cried out. She began to pray to the God she had forsaken. Finally she fell asleep, and when she awoke in the predawn darkness all her pains had ceased. She saw her grandfather standing at the foot of her bed. He wore a white robe and cowl, such as he used to wear on the eve of Yom Kippur when he blessed Akhsa before going to the Kol Nidre prayer. A light shone from his eyes and lit up Akhsa's quilt. "Grandfather," Akhsa murmured.

"Yes, Akhsa. I am here."

"Grandfather, what shall I do?"

"Run away. Repent."

"I'm lost."

"It is never too late. Find the man you shamed. Become a Jewish daughter."

Later, Akhsa did not remember whether her grandfather had actually spoken to her or she had understood him without words. The night was over. Daybreak reddened the window. Birds were twittering. Akhsa examined her sheet. There was no blood. She had not given birth to a demon. For the first time in years, she recited the Hebrew prayer of thanksgiving.

She got out of bed, washed at the basin, and covered her hair with a shawl. Ludwik and Gloria had robbed her of her inheritance, but she still possessed her grandmother's jewelry. She wrapped it in a handkerchief and put it in a basket, together with a shirt and underwear. Ludwik had either stayed the night with one of his mistresses or he had left at dawn to hunt. Gloria lay sick in her boudoir. The maid brought Akhsa her breakfast, but she ate little. Then she left the estate. Dogs barked at her as if she were a stranger. The old servants looked in amazement as the squiress passed through the gates with a basket on her arm and a kerchief on her head like a peasant woman.

Although Malkowski's property was not far from Krasnobród, Akhsa spent most of the day on the road. She sat down to rest and washed her hands in a stream. She recited grace and ate the slice of bread she had brought with her.

Near the Krasnobród cemetery stood the hut of Eber, the gravedigger. Outside, his wife was washing linen in a tub. Akhsa asked her, "Is this the way to Krasnobród?"

"Yes, straight ahead."

"What's the news from the village?"

"Who are you?"

"I'm a relative of Reb Naftali Holishitzer."

The woman wiped her hands on her apron. "Not a soul is left of that family."

"Where is Akhsa?"

The old woman trembled. "She should have been buried head first, Father in Heaven." And she told about Akhsa's conversion. "She's had her punishment already in this world."

"What became of the yeshiva boy she was betrothed to?"

"Who knows? He isn't from around here."

Akhsa asked about the graves of her grandparents, and the old woman pointed to two headstones bent one toward the other, overgrown with moss and weeds. Akhsa prostrated herself in front of them and lay there until nightfall.

* * *

For three months, Akhsa wandered from yeshiva to yeshiva, but she did not find Zemach. She searched in community record books, questioned elders and rabbis—without result. Since not every town had an inn, she often slept in the poorhouse. She lay on a pallet of straw, covered with a mat, praying silently that her grandfather would appear and tell her where to find Zemach. He gave no sign. In the darkness, the old and the sick coughed and muttered. Children cried. Mothers cursed. Although Akhsa accepted this as part of her punishment, she could not overcome her sense of indignity. Community leaders scolded her. They made her wait for days to see them. Women were suspicious of her—why was she looking for a man who no doubt had a wife and children, or might even be in his grave? "Grandfather, why did you drive me to this?" Akhsa cried. "Either show me the way or send death to take me."

On a wintry afternoon, while Akhsa was sitting in an inn in Lublin, she asked the innkeeper if he had ever heard of a man called Zemach—small in stature, swarthy, a former yeshiva boy and scholar. One of the other guests said, "You mean Zemach, the teacher from Izbica?"

He described Zemach, and Akhsa knew she had found the one she was looking for. "He was engaged to marry a girl in Krasnobród," she said.

"I know. The convert. Who are you?"

"A relative."

"What do you want with him?" the guest asked. "He's poor, and stubborn to boot. All his pupils have been taken away from him. He's a wild and contrary man."

"Does he have a wife?"

"He's had two already. One he tortured to death and the other left him."

"Does he have children?"

"No, he's sterile."

The guest was about to say more, but a servant came to call for him.

Akhsa's eyes filled with tears. Her grandfather had not forsaken her. He had led her in the right direction. She went to arrange conveyance to Izbica, and in front of the inn stood a covered wagon ready to leave. "No, I am not alone," she said to herself. "Every step is known in Heaven."

In the beginning, the roads were paved, but soon they became dirt trails full of holes and ditches. The night was wet and dark. Often the passengers had to climb down and help the coachman push the wagon out of the mud. The others scolded him, but Akhsa accepted her discomfort with grace. Wet snow was falling and a cold wind blew. Every time she got out of the wagon she sank over her ankles in mud. They arrived in Izbica late in the evening. The whole village was a swamp. The huts were dilapidated. Someone showed Akhsa the way to Zemach the Teacher's house—it was on a hill near the butcher shops. Even though it was winter, there was a stench of decay in the air. Butcher-shop dogs were slinking around.

Akhsa looked into the window of Zemach's hut and saw peeling walls, a dirt floor, and shelves of worn books. A wick in a dish of oil gave the only light. At the table sat a little man with a black beard, bushy brows, a yellow face, and a pointed nose. He was bending myopically over a large volume. He wore the lining of a skullcap and a quilted jacket that showed the dirty batting. As Akhsa stood watching, a mouse came out of its hole and scurried over to the bed, which had a pallet of rotting straw, a pillow without a case, and a moth-eaten sheepskin for a blanket. Even though Zemach had aged, Akhsa recognized him. He scratched himself. He spat on his fingertips and wiped them on his forehead. Yes, that was he. Akhsa wanted to laugh and cry at the same time. In a moment she turned her face toward the darkness. For the first time in years, she heard her grandmother's voice. "Akhsa, run away."

"Where to?"

"Back to Esau."

Then she heard her grandfather's voice. "Akhsa, he will save you from the abyss."

Akhsa had never heard her grandfather speak with such fervor. She felt the emptiness that comes before fainting. She leaned against the door and it opened.

Zemach lifted one bushy brow. His eyes were bulging and jaundiced. "What do you want?" he rasped.

"Are you Reb Zemach?"

"Yes, who are you?"

"Akhsa, from Krasnobród. Once your fiancée . . ."

Zemach was silent. He opened his crooked mouth, revealing a single tooth, black as a hook. "The convert?"

"I have come back to Jewishness."

Zemach jumped up. A terrible cry tore from him. "Get out of my house! Blotted be your name!"

"Reb Zemach, please hear me!"

He ran toward her with clenched fists. The dish of oil fell and the light was extinguished. "Filth!"

The study house in Holishitz was packed. It was the day before the new moon, and a crowd had gathered to recite the supplications. From the women's section came the sound of pious recitation. Suddenly the door opened, and a black-bearded man wearing tattered clothes strode in. A bag was slung over his shoulder. He was leading a woman on a rope as if she were a cow. She wore a black kerchief on her head, a dress made of sackcloth, and rags on her feet. Around her neck hung a wreath of garlic. The worshippers stopped their prayers. The stranger gave a sign to the woman and she prostrated herself on the threshold. "Jews, step on me!" she called. "Jews, spit on me!"

Turmoil rose in the study house. The stranger went up to the reading table, tapped for silence, and intoned, "This woman's family comes from your town. Her grandfather was Reb Naftali Holishitzer. She is the Akhsa who converted and married a squire. She has seen the truth now and wants to atone for her abominations."

Though Holishitz was in the part of Poland that belonged to Austria, the story of Akhsa had been heard there. Some of the worshippers protested that this was not the way of repentance; a human being should not be dragged by a rope, like cattle. Others threatened the stranger with their fists. It was true that in Austria a convert could return to Jewishness according to the law of the land. But if the Gentiles were to learn that one who went over to their faith had been humiliated in such a fashion, harsh edicts and recriminations might result. The old rabbi, Reb Bezalel, approached Akhsa with quick little steps. "Get up, my daughter. Since you have repented, you are one of us."

356

Akhsa rose. "Rabbi, I have disgraced my people."

"Since you repent, the Almighty will forgive you."

When the worshippers in the women's section heard what was going on, they rushed into the room with the men, the rabbi's wife among them. Reb Bezalel said to her, "Take her home and dress her in decent clothing. Man was created in God's image."

"Rabbi," Akhsa said, "I want to atone for my iniquities."

"I will prescribe a penance for you. Don't torture yourself."

Some of the women began to cry. The rabbi's wife took off her shawl and hung it over Akhsa's shoulders. Another matron offered Akhsa a cape. They led her into the chamber where in olden times they had kept captive those who sinned against the community—it still contained a block and chain. The women dressed Akhsa there. Someone brought her a skirt and shoes. As they busied themselves about her, Akhsa beat her breast with her first and recounted her sins: she had spited God, served idols, copulated with a Gentile. She sobbed, "I practiced witchcraft. I conjured up Satan. He braided me a crown of feathers." When Akhsa was dressed, the rabbi's wife took her home.

After prayers, the men began to question the stranger as to who he was and how he was connected with Reb Naftali's granddaughter.

He replied, "My name is Zemach. I was supposed to become her husband, but she refused me. Now she has come to ask my forgiveness."

"A Jew should forgive."

"I forgive her, but the Almighty is a God of vengeance."

"He is also a God of mercy."

Zemach began a debate with the scholars, and his erudition was obvious at once. He quoted the Talmud, the Commentaries, and the Responsa. He even corrected the rabbi when he misquoted.

Reb Bezalel asked him, "Do you have a family?"

"I am divorced."

"In that case, everything can be set right."

The rabbi invited Zemach to go home with him. The women sat with Akhsa out in the kitchen. They urged her to eat bread with chicory. She had been fasting for three days. In the rabbi's study the men looked after Zemach.

They brought him trousers, shoes, a coat, and a hat. Since he was infested with lice, they took him to the baths.

In the evening, the seven outstanding citizens of the town and all the important elders gathered. The wives brought Akhsa. The rabbi pronounced that, according to the law, Akhsa was not married. Her union with the squire was nothing but an act of lechery. The rabbi asked, "Zemach, do you desire Akhsa for a wife?"

"I do."

"Akhsa, will you take Zemach for a husband?"

"Yes, Rabbi, but I am not worthy."

The rabbi outlined Akhsa's penance. She must fast each Monday and Thursday, abstain from meat and fish on the weekdays, recite psalms, and rise at dawn for prayers. The rabbi said to her, "The chief thing is not the punishment but the remorse. 'And he will return and be healed,' the prophet says."

"Rabbi, excuse," Zemach interrupted. "This kind of penance is for common sins, not for conversion."

"What do you want her to do?"

"There are more severe forms of contrition."

"What, for example?"

"Wearing pebbles in the shoes. Rolling naked in the snow in winter—in nettles in summer. Fasting from Sabbath to Sabbath."

"Nowadays, people do not have the strength for such rigors," the rabbi said after some hesitation.

"If they have the strength to sin, they should have the strength to expiate."

"Holy Rabbi," said Akhsa, "do not let me off lightly. Let the rabbi give me a harsh penance."

"I have said what is right."

All kept silent. Then Akhsa said, "Zemach, give me my bundle." Zemach had put her bag in a corner. He brought it to the table and she took out a little sack. A sigh could be heard from the group as she poured out settings of pearls, diamonds, and rubies. "Rabbi, this is my jewelry," Akhsa said. "I do not deserve to own it. Let the rabbi dispose of it as he wishes."

"Is it yours or the squire's?"

"Mine, Rabbi, inherited from my sacred grandmother."

"It is written that even the most charitable should never give up more than a fifth part."

Zemach shook his head. "Again I am in disagreement. She disgraced her grandmother in Paradise. She should not be permitted to inherit her jewels."

The rabbi clutched his beard. "If you know better, you become the rabbi." He rose from his chair and then sat down again. "How will you sustain yourselves?"

"I will be a water carrier," Zemach said.

"Rabbi, I can knead dough and wash linen," Akhsa said.

"Well, do as you choose. I believe in the mercy, not in the rigor, of the law."

In the middle of the night Akhsa opened her eyes. Husband and wife lived in a hut with a dirt floor, not far from the cemetery. All day long Zemach carried water. Akhsa washed linen. Except for Saturday and holidays, both fasted every day and ate only in the evening. Akhsa had put sand and pebbles into her shoes and wore a rough woolen shirt next to her skin. At night they slept separately on the floor—he on a mat by the window, she on a straw pallet by the oven. On a rope that stretched from wall to wall hung shrouds she had made for them.

They had been married for three years, but Zemach still had not approached her. He had confessed that he, too, was dipped in sin. While he had a wife, he had lusted for Akhsa. He had spilled his seed like Onan. He had craved revenge upon her, had railed against the Almighty, and had taken out his wrath on his wives, one of whom died. How could he be more defiled?

Even though the hut was near a forest and they could get wood for nothing, Zemach would not allow the stove to be heated at night. They slept in their clothes, covered with sacks and rags. The people of Holishitz maintained that Zemach was a madman; the rabbi had called for man and wife and explained that it is as cruel to torture oneself as it is to torture others, but Zemach quoted from *The Beginning of Wisdom* that repentance without mortification is meaningless.

Akhsa made a confession every night before sleep, and still her dreams were not pure. Satan came to her in the image of her grandmother and described dazzling cities, elegant balls, passionate squires, lusty women. Her grandfather had become silent again.

In Akhsa's dreams, Grandmother was young and beautiful. She sang bawdy songs, drank wine, and danced with charlatans. Some nights she led Akhsa into temples where priests chanted and idolaters kneeled before golden statues. Naked courtesans drank wine from horns and gave themselves over to licentiousness.

One night Akhsa dreamed that she stood naked in a round hole. Midgets danced around her in circles. They sang obscene dirges. There was a blast of trumpets and the drumming of drums. When she awoke, the black singing still rang in her ears. "I am lost forever," she said to herself.

Zemach had also wakened. For a time he looked out through the one windowpane he had not boarded up. Then he asked, "Akhsa, are you awake? A new snow has fallen."

Akhsa knew too well what he meant. She said, "I have no strength."

"You had the strength to give yourself to the wicked."

"My bones ache."

"Tell that to the Avenging Angel."

The snow and the late-night moon cast a bright glare into the room. Zemach had let his hair grow long, like an ancient ascetic. His beard was wild and his eyes glowed in the night. Akhsa could never understand how he had the power to carry water all day long and still study half the night. He scarcely partook of the evening meal. To keep himself from enjoying the food, he swallowed his bread without chewing it, he oversalted and peppered the soup she cooked for him. Akhsa herself had become emaciated. Often she looked at her reflection in the slops and saw a thin face, sunken cheeks, a sickly pallor. She coughed frequently and spat phlegm with blood. Now she said, "Forgive me, Zemach, I can't get up."

"Get up, adulteress. This may be your last night."

"I wish it were."

"Confess! Tell the truth."

"I have told you everything."

"Did you enjoy the lechery?"

"No, Zemach, no."

"Last time you admitted that you did."

Akhsa was silent for a long time. "Very rarely. Perhaps for a second."

"And you forgot God?"

"Not altogether."

"You knew God's law, but you defied Him willfully."

"I thought the truth was with the Gentiles."

"All because Satan braided you a crown of feathers?"

"I thought it was a miracle."

"Harlot, don't defend yourself!"

"I do not defend myself. He spoke with Grandmother's voice."

"Why did you listen to your grandmother and not to your grandfather?"

"I was foolish."

"Foolish? For years you wallowed in utter desecration."

After a while man and wife went out barefoot into the night. Zemach threw himself into the snow first. He rolled over and over with great speed. His skullcap fell off. His body was covered with black hair, like fur. Akhsa waited a minute, and then she too threw herself down. She turned in the snow slowly and in silence while Zemach recited, "We have sinned, we have betrayed, we have robbed, we have lied, we have mocked, we have rebelled." And then he added, "Let it be Thy will that my death shall be the redemption for all my iniquities."

Akhsa had heard this lamentation often, but it made her tremble every time. This was the way the peasants had wailed when her husband, Squire Malkowski, whipped them. She was more afraid of Zemach's wailing than of the cold in winter and the nettles in summer. Occasionally, when he was in a gentler temper, Zemach promised that he would come to her as husband to wife. He even said that he would like to be the father of her children. But when? He kept on searching for new misdeeds in both of them. Akhsa grew weaker from day to day. The shrouds on the rope and the headstones in the graveyard seemed to beckon her. She made Zemach vow that he would recite the Kaddish over her grave.

* * *

On a hot day in the month of Tammuz, Akhsa went to gather sorrel leaves from the pasture that bordered the river. She had fasted all day long and she wanted to cook shchav for herself and Zemach for their evening meal. In the middle of her gathering she was overcome by exhaustion. She stretched out on the grass and dozed off, intending to rest only a quarter of an hour. But her mind went blank and her legs turned to stone. She fell into a deep sleep. When she opened her eyes, night had fallen. The sky was overcast, the air heavy with humidity. There was a storm coming. The earth steamed with the scent of grass and herbs, and it made Akhsa's head reel. In the darkness she found her basket, but it was empty. A goat or cow had eaten her sorrel. Suddenly she remembered her childhood, when she was pampered by her grandparents, dressed in velvet and silk, and served by maids and butlers. Now coughing choked her, her forehead was hot, and chills flashed through her spine. Since the moon did not shine and the stars were obscured, she scarcely knew her way. Her bare feet stepped on thorns and cow pats. "What a trap I have fallen into!" something cried out in her. She came to a tree and stopped to rest. At that moment she saw her grandfather. His white beard glowed in the darkness. She recognized his high forehead, his benign smile, and the loving kindness of his gaze. She called out, "Grandfather!" And in a second her face was washed with tears.

"I know everything," her grandfather said. "Your tribulations and your grief."

"Grandfather, what shall I do?"

"My daughter, your ordeal is over. We are waiting for you—I, Grandmother, all who love you. Holy angels will come to meet you."

"When, Grandfather?"

In that instant the image dissolved. Only the darkness remained. Akhsa felt her way home like someone blind. Finally, she reached her hut. As she opened the door she could feel that Zemach was there. He sat on the floor and his eyes were like two coals. He called out, "It's you?"

"Yes, Zemach."

"Why were you so long? Because of you I couldn't say my evening prayers in peace. You confused my thoughts."

"Forgive me, Zemach. I was tired and I fell asleep in the pasture."

"Liar! Convert! Scum!" Zemach screeched. "I searched for you in the pasture. You were whoring with a shepherd."

"What are you saying? God forbid!"

"Tell me the truth!" He jumped up and began to shake her. "Bitch! Demon! Lilith!"

Zemach had never acted so wildly. Akhsa said to him, "Zemach, my husband, I am faithful to you. I fell asleep on the grass. On the way home I saw my grandfather. My time is up." She was seized with such weakness that she sank to the floor.

Zemach's wrath vanished immediately. A mournful wail broke from him. "Sacred soul, where will I be without you? You are a saint. Forgive me my harshness. It was because of my love. I wanted to cleanse you so that you could sit in Paradise with the Holy Mothers."

"As I deserve, so shall I sit."

"Why should this happen to you? Is there no justice in Heaven?" And Zemach wailed in the voice that terrified her. He beat his head against the wall.

The next morning Akhsa did not rise from her bed. Zemach brought porridge he had cooked for her on the tripod. When he fed it to her, it spilled out of her mouth. Zemach fetched the town healer, but the healer did not know what to do. The women of the Burial Society came. Akhsa lay in a state of utter weakness. Her life was draining away. In the middle of the day Zemach went on foot to the town of Jaroslaw to bring a doctor. Evening came and he had not returned. That morning the rabbi's wife had sent a pillow to Akhsa. It was the first time in years she had slept on a pillow. Toward evening, the Burial Society women went home to their families and Akhsa remained alone. A wick burned in a dish of oil. A tepid breeze came through the open window. The moon did not shine, but the stars glittered. Crickets chirped, and frogs croaked with human voices. Once in a while a shadow passed the wall across from her bed. Akhsa knew that her end was near, but she had no fear of death. She took stock of her soul. She had been born rich and beautiful, with more gifts than all the others around her. Bad luck had made everything turn to the opposite. Did she suffer for her own sins or was she a reincarnation of someone who had sinned in a former generation? Akhsa knew that she should be spending her last hours in repentance and prayer. But such was her fate that doubt did not leave her even now. Her grandfather had told her one thing, her grandmother another. Akhsa had read in an old book about the Apostates who denied God, considering the world a random combination of atoms. She had now one desire—that a sign should be given, the pure truth revealed. She lay and prayed for a miracle. She fell into a light sleep and dreamed she was falling into depths that were tight and dark. Each time it seemed that she had reached the bottom, the foundation collapsed under her and she began to sink again with greater speed. The dark became heavier and the abyss even deeper.

She opened her eyes and knew what to do. With her last strength she got up and found a knife. She took off the pillowcase and with numb fingers ripped open the seams of the pillow. From the down stuffing she pulled out a crown of feathers. A hidden hand had braided in its top the four letters of God's name.

Akhsa put the crown beside her bed. In the wavering light of the wick, she could see each letter clearly: the *Yud*, the *Hai*, the *Vov*, and the other *Hai*. But, she wondered, in what way was this crown more a revelation of truth than the other? Was it possible that there were different faiths in Heaven? Akhsa began to pray for a new miracle. In her dismay she remembered the Devil's words: "The truth is that there is no truth."

Late at night, one of the Burial Society women returned. Akhsa wanted to implore her not to step on the crown, but she was too weak. The woman stepped on the crown, and its delicate structure dissolved. Akhsa closed her eyes and never opened them again. At dawn she sighed and gave up her soul.

One of the women lifted a feather and put it to her nostrils, but it did not flutter.

Later in the day, the Burial Society women cleansed Akhsa and dressed her in the shroud that she had sewn for herself. Zemach still had not returned from Jaroslaw and he was never heard of again. There was talk in Holishitz that he had been killed on the road. Some surmised that Zemach was not a man but a demon. Akhsa was buried near the chapel of a holy man, and the rabbi spoke a eulogy for her.

One thing remained a riddle. In her last hours Akhsa had ripped open the pillow that the rabbi's wife had sent her. The women who washed her body found bits of down between her fingers. How could a dying woman have the strength to do this? And what had she been searching for? No matter how much the townspeople pondered and how many explanations they tried to find, they never discovered the truth.

Because if there is such a thing as truth it is as intricate and hidden as a crown of feathers.

Translated by the author and Laurie Colwin

Acknowledgments

"The Death of Edward Lear" from *Great Days* by Donald Barthelme. Copyright © 1977, 1979 by Donald Barthelme. Reprinted by permission of Farrar, Straus and Giroux, Inc.

"The Circular Valley" copyright © 1979 by Paul Bowles. Reprinted from *The Collected Stories of Paul Bowles* with the permission of Black Sparrow Press.

"The Next Room" copyright © 1987 by A. S. Byatt. Reprinted with permission of Charles Scribner's Sons, an imprint of Macmillan Publishing Company, from *Sugar and Other Stories* by Antonia Byatt.

"The Ghost Who Vanished by Degrees" from *High Spirits* by Robertson Davies. Copyright © 1982 by Robertson Davies. Used by permission of Viking Penguin, a division of Penguin Books USA Inc., and by permission of Penguin Books Canada Limited.

"The Third Voice" from *Freedom and Other Fictions* by William Ferguson. Copyright © 1984 by William Ferguson. Reprinted by permission of Alfred A. Knopf, Inc.

"The Lost, Strayed, Stolen" from *Sister Age* by M. F. K. Fisher. Copyright © 1983 by M. F. K. Fisher. Reprinted by permission of Alfred A. Knopf, Inc.

"Up North" from *Home Truths: Sixteen Stories* by Mavis Gallant. Copyright © 1981 by Mavis Gallant. Reprinted by permission of Random House, Inc.

"The Warden" from *The King's Indian* by John Gardner. Copyright © 1974 by John Gardner. Reprinted by permission of Alfred A. Knopf, Inc.

"Letter from His Father," copyright © 1984 by Nadine Gordimer. From *Something Out There* by Nadine Gordimer. Used by permission of Viking Penguin, a division of Penguin Books USA Inc.

"Ghost and Flesh, Water and Dirt" from *Had I a Hundred Mouths: New and Selected Stories* by William Goyen. Copyright © 1985 by Doris Roberts and Charles William Goyen

Trust. Reprinted by permission of Clarkson N. Potter, Inc., a division of Crown Publishers, Inc.

"A Little Place off the Edgware Road" from *Collected Short Stories* by Graham Greene. Copyright © 1947, renewed 1975 by Graham Greene. Used by permission of Viking Penguin, a division of Penguin Books USA Inc.

"Jack's Girl" by Cynthia Kadohata. Copyright © 1987 by Cynthia Kadohata. Reprinted by permission of Wylie, Aitken & Stone, Inc.

"Revenant as Typewriter" by Penelope Lively from *Pack of Cards and Other Stories,* copyright © 1986 by Penelope Lively. Used in the United States of America by permission of Grove Press, Inc. Used in Canada by permission of William Heinemann Ltd. and Penguin Books Canada Limited.

"Ghostly Populations" by Jack Matthews. Copyright © 1986 by Jack Matthews. Used by permission of the Johns Hopkins University Press.

"Marmilion" by Patrick McGrath from *Blood and Water and Other Tales,* copyright © 1988 by Patrick McGrath. Reprinted by permission of Poseidon Press, a division of Simon & Schuster, Inc.

"Eisenheim the Illusionist" by Steven Millhauser from *The Barnum Museum,* copyright © 1990 by Steven Millhauser. Reprinted by permission of Poseidon Press, a division of Simon & Schuster, Inc.

"Old Man of the Temple" from *Under the Banyan Tree* by R. K. Narayan. Copyright © 1985 by R. K. Narayan. Used by permission of Viking Penguin, a division of Penguin Books USA Inc.

"The Others" from *The Assignation* by Joyce Carol Oates, copyright © 1988 by The Ontario Review, Inc. All rights reserved. Published by The Ecco Press in 1988. Reprinted by permission.

"The Ghost Soldiers" reprinted by permission of Tim O'Brien. Copyright © 1981 by Tim O'Brien. First appeared in *Esquire.*

"Family" copyright © 1989 by Lance Olsen. Reprinted by permission of Lance Olsen.

"Letter from a Dogfighter's Aunt, Deceased" from *Typical* by Padgett Powell. Copyright © 1991 by Padgett Powell. Reprinted by permission of Farrar, Straus and Giroux, Inc.

"Spirit Seizures" from *Spirit Seizures* by Melissa Pritchard. Copyright © 1987 by Melissa Pritchard. Used by permission of the University of Georgia Press.

ACKNOWLEDGMENTS

"A Story of Don Juan" from *More Collected Stories* by V. S. Pritchett. Copyright © 1983 by V. S. Pritchett. Reprinted by permission of Random House, Inc.

"The Ghost" from *Words for Dr. Y* by Anne Sexton, edited by Linda Gray Sexton. Copyright © 1978 by Linda Gray Sexton and Loring Conant, Jr., Executors of the Will of Anne Sexton. Reprinted by permission of Houghton Mifflin Co.

"A Crown of Feathers" from *A Crown of Feathers* by Isaac Bashevis Singer. Copyright © 1974 by Isaac Bashevis Singer. Reprinted by permission of Farrar, Straus and Giroux, Inc.

"The Portobello Road" from *The Stories of Muriel Spark* by Muriel Spark. Copyright © 1985 by Copyright Administration Limited. Reprinted by permission of Georges Borchardt Inc. for the author.

"Angel, All Innocence" copyright © Fay Weldon 1981. Printed with permission of Sanford J. Greenburger Associates, Inc.

"Grass" copyright © 1987 by Barry Yourgrau. Reprinted with permission of Barry Yourgrau.